Sophia Singh Sas...
daydreaming to goo...
will give you hope, ...
snort tea from your n...
and has lived in India ...
madness of Washingt...
the Welcome to Bellh... ... ... the Union series.
She loves to read, travel to exotic locations in the name of
research, bake fancy cakes, explore water sports and
watch Bollywood movies. Hearing from readers makes
her day. Contact her through sophiasasson.com

A lover of storytelling in all forms, **Susannah Erwin**
worked for major film studios before writing her first
novel, which won RWA's Golden Heart® Award. She
lives in Northern California with her husband and a very
spoiled but utterly delightful cat.

Discover more at millsandboon.co.uk

MARRIAGE BY ARRANGEMENT

SOPHIA SINGH SASSON

CINDERELLA UNMASKED

SUSANNAH ERWIN

MILLS & BOON

First Published in Great Britain 2020
by Mills & Boon, an imprint of HarperCollinsPublishers,
1 London Bridge Street, London, SE1 9GF

Marriage by Arrangement © 2020 Sophia Singh Sasson
Cinderella Unmasked © 2020 Susannah Erwin

ISBN: 978-0-263-28000-5

0820

MIX
Paper from
responsible sources
FSC® C007454

This book is produced from independently certified FSC™ paper to ensure responsible forest management.

For more information visit: www.harpercollins.co.uk/green

Printed and bound in Great Britain
by CPI Group (UK) Ltd, Croydon, CR0 4YY

MARRIAGE BY ARRANGEMENT

SOPHIA SINGH SASSON

To all the women who've been hurt in love.
Second chances do exist. Trust me.

And to my husband,
who gave me a second chance
and is my happily-ever-after.

This book, and the entire Nights at the Mahal series,
would not have happened without my awesome
editor Charles Griemsman, and my agent
extraordinaire Barbara Rosenberg.
Thank you for believing in me.

Great appreciation to my long-time
critique partner Jayne Evans.
She is never afraid to tell me when it's
time to hit the delete button.

Most of all, thank you to my readers.
Your reviews, emails, tweets and letters
keep me writing.

One

1>He owns the room, even when it doesn't belong to him.

The first bullet point of the memo Rani Gupta had written for her boss was right on target. Everyone around the polished mahogany table stood as Arjun Singh walked through the door. He was tall, confident, impeccably dressed in a tailor-made suit with shampoo-commercial hair and a take-charge stride. *India's hottest hottie.* That's what the South Asian media called him. The title was normally reserved for rising Bollywood stars or sizzling new male models. It was India's version of the most eligible bachelor. For the first time in twenty years, the coveted title had gone to a businessman. Hotelier Arjun Singh, hopefully RKS Architecture's new client.

"Let me do the talking," Rani's boss, Delia Dietz, leaned over and whispered to her.

Like hell! Rani clenched her jaw but resisted the urge to

argue. Her promotion paperwork was on Delia's desk. *The promotion that should have been mine two years ago.* It was best to seethe internally; she didn't want to give Delia an excuse to turn down her promotion. Again.

Arjun Singh greeted the bigwigs at the table. His voice was rich and deep with an Indian-tinged British accent that came from being educated in an English boarding school. She tried not to swoon at the way he enunciated each word and rarely used contractions. He gestured for everyone to sit. Rani sank into the buttery leather chair and took a sip of the coffee that an assistant had placed there just moments ago. *Even the coffee is better up here.* The boardroom of RKS Architecture was designed to impress. Floor-to-ceiling windows glittered with a bird's-eye view of the Vegas strip. Every surface of the room gleamed with the shine of money.

They began the meeting with introductions. Arjun's golden-brown eyes moved quickly around the table but stopped when Rani introduced herself. Delia was talking but Arjun kept his eyes locked on Rani. She stared back at him, mesmerized, grateful that her medium-brown complexion hid the heat rising in her cheeks. His right eyebrow went up ever so slightly and she swallowed, her throat suddenly tight. *Damn.*

He broke eye contact and she let out a breath. *What was that?* If she didn't know better she would've sworn she'd caught his interest, even if just for a second. She shook off the thought. A man like Arjun Singh didn't notice women like her. India's hottest hottie had the most gorgeous women in the world lining up for him. An average-looking, slightly overweight woman like her would never register on his radar. Obviously she was reading too much into his attention. Her experience with men was so limited that she'd only ever been intimate with her ex-husband. What did she know about flirtation?

Delia started with pleasantries. "Namaste, Mr. Singh." Delia's voice had dropped low and she stretched out the word *Namaste* like she was a yoga instructor encouraging her students to find inner peace. Rani fought the urge to roll her eyes and got the feeling Arjun was trying to do the same. Indians used *Namaste* as a respectful greeting of hello or goodbye, not a new age chant.

"It is so nice to have you here all the way from India. My neighbor is from Bangalore and I was just talking to him about taking a trip there, though I understand you are from Rajasthan, which is in the north, of course…"

Ten, nine, eight… Rani silently counted down the seconds. She got to five before Arjun Singh raised his hand gesturing for Delia to stop. "With all due respect, my time is limited so let's get started with our business."

2>Don't try to regale him with stories of India or Indians you know. He finds it patronizing.

Obviously, her boss hadn't bothered to read her memo.

Delia cleared her throat and pressed a button on the remote. Two wood panels parted to reveal a TV screen. As Delia talked through the PowerPoint slides in a crisp voice, Rani's shoulders dropped. Delia had decided not to go with her ideas for the lobby, casino or guest rooms. Not only was all of Rani's work wasted, the generic Vegas design Delia presented was all wrong for Arjun's hotel. Rani snuck a look at him. Arjun silently drummed his fingers on the table and Rani admired how graceful they were: long, slim and perfectly manicured. She curled her own bitten nails into her hands. *Does he like these uninspired designs?* Then Delia got to the owners condo and Rani was pleased that they had chosen her plans. The condo was unusually large for a typical Vegas hotel. *You probably didn't have any designs you could recycle.*

Delia was barely finished with the presentation when Arjun raised a hand again. "Stop. I do not need to hear any more." Everyone in the room stilled. "With one exception, these are the same rubbish designs that every other firm in Vegas has peddled. Including the one I fired."

3>He's known for his sharp tongue and ruthless business practices.

Delia shifted on her feet. Rani would have enjoyed seeing Delia brought down a notch but her own mouth was sour. Was he trashing her idea for the owners condo? He hadn't even seen her full design.

"Mr. Singh, could you elaborate on your concerns?" Delia asked diplomatically.

"The only original part I see is the design for the owners condo. What inspired you to use a *jaali* theme?"

Rani's pulse jumped and she looked pointedly at Delia, resisting the urge to raise her hand like a schoolgirl. Her boss ploughed on. "Well, we wanted something as grand as the Taj Mahal and…"

Rani inwardly groaned. Arjun Singh closed his portfolio. "Obviously you have no idea what you are talking about and this meeting was a waste of my time." He pushed his chair back.

"Your requirements stated that you want a design that allows for both an open concept and privacy. As I'm sure you know, the *jaali* model has porous walls to let light and air pass through but still maintain privacy. The pattern can be intricately carved into stone or wood. The design choices are endless, and can provide a unique touch for the hotel." All eyes turned to Rani, and Arjun Singh slowly pulled himself back to the table. His stare was fixed on her and her nerves tingled. *Delia will kill me, but if I'm going to commit career suicide, I might as well go for broke.*

"You said you wanted the owners condo to feel like home, so we took inspiration from the old Indian-style houses." She went on for another five minutes, careful to use "we" instead of "I" to describe her work. Arjun didn't take his eyes off her the entire time.

When she was finished, Delia jumped in. "Rani Gupta works on my team and helped with this portion of the design."

Arjun's eyes flicked to Delia in irritation, giving her a universal *oh please* look.

4>He is very good at reading people and hates credit-hogging bullshitters.

This last bullet point wasn't actually on her memo but it should've been.

"Most of your ideas are stale and overused. I want more original thought like the *jaali* design."

Rani's heart stopped in her chest, matching the stunned silence in the room.

"Mr. Singh, I assure you all our ideas are unique. If you didn't like these, we can develop some additional options for you to consider," Delia sputtered.

"This hotel needs to be completed in six months. I do not have time to dawdle with more presentations. What assurance can you give me that your firm can understand my vision for this hotel?"

"Mr. Singh, given the importance of your project to us, we will have our best staff on your contract. In fact, Rani Gupta will lead the project." The soothing compromise was offered by the company CEO, Ian Rabat. He was a small, thin man with square glasses and a goatee. His father had founded the company and was the R in RKS While everyone else referred to each other by first names, it was always Mr. Rabat for him.

"But…" Delia started to say something but a sharp look from Mr. Rabat silenced her.

Rani's pulse raced. *Is this really happening? I'm going to lead a big contract?* Arjun's eyes sought her out and he lifted his chin. *Is he asking me if I'm okay with this? Can't be!* In her experience, wealthy Indian men didn't ask permission, they took what they wanted. Her ex-husband, Navin, immediately sprang to mind.

She met Arjun's gaze and gave him a slight nod, trying to look nonchalant as if she was asked to lead big projects every day. But panic seized her. Could she really handle a client like Arjun Singh?

"I am willing to do a limited contract with your firm for the construction of the owners condo, plus blueprints and a 3D interior design for the lobby that mimics the one Ms. Gupta presented for the owners condo. Further business will depend on how quickly you complete this work, and your ability to impress me with ideas for the rest of the hotel. Send me a cost proposal by the end of the day. As long as it is reasonable, you will have a signed contract by the morning." Arjun stood and left the room without even a goodbye handshake. There were ten seconds of silence, and then everyone spoke at once. Delia stood and went to have a private word with Mr. Rabat.

Rani slipped out and caught up with Arjun at the elevator banks, her heart beating wildly.

"I look forward to working with you, Mr. Singh." She held out her hand and he looked at it for a second before taking it. Her hand felt small enveloped in his firm grip, and a delicious current danced through her body. She was five-foot-four and wearing two-inch heels but had to tilt her head far back to maintain his gaze. She met his eyes and her legs turned to Jell-O.

"Call me Arjun." His lips twitched. "Is it okay if I call

you... Rani?" He said her name slowly, like it was a sip of fine wine tantalizing his tongue.

"Um, sure." She tugged on her hand and he let it go but his eyes stayed on her. The man vibrated with sexual charm. *Careful, Rani!*

"How much of the condo design was yours?" he asked.

Rani resisted the urge to look back at the boardroom. "All of it."

He smiled. Not the clipped polite smile she'd seen him give when reporters thrust a microphone in his face or the fake one he gave at the meeting. This one was wide, revealing a tiny dimple in his right cheek. Rani's stomach flipped, and then flipped again. She'd looked at hundreds of photos of this man in the course of her research and there wasn't a dimple in any one of them. *Can this man get any hotter?*

"I have been meeting with architectural design firms for months and no one has come close to what I want. You're quite talented, Rani. I cannot wait to see what you come up with for the lobby."

Now it was Rani's turn to smile.

"I already have your lobby designed. I think you're going to like it."

His lips twitched again. The elevator doors dinged open and he stepped through, then turned to face her and smiled. A full-wattage smile with the little dimple. "I think we are going to work really well together." He joined his hands together as the elevator doors closed. "Namaste, Rani," he said in a silky voice that melted her insides.

Namaste, hottie! Rani stared as the doors closed. Then the sound of someone clearing their throat caught her attention. She turned to see Delia standing behind her. Her chest deflated.

"Rani, I see you're getting to know Mr. Singh."

"I spent a lot of time researching him. I thought I'd take a minute to get a sense of him in person if we're going to be working together," Rani said cagily. Why did Delia question her every move?

Delia nodded. "I read the client memo you wrote on him. I didn't agree with your assessment, but given how things went, I think you researched him well."

It was the closest Rani would get to an apology but she'd take it. There was no mention of a dimple in the memo. Still buzzing from her encounter with Arjun, Rani put her hands behind her so she wouldn't fidget.

"Congratulations. You're leading this project as far as the client is concerned, but you'll still be reporting to me and I'll be watching your every move."

Rani sighed inwardly. Any failures would be blamed on her and successes would be credited to Delia. But that was a problem for another day. She wasn't going to let Delia bring her down.

"Great. I look forward to working with you," she said with fake enthusiasm. Then it struck her. She finally had a modicum of power over Delia. Mr. Rabat had already announced to the client that she would be leading the project. "Can I assume that my promotion will be made official soon?"

"We'll see." Delia said noncommittally.

But Rani wasn't going to let it go this time. She had worked long hours on the proposal, hadn't reused old ideas like her colleagues, and had won her firm the contract because of it.

"I think leading a contract like this is well beyond the job description for a *junior* architect." Rani crossed her arms.

"I guess you're right," Delia admitted grudgingly.

Yes! Finally! Rani couldn't help but grin.

"Rani, this is a big step for you so let me give you some advice." Delia's voice was sharp. "Architecture is a man's field. It takes a lot to succeed as a woman, especially in Vegas. You have the talent to make it to the top but you already have a black mark against you. This project can catapult your career…" She paused and looked meaningfully at Rani. "If you don't get involved with the client."

"Excuse me, Delia…"

Delia rolled her eyes. "Spare me. The way you two were making eyes at each other in the boardroom didn't go unnoticed. I'm simply reminding you that this firm has a very strict morals clause in our employment contracts. We didn't invoke it two years ago but you won't get another chance."

Shame pricked through her body at Delia's not-so-subtle hint about Rani's past at the firm. Her ex-husband had wreaked havoc on her work life. Right after she filed for divorce, her ex had shown up at RKS and blown her relationship with her former boss out of proportion. A good man had gotten fired. What Delia didn't know was that Rani had a lifetime of pain gathered in her heart. Her previous marriage had left her caged in a traditional Indian home, stripped of her freedom and dignity. Her judgment in men had cost her emotionally, financially and professionally. She had no intention of letting a man have any control over her ever again. Especially not an Indian man. Marrying an Indian man meant marrying his family. She'd learned *that* lesson the hard way. She was done with traditional Indian families.

Arjun's project was her ticket out of the career rut she was in. He had already fired the best interior architecture firm in Vegas. If she succeeded where they had failed, people would stop talking about her past mistake and focus on her talent. She could finally pursue her dream of opening her own consulting business.

"Delia, nothing is more important than my career. Arjun Singh will never be more than a client."

She looked back at the elevator doors. Dimple be dammed. This was her big chance to get control over her life and she wasn't going to blow it.

Two

"So you finally hired a firm?"

"Yes, Ma," Arjun said into the phone. He'd just finished updating his mother on the progress with the hotel. "Their lead architect is Indian so she really understands the look I'm going for." Arjun smiled as he remembered he'd be seeing Rani tonight. RKS was throwing a reception to celebrate the signing of the contract.

"That is excellent. How long until the hotel is completed?"

He was glad his mother hadn't gotten comfortable with video chatting and they were just doing a voice call so he didn't have to hide his eye roll. He knew what was coming next.

"I'm not sure. The designs have not been finalized yet."

"Arjun, do not lie to your mother. You would not have signed the contract without an end date." Arjun swore under his breath. His mother knew him too well.

"They have six months. With a bonus for doing it in five."

"That is good news. You know, *pandit-ji* told me that there is an auspicious date in March for your wedding to Hema."

Arjun sighed into the phone. "Ma, again the same old thing."

"*Aaare, pandit-ji* believes such an auspicious date won't come for another two years. And look, the timing works out with your hotel. All the stars are aligned."

Of course, the *pandit*, his mother's well-paid priest, had managed to find an opportune date that corresponded to the exact amount of time his mother needed to plan a big fat Indian wedding.

"I don't understand the rush, Ma."

"Rush! Hema and her family have been waiting patiently for you for five years. And now that we are business partners, it's not right to keep delaying. Best to solidify our relationship with Hema's family. Come home in a month for the Diwali holidays and we will do the official engagement."

Arjun rolled his neck to ease the tension out of his shoulders. He was running out of excuses with his parents and with Hema's. It was his dream to expand their empire globally but his family's wealth was tied up in assets. He didn't have the liquid cash to make it happen. Hema's family were close friends and had approached him about a billion-dollar deal that was hard to pass up. The Vegas hotel was the first in a planned chain of high-end luxury hotels around the world. The arranged marriage with Hema had been suggested by his parents as a way to ensure that their business relationship was cemented with a personal one. Arjun had agreed. Hema was a nice woman, well versed in his family traditions, and he'd already had his heart broken. He wasn't going to marry for love, so why not marry someone who was guaranteed to fit in with his family?

"Why can't we just wait until the hotel is finished and

do the engagement and wedding all at the same time? I'll be really busy the next few months."

While he intended to marry Hema, a formal engagement took the commitment to the next level and he didn't want to go there. Yet.

"If we do the engagement during the wedding week, it will be one more party that nobody will remember. This way it will be special. I will send the jet. You can fly overnight and be back in two days' time."

"Ma…"

"Come on now, haven't you sown enough of your wild rice, as they say in America?"

Arjun smiled. "The expression is sowing wild oats, Ma."

"Yes, yes, wild oats." She softened her tone. "It would be good for you to come home, *beta*, even for a short trip. Your sisters are giving me daily heartburn. Now Divya is on a new kick saying she wants to get a job in Delhi and live by herself. And then there's Sameer…"

Arjun sighed. There was a constant tension in his household between his very traditional and strict parents and his rebellious brother and three sisters. He talked with his mother for a few more minutes about the brewing problems with his siblings.

Ten seconds after he hung up with her, his phone zinged with the melody of "We Are Family."

It was a text from his sister Divya. Please talk some sense into Mom. I'm an educated, grown woman with life goals. She expects me to sit at home waiting to get married.

Divya had obviously overhead his mother complaining to him about her. Subtlety was not his mother's strong suit. He hated being caught between his parents and his siblings but it was the role he had to play to keep the household peace.

Give me some time, I will figure something out, he texted back.

His sister wasn't easily placated but she agreed to give him time to think of a solution.

The rest of his afternoon was a blur of decisions that needed to be made for the hotel. He welcomed the distraction because they were problems he could actually solve. At five thirty, he asked his chauffeur, Sam, to drive him to RKS Architecture.

He exited the Lexus ES at the precise invitation time and instructed Sam to stay close. He hated corporate receptions and didn't plan to stay long.

When he walked through the doors of the firm, he stopped short. A few weeks ago when he'd first come to hear their pitch, the lobby had been unmemorable and generic. Today, it was transformed. Silk curtains in royal blue and gold hung across temporary walls that created cozy gathering places. Hand-carved wooden settees with rich fabric cushions were set between the curtains. A jeweled chandelier hung over each area, throwing glimmering beams of light that created intimate shadows.

His feet were glued to the floor, taking in the breathtaking scene. It was like the *darbar* of an old Indian palace. It almost looked like a painting that hung in his home of what the house's grand hall looked like back when his great-great-great-grandfather was a king, and used the space as his court.

"Do you like it?"

He turned to see Rani Gupta smiling at him. Her hair was pulled back into a chignon and her dark eyes were lined with black kohl. Her lips had a slight tinge of gloss. He liked that her makeup was minimal; she was a natural beauty.

He nodded, barely able to contain his excitement. "I want this for my lobby."

Rani's smile widened and he tried not to stare. For the

past year and a half, every business contact whose palms he'd greased to get his hotel built in record time had set him up with the most stunning women Vegas had to offer. None had caught his eye. But Rani Gupta had captured his attention from the moment he first saw her. Maybe it was the fact that she'd seen his vision for the hotel like no one else. Or maybe it was her big round eyes that sparked with a mixture of intense yearning and dark sadness. She was dressed in a generic black pantsuit with a cream blouse. As boring an outfit as a woman could wear, and yet heat burned deep in his core.

Speaking of wild oats. He smacked the thought from his mind. He didn't enter into a relationship unless there was an easy exit strategy. And getting involved with a woman at work violated too many boundaries.

"I was hoping you'd like it. I have some *jaali* walls to show you, as well. I was thinking we could use the same design throughout the hotel to give it a sense of connected flow."

Rani Gupta, you've managed to do something rare. You've surprised and impressed me. He had been expecting the usual corporate reception with mediocre wines, bloated executives and bland food.

As if on cue, several of the firm's senior partners showed up. Rani faded into the background as Arjun was introduced around the firm. The CEO, Ian Rabat, spoke with an authority that belied his slim five-foot-six-inch frame and took charge of introducing Arjun to his senior staff. Arjun didn't bother to keep track of the names of the men, who wore almost identical gray or black suits with patterned ties. Arjun vaguely remembered them from the original pitch meeting. Each man was the vice president of one thing or another. "Every significant member of the RKS team is here for you tonight, Mr. Singh," Ian Rabat roared with his arms spread. Arjun nodded as if he were impressed but knew that like him, each of the executives was wondering when they could clock out. They talked about the weather, the traffic and the stock market.

"Tell me, Mr. Singh, why choose Vegas for your first US hotel?" The question came from a rotund man with a jovial smile and thinning hair. Arjun remembered that he was the head of the accounting department.

"Honestly, it was about opportunity. I have been considering expanding to America for years. Then the Sandaway went up for sale. It was the right size, and I thought remodeling and rebranding it was the fastest way to get into the US market."

"You're an astute businessman. The hotel is well built and in a prime location. With our designs, it truly will be spectacular and attract the kind of high rollers you want," Ian Rabat said grandly. Arjun stifled the urge to roll his eyes. It had taken him more than a year to find the right property, and even longer to find the right design firm. Scratch that, the right architect.

"Why call it the Mahal hotel?" The question came from a gaunt-looking man named Pierce Waters, who headed the legal department.

"*Mahal* in Hindi means *palace*..."

"Ah, like the Taj Mahal," exclaimed Pierce. "I took a trip there six years ago with my wife. Let me tell you..."

Arjun stifled his boredom and let the man talk till he found his chance to excuse himself to go to the bathroom. He would've left the party but he wanted to talk to Rani one more time.

He found her fussing with pillows. "You know you're an interior architect, not a decorator. Surely you have people to do this?"

She turned and smiled. "I think interior architecture and decorating go hand in hand. Especially for a project like this." She held up a pillow and then pointed to the intricate design on the wall. "The pillows are embroidered in the same pattern that'll be carved into the wall. When done right, interior decoration flows from the architecture. What do you think?"

The light from the jeweled chandelier threw a soft glow on her face, and he found himself drawn deep into her eyes. He smiled. *Rani Gupta, you really have my attention now.*

"You've impressed me. I think you have a lot of talent."

"Thank you, Mr. Singh."

It's Mr. Singh now. "Rani, I insist you call me Arjun."

Her eyes widened for a fraction of a second before a neutral expression settled over her features. "I prefer we keep things formal. A wise man once said that it's best not to let business get personal."

She'd quoted him.

"I feel a distinct disadvantage. You've researched me, yet I know nothing about you."

He took a step closer, into her personal space, to allow a waiter to pass behind him. Her lips parted slightly, her pink mouth seductively lush. The pillow fell from her hands. A hot thunder raged deep in his core and he was tempted to kiss her senseless.

He stepped back, mentally scolding himself. They'd be working together for months, and he was her client. He didn't want to put her in an awkward position, especially not with her bosses in the same room. He gave himself the same admonition he often lobbed at his brother: *keep it in your pants.*

"Is your phone playing 'We Are Family'?" Rani asked with amusement in her voice. Arjun realized his phone was chirping. He looked at the message; it was from Hema. Your mom is planning a Diwali engagement. Do something, please!! Delay another year++

Annoyance churned through him. Hema wasn't ready to get married any more than he was, but she never expressed her feelings to anyone but him. He was in an awkward situation since Hema's father was a major investor in his hotel. Yet she left it up to him to solve their problem. Just like his sisters did.

"Everything okay?"

Rani's voice pulled his attention back to her. He gave a dismissive wave. "Yes."

"You seem a little upset. Was the message from one of your family members?"

Had he let his emotions show so blatantly? He prided himself on his poker face; it was essential for his business success.

"Do you have brothers or sisters, Rani?"

She nodded. "One brother and one sister."

"Are they younger or older?"

"I'm the eldest."

"That must be a lot of responsibility."

"You know how being the eldest is a lot of pressure in an Indian family. Parents expect you to bring the younger ones to heel when they get out of line, and the siblings want the older one to fight their battles with the parents." She gave a small smile and a knowing gaze that pierced through him. He had the feeling that she knew what he was going through and was inviting him to unburden himself. He could picture it, them sitting down on the pillowed *diwan* and talking to her about the crises brewing in his house. *Have I gone mad?* He did not share information about his family with anyone. Nor had he ever been tempted to.

Rani was still looking at him with her deep dark eyes and he felt a magnetic draw to her.

Rani is off-limits!

He straightened his back and changed the subject. "I think you're off to a great start with this project."

"Thank you. We should set up regular meetings so we can finalize the designs and start construction in parallel.

We're on a tight timeline, and I hope to work closely with you over the next few weeks so we can meet your deadlines."

Work closely? He had enough complications in his life. He didn't need one more. Rani pulled at his heart strings in a way that made him want to get close to her. Not only was he going to be working with her, he wasn't sure he could delay his engagement and marriage to Hema any longer.

"I'm pretty busy so you'll be dealing with my staff from here on out."

Three

Rani anxiously paced the marble-floored lobby of Arjun's office. *Will he attend the meeting?* It was a question she hadn't been able to get a straight answer to. It had been two weeks since the reception. Since the moment when he'd really come close to her, when she'd felt something she didn't know she could experience: desire. Even now, standing in the cool lobby with its funky wall art and bright white lighting, the thought of him made her warm all over.

What happened at the RKS party? They'd been having a nice conversation but then all of a sudden he'd said goodbye and walked out. The next day, Vanessa Knott had emailed to say she would be Rani's primary contact. While Rani didn't expect Arjun to be involved with every little detail, he seemed to have disappeared.

What did I do wrong?

Had he read her mind that night? Seen her studying him? Lusting after him?

She'd slept fitfully the entire week. She was either tossing and turning, thinking about seeing him again, or dreaming of Arjun when she was asleep. *Dreaming* was the wrong word. Fantasizing. She had woken up hot, with an ache that screamed for relief. In all her research, there wasn't a single picture of him shirtless, yet in her dreams he had appeared naked.

What is wrong with me? She was acting like a horny teenager. Then she thought back to the advice her mother had given her the night before her wedding. *Sex is something women endure to hold on to their husbands and have children.* Like a good Indian girl, Rani had saved herself for marriage, but she wasn't uneducated. At the time Rani had thought about how traditional and reserved her Indian mother was, and felt sorry for her. But after five years of marital relations with Navin, she realized that her mother's advice had been very sage. It wasn't that the sex had been bad, it just hadn't been good enough to inspire sleepless nights. Navin had always said that she was sexually repressed. She figured that either years of her parents' inhibitions had seeped into her, or the fact that she hadn't lost her virginity in high school like all her friends had retarded her sexual growth.

So what's happening all of a sudden?

Whatever was going on with her, she would push it aside. Navin and his traditional Indian family had given her a lifetime of wounds to contend with. She wasn't going to get romantically involved with another Indian man. Ever. And the fact that Arjun was her client made it all the more dangerous. She was so close to achieving her career dreams, she wouldn't risk it for some sexual satisfaction.

"Sorry for the wait. Here you go." A security guard swiped his badge against a panel on the wall and led her into a private elevator. Rani checked her reflection in the stainless steel doors as they closed. She was wearing her standard black suit but had bought a silky pink blouse to wear underneath. She'd gained some weight with the stress of the last few years and the only clothes that fit her were her shapeless shirts. The new shirt was her one splurge to celebrate her new salary. Standing straight, she squared her shoulders. She looked good. Her makeup and hair were perfect, her suit was crisp.

I'm a professional woman, and I'm going to act like it.

She was sick of begging for well-deserved promotions at RKS. Arjun's hotel would put her on the map. She hadn't dared dream big, not with her reputation still shadowed by the incident two years ago, but Arjun's hotel would change everything. She'd be the architect who succeeded where the best had failed. There was no other choice but to be totally professional with Arjun.

No more drooling over his dimple.

When the elevator stopped, she braced herself. She stepped into a polished foyer that featured an oval table with a giant vase filled with fragrant fresh flowers. The only other furniture was two pairs of stylishly rugged leather chairs. The walls were the palest shade of blue. There was no reception desk, but a screen touch pad invited people to check in. It was minimalist but warm, modern yet comfortable. Rani knew these were rented offices, but she could clearly see Arjun's style showing through.

"Good afternoon, Rani. I'm Vanessa Knott."

Rani looked up to see a young woman dressed in an elegant white shift dress with high nude-colored heels. They had talked and emailed several times a day for the past two weeks. She'd pictured someone petite and librarian-like but Vanessa was tall, elegant and looked like she'd just stepped out of a *Sex in the City* episode. Rani didn't want to think about how frumpy she looked in comparison.

Is Vanessa also Arjun's style?

Rani shook hands with the other woman. "Come, we

are all eagerly awaiting your presentation in the conference room," Vanessa said crisply.

Did the "all" include a certain hottie? Rani's heart thudded hard inside her chest.

Beyond the gleaming waiting room was a more traditional office setup. A maze of cubicles filled the center of the space and offices lined the periphery. The sounds of typing and muted voices filled the air.

They walked into a glass-walled conference room where a dozen people were already seated. It took her less than a second to lock eyes with Arjun. He stood when she entered. She bit her lip and willed strength into her legs as she crossed the room to shake hands with him. He gave her a small smile. "Welcome, Ms. Gupta."

It's Ms. Gupta now?

"Please call me Rani," she said, bemused. The grin he shot back told her he'd done that on purpose and it had the desired effect of setting her at ease. Once again he was impeccably dressed in a gray suit and a blue shirt with French cuffs. His staff were a little more casual, in collared shirts without ties; some of the younger men were even in jeans. The women, however, were all fabulously attired in fashionable dresses and suits. She smoothed down her skirt, wishing she had also splurged on a new suit.

The slides she'd emailed Vanessa just an hour ago were already projected on the wall screen. Rani took a breath and launched right into business. She kept her eyes on everyone except Arjun.

"Rani, how will you acquire the custom fabricated items in your designs given the deadlines in the contract?" Vanessa asked the cutting question and Rani noted with some irritation that Arjun gave a small nod and leaned forward. Rani could tell this was going to be a long day.

By the time the meeting ended four hours later, she was exhausted. There were a lot of questions and several suggestions for design changes, mostly from Vanessa. It was a normal part of the process but Rani had no idea what Arjun was thinking the entire time. Had he liked her ideas? He'd sat back and listened, letting his team do the talking, until a decision needed to be made. Then he took full control. She silently added to her growing dossier on him.

5>*He is very good at giving you the illusion that you're in charge.*

One by one, Arjun's staff members left and then she, Arjun and Vanessa were the only ones remaining. The hum of activity outside the conference room had stopped. The workday had ended.

"That's some really good work, Rani. Keep it up and your firm might just get the contract for the full hotel," Arjun said. Rani beamed, his compliment sliding over her like cool shade on a hot, sunny day.

Vanessa chimed in. "We made some good progress but there's still work to do. It's almost dinnertime. How about we eat together and go over the final list of changes and contract modifications?"

"That's a great idea. It'll be my pleasure to take you guys out. There's an excellent Italian restaurant right around the corner." Rani tried to inject as much sincerity as she could muster into her voice. It was an expected part of the job to take the clients out to dinner. RKS spent a small fortune in buying client loyalty through wining and dining.

"Do you mean Portofino's?" Vanessa asked.

Rani nodded.

"We go there all the time." Vanessa touched Arjun's arm. *Did she just pout?* "How about that Indian place you keep telling me about? We haven't been there yet."

We? Was there a "we" in Arjun and Vanessa?

Arjun tapped his smart watch. "Sam, please bring the car around."

He gestured towards the doors. "Let's go, ladies."

The restaurant was not what she would've selected for a client dinner. And judging by the creases on Vanessa's otherwise perfect forehead, she felt the same. It was a small place with five plastic tables and a large counter that seemed to have a bustling carryout business. Several white plastic bags full of takeout containers were sitting on the countertop and at least ten people stood in the cashier's line. The vinyl floor looked like it had years of scuff marks permanently tattooed on it. A waiter waved to them as he dropped water glasses at the only other table that was occupied. Arjun led them to a table in the corner. Vanessa brushed the chair with her hand before sitting down. Rani caught Arjun's eye, and smiled with shared amusement.

The waiter appeared seconds after they'd sat down and beamed at them. "Mr. Singh, eating in today? No carryout? And with lovely ladies?"

"These are my work colleagues, Venkat. Could you please bring us some waters and menus?"

"So the food is good here, then?" Vanessa ventured.

Arjun smiled. "It's the best Indian food in Vegas."

Venkat returned and plopped down menus and overflowing glasses of water that splashed as he set them down.

"Why don't you order for us, Arjun, since you know what's good," Vanessa said. She pronounced it *Aaah-arr-jun* with a slightly breathless quality.

Rani cleared her throat. "I prefer to order for myself, thank you."

Arjun's lips twitched and she got the feeling he was trying not to smirk.

Rani took refuge behind the menu, taking some deep breaths. *I can get through this.*

Venkat was hovering, so Arjun called him over and ordered naan, rice, tandoori chicken, fish curry and *daal makhani*. Rani had to admit it was a pretty good order.

"I'll have the lamb *saag*," she started, but Arjun shook his head. He pointed to a picture on the front cover and she sighed. "Delete that, I'll have the chef's *thali*."

"Good choice, madam." Venkat scurried off with their menus.

"What's wrong with the lamb *saag*?" she asked when the waiter was gone. The lamb and spinach dish was one of her favorites.

"They use really substandard lamb and it's not very good. You will like the *thali*, it has the best of everything."

Vanessa had the grace not to smirk, and Rani reminded herself that she needed to focus on business and not on whatever was going on between Arjun and Vanessa. Rani pulled out her notebook and steered the conversation back to their meeting and the design changes they had requested.

Their food arrived, and Rani's mouth watered as Venkat put down a basket with fresh-baked naan. Next he set down the bright red grilled chicken that got its name from the clay tandoori oven it was cooked in, a steaming dish of fish curry, and a pot of lentils. Rani's order was a large round steel *thali* with ten smaller round containers arranged inside that had a sampling of various dishes. The chef's plate.

Arjun and Vanessa's order was served family-style and Arjun went about ladling the food onto each of their plates. Despite the delicious aroma coming from her own plate, Rani couldn't eat. She returned to the notebook. "From the list of design changes, I think we need at least three contract modifications." She started to describe them as Arjun and Vanessa dug into their food.

"Wow, that's spicy!" Vanessa interrupted. Rani looked up from her notebook to see that her flawless complexion was flushed pink. She was waving her hand in front of her mouth.

Rani picked up the small round container of yogurt on her plate and thrust it forward. "Here, eat the yogurt, don't drink water. Water circulates the spices on your tongue. The yogurt will calm them."

Vanessa grabbed the yogurt and finished it in two unladylike bites, then gulped down the rest of her water glass.

"I think I need to wash my mouth out. Where is the bathroom?"

Arjun's face was totally impassive as he pointed her in the right direction.

As soon as they heard the tapping of Vanessa's heels receding in the distance, Arjun turned to Rani and grinned. Rani sighed internally. *That dimple.*

"You could've warned her, you know." Rani was trying and failing to hide her own smile.

"She is very good at her job, but she hasn't gotten the message that I do not dip my pen in the company ink."

So he wasn't completely oblivious to Vanessa's flirting.

"You've never dated anyone you work with?" Rani asked.

He shook his head. "I like my personal relationships to be uncomplicated."

And I seem to be drawn into complications.

"It's a good rule. So who do you date?"

He leaned forward. "Why are you so interested in knowing?"

She bit her lip. *Busted.* "I need to know whether I should furnish the master bedroom for one or for two in the owners condo."

"For two," he said, his lips doing that sexy twitch they did when he was trying not to smirk.

"I see." Her throat was suddenly dry and she took a sip of her water.

"I'm not seeing anyone right now, but I plan to have a family someday."

Arjun with a family. Two-point-five kids and a dog. Scratch that, no dog. Three kids, two boys that look like him when he frowns and a girl with dimples when she smiles.

She ripped a piece of the naan from her plate and stuck it in her mouth.

"What about you, Rani? Have you ever dated anyone you worked with?"

Rani nearly choked on the naan. *Shit. Do I lie?* Unfortunately her disastrous relationship with her former boss was well known among the Vegas design and build world. He could easily find out from one of the mouthy contractors or vendors. She could evade but she'd hesitated long enough that he'd know something was up. Better he hear it directly from her, then dig up the unsavory version from someone else.

"I did date someone at RKS. It didn't end well, and I learned my lesson. I won't be dipping my ink in the company well ever again."

"Why was it so bad?" Arjun asked softly.

A lump formed in her throat. She hadn't talked openly about what had happened with anyone except her best friend, Em. "Let's just say that a good architect, and more importantly a good man, lost his job and it wasn't his fault."

"Are you talking about Bob Seagel?"

How had Rani not heard Vanessa come back? She said down, once again fully composed.

"How do you know Bob?" Rani asked.

"Before I started with Arjun, I worked with Gankle Architecture. Bob applied for a job, but there was a rumor going around that he got fired from RKS for sexual harassment. You must be talking about him. It's not often that an architect gets fired around here."

Rani took a breath. She didn't want to have this conversation in front of Arjun but she wasn't going to let one more person continue to think it was Bob's fault. "First of all, Bob didn't get fired. He resigned. And there was no sexual harassment. He was my boss and my friend. We had just started dating when things got blown out of proportion." She wasn't going to get into how she'd been going through a messy divorce and her ex-husband had hired a private eye who managed to snap a picture of the one and only time she and Bob had kissed.

Vanessa learned forward, clearly relishing getting the firsthand story. "If it was mutual, why did he resign?"

"Relationships with subordinates are against the rules at RKS."

"But this is Vegas. Surely this type of thing is common," Arjun said. Rani felt a small measure of relief to hear no judgment in his voice.

"Yes and no. RKS is a conservative firm and finding out that a male boss is having a romantic relationship with a female subordinate had to be taken seriously. Plus our personal relationship was so new, we hadn't gotten around to filling out the required HR paperwork stating it was mutual. I'm not saying it's fair and I tried to stand up for Bob, but ultimately he decided it would be better for him to resign."

What she didn't say is that RKS would have overlooked the relationship had her ex not made a big deal about it. Navin's motivation had been to get her fired but Bob had taken the hit.

"Poor Bob. I hear he had to go to New York to find another position."

Rani had heard the same thing and it just added to her guilt.

"Sounds like the whole thing was not easy on you," Arjun said softly. She met his gaze and felt a comforting warmth flow through her.

Vanessa followed the look between them. "Well, I think I've had it with Indian food for tonight so I'll just get an Uber home." She pushed her chair back.

Arjun stood. "Nonsense. Sam will take you home and then come back to get us."

Arjun walked Vanessa to the car, then returned to their table. Rani didn't know whether to feel relieved Vanessa was gone or nervous that she was now alone with Arjun.

"You have hardly touched your food. Too spicy?" He grinned.

She smiled then shook her head. "I love spicy food, but nothing beats homemade Indian food."

His lips curved up. "Do you cook?"

What a typical question from an Indian man. She shook her head. "Another virtue that this Indian does not have. I'm a disaster in the kitchen. The only thing I know how to make is masala chai."

"My sisters are the same way. My mother tells them that they had better marry someone rich who can hire a cook for them, or else they'll starve."

Rani laughed mirthlessly. "That's the same advice my mother gave me. And I took it and married someone rich."

Arjun stopped mid-chew. "You're married?"

Was it wrong that she felt a tingle at the surprise and disappointment in his voice? "Divorced," she said simply, then waited. While divorce was much more common than it used to be, it was still a little taboo among Indians. And the inevitable *what happened* question was not easy to answer. *No, he did not leave me. No, he did not beat me. No, he did not have an affair.* Apparently those were the only acceptable reasons for an Indian woman to divorce her husband.

"I'm sorry to hear you had to go through something like that. It's sad that even in this day and age it's difficult to be divorced in the Indian community."

Is this man for real?

"It's getting late, I should head back." She didn't want to get to know Arjun any better. They'd already gotten too personal.

"What's the rush? We have to wait until Sam returns with the car anyway."

She could take an Uber. But she was supposed to be taking the client out to dinner. How could she walk out? *Be professional, get back to the contract.*

"Do you regret having dated at work?"

Rani was jolted by the non sequitur. Arjun's soft brown eyes looked at her with such intensity that her nerves tingled.

"Yes, I do. It was the first and last time I'll ever get involved with someone at work."

Arjun stared at her for a few seconds and as much as she wanted to, she couldn't break the eye contact. It was as if he was trying to convey something without saying it out loud.

"It's getting late. Would you mind if I paid the bill, then took an Uber back to my car? I have a lot of work to do on these contract modifications."

"Don't worry about the bill. I will take care of it, but do wait for Sam. You should not be out alone at this time of night."

Excuse me? Now there's the Indian man I was expecting. She knew only too well what he meant. Her ex in-laws had been the same way. *Girls from good families don't go out alone at night.* Translation: *we feel more comfortable being in control of your whereabouts.*

Rani gestured for the check. Venkat pulled out a piece of paper from his apron pocket, then handed it to Arjun without a second glance at Rani.

"Dinner is on RKS," she said forcefully, holding out her hand for the bill.

"It's okay, Rani." Arjun extracted some bills from his wallet and handed them to Venkat, brushing off Rani's gestures to hand her the check.

Well isn't that typical. Always needs to be in control.

She pulled out her phone and tapped on the screen.

"My Uber will be here in a few minutes. Thank you for dinner, Mr. Singh. I'll send over the revised contract in the morning." She stood and walked out.

"Rani, wait!"

She resisted the urge to walk faster. Her Uber was still ten minutes away and it was pointless to get too far from her pickup location. Arjun strode up to her.

"What just happened? I feel like I offended you and I have no idea why."

She turned to face him and took a sharp breath. *He's your client, Rani. Watch it.* "Not at all, everything's fine. I just realized how late it is and I'd like to get home," she said in a high-pitched voice.

"Rani, you originally suggested we go out to Portofino's for a three-course meal. Please don't be formal with me. Just tell me what I did to upset you."

"I specifically asked to pay the bill and I don't like how you ignored me."

To his credit, he didn't smirk or say *is that all?* He placed his hand on his heart. "My apologies, Rani. My chivalry got the better of me. I don't ever let a woman pay."

"We aren't on a date. You're my client. Did it occur to you that RKS expects me to take clients out to dinner and I'll need to explain why I didn't?"

Before he could say anything, Sam pulled up to the curb next to them. "Seeing as your ride isn't here, could I do my *colleague* the courtesy of giving her a ride?"

It would be childish to resist. She nodded and slid into the plush leather seats of his Lexus. They rode to Arjun's office in silence but she was acutely aware of him next to her in the back seat. On the ride to the restaurant, Arjun had ridden up front with Sam while she and Vanessa shared the back seat. Despite the spaciousness of the car, Arjun felt too close. She could sense his breath as he exhaled, smell his spicy aftershave, feel the heat from his body. The short ride back to her car felt interminable.

There were no empty spots next to her car in the garage, so Sam pulled up a few feet away. "Thank you again, I'll be in touch," Rani said. She collected her laptop bag and had scarcely gotten her door open when Arjun appeared on her side, pulling the door wider for her. They walked to her car in silence.

As they neared her car, Rani pulled out the keys and hit the unlock button.

"You owe me forty-six dollars and twenty-two cents."

Rani turned towards Arjun. "What?"

He held out the receipt from the restaurant. "Plus whatever you would have tipped."

Rani raised her eyebrow and took the receipt. "How much did you tip?"

He smiled. "I rounded up to an even hundred."

"That's more than a hundred percent," Rani exclaimed. No wonder Venkat was so attentive.

"Venkat has a sick son. Everything he earns, he sends home to India. That's why I ignored your request."

Now she felt like shit. Smiling, he joined his hands together in a gesture of apology. His dimple struck a fatal blow to the last of her irritation.

"Mr. Singh, RKS would not approve a hundred percent tip as a business expense, so why don't I take you out to dinner another night? When might you be free?"

"How's this coming Saturday?"

That soon?

"Would Vanessa be available on such short notice?" she

asked stupidly, knowing full well he wasn't including her in the dinner plans.

"I think this one will just be the two of us. You pick the restaurant, I'll get the show tickets."

"Show tickets?"

He grinned. "My favorite comic, Russell Peters, is doing a show. I was hoping you would come with me."

Her heart jumped. *As in a date? No, that can't be right.* "I don't think it would be appropriate for us to see each other socially."

"We can go as colleagues, or two random Indians who have a sense of humor and want to support a politically incorrect comic."

She couldn't help but smile. "When you put it that way, how can I say no?"

"Great, text me your address and I'll pick you up."

This is sounding a little too much like a date.

Rani looked at the receipt that was still in her hand. "How did you know Venkat had a sick son?"

Arjun shrugged. "I noticed him crying outside the restaurant one night when I stopped to get carryout. I asked him what was wrong."

He stopped and asked what was wrong.

"Before you get the wrong idea about me, I'm not a bleeding heart, just a little homesick, and Venkat reminds me of one of my favorite servants."

A favorite servant. Rani resisted the urge to roll her eyes.

Arjun opened her car door. She threw her laptop bag on the passenger seat and got in. He leaned down through the doorway as a car tire screeched in the distance. His face was inches from hers, backlit from an overhead light. His aftershave smelled of a sultry mix of sandalwood and spice. A five o'clock shadow darkened his face. His lips were close. *So close.* All she had to do was lean forward

a few inches. She bit her lip and heard the sharp intake of
his breath.

"I have to warn you, Rani, you're making me reconsider
my policy about the company ink."

*6>Just when you think you understand him, he sur-
prises you.*

Four

"Then he just left?"

Rani heard the incredulity in her roommate and best friend Em's voice. She nodded.

"What did he mean?" Em demanded.

"If I knew, I wouldn't be asking you to translate man-speak for me."

Em took a big gulp from her can of soda and Rani smiled, amused by her friend's new lime-green hair. She was a pediatric oncology resident and she changed her hair color every time she discharged a patient. The other kids who remained on the unit picked the color. It was her way of giving them hope.

Rani held out a black dress in front of her. Em shook her head. "Do you have anything that's not black and conservative?"

Rani frowned. Sadly she didn't. It had been two years since she'd really been out on a date. *Not that this is a date.* The only clothes she had were business-appropriate.

Em went to her own room and returned with a strappy red dress. Rani shook her head. "That'll send the wrong message."

"And what message are you trying to send?"

Rani stepped into the black dress Em had rejected and studied her image in the mirror. The simple shift looked proper and boring and very businesslike. She thought of Vanessa and the other women from Arjun's office.

"I want to show him that I can be sexy. But I want to make it clear this is not a date."

Em raised a brow then walked out of the room. She returned a few minutes later and slipped a sparkly necklace around Rani's neck that fell between her breasts and handed her a pair of dangly earrings. She began pulling the pins out of Rani's chignon.

"What are you doing?" Rani protested, ineffectively batting Em's hands away.

Em fluffed Rani's hair, then pointed at the mirror.

Rani had to admit the effect was pretty good. Her shiny shoulder-length black hair fell in waves, naturally curly from being tied up all day. She put on the earrings. "You don't think this is too unprofessional?"

Em smacked her hand on her forehead. "I thought we were going for business sexy!"

Rani blew out a sigh and sat on the bed. "I should've canceled."

"Rani, it's been forever since you did something fun. Why don't you stop overanalyzing and just go out and have a good time. You love Russell Peters. Have a few laughs, enjoy the company of a handsome, intelligent man and let things happen naturally."

"I can't let anything happen. He's a client. If I get the contract to design his full hotel, it'll set me up on the fast track to start my own firm. I can't risk all of that for…for…"

"Toe-curling sex?"

Rani nodded, too embarrassed to say it out loud.

"I've known you since high school. Not once have you done anything risky. You were a virgin when you got married. Probably the only one in our entire school. Somehow I don't see you losing your panties tonight. But if you wanted to, there's nothing wrong with it. This is Vegas. You know how the saying goes."

Rani smiled. Em placed both hands on Rani's shoulders, her slate-gray eyes serious. "Every day I deal with children who would give anything just to go outside and play, eat ice cream and do the simple things that you and I take for granted. You've been living with an enormous weight on your shoulders. First your parents' expectations, then your in-laws'. When have you ever lived? When have you done something that brings you joy?"

"It's easier said than done."

Em fluffed Rani's hair a little more. "I know you're worried about your career, but you're not in the same situation as you were two years ago. There's no one out to get you."

Before Rani could think about it any longer, there was a knock on the door. Her apartment building was too low-rent to have a working buzzer, so the residents frequently propped open the front door to the building, letting anyone off the street just walk in.

"That's Arjun. He's right on time! I need shoes!" Rani said, panicked.

"Go let him in. I'll get you heels."

Rani opened the door to find Arjun standing there, ready to take her breath away. He wore his usual perfectly cut black suit, but his shirt was unbuttoned at the collar, revealing a hint of chest hair. His face was freshly shaven and she hoped that if she stepped closer, she might catch a whiff of that intoxicating smell from last night.

"Wow, Rani, you look beautiful."

She blinked. "Um, thank you. I'm ready to go, I just need…"

She looked down to see that Em had surreptitiously placed a pair of red-and-black heels near her feet. *There is no way I can wear those shoes.* She looked around for the sensible ones she wore with her business suit and noted they were gone from their usual place.

"Your purse," Em whispered.

"Is that your flat mate?" Arjun asked.

Em stepped forward. "Emmaline Roberts. Nice to meet you."

"Arjun Singh."

"I don't want to keep you two. I know it's hard to squeeze dinner in before a show." Then, turning away, from Arjun, Em mouthed, "He's hot. Go for it."

Rani put on the red-and-black heels, wondering how long it would be before she took an embarrassing spill.

She teetered down the stairwell to Arjun's waiting car, wondering what he must think of her. Vanessa probably did jumping jacks in her four-inch heels.

Rani had picked an upscale Malaysian restaurant for dinner, and she filled the silence in the car by telling him about the chef and the menu. "This particular chef combines not just Indian, Chinese and Thai flavors but also uses a lot of African and Arabian spices."

"It sounds right up my alley."

"I know."

"You were quite thorough in researching me."

"Everything I know about you is what you allow the media to report."

He raised an eyebrow, and the corner of his mouth lifted up in a look so sexy that Rani found it hard to breathe. "That's right, Ms. Gupta."

"So, how about telling me something real."

"Well, you've read about all my favorite foods. What you don't know is that I like cooking the dishes myself."

He cooks? Arjun Singh had grown up with the kind of wealth and privilege that most people could only dream of. He'd been surrounded by servants all his life. She couldn't imagine him doing something as domestic as cooking a meal.

They arrived at the restaurant and were seated immediately. Rani was pleasantly surprised since it was a popular place and the bar was packed with waiting customers. They were shown to a quiet table in a back room where there were only two other couples seated. Rani wondered if that was why they hadn't had to wait: they were being shown to the loser seats.

Arjun didn't seem to mind, so she didn't say anything. They shared an appetizer of mango and tofu salad, then moved on to a family-style dinner of *roti canai*, chili chicken, crispy squid and Singapore noodles. They talked about their favorite foods, movies, TV shows and books. Rani discovered that Arjun was a fellow fan of political and psychological thrillers.

They shared mango sticky rice for dessert. Arjun put his hands up when the check came and Rani deftly set down the RKS business card, guiltily realizing she'd forgotten it was a business dinner. They hadn't talked about work at all.

Arjun had secured box seats for the show, giving them a bird's-eye view of the stage, where an opening act band was playing. "What, no front row seats?" Rani quipped. Arjun shook his head. "Comedians always pick on the front row, and then your embarrassment can live in perpetuity on social media."

Rani hadn't even thought about that. "It must be really hard for you to constantly worry about the media."

He nodded.

"At the restaurant, they purposely sat us in the back room?"

He smiled sheepishly. "Before I go out, my assistant always calls the restaurant to make sure there won't be any reporters, and to secure seats in a private section, if possible."

Rani couldn't fathom living that way. "So Venkat was overseeing the VIP section yesterday?" she quipped.

"Impromptu dinners are different. And Venkat keeps an eye out for anything shady." As they settled into the conversation, Rani found herself relaxing. Truth be told, this was the best date she'd had in her life.

She mentally slapped herself. *This isn't a date, Rani!* When a waiter appeared and took drink orders from them, she asked for sparkling water. This was a work dinner, after all. *But what if it could be more than that?*

Arjun's phone buzzed just as the waiter set down their drinks. He looked at the text to see it was another one from Hema. Whatever you said to your mom didn't work. She's in full scale Diwali/engagement party planning mode. Do something! Arjun clenched his teeth. Hema was a grown woman. Why couldn't she just tell her parents she wasn't ready to get married? His phone buzzed again, this time with a text from Divya. Arjun hit the Do Not Disturb setting on his phone. He deserved a night of peace.

"Where did you disappear to?" Rani's soft voice broke through his reverie, drowning out the sound of the warm-up comedian who was introducing himself on stage. Arjun tried to give her his fake smile but stopped short when he looked into her eyes.

She reached over and touched his hand, which was on the armrest between them. Her touch was soft and delicate and immediately calmed the storm raging inside him. He dealt with thousands of problems each day and none of them twisted him up in knots like his family did.

"Are you okay?" Rani asked.

The changing stage lights threw seductive shadows across her face, and he felt himself gazing into her dark eyes. He'd always thought she was beautiful but tonight she looked spectacular. He knew she wasn't wearing a designer dress, and if he had to guess, she probably hadn't spent all day at the beauty salon getting her hair and makeup done. Yet she looked more stunning than any woman he'd ever met. Those heels that she clearly hated showed off her long, shapely legs and the way her hair framed her face made him want to weave his fingers into it. She was looking at him with such intensity, it seemed she could see into his soul.

"Just family drama," he said, surprising himself. He pulled his hand away from hers before he was tempted to take things further. Last night when he'd said goodbye in the car, he'd felt such an urgent need to kiss her that he'd almost canceled their plans tonight. He prided himself on always being in control.

He took a sip of the neat whiskey he'd ordered, hoping the raw burn down his throat would bring him back to his senses and shake loose an idea on how to deal with his family.

"Tell me about it." Rani leaned in close to him, and he caught a whiff of her vanilla scent.

Where do I start? With Divya or Hema? Hema was a not a problem to solve. She was an obligation he had to come to terms with. "My sister Divya has been offered a job in Jaipur and wants to take it, but that's not done in our family."

"Why not?"

He shifted in his chair.

"What I mean is, what is your parents' specific concern beyond the fact that it's not the tradition? The *parampara*?"

He looked at her in surprise. *She gets it.*

"I think they fear that if she's financially independent, she won't follow the house rules." Even as he said the words, he realized how horrible it sounded. "You have to understand that my parents are doing what they think is best for her."

"They're trying to control her."

"They are trying to protect her."

"I don't think we'll agree on that point. So what do you plan to do?"

"I'm thinking of secretly increasing her allowance. That way she can buy what she wants without having to ask my parents' permission. That's how this whole job thing started. She wanted to buy a car for herself and they questioned her spending."

Rani shook her head. "You're not understanding her."

He frowned. While he wanted Rani's perspective, she didn't know Divya. Arjun talked to Divya almost every day. How could Rani be so confident in saying he didn't understand his sister?

"Divya doesn't want to work just to buy things. She wants to work to have a sense of purpose, of independence. To do something meaningful with her life. I don't think you can appreciate what it's like for an intelligent person to sit at home all day with nothing to do. It's maddening."

"She has lots of things to do. There is staff to manage, social events to plan, charity work. My mother is always complaining about how busy she is."

"But those aren't things that satisfy a young, educated woman who doesn't want to be a socialite. She wants do something that is uniquely hers, and have control over some aspect of her life."

"It seems you're speaking from personal experience."

She nodded. "My ex-husband's family didn't have your kind of wealth but they were comfortable. My in-laws asked me to quit my job, which I foolishly did. My days were filled with shopping and social events that I couldn't care less about. I'm guessing your sister lives a similar life.

Working is not about the money, it's about independence. Of the many things I lost during my marriage, the one I lament the most is my career. I was almost at the point of making senior architect at RKS when I left. After the divorce, I had to start at the bottom of the junior level because I'd been out of the game so long. Divya doesn't want to become obsolete."

Arjun spread his hands. "So what do you suggest I do? My mother will not agree to let her get a job. I've already tried to convince her and she is firm on this point."

"What is Divya qualified to do?"

"She studied law."

Rani chewed her lip, and he found himself staring at her. "Your business is big enough that you surely need lawyers."

He nodded. "Of course. I have a couple in every city that we have a hotel."

"So hire her for your legal team in the Jaipur office."

"Jaipur is an hour away from our home."

"Do you do the commute?"

He rubbed his neck. *It could work.* "We have a trusted driver who could take her every day."

It was a nice idea. His brother, Sameer, had no interest in working for the family business, and Arjun could use a trusted person to take on some of the responsibilities of the company while he was in Vegas. He was tired of having to wake up in the middle of the night to get on the phone with someone in India.

"It's a potential solution. Thank you, Rani."

The crowd became louder as the warm-up act wrapped up and introduced Russell Peters. Rani started laughing at one of the jokes. Arjun hadn't heard it. All he could focus on was the way her mouth crinkled, and the happy sound of her giggles and laughter. He'd been with a fair number of women in the last several years; all of them had been socialites who clearly understood that he wasn't looking for an emotional attachment. His relationships were always physical. None of them had made him want to connect emotionally like this.

"Am I really more amusing than the comedian?" Rani turned to him, grinning.

He smiled sheepishly. "You certainly are more beautiful."

Her eyes widened and her mouth opened slightly. He took a breath to keep from leaning over and kissing her irresistible lips. As if reading his mind, she suddenly snapped her head back towards the stage. He took a long slug from his glass of whiskey.

So what if we work together? The project would be over in less than six months and he'd be returning to India to a lifetime of obligation. If she was attracted to him too, what was wrong with a brief affair? He knew how to be discreet; he would protect Rani, and make sure there would be no fallout for her at RKS. *After all, what happened in Vegas could stay in Vegas.*

Five

The show was over but Rani didn't want the evening to end. The warm October night and the irresistible sparkle of the Vegas strip made her link her arm with Arjun's as they walked down Las Vegas Boulevard. The streets were packed with crowds spilling from all different directions, loud and clumsy and infectiously happy.

"How about a walk to the Bellagio fountains? It's about a mile," Arjun suggested.

Rani had easily done the walk before but not in killer heels. She almost refused but she didn't want the evening to end. The only thing waiting for her at home was an on-line movie.

As they walked, their conversation turned back to food as Rani recalled her favorite dishes at the endless eateries and hotels lining the Strip. When they got to the New York-New York hotel and casino, Arjun looked at the large Statue of Liberty dominating the fake city skyline.

"Do you think I should've built a large replica of the Taj Mahal?"

Rani laughed because she knew from the look on Arjun's face that he was joking. It was funny how in the short time she'd known him, she could already read so many of his facial expressions.

"You still can. We can add a giant dome to the roof and four pillars at the corners of the building. Then we can have it painted in a faux marble look. I could do the architectural drawings tomorrow if you like. The only thing is, you'll have to change your plans for the restaurant from a Michelin star chef to a team of short order cooks that can put out large buffets. And you'll have to change the plans for the casino. Forget the high roller tables. Think quarter slots." They both laughed at the thought. The Mahal hotel wasn't going to cater to regular tourists like most of the hotels on the strip. The casino was for serious players only. The rooms were luxurious and exclusive. The restaurant would cater to the most discerning foodies. High class all the way.

"Shit." The Bellagio fountains were in sight when Rani's heel got stuck in a pothole. Just in time, Arjun caught her from falling face-first onto the sidewalk.

"Ouch, ouch!" Her heel was wedged into the sidewalk so tight that she couldn't lift her foot out. Arjun bent down and unstrapped her shoe. She stood on one leg while he extricated her shoe from the hole. Then he half carried her to a nearby bench. He bent down on one knee and gently lifted her leg.

His warm hand on her foot sent a delicious signal right to her core.

"You're ankle is bleeding and swelling up. I'm calling Sam to come get us."

"Good idea." It didn't feel like she'd broken anything

other than her pride, but her ankle was hurting. She shouldn't have worn the stupid heels.

While they waited for Sam to make his way through the clogged traffic, they watched the Bellagio fountains from afar. It was a spectacular show of water and light timed to music. Arjun put his arm around her shoulders and she leaned against him to keep the weight off the ankle. For the first time in years, Rani felt weightless.

When Sam pulled up, Arjun helped Rani half hop, half walk to the car. As soon as they were seated, Sam roared back into traffic.

"My condo isn't far from here. We will go there first and get you bandaged."

"There's no need to do that. My roommate is a doctor. I'll be better off going home."

"Your apartment is a fifth floor walk-up. No way are you hobbling up that many flights of stairs without us icing that ankle and making sure it's okay."

"Are you always this bossy?"

"Do you even have to ask? I promise I'll be a perfect gentleman."

"Is that a promise that needs to be made?"

He gave her a big smile and her resolve melted. *That dimple!*

They arrived at a shimmering glass high-rise building with yellow accents in the city center. Rani knew it was one of the most exclusive residential condos in the city. Sam pulled into an underground garage, and once again Arjun supported her as they made their way to a private elevator.

Her heart skipped a few beats as they got to his floor and he punched in a code to open the door to his condo. *I'm going to be alone with him.* In all of her naughty dreams, she had not pictured him in bed, but now that was all she could think about.

She gasped as she entered the apartment. The doors

opened to a great room with thirteen-foot ceilings and a wall of windows that offered a breathtaking view of the Eiffel Tower, and the south Strip. *This is his rental?*

"Let's get you on the couch." His arm was around her, his body close to hers as he helped her across the room. His closeness made her heart flutter.

He made quick work of getting a first aid kit and cleaning and bandaging the cut on her foot. Her ankle was swollen but she rotated it and it didn't hurt.

"I don't think it's twisted. It just looks worse than it is."

He pulled an ottoman close, lifted her leg and set her foot on it. "How about you elevate it and I'll get some ice."

Arjun went into the kitchen and returned with a bag of frozen peas, which he placed on her ankle. She winced at the cold.

"This is quite a rental."

He smiled. "It belongs to a friend of mine. He's letting me use it while I'm here. The building is run like a hotel with full concierge, room service, all sorts of amenities."

"Are you going to miss Vegas when you go back to India?"

He shrugged and stared out the window. "I'm looking forward to being on my land again."

"Well, the Vegas lights are only fun for so long. I've had a hard time feeling at home here too."

"Where do you consider home?"

"California, I guess. It's where I was born and grew up."

"Why don't you feel like you belong there?"

She looked up into his honey-brown eyes. She'd never said out loud that it didn't feel like home. "I'm from a very traditional Indian family. When I went to school, my friends were American and I wanted to do the things they did but it's not the way my parents lived at home. I couldn't have boys call me, even if they were just friends. I wasn't allowed to go out after dinner, even when I was in high school. In the end I was always torn about whether I was Indian or American and no place felt like I belonged."

"Have you been to India?"

"Yes, I have some aunts and uncles in Delhi. India feels even less like home. Everyone there treats me like an NRI—nonresident Indian. To them I'm too Americanized and to my American friends I'm too Indian."

She hadn't meant for the conversation to get so serious and personal. She looked away from him towards the view.

"I guess that means you're what they call an ABCD. An American-Born Confused Desi."

She laughed at the expression, with its use of the colloquial Hindi term for Indian people. "Yes, that's exactly what I am."

"Well the way I see it, home is a feeling. A place where you can be yourself, feel at ease, shed the persona you show the world. For now, make my temporary home yours."

He shrugged off his jacket, then rolled up his sleeves. She watched his chest muscles flex underneath his shirt and felt a little light-headed.

"Are you hungry?"

She hated to admit it, but she was. The show had run late and it had been more than three hours since they ate dinner.

"I could eat. Maybe we can order a pizza or Chinese?"

"No way." He strode over to the open kitchen and she turned so she could watch him. He busied himself taking things out of the refrigerator. "I think I have everything I need to make lamb *saag*."

Her jaw dropped. She'd shared with him that it was her favorite dish. "You're going to try and make lamb *saag* now?"

"Why not? I'm not as bad as you think. I hired one of the best chefs in India to teach me how to cook."

She still couldn't fathom it. "You have room service, and

I'm sure you could hire a cook if you want. Why would you want to toil away in the kitchen?"

"So I can cook for a beautiful woman with the hopes of impressing her."

Beautiful woman, ha! The charm sure is on tonight. But she couldn't deny the fact that she was enjoying his attention, as fake as it might be. He was surrounded by fine-looking women every day, yet he'd made her feel like she was one in a million tonight.

"Thanks for the compliment but it's not necessary. I'm hardly in the class of women you're used to being with."

"And what class might that be?"

"Women who are tall and skinny enough to be on the cover of the Victoria's Secret catalog."

He rolled his eyes and shook his head. "That may be your idea of beauty but it is not mine." He began chopping an onion.

"What's your idea of beauty?"

He stopped what he was doing and looked straight at her. "You, Rani. You are my idea of beautiful. You're intelligent, talented, and don't need a pound of makeup or fancy clothes to make you attractive."

Her heart thumped so hard she could feel the pounding in her ears. She was glad he wasn't close to her to see her tremble at the very idea of him wanting her. Not even in her wildest fantasies did she imagine this conversation with him.

"Your idea of beauty is not only different than every man on the planet, but also every Indian. Especially every Indian." She could tell from the way he averted his eyes that he knew what she was talking about. In India, complexions ranged from almost white to almost black and the fairer a woman, the more beautiful she was considered. Growing up, she'd been told, *Rani, you are not fair, tall or slim so you must be smart if you want to marry a good man.* Her mother's words were not malicious but matter-of-fact. And they'd been echoed by every well-meaning aunt in her family.

It was a part of her culture that Rani both loved and hated. People were brutally honest. An American aunt would disingenuously reassure her if asked whether she looked fat in a pair of jeans. An Indian auntie would point out her big butt before she even asked.

"I don't view things that way. What you're referring to are the antiquated beauty standards of my parents' generation."

It was the perfect answer. One she wished she could have taped and replayed to her mother and every Indian woman of a certain generation. While the choice to marry Navin had been hers, the prejudices she had grown up with had influenced her decision-making. Navin was a successful, well-off Indian man who was much darker complected than she was. She'd liked the idea of joining a family where she was the lighter-skinned one, rather than the one who was constantly being handed skin bleaching creams.

Arjun held up a wineglass and she shook her head. She did not want to feel uninhibited with Arjun. She was already drunk on him.

"Mango *lassi*, then?"

She nodded and he retrieved a crystal glass containing the yellow beverage from the refrigerator.

She stood and gingerly put weight on her ankle. It seemed better. She made her way to the island and perched herself on one of the stools.

"Are you sure you're okay on that stool?"

She nodded and he handed her the glass.

She took a long sip and sighed with pleasure. "Wow, this might just be the best mango *lassi* I've had. Did you make this?"

He shook his head. "The head chef at one of my hotels in India made it. I had him overnight it."

"You had him mail mango *lassi* from India?" She laughed as she pictured a dripping FedEx envelope making its way across the Pacific Ocean.

"Why not? People have special meals shipped all the time."

Normal people did not have their meals shipped across the globe. They eat mediocre takeout or go to the frozen section of their grocery store to get their exotic fix.

He threw onions into a pan and while they sizzled, he added a bunch of spices. Then he began chopping tomatoes and garlic.

"The mango *lassi* alone is fine for me. You really don't have to go through the trouble of cooking."

"Rani, I'm trying desperately to impress you."

He did not just say that! She took a sip of her mango *lassi*, not trusting herself to speak. Her lips quivered on the glass and she barely tasted the cold liquid.

He added garlic and tomatoes to the pan, then some cubed lamb. The air filled with the smell of spices and sizzling meat. Rani's stomach growled as the familiar smells permeated her breath. It had been two years since she'd had her mother's home-cooked Indian meals. Two years since she'd talked to her parents.

"Is everything okay?" Arjun was looking at her over the steam rising from the pan.

She realized there were tears in her eyes. "Yes, it's just that my mom's kitchen smells like this and it's been a while since I've seen my parents."

He lifted the spatula from the pan and walked around the island to where she was seated. "Here, try this." He blew on the spatula before holding it to her lips. She carefully took a bite. The spices tingled on her tongue.

"Mmm, yum. Maybe a touch more salt."

He took the spatula and finished the bite that was left on it. "Yes, I think you're right."

They chatted easily about the comedy show while Arjun cooked. He made some basmati rice as the meat simmered. When the lamb was almost done, he cut some spinach and added it to the pot.

While waiting for the rice to cook, Arjun checked her ankle.

"Don't worry, it's still attached to my leg."

He let his hand linger a second too long and Rani's nerves jangled. She switched to talking about the hotel, desperate to remember that he was her client. When the food was ready, he spooned some rice and lamb *saag* onto a plate and handed it to her.

"This smells amazing."

He sat on a stool kitty-corner to her and they dug in. From the first bite Rani knew she was in love. "Wow, that's the best lamb *saag* I've ever had." She closed her eyes and savored the spices. When she looked again at Arjun he was staring at her, his honey-colored eyes completely dark.

"That face you just made, that is the reason I like to cook," he said thickly.

She turned back to her food, hoping he hadn't noticed the heat in her cheeks.

Once they were finished eating, she helped him clear the dishes and began washing the pots. "Rani, my housekeeper will be here tomorrow. You should rest your foot."

"Those of us who don't have housekeepers can't stand the thought of going to bed with a dirty kitchen," she joked.

"Is that your way of saying you'd like to go to bed here?"

Her hand flew to her mouth to shove the words back in. "That's not what I meant at all."

He laughed. "I'm just joking with you."

"How about I make us some masala chai?" she offered hastily to get off the topic of her spending the night.

"You really should rest your foot."

"I'm fine!"

"I do have a soft spot for homemade masala chai."

He helped her find what she needed, then leaned over her shoulder as she added cardamom, cloves, cinnamon and milk to a pot of water. She added a touch of black pepper, keeping up a chatter about how she'd bribed a *chai wallah* in Delhi to give her his recipe. Arjun stood so close to her that if she moved an inch, she'd be touching him. *Just a tiny step back and I'll feel his solid chest against me.*

"Are you learning to make masala chai now?"

She felt him nodding. "Lamb *saag* takes a while to prepare. Masala chai is much more efficient for the purposes of impressing women with my domestic prowess."

"I don't think you need to cook to impress women. I think every woman in India would gladly marry you."

"Ah, but I'm not interested in all those women in India. Right now I would really like for this ABCD to notice me."

Notice him? Her heart jumped into her throat. *The* Arjun Singh was trying to get her attention?

She took a tiny step back towards him, then turned so she was facing him. Her breasts brushed against his solid chest. A longing took hold of her, curled down her spine and lit a fire deep in her core. For just a moment, she wanted to be the woman a man like Arjun desired. To be the type of confident woman who could take control and seduce a man.

She looked up at him. Arjun's eyes widened as she lifted herself on tiptoe and touched his lips with hers. His kiss was featherlight, teasing, probing, testing. She circled her arms around his neck and opened her mouth to deepen the kiss. He obliged, letting his tongue explore her. His hands were loose around her waist. She felt the hard ridge of his desire and the molten heat in her own core. She moved against him and heard him groan, which sent a new pulse of electricity through her.

What am I doing? The temptation to see what he felt like had been all-consuming, but suddenly her brain kicked in. *He's a client.*

She made a sound and he slowly excruciatingly, ended the kiss. He moved his arms from her waist to her arms, unmolding their bodies, then rested his forehead on hers. "Rani." His voice was husky, and never in her life had her name sounded so sexy. *This was what it was supposed to feel like.*

But did Arjun think the kiss was special too, or was every kiss like that for India's hottest hottie?

"Oh no!" He pushed her aside just as the tea boiled over and splashed out of the pot. He turned the gas off, getting some of the hot liquid on his hand. He grimaced and shook it off.

Rani took a breath to force her mind back to reality. The kiss with Arjun had been a fantasy, one that she couldn't indulge in again.

What is wrong with me? Arjun prided himself on being in control. He hadn't planned on kissing Rani, let alone letting the kiss get so intense that he was seconds away from lifting her up and carrying her to his bedroom. That wasn't his style. He liked to take things slow with a woman, and until tonight he'd never had a problem keeping his desire in check. Especially for someone he worked with.

Rani ran the faucet, grabbed his hand and stuck it under the cold water.

"I'm so sorry, I totally forgot about the tea." Rani's face was inches from his; she looked stricken.

He smiled. "For that kiss, I'd happily burn my hand again."

She opened her mouth, then let her hand fall away from his.

"Arjun, I can't."

He turned the faucet off. His hand stung but he didn't care.

Rani was putting distance between them. *Damn it. Why didn't I stop myself?* He sensed that Rani was not very experienced with men. If he felt unsettled by that one kiss, he could only imagine how jolted she must be.

She bit her lip. The nervous gesture was so sexy that he had to resist the urge to run his thumb over her lips.

"Our firm has a very strict morals clause. I can be fired for getting involved with a client. I'm sorry, our relationship has to be business only." She grabbed her jacket and put it on.

"Because your firm has a morals clause or because you aren't interested?" Since when did he need to question a woman's interest in him?

She shifted on her feet. "I don't think there's a woman in this world who wouldn't be interested in you, Arjun. But I have my reputation to consider."

"I understand your concern. But know that I'm very discreet. This would not affect our work together on the Mahal."

"I don't know…" she said uncertainly.

He stepped closer to her but didn't touch her. "Tell me that kiss was nothing. Because I'll be honest with you, I've had my share of women, and that kind of earth-shattering kiss is not common."

The hint of a smile played on her lips and he knew he had her.

"It was earth-shattering, Arjun. And if you weren't my client, I would love to see more of you. And I mean that literally and figuratively."

The intense longing in her eyes was enough to make him want to pull her close, but she crossed her arms, clearly fighting with herself. "This isn't the right time for us. Maybe after I'm done with your hotel."

After we're done with the hotel, I'll be married. While

he and Hema had agreed to date other people before they were formally engaged, he had no intention of being with someone else once things became official between them.

He hung his head. "I'm sorry to hear that, Rani, but I understand. It'll just be business between us, then."

Six

Rani didn't know how she managed to focus on work for the next four weeks. Her nights were spent tossing and turning as she tried not to think about that kiss, and fantasize about what more Arjun could do with his mouth.

She still hadn't gotten over the fact that Arjun Singh was attracted to her. Plain old Rani. How she'd had the fortitude to turn him down was still a mystery.

The only thing saving her was work. As lead architect, she had to do more than just come up with the designs. She had to oversee the contractors and supply vendors, and take care of a thousand details. Enough to keep her traitorous mind from wandering.

Since the night of their kiss, Arjun hadn't attended any of the meetings for the project. He'd sent Vanessa. Each time a meeting was about to start, Rani had waited breathlessly for him and he hadn't come. She had politely asked about him only to be told that he was busy. She should've been relieved but was irritated. *Is he avoiding me? What the hell!*

She signed the last invoice on her desk and turned to her email. Despite being an architectural design firm, RKS's offices were as bland as a government building's. Her ten-foot-by-ten-foot space included a black functional desk, a gray mesh chair for her, and two guest chairs. The bookshelves were empty. With the promotion, she'd moved out of her cubicle and into the office and hadn't had time to personalize it other than to put a picture of her parents and siblings on the desk.

Her office phone rang and she answered it, expecting it to be Vanessa again. The woman called no less than three times a day.

"Rani, it's Bob."

The voice was familiar but it took Rani a second to realize it was *the* Bob. Bob Seagel. She hadn't spoken to him since he'd left RKS. The extent of their contact had been the occasional comment on a Facebook post.

"Bob, this is a surprise. How are you?"

"I'm great, Rani, how are you?"

She bit her lip. Why was Bob calling her out of the blue? "Fantastic. I finally made senior architect and am leading the remodel on the Mahal hotel. It's keeping me busy."

"I heard. Congratulations! That's actually why I'm calling. A Vanessa Knott called me asking about you."

Rani straightened.

"She made it sound like they hadn't fully signed with RKS and she knew you'd worked for me and was checking a reference. I saw right through her of course. Every major firm in the country knows RKS managed to win the contract for the Mahal."

That witch! What is she playing at?

"What did you tell her?"

"That you're the best architect I've ever worked with. She kept digging, though, trying to get at our personal relationship, but I didn't give her anything."

Rani's mouth was dry. "Bob, I appreciate you looking out for me. You left so fast two years ago we never got a chance to talk. I want you to know that I tried to stand up for you, to let them know you did nothing wrong. There's not a day that goes by that I don't feel terrible about what happened to you because of me. I'm so sorry for…"

"Rani, stop."

Rani bit her lip. She deserved whatever harsh things he had to say to her.

"I know you tried to protect me. Me leaving had nothing to do with our relationship."

What! "Then why did you resign in such a hurry?"

Bob sighed. "Ian Rabat wanted me out. And not because of you. That was just a pretext. He offered me a really lucrative severance package to leave right away so he could promote Delia."

"What? Why would he go to such lengths to promote her? She started a year before I did." What Rani didn't say is that Delia wasn't even that good. Despite her years of experience, her designs were bland and her technical expertise was dated.

"Oh, you don't know? Delia is Ian Rabat's daughter from an affair he had almost forty years ago."

Rani gasped. For all the sanctimonious advice Delia gave her about morals, she'd gotten the promotion because she was the boss's illegitimate daughter.

"I found out when I was digging around for why Ian wanted me gone. Turned out that Delia was planning to leave for another firm so Ian needed to find a way to promote her so she'd stay."

"And you agreed to this?"

"It was a good deal for me. And he hooked me up with a lucrative position at my current firm. But one of the conditions Ian had was that he wanted everyone to think I left because of you so Delia wouldn't suspect he was pulling strings to get her promoted."

"Does she know she's his daughter?"

"Yes."

Suddenly exhausted, Rani leaned back in her chair. "I wish you'd told me two years ago."

Bob was silent. "I should have. At the time I was thinking very selfishly. Ian's wife doesn't know about Delia so he asked me to keep it quiet. I'm sorry you've been carrying the guilt around for so long, Rani. I would've told you if I knew you'd taken it so hard."

"Well, thank you for telling me now. You can count on my discretion."

"Oh, you don't have to be discreet. Vanessa was nice enough to tell me the rumors Ian spread around Vegas once I left. He's ruined my reputation in that entire town. By the way, watch out for Vanessa. After she called, I asked around about her. She's Vegas all the way. Always after something better for herself."

That's rich coming from you.

Rani somehow found the words to politely end the call. Bob promised to keep in touch, though she had no intention of staying friends with him. *All that time feeling guilty about Bob, standing up for him no matter how detrimental it was to my reputation, and he's only been looking out for himself.* Her entire life had been spent fulfilling other people's needs. First her parents', then her in-laws', and then RKS's. She'd let the company use her. She was done with that. It was time for her to get what she wanted, to take control of her life. She was going to do something for herself.

Seven

It had been another night spent tossing and turning. Despite cranking the AC so high that Em had threatened to throw her out, Rani woke up hot and tortured with the feel of Arjun's kiss burned into her soul.

She'd written a terse email to him yesterday asking whether he knew Vanessa had called Bob about her. His response had come immediately to ask whether they could move today's owners condo walk-through to seven o'clock in the evening. Vanessa had emailed to say she wouldn't be coming.

Rani was proud of how the condo had turned out. RKS had allowed her to call in every contractor favor they were owed, not because they were trying to help her, but because they wanted to secure the contract to design the rest of the hotel, including its five hundred guest rooms, the conference rooms and the casino. Every architectural firm in Vegas was still courting Arjun and RKS didn't want to lose out.

She looked around the room one last time. She had asked the contractors to leave so she could take the meeting alone with Arjun. There was a knock on the door just as the clock struck seven.

Her heart thundered. She checked her reflection in the antique mirror in the foyer. She had splurged and bought herself a skirt suit with a stylish short jacket, and paired it with a sleeveless crimson blouse with a deep V-neck. She took a breath and opened the door.

And there he was! Dressed in jeans and an open collared shirt, Arjun looked effortlessly hot.

"Mr. Singh," she said with a purposefully mischievous tone, "I'm glad this meeting is worth your time." Rani would never have spoken to another client that way, but a familiarity hummed between them as he gave her a dimpled smile.

"Ms. Gupta." His tone was measured but his eyes unabashedly traveled the length of her body. And just like that, eating ramen noodles for a week to afford the new clothes was worth it.

She waved him inside. The antique mirror reflected the *jaali* wall that separated the foyer from the great room. A staircase led to the upper level with the bedrooms, which had a balcony overlooking the large living area and kitchen below.

He cleared his throat. "I'm sorry I haven't been able to attend our meetings. I ran into an issue with the gaming commission that's taken up my time."

"No apologies necessary. Vanessa is highly capable. Why didn't she come?"

"I suspended her, and am thinking of firing her."

Rani's hand flew to her mouth. "Not on my account, I hope? I didn't mean for her to lose her job, I just wanted to know whether you had put her up to it." Though if she was honest with herself, she never suspected Arjun would have done something like that. She'd wanted him to put Vanessa in her place.

"Of course not. And I don't allow my staff to behave that way."

Rani took a step back at his tone. "It isn't bad enough to fire her."

"She called your former boss to get dirt on you. I suspect it's because she was jealous. It was highly unprofessional."

"Why would she be jealous of me?"

Arjun rolled his eyes. "Because she could see I was interested in you, Rani. She called me on it after our dinner at Delhi Dhaba."

"And what did you say?"

"I told her it was none of her business. And speaking of business, let's get through ours, shall we?"

Rani's heart sank at his crisp tone. "Okay, then. As you can see, we have the main living areas finished. Upstairs, only the master bedroom is finished, but the other four will have the same look and feel."

He ran his hand over the wood carvings in the antique mirror frame, then walked to the living room. RKS had an excellent interior decorating team, but Rani had overseen every selection here. Divans upholstered in a rich royal-blue-and-silver pattern lined the walls underneath the balcony overhang. In the center of the room were two long couches facing each other with two large armchairs on either side forming a square. Silver hammered coffee and end tables provided an accent. The floors were a dark hand-scraped wood. Beyond the living room, the open kitchen had copper pots offset by antique white cabinets with brass handles and quartz counters. The furniture was minimal but traditional.

Arjun walked through the space, examining each piece of furniture, light fixture and decoration. Rani stood back, enjoying the silent smile that played on his lips when he touched a carved wood elephant that was her favorite piece. She should've been anxious about whether he liked her work but she was enjoying the luxury of watching his athletic figure flex and bend as he examined things. Was it really wrong to want him? Just once, maybe twice? To feel like a woman sexy enough for a man like him?

She cleared her throat. "How does the space feel?"

There was no hesitation in his reply. "Like home."

She smiled. "Your home maybe. My home has Ikea furniture and a stove from the seventies."

He smiled. "You're right. My house does have extraordinary luxuries. But what I mean is the colors, the fabrics and the wood. It all reminds me of Rajasthan. Thank you, Rani. This is what I wanted, the feel of my home."

"I can't even imagine the astronomical price you will charge for this condo."

"I don't plan to rent it out."

Rani tilted her head. "After what you've spent on this?" Arjun's budget for the owners condo was double the typical amount per square foot at similar luxury hotels. Rani assumed it was an investment he'd make up by using it to attract high rollers to the casino. How else was he going to make money on this extravagant unit?

"This is for me. For my sanity when I need to be here."

"So you won't live in India?"

"India is my home. It's where my family is and where my life will continue to be. I will never leave there. I can't imagine anyplace else being home. This is my…" he clicked his fingers as if searching for the right word "…my…"

"Escape?"

A wistful smile crossed his lips, and he looked so lost that Rani stepped towards him and touched his arm to bring him back. He smiled down at her. "Yes, my escape." He met her gaze. "Rani, you've made this as close to home as I could possibly feel. It's beyond my expectations."

His voice was thick and her heart filled with joy. Arjun's praise was hard to come by and she was exhilarated by the fact that she'd met his exacting standards for a space that was so personal to him. She released a long held breath. For years she'd been beaten down, first by Navin convincing her that she was screwed up inside, and then Delia making her doubt her abilities to lead this project. It was nice to hear someone build her up rather than cut her down.

"Shall we see the bedroom?"

Her words hung in the space between them. She focused on his lips as her nerves tingled and sparked. *He's only here for four and a half more months. This wouldn't be anything permanent. Something just for me.* It was a chance to explore a side of herself that had never surfaced before. What was wrong with that?

"I don't need to see any more. I think you've earned your firm the contract for the rest of the hotel."

Rani pulled out of her salacious thoughts and grinned at him, silently whooping with joy. The commission from this contract would put her on the path to opening her own firm.

"Before you hand me the keys to the hotel, are you sure you don't want to see the master bedroom?"

His smile flickered. "I'll see it later."

"Without me?" She couldn't keep the disappointment out of her voice. This entire project was her baby. Yes, the great room was an example of her best work, but the bedroom was her masterpiece. She'd personally picked out the sheets for the bed. Egyptian cotton.

He shook his head. "I should get going."

Rani couldn't believe what she was hearing. Where did he have to go? It wasn't even eight o'clock yet. "Arjun, it'll only take a minute. I've been killing myself trying to get it ready for tonight. The least you can do is come see it."

He stepped back from her and shook his head. "I told you that it would just be business between us. Rani, I cannot walk into a bedroom with you and keep that promise."

Eight

So he still feels it. A frisson of excitement sparked through Rani. One way or another, she was getting him into that bedroom.

"Mr. Singh, you assured me that your personal feelings would not affect our working relationship." Rani put the right amount of force in her voice.

He sighed, then swore under his breath. "Right. But what do you want me to do? You are doing a fantastic job with my hotel. In fact, you're the only one that can achieve the vision I have for this hotel and more. You just proved it with what you've done here. I want you to finish my hotel, but…" He took a heavy breath. "I have not stopped thinking about you, and that's why I've been avoiding you."

Her heart was doing cartwheels. *I'm not the only one who's obsessed with that kiss.* It made sense for her to swoon over him, but the fact that he—a man who could have any woman he wanted—was thinking about her was just too heady.

"Follow me, we're going to the master bedroom."

She didn't wait for him as she walked to the corner stair-case that led to the upper level. He soon caught up to her but didn't say a word as she opened the hand-carved double doors. She had planned to point out how the carvings depicted the homecoming of Lord Rama, the event from Hindu mythology that formed the basis for Diwali. As the story went, the festival of lights came to be when Rama returned victorious after a battle against evil and all of the households in his kingdom lit *diyas* or candles to illuminate the way for him. She remembered from an interview she'd read that Diwali was Arjun's favorite holiday. The doors had cost more than her annual income but she knew Arjun would appreciate the craftsmanship. Now she breezed past them into the master bedroom.

It consisted of a main room, a luxurious bathroom suite and a sitting area. A four-poster bed with rich velvet drapes was the centerpiece of the space. Large windows along one wall glittered with the lights of the Vegas Strip. The windows had been finished with built-in privacy shades that could be opened and closed with the push of a button.

She turned to him, expecting him to explore the room like he had downstairs. She'd handpicked every piece of furniture, including the antique silver side tables, a richly upholstered chaise longue, a couple of well-placed chairs, and a TV cleverly hidden behind a painting that slid aside by remote control.

But Arjun wasn't looking at the room. His eyes were on her. Dark and penetrating.

"A month ago I was sure that I didn't want to get personally involved with you," she said tentatively. She bit her lip, trying to formulate her next words.

"But now?" His voice was thick, the anticipation heavy.

Rani had done a lot of thinking in the wake of Bob's confession. She was done blaming herself; she had done nothing wrong. She hated working at RKS. Her stock in the company had risen and she realized that the respect she was getting now should have been hers all along. Word was already spreading that she'd won Arjun's business for RKS, and firms were making subtle overtures towards her. With Arjun giving her the contract for the full hotel, she had even more power in the company. If they wanted to throw the morals clause at her, let them.

She met his searing gaze, her chin up, her shoulders square. "Now I want to feel the way I did when you kissed me the first time."

He made a guttural sound. "You need to say the words, Rani. Do not play with me. Tell me what you want me to do to you." His voice slid over her like hot fudge on a sundae. It melted any last doubts she had.

"I want you. I need you to make love to me." *Who is this talking?* Rani didn't know where the words had come from. She'd never spoken to a man like that. Not even in her wildest Arjun fantasies.

He didn't waste a second. He closed the distance between them, cupped her face in his hand and brought his mouth down on hers. This time the kiss was exactly as she expected it to be, hard and bruising. She stood on her toes to get even closer to him and he bent down further. Every nerve inside her was alive, begging for his touch. She ran her hands along the muscles of his back, scratching lightly with her fingers, letting him know that she was ready for more. He groaned into her mouth and she pressed her body into his.

Oh, he's definitely feeling it too.

Arjun had meant to kiss her lightly and sweetly, something to tempt her into what he really wanted from her. But his lips had a mind of their own. They pressed against hers with naked need. His tongue darted out and plunged into her mouth, hungry for a taste of her. She fit perfectly into him and moaned when she felt his arousal. He shifted to mold himself to her body, all the while hungrily plundering her mouth. He dropped his hand from her cheek and ran it down her shoulder and over her waist. Her hands were in his hair, tugging and pulling. He reached underneath her blouse and cupped her breast through the lace of her bra. It was soft and round and heavy, her nipple taut.

He wanted her. Bad. Unlike his brother, who partied and had one-night stands, Arjun enjoyed short, discreet affairs. He always selected intelligent, career-minded women who understood from the start that their relationship would be short-lived and most importantly, needed to be kept private. His girlfriends were secure enough in their lives not to fall in love with him. Did Rani meet the last criterion? Could she be with him without losing her heart?

A plaintive moan escaped her throat and the sound was desperately sexy. "Are you sure you want to do this here? Like this?" He half hoped she'd ask him to stop. When he'd imagined their first time—something he didn't care to admit doing—he'd envisioned champagne and fine chocolates. And room service breakfast. Though now that he was in this room, there was poetry in christening it with the woman who was making his dream hotel come true.

She reached into her jacket pocket and took out a condom. "I want this, Arjun." Her voice was barely over a whisper. He took the foil packet from her hands and strode over to the nightstand, barely noticing the Calacatta marble top. He turned to her with a smile on his face. "I don't think we'll be needing that for a while. I plan to make sure you are good and ready before we get to that part."

Her mouth fell open and her eyes went wide. The prim shirt did little to conceal the peaks of her nipples as they thrust forward.

He shrugged off his jacket and draped it on the bench

at the foot of the bed. Rani stood frozen, so he stepped behind her and kissed the back of her neck, enjoying the little shiver she gave up. He kissed her earlobe as he pushed her jacket down over her shoulders. He flung it onto the bench next to his. Then he lifted her shirt over her head and took it off. She gasped as he cupped her breasts, teasing her nipples through the thin lace of her bra. He unzipped her skirt and let it fall to the ground.

"Um, there is one thing I need to tell you."

He took a breath. She'd been married before so he knew she wasn't a virgin. That was a line he refused to cross. There were plenty of women in India who still believed in saving themselves for their husbands and he would never be the man to take that away from them.

"I've only been with one man."

Arjun's hands stilled. Somehow that didn't surprise him. But it did complicate things. Would sex mean more to her than it did to him?

Will she expect something from me?

"Do you want me to stop?"

"No!"

She turned around so she was facing him and stepped close enough that her breasts were touching his chest. "I just wanted you to know that I'm not very experienced in how to treat a man in bed."

He touched her cheek. "I don't think you need to worry about my pleasure." He looked pointedly down to where his arousal was plainly visible. "But you do understand that there is no long-term future for the two of us. This is temporary."

She nodded vehemently. "I'm not looking for a relationship. I've done the Indian marriage and in-laws thing and it's not for me. My career is my focus right now."

He should have been relieved, yet for some reason her words twisted in his heart. What did it matter anyway?

She was on the same page as him, and that's what was important.

"Good, let's show you what you've been missing." He moved his hands to her bottom, then lifted her into his arms, causing her to squeal in surprise. He walked over to the bed and set her down. He went to unclasp her bra but her hands flew to her breasts.

"You are beautiful, Rani."

She reached over and flipped the light switch on the wall, throwing the room into darkness. There was enough light from the windows that he could see Rani perched on the edge of the bed, her arms protectively around her chest. She truly was beautiful with just the right amount of womanly curves that stoked the fire already raging through his body.

He didn't need to ask her to know that her sexual experience hadn't been great. It was obvious from the way she fought with herself, responding to him with open desire, then shutting down just as quickly. *What's the right move here?* She was like a newborn kitten, eager to explore but afraid to approach. He was used to women who were sexually liberated, who told him how to deliver them pleasure. Women who knew what they wanted and weren't shy about it. But with Rani, he'd have to figure out what drove her wild without scaring her away.

He was up for the challenge.

What was I thinking? Rani had waxed, bought lacy underwear and packed a condom. Actually, a whole box of condoms. She'd spent a month of sleepless nights fantasizing about Arjun running his hands over her, imagined his naked body pressed against hers, his mouth ravaging her. In the cold light of day she'd had agonizing arguments with her heart about whether the risk was worth it. Finally she came to the conclusion that Arjun wasn't from Las Vegas, or even an American. He wasn't going to be around long-term so she didn't have to think about what life with him would be like. This project would be over soon enough. Surely she could indulge herself, especially now that she knew Delia's hypocritical secret.

So tonight she'd been prepared, physically and mentally, for the kind of toe-curling sex Em talked about. And here she was, her entire body tingling in anticipation of his next touch, and yet she was letting Navin's words worm into her thoughts.

Some women don't like sex. I think you're one of them.

Arjun came towards her and placed his arms on either side of hers. The lights from the Strip glimmered in his eyes. "Are you okay? We can stop now if you want."

Why does he keep asking me that? Was her nervousness that obvious? Or was he having doubts himself? In response, she began unbuttoning his shirt. It was time to see how well her mind had conjured his naked body in her dreams. When she was done with the buttons he shrugged off the shirt and leaned forward again, placing his palms on the bed. His face was a mere inch away from hers. She looked straight into his blazing eyes and unbuckled his belt. Very carefully, she unzipped his pants, touching his length with her hands as she went. He closed his eyes and took a sharp breath. She pushed his boxer briefs down with his pants and he kicked them off. She got her first look at him in the shadows and wished she hadn't turned the lights off. *Magnificent.*

Her imagination had not done him justice. Dark hair covered his chest. His legs were pure muscle, his arousal long and thick. She licked her lips, her mind completely emptying of all coherent thought. He stepped towards her, bent his head and kissed her. This time she kissed him back with abandon, sucking on his tongue the way she wanted to suck on him, letting him know just how much she ached for him.

He ran his hand down her body, stopping to caress her breasts, then continued down to her stomach and—*oh, thank you*—right between her legs. Her bud was throbbing and his finger found it with ease, applying just the right amount of pressure to make her moan and feel a welcome rush of heat. For once in her life, she knew exactly what she wanted. She pushed her black lace panties down, then took hold of Arjun and guided him towards her. Just when his tip touched her swollen bud, he put his hands on top of hers and retreated.

A moan of protest escaped her lips.

"Not so fast."

She didn't have the words to tell him she couldn't wait, that the heat coursing through her was so intense that she would internally combust. He gently pushed her shoulders back until she was flat on the bed. When he nestled his head between her legs, she gasped. His tongue found her throbbing need and circled and sucked it. Then his fingers pushed into her gently, slowly, *too damn slowly.* She rocked against his finger, letting him know that she wanted it faster, harder.

"Rani..." His voice was thick and husky and so wonderfully sexy but all she could think about was getting his mouth back on her. She lifted her head and weaved her fingers through his hair, grabbing a fistful. He got the message and pushed three fingers inside her. Suddenly an overwhelming crescendo seized her body, giving her that sweet release she'd been thirsting for. Her mind and body exploded and she didn't know how much time passed before she came down from the stratosphere and back into the real world.

Wow. She thought she'd had orgasms before but it was like comparing the intensity of a candle flame to that of a roaring fire. *I've really been missing out.* Once again, Navin's voice pierced her head, telling her that she was too reserved in bed, too unwilling to experiment. *Too cold.* She pushed Navin firmly out of her mind. She wasn't going to let him spoil this glorious moment for her.

She propped herself on her elbow to find Arjun laying a trail of kisses up her belly toward her breasts. He took one nipple in his mouth and teased it with his tongue. *Whoa, whoa, whoa.* The inferno inside her was ramping back up. His tongue was doing things that restoked that very delicious but raging fire deep within her. By the time he made it to her neck, she was writhing underneath him. A smile played on his lips as he lifted his head and looked at her. *That damn sexy mouth.* She reached up and kissed him, smelling herself on his lips. The scent drove her wild, as did the feel of his hardness against her. She reached between them and grabbed him. He put his hand on hers and stilled her. *Am I doing it wrong?*

"Rani, if you'd like me to last a little while longer, you need to stop touching me."

What? I'm affecting him?

"I want you inside me. Now." She colored at the nakedness of her words.

He groaned and lifted himself off her, grabbing the condom off the nightstand. He slipped it on as she watched. She expected him to plunge right into her but he returned his lips to her breast, suckling and teasing. She raised her pelvis, an open invitation, but he kept torturing her with his mouth and then his fingers. Finally, unable to take it any longer, she grabbed him and thrust upward, so he was inside her. She clenched against him. He rocked faster and faster, matching her rhythm. Then suddenly it came, the explosion that lit her world. Even more intense than the last, it took a while for her to come down from the high.

When she opened her eyes, Arjun was leaning toward

her, his forehead touching hers. *Did he enjoy it? Did he fin- ish?* She'd been so focused on her own pleasure that she hadn't paid attention to his. Now she noticed that he was soft inside her.

He lifted his head and dropped a gentle kiss on her lips.

She wanted to tell him how much this had meant to her. To know that she was capable of enjoying sex like a nor- mal woman. That nothing was wrong with her. She could arouse a man like him and have the kind of mind-blowing orgasms that other women always talked about.

Most of all she wanted to thank him for showing her that she wasn't broken.

7>He will rock your world. If you let him.

Nine

"Well." Arjun spoke first. "We can't sleep here tonight."

She nodded. "The workers may show up really early to start on the other bedrooms. Um…it was a great. I guess I'll see you around."

He laughed and pulled her close. "Oh no, you're not getting away that easy. I'm spending the night with you." Her heart kicked at the fierceness in his voice. "We will go back to my place."

Rani wanted to object to the plan but the thought of spending the night with him was too tempting.

They dressed quickly, then made the bed together. He stealthily held her hand on the way down to the almost completed lobby, then let go when they reached the circular driveway out front where Sam was waiting with the car. She appreciated Arjun's caution; the last thing she needed was for RKS to suspect what had just happened between them. While she wasn't so worried about losing her job anymore, she didn't want people to think she got the hotel contract because she was sleeping with Arjun.

She followed his car and parked in the visitor's lot. He met her in the lobby. As soon as they got inside his condo, he kissed her. She knew without a doubt that he was ready to make love to her again and that knowledge gave her a rush. It had been such a struggle to arouse Navin; she'd constantly felt inadequate.

In one night, Arjun had elevated her confidence, in and out of bed. A month ago a promotion was the best she could've hoped for with her career. Now, a world of possibilities lay at her feet. All because Arjun believed in her. When she was done with his hotel, all of Vegas would know her name. And this time for the right reasons.

Then doubt snaked through her.

He began undressing her but she stopped him. "Arjun, I need to ask. Did you give me the hotel contract because you'd hoped we would get together tonight?"

He frowned at her. "How could you ask me that, Rani? I gave it to you because you earned it. You did an extraordinary work with the owners condo. And I had no idea you were even interested in us getting together. You did a good job convincing me I was not worth your time."

She laughed. "Not worth my time? You've been consuming my every dream since we met."

He grinned, and she kissed that dimple that had been driving her mad.

"Well then, how about we make some more dreams come true." And with that, he led her into the bedroom.

When she woke in the morning, all she could think about was how unreal it was to be in Arjun's bed and not starting at the popcorn-textured ceiling of her apartment. She rolled over, expecting to find Arjun, but the bed was empty. She sat up. He wasn't in the room. She looked for a note on the nightstand but there was none.

Is our time over? She quickly wrapped a sheet around her and raced downstairs to the great room. A room service cart next to the dining table where Arjun, dressed in a bathrobe, was seated with a cup and saucer in his hand. She let out a breath.

"Good morning." He grinned when he saw her. "What do you eat for breakfast?"

"Usually it's coffee and an oatmeal bar."

"Well, today you have your choice." He waved to the cart where there were no fewer than ten dishes covered by silver domes.

She gasped. "That's enough food to feed half the building."

"Well, I didn't know what you liked, so I ordered one of everything through room service. There's omelets, French toast, eggs Benedict, pancakes, Belgian waffles, oatmeal…"

Room service was a luxury she didn't allow herself even when she traveled for work on an expense account. The very thought of how much all this food must've cost made her head spin.

"Okay, let me get some clothes on."

"How about a bathrobe? It'll save me some time when I take it off later. There's one for you in the bedroom."

A shiver of anticipation went through her as she went and got the bathrobe, then joined him at the table.

"I don't have any morning meetings. How about you?" Arjun poured her a cup of coffee as she lifted the domes off the breakfast dishes.

"My first meeting is in an hour and a half, but I have to go home and change. I can't show up in the same clothes I was wearing yesterday."

"What size do you wear?"

"Um…none of your business."

He rolled his eyes. "There are some nice stores downstairs in the building complex. Let me call down to the concierge."

Rani stared as he called and got connected to the store he wanted. "Yes, this is Mr. Singh in P241. I need you to send up a few complete business outfits for my guest to select from. I'll give you a credit card now for anything she decides to keep."

He handed the phone to her. "I'll give you some privacy."

Was he for real? Did he really expect her to order clothes like it was room service?

"Rani?"

She realized he was still holding the phone. As soon as he handed it to her, he disappeared upstairs. The woman on the other end efficiently asked her about size, color preferences and whether she preferred any designers. *Designers?* Her clothes came from discount department stores.

She hung up the phone and found Arjun. "I'm not letting you buy me clothes," she said.

"Why not?"

"Because I'm not one of those women who lets a man buy her things and tell her what to wear." She crossed her arms and a minute of silence passed between them.

"It's not that, Rani. I just figured that it'll give us more time together. Every minute I get to spend with you is precious." He touched her arm and her heart squeezed. It was a sweet gesture and the words were even sweeter, but a part still stung. Every minute together was precious because they wouldn't have too many. She knew this was temporary and was really okay with it when all it was about was hot and lusty sex. But his tenderness was something else.

She shook her head. "Let's not waste time arguing over this. I need to leave in forty minutes."

He opened his mouth to object but then gestured to

the dining table instead. They dug into the scrumptious breakfast.

"Tell me about your family," he asked after a minute of silence.

A piece of egg stuck in her throat and she coughed. "What do you want to know?"

"How about telling me more about your siblings."

She relaxed and a smile spread on her face. "My brother, Sohel, is two years younger than I am. He's trying to break into Hollywood as a screenwriter and director. My sister, Anaya, is much younger. She's still a teenager. What about your siblings?"

She already knew he had three sisters and a brother but she wanted to see how he described them.

He took a sip of his tea. "Well, my brother, Sameer, is three years younger than me and is proving to be a handful. We are so careful about our media image and he is constantly getting in trouble. I have a budget just to pay off reporters, a full time IT guy to sanitize his social media accounts, and an entire PR team that monitors all the news outlets."

His family did do a good job of keeping the dirty laundry under wraps but she didn't realize how much it took. "And your sisters? Are they just as much trouble?"

He sighed. "Divya, Karishma and Naina. They are harder to handle than Sameer. My mother is constantly calling me about some issue with them."

"Like what?"

"Well, yesterday, just before I got to the hotel, she called because Karishma and Divya snuck out of the house to go to a nightclub with their friends and Naina, who is the youngest, put pillows under their bedsheets to cover up for them."

Rani tensed. "Why did they have to sneak out?" She

knew that his sisters were only a few years younger than him. Definitely old enough to be independent.

"Because it's not safe for *girls* to be out late at night by themselves in India."

Rani set down her fork a little harder than she intended and it clanked on the plate. "But it's okay for the *boys* to go out late?" Her tone was sharp but she didn't regret it.

He looked up. "It's different in India. Police enforcement is not what it should be and harassment is not punished the way it is in America so the bad elements are a little more aggressive."

She was well aware of the horrifying statistics regarding women's safety but it was not an excuse to curtail their freedoms.

"And do you know how many men get murdered every night around the world? No one uses that as an excuse to lock them at home at night."

He opened his mouth, then closed it. "You're right. I know how chauvinistic it sounds. My parents are very traditional. There are rules in our house that have existed for generations. And yes, they are sexist, but I have to choose the battles I fight. My role in the family is to run the business. My battle with my parents has been to expand outside of India—they were very reluctant to go that route. But one of the benefits is that it will open up so many opportunities for my sisters to experience the world."

Your parents sound as bad as my ex in-laws. Rani would never say the words out loud to him; it wasn't her business. They weren't in a relationship. She had fought her own battles, and paid the price for her freedom. What did she care what Arjun's family was like? It wasn't as if they were ever going to meet.

He leaned forward and placed his hand on hers. "I know my parents are old-fashioned. It's something I deal with every day in our house. I'm working on them, one day at a time." He smiled. "Luckily they are far away and the only thing we need to worry about right now is how to delay your first meeting."

She sighed, feeling herself give in to his charm once again. After all, what did she care about his family? She wasn't going to marry him. This was just a casual affair.

Ten

Arjun rubbed his temples. He'd been hoping to see Rani tonight but it didn't look like he'd make it out of the office before midnight. He was having trouble with his liquor license in addition to the red tape being thrown up by the gaming commission. It was the usual headaches that came with opening a hotel. Whether it was India or America, the last-minute troubles were the same. He'd hired a Las Vegas firm to make sure the right palms were greased and the appropriate people wined and dined, but he had to personally show face and kiss a few rings to make it all work. He half suspected that since he'd used the gaming commission as an excuse not to return to India for the Diwali holiday, effectively postponing his engagement, it was the universe's way of making him pay.

He couldn't stop thinking about Rani. He'd only seen her once since their first night together. He'd taken her out to dinner at an exclusive Japanese restaurant on the outskirts of the city. The food was amazing, and her face glowed in the soft lights.

They'd talked about politics, religion, even his problems with the gaming commission. Normally Arjun kept to superficial topics with his dates, like food and travel. It was his stress-relief time, when he didn't have to think, plan, solve a problem or make an impossible decision. But with Rani, they lapsed naturally into meaningful conversations. He asked her opinions about how to resolve the problems he was having with the hotel and she offered solutions and helped him think through thorny issues. She was a good strategist and he liked talking things over with her.

He looked at his calendar again to see if there was something he could move to make time for Rani. While he enjoyed the company of women, he fit them in during holes in his schedule. He never arranged his meetings around them. But Rani was special. He wanted more time with her, in and out of bed. It was the last time he'd get to be with a woman because he wanted to be, not because he had to.

His mother had made it very clear that she was planning the wedding as soon as the hotel was done and she would not accept any more excuses from him. Hema was sending him daily text messages freaking out. He had finally told her that she had to accept the inevitable just like he did.

His assistant buzzed to let him know that Rani was downstairs and he asked for her to be sent up immediately.

"This is a nice surprise." He greeted her from behind his desk. His office walls were all glass and he didn't want to give his staff a show.

She smiled and took a seat opposite him. Her demeanor was professional but her eyes glinted with excitement. "I have the final designs for the guest rooms. Your team has already approved them but I wanted an excuse to see you." On Rani's advice, Arjun hadn't fired Vanessa, but he had read her the riot act and she'd been much more pleasant to work with.

"I'm glad you came. I have yet another dinner with the gaming commission tonight."

She held up a brown bag. "Then how about lunch with me?"

He smiled. "That depends on what you brought me."

"The best drunken noodle you'll ever have. This Thai food truck near me is amazing, just the right amount of spice and heat."

He smiled. *Just like you, Rani. The right amount of spice and heat.*

She took out a container and handed it to him with a plastic fork. He stared at it, the foil tin with the paper lid stinging him with a long buried memory.

"Is something wrong?"

He shook his head. "The last time I ate out of a container like this was eleven years ago."

Her face fell and she set the container on the table. "I'm sorry, I should've thought about the fact that you're not used to eating food out of plastic."

He shook his head. "It's not that. It reminds me of this time in Mumbai with my ex-girlfriend. It didn't end well."

Rani tilted her head, her eyes begging him to tell her more.

He sighed. Why was he thinking of Lakshmi now? The last time he had talked about her was five years ago, when he'd agreed to marry Hema.

"I'm so sorry. That must have been so painful for you." Rani extended her arm across the table and put her hand on his.

"I was going to marry her. Her parents didn't approve and neither did mine so we were going to elope." He waited for the familiar ache to settle into his heart but it didn't come.

"Why didn't the parents approve?"

"Hers did not approve because they knew my parents would never accept her and they were worried that I'd dump her. Mine took issue with the fact that Lakshmi came from a poor, unknown family."

"Ah, truly the makings of a Bollywood film."

He smiled. "We thought so too when we decided to elope. We were meeting in Juhu Beach to plan the details. I stopped at her favorite restaurant to pick up *hakka* noodles. We were sitting on the sand eating out of containers exactly like those." He pointed to the takeout food she'd brought. "Then she broke my heart."

Rani didn't say anything, giving him the space to tell his story.

"She decided she didn't want to marry me."

"Why not?" Rani's voice had the same incredulous tone his had when he'd asked the question of Lakshmi.

"That day she'd auditioned for a role in a Bollywood film and she was offered the part. It was her life's dream."

"I understand such a profession wouldn't have been acceptable in your family, especially eleven years ago, but was it worth letting go of the woman you loved?"

He sighed. "She never gave me the chance to make that decision. That role had been offered to her on the condition that she leave me. My mother orchestrated it. Ma challenged me with the idea, and not in a million years did I think Lakshmi would take that offer so I told my mother to try it. I wanted to prove to Ma that our love was real. But Lakshmi came to tell me that it was her big Bollywood break and she couldn't give it up for me."

Rani bit her lip. "How could your mother do that to you?"

He bristled at her tone. "My mother has always had my best interest at heart."

Rani's lips thinned and Arjun could see the disapproval

in her eyes. He didn't want her to get the wrong impression of his mother. "I'm going to tell you something that only my family knows." He swallowed to ease the lump in his throat, wondering why he wanted to share something so personal with Rani when he wasn't yet ready to tell her about Hema. "My biological mother died giving birth to me."

Rani gasped and squeezed his hand. "This is something I didn't know until recently," he continued. "My mother gave me so much love that not once did I question whether she was my real mother. My siblings who are her biological children still say I am my mother's favorite. She was heartbroken when I found out." So much so that his mother hadn't spoken to her own brother for years for telling Arjun.

"You would do anything for your mother, wouldn't you?" Rani's voice held no judgment. Just soft understanding. Arjun nodded.

"Do you still think about Lakshmi?"

"Enough time has passed that I've let go." Or at least he did a good job pretending he had.

"It doesn't seem that way to me."

His heart stopped in his chest. On the pretense of taking the Thai food container, he extracted his hand from Rani's.

"So let's try this. I really miss street food."

"You're changing the subject."

He opened the lid of the container, and Rani passed him a fork. He chose his words carefully. "No one can take Lakshmi's place. She was my first love and you know what they say about first loves."

She nodded and a thought struck him. "Do you feel like you can never love someone the way you loved your ex?" The very idea of her confirming such an idea soured his mouth.

She took a bite of her food and chewed. He did the same, knowing that she needed time to formulate her answer, just as he needed a minute to prepare for it.

"I don't think I ever truly loved Navin. But he was the best among the choices I had. My parents expected me to marry an Indian and I wanted someone who understood what it's like to be an Indian American."

"And Navin was like that?"

"He was. But his family wasn't." She paused, clearly weighing her words. "They were very traditional and it was hard for us to see eye to eye on a lot of things."

"Like?"

"They asked me to stop working because they didn't want people to think Navin didn't earn enough to support us. They were constantly harping on my weight. My mother-in-law would make me get on the scale to prove I was trying to lose weight. She would check the food in the kitchen to see what I'd eaten. They had access to Navin's bank accounts and constantly questioned the littlest purchases. It was suffocating."

Tears glittered in Rani's eyes and Arjun wanted desperately to get up and comfort her, but her story was hitting a little too close to home for him. His sisters' complaints echoed those of Rani.

"At first I resolved to work it out because I don't believe in divorce and Navin promised me that we'd only live with my in-laws for the first year so we could buy a big house of our own. As it turned out, his parents moved in with us when we did buy our house. And things were getting worse between me and Navin. He was constantly angry with me for every little thing—the way I hung my towel in the bathroom, if I sneezed too loudly, and on and on."

"I'm sorry, Rani."

She shrugged. "It's over now. I've learned my lesson—that you don't marry an Indian man, you marry his family. I wish I'd taken the time to get to know Navin's parents before I married him."

He nodded. That was one of the reasons why he had

agreed to marry Hema. She was a family friend and familiar with the traditions of his house. He'd been in denial about the fact that he really had no choice in whom he could marry. Maybe that's why he hadn't told Rani about Hema. Telling Rani would make it a little too real, too inevitable for him.

He leaned forward. "Don't blame yourself, Rani. It was Navin's job to protect you from his parents."

She gave him a small smile. "It's very easy to say, but you know that's not how things work in Indian households. Navin would always remind me that I can walk away from him because I'm not blood but his parents will always be there for him. In the end I proved him right."

Arjun had no words. She may as well have been talking about his own parents. The *parampara* of his household were not just old fashioned, they were stringent. There weren't many intelligent, educated women who would be happy in such an atmosphere. But was it enough of a reason to marry Hema?

His assistant buzzed to let him know it was time for him to leave for a meeting. Rani stood and handed him the design folio she had arrived with. She held out her hand and he took it, holding onto it. "Rani, you are intelligent and beautiful, inside and out. Navin was a fool to let you go."

She gave him a brilliant smile and retracted her hand.

As he watched her leave, Arjun realized that Navin wasn't the only fool. He could no longer deny the fact that he was falling for her, and at the same time realized that there was no way they could be together.

Eleven

As soon as Arjun opened the door, Rani could tell he was stressed. They had a rare evening off from work obligations and she'd just arrived at his condo so they could go out to dinner. His eyes were focused on her but had that faraway look like his mind was elsewhere.

He looked magazine-worthy in a perfectly cut black suit and an open-collared blue shirt. He kissed her lightly on the lips and her stomach fluttered. The more they were together, the hungrier she got for him. Part of her wanted to slow down on the hotel work and make him stay longer, and another part wanted to hurry up and get it done even faster. Ultimately, she had landed on the side of speed. The longer she spent with him, the harder it would be to give him up. They'd been together for three months now and she still couldn't get enough of him.

She'd resolved to talk to him today about how much longer he envisioned their affair lasting and what the terms of their breakup would be. While most of the work for his hotel would be completed in the next month, there would be follow-up items that could last for several months after he returned to India. She wanted to be prepared for the end, and to know with certainty when it was coming.

"We still have some time before dinner." He nuzzled her neck.

"How should we entertain ourselves?" she murmured as she untucked his shirt. She made quick work of the buttons then ran her hands over his abdomen, feeling the ripple of muscle and coarse line of hair that ran down the center of his belly and disappeared beneath his waistband. She popped the buttons on his pants and slid them down along with his boxer briefs. He was fully erect and she touched him, gently at first, then harder. She had never initiated sex before, always too unsure of herself to risk doing it wrong. But something had taken hold of her. Maybe it was the hungry way in which Arjun responded to her, mirroring the desire she felt for him. Or maybe it was the knowledge that their time together was winding down.

Whatever the case, she still couldn't believe how this sex symbol was enjoying what she was doing to him.

She had never gone down on a man before, had always felt it was awkward and a little on the disgusting side. But now, looking at Arjun's velvety skin, she wanted to drive him mad with pleasure, to be a seductress.

She knelt down and took him in her mouth. His low groan spurred her on until he stopped her. She looked at him. *Am I doing it wrong?*

"I want to come inside you, Rani," he said.

She wanted that too. She was strung tighter than a guitar wire. He moved to pick her up to take her to his bedroom, but she shook her head and directed him to sit on the couch. She lifted her dress, pushed down her panties and unhooked her bra. Navin would have looked at her naked body with disappointment. Arjun gazed at her with such feral hunger, it was easy to forget the past and focus on her fantasies.

She tore open a condom wrapper, sheathed him, and then straddled him, using her hand to guide him inside her. She rocked against him, focusing on the exact spots that pulsed inside her.

"Rani!" His voice was thick against her neck. "Slow it down."

She shook her head, unable to speak. She guided his hands towards her breasts. He squeezed them lightly. "Harder," she whispered urgently, rocking faster against him, taking him deeper inside.

Her body trembled as she climaxed. She always orgasmed with Arjun, but this time it was different. This was on her terms and she liked that. It was the first time she'd been in command of her pleasure. It was the most exhilarating and frightening experience of her life.

He pressed his forehead between her breasts. "Wow. When are you going to stop surprising me?"

She didn't answer him. Under the pretense of needing to use the bathroom, she took her leave so she could bring her quivering body under control. When she came out, he called for her to join him in his bedroom. Rani had been there a few times. Like the rest of the condo, it was minimally but comfortably furnished. There was a king-size platform bed with a navy velvet duvet. The side tables were gray and a white-and-gray rug accented the gray wood floor. It was a quintessential bachelor pad.

Arjun had already put his stylish Brioni suit back on. His shirt was miraculously wrinkle-free, though Rani suspected he had a closet full of them and this was just a fresh one.

"I want you to wear this dress for me."

He presented her with a black lace tea dress with a cowl back that dipped down low, leaving most of the back exposed. It was a stylishly retro dress by a designer that Rani could never afford. She'd spent a fortune on the dress she was wearing but apparently it didn't meet Arjun's expectations.

A familiar feeling of unease washed over her.

"It's beautiful, Arjun, but…"

He put a finger to her lips. "I saw it hanging in a shop window and couldn't stop thinking about how incredible it would look on you. I showed the saleswoman your picture and she guessed your size perfectly. Indulge me this once."

His phone rang and he stepped away. She eyed the dress, then slid it on. She had to admit it looked amazing on her, even if it wasn't her style. But something about accepting the dress didn't sit right. It reminded her of a time when she was in middle school and asked her mother if she could wear makeup. Her mother said no so Rani's friend suggested Rani use hers. Her skin itched but she wore the makeup anyway because she wanted so badly to fit in with the girls at school.

When Arjun returned, his gaze was so appreciative, Rani didn't have the heart to decline the dress. He took her to Joël Robuchon. Rani had never been there before; it was the only restaurant in Las Vegas that was so expensive that RKS staff had to get special permission before they could wine and dine clients there. The decor was 1930s French, with royal blue cushioned seats, thick, dark curtains and elaborate chandeliers. The wait staff were formally dressed and fell over themselves to show Arjun and Rani to a private room that could've held at least ten people. The head waiter explained that Arjun had reserved the entire room and ordered a sixteen-course tasting menu.

Rani gasped. "How will we eat that much food?"

He leaned over and whispered, "It's French. As my mother says, an Indian woman would be embarrassed to serve such small portions to dinner guests."

Rani laughed. Her mother would say something similar.

Before the meal even started, a waiter rolled out a bread cart with twenty different kinds of bread, served with hand-churned Normandy butter. Rani chose a saffron focaccia and Arjun took a rosemary brioche.

"I could be happy just with the breads on this cart." She buttered a piece and held it out to Arjun. He opened his mouth and sucked on the tips of her fingers as he took the bread. At her surprised gasp, he grinned. "Now I'm regretting the sixteen-course meal."

She pointed to the glass of wine the waiter had poured for her. Each course came with a wine pairing. "I'm actually looking forward to having a leisurely dinner where we can talk and enjoy each other's company."

"I think it's obvious how much I enjoy your company." His voice was low and seductive as he leaned over and brushed his lips across her earlobes.

Her nerves instantly tingled but she wasn't going to let him turn the conversation back to their sexual relationship.

"When I came to your condo, you looked very serious. Is everything okay?" she asked.

He sighed. "Solving everyone's problems in the family can be exhausting."

"Being the eldest is tiresome, isn't it?"

"What's it like for you?" he asked as the first course was served. The waiter described it in flourishing detail as a pan-seared foie gras with a grapefruit chardonnay reduction.

"It's different for me. My family is very middle class. My dad works in information technology and my mother is a schoolteacher. I don't have an empire to run. But I know what you mean about carrying the family burden. I thought my divorce was about my life and my happiness but my parents considered it to be a family decision. They haven't spoken to me in two years."

"Because of the divorce?"

She nodded. "It's bad enough that I divorced. It's even worse because I'm the eldest. They fear it'll reflect badly on the family and they'll have a harder time finding a *rishta* for my brother and sister."

"I know these things are important in India, but I thought living in America, it wouldn't matter so much. Divorce is pretty common here. Most of the Indian Americans I meet are quite progressive."

She sighed. "My parents are ultra-traditional. They immigrated almost forty years ago but are still holding on to their customs hard and fast because giving even an inch means losing too much of themselves."

He nodded. "I understand only too well. My parents are the same. They've seen a lot of modernization, which is good for India, but they're having trouble accepting the social progress." He took a bite of the food and then a sip of his wine. "Do you keep in touch with your brother and sister?"

Rani nodded. "We're pretty close. And ironically, as much as my parents worry that I've sullied our name and no one will want to marry into our family, neither one of my siblings will accept something as archaic as an arranged marriage."

Was it her imagination or did the wineglass in Arjun's hand tremble ever so slightly?

"There are some good reasons to have your marriage arranged."

Rani looked at him, an uneasy feeling creeping deep into her belly. "Like what?"

He swallowed. "Like knowing that two people share the same family values and expectations."

Rani stopped midchew. Why did Arjun sound like he wasn't just talking hypothetically?

"Would you accept an arranged marriage?"

"I already have."

Rani dropped her fork and it clanked loudly as it hit her plate. She must not have heard him correctly. "Excuse me, what?"

"There's an arrangement between my family and good friends that I'll marry their daughter Hema."

Rani's heart dropped to her toes. *I'm not hearing this right.* "You've been cheating on your fiancée with me?"

Her stomach roiled and for a minute she thought the delicious food she'd just eaten would come back up.

"Hema and I aren't engaged. She knows I date, and so does she. Our families went into business together five years ago and our parents want to solidify our relationship with a marriage. Eventually."

"And you didn't think to tell me this before?"

"I didn't think it mattered. We decided early on that this is a temporary affair."

Rage boiled through her veins. "Excuse me, I decide what matters to me. I don't sleep with another woman's man."

"Rani, Hema and I are not together in the traditional sense. We've never been physical with each other. If I had to characterize our relationship, I would say she's like a family member, almost like my sister. Our impending marriage is an obligation. One that I only agreed to because after what happened with Lakshmi, I'll never fall in love with anyone again."

Rani tried to ignore the searing pain that cut through her heart. He had made a part of her blossom that she'd never thought existed, given her a new sexual confidence. She'd hoped she had opened his heart enough to believe that he could love again.

The waiter placed a second course before them with some fanfare. At another time Rani would have admired the artfully presented charcuterie but she was quaking with anger.

Arjun tried to take her hand but she snatched it away.

"How dare you keep something like this from me."

"It is not relevant to our relationship."

"You don't get to decide that for us! Am I just a roll in the hay for you? A sex partner?"

"Rani, I've come to care for you. More than I've cared for anyone since Lakshmi. It was not my intention to deceive you. The arrangement with Hema is not mine to share. Her parents invested a billion dollars in a partnership with me to expand our hotel chain globally. While my company is privately held, Hema's family business is traded on the Bombay Stock Exchange. We have to carefully control our wedding announcement. Even an accidental slip to the media could have repercussions. No one outside my immediate family knows about it. It's not something we discuss with outsiders."

An outsider. That's how he thinks of me.

Rani speared whatever was on her plate and stuck it in her mouth to keep from screaming.

"Say something, Rani."

She cleared her throat. "I need to use the restroom." She needed to get away from him. To have a minute to regain her composure.

In the bathroom she stood in front of the mirror and splashed cold water on her wrists. Her stomach twisted into a thousand knots.

What did I expect? He's an Indian man who thinks he knows best.

She'd been a fool to think she was sophisticated enough to have an affair with a man like Arjun and come away unscathed. To think herself capable of separating the physical from the emotional. What had she been expecting? That he'd fall in love with her? And then what? Forsake his family and live with her in Vegas? She wasn't about to move to India and play the dutiful wife and daughter-in-law. There was no scenario where she and Arjun would have a happily-ever-after.

So why was she upset? This wasn't news to her. She'd wanted to talk to him about when their affair would end. Now that she knew about Hema, she had her answer. It was best to end it now before someone got hurt.

"Rani?" She looked up to see Delia come out of one of the stalls. Could this dinner get any worse?

"What are you doing here?" Rani flinched at the high pitch in her voice.

"Mr. Rabat and I are here with a client we're courting," Delia replied evenly, looking Rani over. "Are you here on a date?"

Rani shook her head. There was a good chance they'd see her with Arjun. "I'm here with Mr. Singh."

Delia lifted a brow. "I don't remember giving approval to dine him here."

"He invited me," she said, her throat dry.

"Well that certainly explains the dress."

"Excuse me?" The dress might be a touch revealing but it wasn't that risqué.

"I'm no fashionista but that has to be couture. Is it a gift from a certain wealthy client?"

Rani's cheeks burned. "Is your dinner going well?" she asked, trying to change the subject as Delia washed her hands.

"I think so. But it's not as big a contract as you got out of Mr. Singh. Quite an accomplishment. I see you're working hard at it." She gave Rani a thin smile in the mirror, then straightened and dried her hands. "Enjoy your dinner."

As Delia breezed out of the room, Rani leaned on the sink. She wanted to hate Delia but she couldn't blame her. Everyone would see it the way Delia obviously had: that Rani had slept with Arjun to get the contract. While her job might be safe, once again her talent would be overshadowed by rumor and innuendo. *And for what? Some good sex with a hottie? Okay, mind-blowing sex with a damn hot hottie.* But what would come of it? He would leave and marry someone else and she'd be left with her heart in tatters and a reputation to repair.

8>He stops at nothing to get his way.

She squared her shoulders. There was only one thing left to do.

Arjun tried not to look at his phone to see how long Rani had been gone. It felt like forever. She seemed really upset about Hema. Maybe Rani was getting too attached. He never started an affair without an end date in mind and would cut things off even earlier if he sensed that they were getting tired of each other. With Rani, he figured the hotel opening would be their last night together. They wouldn't be working together anymore and he'd be returning to India. But he was more bothered by her behavior than he should be. He had gotten too close to Rani. Their affair had crossed the boundaries he normally set for himself.

When she returned to the table, he didn't like the expression on her face.

"I insisted that we get a few courses at one time. I'm pretty sure the chef is so appalled that he'll never let me back into this restaurant again." He kept his tone lighthearted.

Rani took her seat. He reached out for her hand but she busied herself placing her napkin on her lap.

"What's wrong, Rani?"

She sighed. "I'm wondering how long you'd planned for our affair to continue."

The question caught him off guard. "Why do we need a specific date? I have been enjoying what we have. We can continue for as long as we are both liking each other's company."

What am I saying? Am I really going to continue on with Rani when I get back to India? He usually knew his mind, and didn't give in to temptation. So why couldn't he just tell Rani what he had planned for them?

"What about when the hotel is finished?"

"I'll go back to India but I will be coming back to Vegas to check on things. And I have a great owners condo that'll feel just like home." He gave her his best smile.

"So, what, you want to continue this indefinitely?"

No, I don't. He knew what she was asking and he was prepared with a response. So why was he hesitating? The answer became clear to him as she looked up at him with shining eyes.

"I don't know, Rani. Obviously it cannot be forever. I'm going to marry Hema and I'm not a cheater. That wouldn't be fair to you or her."

"Now you're thinking of Hema? You didn't consider her when we first got together? Or of how I'd feel about her?"

"I've told you, Hema and I are just friends right now. She knows I sleep with other women."

Rani blanched. "I can't do this anymore, Arjun."

"Do what exactly? Have dinner with me? Sleep with me? Work with me?" Why was his voice so sharp?

A tear threatened to escape the corner of her eye and he longed to touch her, but she scraped her chair back and stood.

"I think you and I both know that we can't continue this affair."

And with that, she walked out. He wanted to go after her, at least drop her back at her place, but his feet seemed nailed to the floor.

Because it was best to let her go.

Twelve

I'm okay, I really am.

It had been two weeks since Rani's ill-fated dinner with Arjun. They had managed to avoid each other as she threw herself into working feverishly to get his hotel finished. Contractors were already finalizing the guest suites, a feat that had been accomplished by Arjun offering a hefty bonus for early completion. But there was no avoiding him at this afternoon's meeting at the hotel to review the progress that had been made. She had most of her team attending to serve as a buffer between them.

"Rani, I need to talk to you." Delia shut the door as she entered her office.

Rani took a deep breath.

"I talked with Mr. Rabat and he's in agreement that I will run the meeting this afternoon with Mr. Singh."

"Excuse me? This is my project."

"Given your personal involvement with Mr. Singh, we don't think you should continue as the project lead."

"There is nothing going on between me and Mr. Singh." It was technically true. She had purposely used the present tense.

"But something did happen."

Rani closed her eyes and took a deep breath. Maybe she should let Delia take over the entire project. Then Rani wouldn't have to see Arjun again.

No. Damn it. She had an ace up her sleeve. She could throw Delia's hypocrisy in her face by reminding her that she was Rani's boss because of her own personal relationship. But she wasn't going to stoop to her level.

"We don't want to be late. You want to run the meeting, fine. I hope you've walked the space, cataloged the progress and talked to all the contractors so you're prepared." She walked out the door, leaving Delia no choice but to follow.

When Rani got to the hotel, she saw that Arjun had armed himself with an entourage. The smells of paint, dust and cut wood filled the air. Delia led the tour, but Rani constantly interjected, pointing out the areas where they were ahead of schedule and the ways in which they had incorporated unique architectural details. Just a few months ago, Rani wouldn't have dared to act so brazenly, but she was tired of everybody making decisions for her. Maybe Arjun had rubbed off on her. It was her project and Delia had no right to take it over.

Arjun stayed toward the back of the group. When the tour was done, they gathered in the newly finished lobby. "Any questions?" Delia asked crisply.

"Yes." The sea of staff parted so Rani had a complete view of Arjun. Her chest tightened, making it hard for her to take the breath she desperately needed. He was wearing jeans and a polo shirt. He'd come casual today as they'd been asked to do; they were all required to wear hard hats and there was no avoiding getting dusty. She loved how he looked in jeans and there was no stopping her mind from picturing the muscular legs underneath the fabric.

"Yes, Mr. Singh?"

Arjun had a number of technical questions, none of which Delia could answer, so Rani answered them for her.

"I have a final question," Arjun persisted. "Why are you running this meeting when Ms. Gupta has all the answers?"

Rani wanted to kiss him.

"I'll be leading the project from this point forward," Delia stated matter-of-factly.

Rani's head snapped towards Delia. *What? How dare she!*

"That is unacceptable," Arjun said simply. "Ms. Gupta has done a tremendous job and I prefer to work with her."

Rani froze and so did every member of the RKS team. Mr. Rabat was also there, eager to make sure everything went well because Arjun had managed to negotiate an unusual clause in the contract that allowed him to fire the firm with little notice.

With courage she didn't know she had, Rani calmly said, "We felt you might want a more senior member of the team at this critical juncture, but you are the client and RKS wants you to be happy." She looked smugly at Mr. Rabat, who reluctantly nodded.

After everyone had left, Rani felt drained but there was one more thing she wanted to do. She walked into the owners condo, which hadn't been toured or discussed today because they'd already been signed off on. As she did, her phone buzzed with two missed calls from her brother, Sohel. She dialed his number but he didn't answer.

Her feet carried her into the master bedroom. The place where she'd made love to Arjun for the first time. She touched the bedspread, her body warming at the memory of the textured fabric on her naked back. And the warmth of Arjun's body on top of hers.

"What are you doing here?"

Rani whirled, her phone falling from her hands as she did.

"I'm sorry, I didn't mean to startle you." Arjun stood there looking at her with a pained expression on his face.

"I… I just wanted to… I… Sorry. I'll leave." She felt like a trespasser. She picked up her phone and moved past him but he caught her hand. She stopped, hating the way she liked the warm feeling of his touch.

"Mr. Singh, I don't think this is professional."

He let her go. "Fine, then. I'll tell you why I came. I couldn't stop thinking about our night here. About how good it felt to be with you, how right we were together. I came back to convince myself that you meant nothing to me."

A strangled sound escaped her throat but before she could say more, her phone vibrated. She glanced at the screen. It was her brother, Sohel, again.

"I'm sorry, I need to take this."

"I don't like how we ended things, Rani. We need to talk."

That was the last thing Rani wanted to do. He would tempt her back into his bed and she couldn't do that. It wasn't just that he was promised to someone. It was the fact that he hadn't told her. He'd made the decision about what she needed to know. He'd been controlling their relationship right from the start, and she'd let him. Just like she'd let everyone around her walk all over her for her whole life.

The phone buzzed incessantly in her hand. Arjun sighed in frustration as she answered it and walked into the hallway.

Her brother didn't waste time with pleasantries. As soon as she heard what he said, her stomach bottomed out.

"Oh my God. No! I'll be there as soon as I can."

"Is everything okay?" Arjun asked as soon as she stabbed the End button.

She shook her head, unable to stop the tears burning her eyes. He came to her and pulled her into his arms. She collapsed against him, hating herself for needing his strength. "That was my brother. My father had a stroke. He's critical." She choked on a sob. "He might not make it through the night. Sohel asked me to come immediately to say goodbye."

She pushed against Arjun and tapped her phone. "I need to find a flight to Los Angeles."

Rani called the travel agency that RKS used. Even after explaining the situation, the best the travel agent could do was put her on a standby flight; she would have to wait hours to get a seat. Rani cursed in frustration, bile rising in her throat. What if her father died before she could see him? She shook her head; she couldn't think that way. She had to find a way to get to Los Angeles.

Arjun gently took the phone away from her and ended the call.

"Arjun no. I have to…"

"Rani, I have a flight for you."

She looked at him wide-eyed.

"I have a membership with an aviation company. They'll have a private plane ready for us at Henderson Executive Airport in thirty minutes. Henderson is a lot less busy at this time than McCarran so we can get underway faster."

She sagged in relief and then it hit her. *"We?"* Her voice was a squeak.

"Yes. I'm not letting you deal with this alone. I'll fly you there."

"You don't have to do that. I appreciate your help in getting me a flight. I'll pay you back."

He shook his head. "Whatever else we are or are not, I

insist that we are friends and I will see you safely to LA. It's only a little more than an hour's flight." He firmly led her out. "Let's get going."

As much as she wanted to resist, the words of protest didn't come out. There were so many emotions wreaking havoc with her, she didn't have the energy to think about why Arjun was coming with her.

"I'll have one of my assistants retrieve your car and drive it to your house."

She nodded, glad that he was calm enough to think through the logistical details.

A Cessna Citation XLS was waiting for them when they arrived at the small airport. Rani had never been here. Then again, she'd never flown in a private plane.

They wasted no time climbing into the cabin. There were seats along both sides of the plane, facing each other, eight in total, clad in luxurious cream leather. Arjun took the seat opposite Rani and buckled in. Rani noticed a refrigerator that contained refreshments.

The pilot greeted them and went over safety instructions, and then they were on their way.

"Sorry this plane is a little basic. I have a Gulfstream back in India but it was impractical to station it here for the few trips I take in the US"

She looked at him incredulously. "Are you kidding me? I was going to spend most of the night at the airport getting bumped from one standby flight to another and then cram myself into a middle seat that's only comfortable for a small child. This is not basic. This is luxury that common people like me only read about in books or hear about from wealthy clients like you."

He winced and Rani regretted her tone. "Do you have any updates on your father?" he asked, changing the subject.

She shook her head. "I just texted Sohel to let him know

that I'm on my way. He's in the ICU. He hasn't told my mom that I'm coming. He thinks it's best that I just show up."

"Do you think your parents will refuse to see you, even now?"

The tears she'd been holding back spilled onto her cheeks. She turned her face away from him. "I don't know. The very fact that Sohel isn't telling my mother that I'm on the way to the hospital means he doesn't think she'll see me." Rani remembered the last time she'd shown up at her childhood home. Her parents had refused to open the door. They'd left her knocking, and then sitting on the porch for hours.

Arjun reached out and touched her hand, which was resting on her lap. "When I was little, there was a time that I broke this crystal statue that Ma kept on her dresser. It was her favorite—she told me many times that it was a special present from my grandfather who had died a few years before. I was forbidden from touching it, but of course I was curious, and one day I broke it while playing with it. She was so angry. She told me to leave her room and wouldn't talk to me for the rest of the day. I was so upset and inconsolable. I was sure she didn't love me anymore. But then she came to tuck me into bed, like she did every night, and told me that no matter what I do, or how I hurt her, she would always love me. You have to believe that your parents are the same way, Rani. They may be unable to see past their anger right now but they love you, and always will."

She nodded through her tears but then the sobs took over her body, and the grief she had bottled away came pouring out. He unbuckled his seat belt, went to her side and pulled her into his arms, holding on to her as she clung to him.

When they reached Los Angeles, they took the private car Arjun had already arranged for them to Cedars-Sinai hospital. They found Sohel and Rani's sister Anaya in the ICU waiting room. The siblings hugged for several minutes, crying into each other's shoulders.

Rani's brother was nearly six feet tall. He was dressed in a black T-shirt and jeans and his thick hair was unruly. Anaya was a petite version of Rani, barely five feet tall. She had glossy black hair pulled back into a ponytail and big dark eyes. She was similarly dressed in jeans and a T-shirt.

Arjun stepped away from them, not wanting to intrude on the family moment, and he didn't want to put Rani in an awkward position by having to explain his presence.

"What are you doing here?"

They all turned when they heard the harsh question. Arjun guessed that the woman in the *salwar kameez*—the traditional Indian pants with a long tunic top, and a scarf called a *dupatta* covering her head—was Rani's mother. He could see the family resemblance.

"Mum!" Rani stepped towards her mother, who held up her hand.

"You should not be here, Rani. Your father is in no condition to deal with you. Please, go away."

Rani shrank back. The look of sheer pain on her face propelled Arjun forward to make sure she didn't collapse. Her mother eyed him.

"Namaste, Auntie." He joined his hands together in front of him and bowed his head in a sign of respect. He could have called her Mrs. Gupta rather than using the more intimate, common term for older women in India. But this would identify him as a friend rather than as an outsider.

Mrs. Gupta appraised him. "And who are you?"

"Arjun Singh. I'm Rani's...colleague."

Her eyes widened and she looked between Arjun and Rani. "I see," she said wearily and sat down in a chair.

Rani sat beside her and clasped her mother's hand. "Mum, what good will come of sending me away again?

Please, I'm begging you, I don't want to leave Dad like this."

Her mother closed her eyes and put her head in her hands. Before she could say anything, a man dressed in scrubs appeared.

"Mrs. Gupta?"

The entire family stood, dread written on their faces.

The man turned to Mrs. Gupta. "I'm Dr. McNeil, the neurologist who's been taking care of your husband since he arrived. I have an update."

Mrs. Gupta placed a hand on her chest.

"You were very wise in bringing Mr. Gupta right after his symptoms began. We were able to give him medication that only works if you administer it within three hours, and ideally within the hour after a stroke. Early tests show that he's responding well. He's awake now, which is a really good sign. You can go see him, but please keep it short."

They all breathed a collective sigh of relief.

Rani rose, but one look from her mother had her collapsing back in the chair. Mrs. Gupta, Sohel and Anaya followed the doctor through the ICU doors.

Rani sobbed into her hands. Arjun sat next to her and put an arm around her. She rested her head on his shoulder. "What will it take for them to forgive me? I did everything I could to work it out with Navin. I really did."

"Just be here, Rani. Be here for your parents. Even if they don't want you around, show them that you haven't forsaken them. That you are here for them. Eventually they will remember their love."

"I don't think they'll ever forgive me. Today is the test. If my father still refuses to see me then I really am dead to them."

"When I told my mother that I loved Lakshmi and was going to marry her despite what they said, she threatened to disown me. And she meant it too. She didn't speak to me, had the servants pack my bags and wouldn't let me in the house. I had to go stay in the guest cottage. Even after things ended with Lakshmi, she wouldn't talk to me, not even to say I told you so. I understand how you're feeling. Like a piece of your heart has been cut out from your chest and you're left to bleed on the street. But I showed up to ask my mother's forgiveness every day for a month. And I didn't stop until she finally let me in the door. She did not talk to me for another two months but eventually she did. There will come a point when your parents will also realize they are not as angry as they want to be."

"That's good advice," said a voice from behind them. They both turned to see Sohel, who was smiling. "Dad wants to see you, Rani. When he opened his eyes and saw all of us standing there his first question was to ask where you were."

Rani stood so fast that she nearly tripped. Arjun steadied her, then she followed Sohel into the ICU.

Arjun smiled, relief flooding through him. Rani's anguish had torn him apart. He knew what it felt like to make a choice that hurt the people he cared about. He had felt so selfish for wanting Lakshmi at the expense of his family. At the time he was young, and nothing felt more important, but could he make the same choice now?

Rani was not just an affair, that much he had come to understand in the last few weeks. No matter how many times he went over the reasons they couldn't be together, all he could think about was how much he missed her. He'd been so happy to see her at the hotel walk-through that he'd spent the entire meeting thinking of frivolous excuses to extend the work on the hotel so he'd have more time in Vegas. More time with her.

He rubbed his forehead with the tips of his fingers. There had to be a way for the two of them to be together. He was a good problem solver so why couldn't he solve this one?

Because there is no reasoning with Ma. He loved his mother but emotion and tradition were a big part of how she made decisions. Did that emotion also apply to forgiving her son? She had eventually forgiven him for falling in love with Lakshmi, hadn't she?

The answer was no. Their relationship had never been the same after that. Where before there had been implicit trust, after the affair with Lakshmi his mother needed constant validations that he would follow through on basic promises. *You're sure you'll come to the party? When exactly will you talk to your sister about that problem?*

And of course the big one: *You promise you'll marry Hema the second you return from Vegas?*

Thirteen

Fifteen minutes later, Arjun didn't have any answers as Rani came out of the ICU doors with tears in her eyes. He stood and went to her side, putting his arms around her, and she sobbed against his chest. "He still hasn't forgiven me."

Arjun's heart sank. How heartless could Rani's father be? Surely facing mortality would have softened him just a little.

Rani folded herself into the waiting room chair. Arjun sat next to her and put a protective arm around her. Sohel and Anaya joined them a few minutes later.

"Excuse me." Arjun turned to see Anaya eyeing him shyly. "Are you *the* Arjun Singh? India's hottest hottie?"

Rani stiffened. He looked down to see a small smile tug at her lips. Then she touched her hand to her forehead in a face-palm. Anaya's voice was so teenage fangirl that in this austere environment, it broke the tension.

He smiled and nodded. "That's me."

Anaya clapped a hand to her mouth. "I knew it. I didn't

want to say anything before but I just knew it was you." She pulled out her phone and swiped. "Do you mind taking a selfie with me? My friends at school will be soooooo jealous."

The slight shake of Rani's shoulders and the amused expression on her face were well worth the ten pictures Anaya proceeded to take, stopping in the middle to put on lipstick and change locations because the light wasn't hitting her right.

"You should get going," Rani told Arjun.

He shook his head. "I'm not leaving you, Rani."

"But you must have a million things to deal with."

He took Rani's hand and squeezed it. "None of that is important. The only thing that matters to me right now is taking care of you."

Her eyes glistened. "Don't do this, Arjun," she whispered. His heart dropped into this stomach. Were they so far gone that he didn't have the right to see her through something so difficult?

In the end, Arjun prevailed. They spent the night in the hospital. Sohel and Anaya curled up on the waiting room chairs. Rani let her head drop onto Arjun's shoulder and dozed off. They woke early the next day as the morning shift arrived at the hospital.

"Why don't I get you guys some coffee and breakfast," Arjun volunteered. He found the hospital cafeteria and bought food for everyone. When he returned to the waiting room, Rani's mother was there too. They were all sitting in a circle with their heads bowed. At first Arjun feared the worst, but then he realized they were praying. His mother had done enough *pujas* for him to recognize that the Sanskrit prayer they were uttering was one of thanks, not of mourning.

He stood a few feet away. It was one thing for him to have been here yesterday when Rani first arrived, but his presence this morning would raise uncomfortable questions with her mother. He knew how an Indian parent would perceive their "friendship."

Anaya looked up and saw him first. She rushed over to help him with the two cafeteria trays he carried laden with food and drinks. "You won't believe it. Dad's doing much better. The doctor's just told *Amma* that he's taken a turn for the better. BTW, what should I call you?"

"That's great news, Anaya, and you can call me Arjun."

They all thanked Arjun for the food and dug in, their spirits clearly resorted.

"Arjun, in what capacity are you here?" Rani stiffened at her mother's question, and Arjun's pulse quickened.

"They are in love, *Amma*," Anaya bubbled.

"Anaya!" Rani called out sharply.

"Oh, don't try to hide it. I heard you guys talking. He said you were the most important thing to him and he was going to take care of you. You're in loooooove with India's hottest hottie," her sister said in a singsong voice.

Arjun's mouth went dry. He was normally so vigilant about appearances. Why hadn't he been more careful around Anaya?

"Anaya, stop it." Rani said in a high-pitched voice. "We are colleagues, that's all."

Arjun caught Mrs. Gupta's eyes and his heart sank. She was looking at him appraisingly. It was a look he was very familiar with, one that Indian aunties with eligible daughters often gave him. He wanted to say something, to correct Anaya, but his tongue was stuck in his mouth. Anything he said would make things worse for Rani. He needed to let her handle it.

"Rani, why don't you tell us what your relationship is to Arjun," her mother said quietly.

Rani gave him a stricken look. "We're friends, *Amma*.

Yesterday when I heard about Dad, Arjun helped me get a flight here."

"Did you come on a private plane?" Anaya asked eagerly, totally oblivious to Rani's discomfort.

"A very small one," Arjun replied. Hoping to give Rani some time to think, he went on to describe the aircraft, which led to questions about the one he owned in India. He took his time talking about that one, as well. He'd hoped once they'd exhausted the subject, the conversation would steer toward a topic other than their relationship, but Rani's mother was not to be deterred.

"You must be very good friends for Arjun to help you like that. I'm guessing you're a very busy man, yet here you are bringing us food and keeping Rani company."

Rani looked down, fidgeting with her purse.

"Rani, it would ease your father's mind to know that you are engaged to someone else. Especially someone as suitable as Arjun." Rani's mother gave her a hard look.

Rani shrank in her chair and looked at Arjun in alarm. "We're not getting engaged, Mum," she finally said, her voice leaden.

Her mother looked between Rani and Arjun then sighed. "After you left yesterday, your father was so upset. Every time he sees you, all he can think about is how you've ruined your life." Rani opened her mouth to say something but her mother raised her hand sternly. Mrs. Gupta would get along really with his own mother. She had a way of making everyone feel like they were still little children being scolded for having dirty hands.

"It will make him so happy to know that you have found a way to be happy again. With one decision, Rani, one announcement, you can erase everything that's happened in the past and focus on the future."

Tears streamed down Rani's face and Arjun's chest hurt. She was in so much pain and he couldn't bear it. "It's not my decision to make, Mum." Her voice was small and very quiet, as if she had no breath left in her body.

"Rani's right, Auntie, the decision is not hers, it's mine." Arjun said. *What am I saying?* The right course of action here would be to explain that they were just friends, which was technically true of their current relationship status, and then extricate himself from the situation.

Instead, he couldn't believe what came out of his mouth next.

"The time is not right, but I think it would be best if I talk to you and Uncle privately so I can ask for Rani's hand in marriage."

Rani's eyes widened. Anaya squealed and clapped, and Mrs. Gupta wiped her eyes with the end of her *dupatta*. "Bless you, my son. This news will have Rani's dad out of this hospital in no time." She stood and hugged Arjun while Rani stared at him openmouthed.

What have I done?

Fourteen

How dare he! Everything was happening so fast that Rani couldn't process the flood of emotions drowning her, but the one bubbling through her body was anger. He had no right to interfere with her family, especially without consulting her. Has he forgotten that he's scheduled to marry another woman?

"I'm going to ask if your father can have visitors." As soon as Rani's mother left, Rani pulled Arjun into the corner, out of earshot of her siblings.

"What the hell did you just do?" she snarled.

He placed his hands on her shoulders. "I couldn't stand to see you hurt like that, Rani. I have a solution. I'll tell your dad that I want to marry you. He will forgive you and you can finally reunite with your family."

"Are you kidding me? How dare you think you can be my savior? What's going to happen when they realize we lied to them? They'll hate me for the rest of my life. You had no right to get involved. This is my situation. I'll handle it!"

"There you are. The doctor says we can go right in." Rani's mother was back, grabbing Arjun's hand and pulling him towards the ICU doors.

Rani followed hurriedly behind him. "*Amma*, I don't think this is the right time to be discussing all this with Dad. Let him come home and then I'll explain everything."

Rani's mother had already pressed the doorbell requesting access to the ICU, and the large double doors swung open. "Don't be silly, Rani. There is no time like the present. Your father will be so happy."

"No, *Amma*, you're not listening…"

"Rani, I know what's best for you." With that her mother went barreling down the hallway towards her father's bed. She looked at Arjun, who squeezed her arm. "It'll be fine, Rani, trust me," he said softly.

Her mother turned and gave an impatient wave for them to follow.

Rani stood there feeling like she was fourteen years old again, being told by her mother that dating was for American girls. Rani would be a good Indian daughter and marry one of the men her parents introduced her to after she graduated college. *Trust me, Rani, I know what's best for you,* her mother had said.

Her father's room had clear glass doors. The incessant beeps of medical machines assaulted them as they entered. Bright white lights cast an unnatural pallor on all their faces.

Rani stepped towards her father's bed but her mother stopped her, pushing Arjun towards him instead. Rani needed to stop this. But even as she formulated the words, she knew it was too late.

As Arjun began speaking to her father, a hysterical laugh bubbled inside Rani but she stifled it. Most American men would introduce themselves first but Arjun started by presenting his family history, listing the members of his current family, then detailing his family business, alluding to but not outright proclaiming his wealth. And *then* he talked about himself. It was exactly what her parents expected, and by the adoring looks they gave Arjun, they were already smitten.

The beaming smile on her father's face should have brought her joy, but her heart sank to her toes. From her parents' perspective, Arjun was a catch. He came from a good family, was wealthy, cultured and traditional.

The words her mother didn't say in the waiting room didn't escape Rani: that Arjun would erase Navin from their lives. When her parents talked about her, they wouldn't have to explain that she was divorced and answer the inevitable string of questions that followed. Navin's family had spared no hatred in portraying Rani as a spoiled, Westernized woman who left the marriage because she didn't want to give her in-laws the respect they deserved. *Must be her upbringing, her parents didn't teach her right.* But if she remarried, the community would no longer point fingers.

"Rani, you have made me so happy. Come here." With heavy feet, she stepped towards her father's bedside and leaned down to give him a hug. It had been three years since he'd held her. The last time was when she'd come home crying, her packed bags in the car. She'd sobbed her troubles to her parents and they'd listened, her father holding her and letting her smear her makeup into his shirt. But then they'd told her to go back to her marital home. To find a way to work it out with Navin and her in-laws. *In a marriage, you must sacrifice yourself, Rani. Learn to suffer, they'd said.*

"When will the wedding be?" Rani's mother asked.

Rani opened her mouth to say there would be no wedding but her throat was too tight. Her father looked so happy; there was even some color in his face.

"I'm not sure yet, Auntie," Arjun said evenly. "I have to finish my hotel in Vegas, and then of course I will have to take Rani to India to meet my parents, and we can make decisions after that."

Her mother pursed her lips but said nothing. Arjun had that way about him, of respectfully brooking no argument. He was used to taking charge; in fact, just like her parents before him, he'd taken charge of her life.

"Well don't wait too long, I'm sure you'll be wanting children." The response came from her father and Rani reddened.

"Your family is so traditional. How do they feel about Rani being divorced?" her mother asked.

Rani closed her eyes and sighed. Being divorced did not make her a damaged commodity but as she'd told herself countless times, her parents had grown up in a different generation, at a time when being divorced was a character flaw.

"I don't have a problem with Rani being divorced. From what she's told me, it sounds like it was a terrible situation and I'm glad she got herself out. She's an amazing woman and her ex-husband was a fool to let her go."

Rani softened a little at Arjun's words. Her mother nodded as if she agreed with him but Rani knew it was a nod of relief.

"My parents don't know I want to marry Rani, which is why we need to wait until Rani and I can travel to India so that I can have the opportunity to tell them in person and explain the situation."

How would his parents react? Rani had never allowed herself to think about the fact that even if he refused to marry Hema, his parents might not accept a divorced woman for Arjun.

What am I thinking? All this isn't real! He's still going to marry Hema. This is all an act. One that Arjun had planned without consulting her. He would go back to India and leave her with a big mess to clean up.

"What if they don't accept?" Rani's father asked.

"We will cross that bridge when we come to it," Arjun said diplomatically. "What's important now is that Uncle gets better."

"We'll need to celebrate. As soon as you are out of the hospital, we should throw a dinner party at our house," Rani's mother gushed.

Arjun shook his head. "Let's not get ahead of ourselves. Once Uncle is well, Rani and I will need to rush back to Vegas to finish the hotel."

Her mother nodded. "Yes, the sooner you finish that hotel, the faster you can go back to India and firm things up with your parents."

And then it struck Rani. That was Arjun's ticket out. He would say that his parents didn't agree. For now she was back in her parents' fold, and when he dumped her later on, it wouldn't technically be her fault. Her stomach bottomed out.

"We should go and let Dad rest," she said, desperate to get out of there before things got worse. She would make Arjun leave tonight and tell her parents he had an emergency at the hotel. The less time her parents spent with Arjun, the better. She didn't need them falling in love with him too.

When they stepped outside, Sohel and Anaya were eager to know how things went. Rani brushed past them and ushered Arjun into the hallway to the elevators. She had to get away from her family. When they got to the lobby, she spotted a sign for the hospital gardens and dragged him outside with her.

The garden consisted of a courtyard with some flowering plants and metal picnic tables. It was relatively empty save for a few patients nursing cups of coffee and eating off cafeteria trays.

She didn't bother sitting down; her entire body was shaking with anger. "What were you thinking? Do you know what'll happen when our fake engagement breaks up? My parents will blame me again. They'll point out how my past has come back to haunt me and how I'll never have happiness. You'll play right into their beliefs that a divorce is a lifelong sentence for loneliness."

She was flailing her arms, her emotions raw and uncontrolled. The stress of the last few days had unraveled her.

Arjun captured her hands in his and pulled her close. "Rani, why do you think this is all fake?"

Her heart slammed into her ribs. *Wait, what?*

She stared at him, her throat tight.

"The last few weeks without you have been hell on me. I'm in love with you, Rani, and I don't want to be without you. I wasn't lying to your parents. I want us to be together."

She had to be hallucinating. The stress had finally gotten to her and she was about to crack. There was no other explanation for the words she was hearing from Arjun's mouth.

"What about Hema?"

"I agreed to marry Hema because it was good for business. Hema doesn't want to marry me. She's doing it out of obligation."

"What about your parents?"

"It will not be easy. None of this will be easy. For me or for you. But right now we don't have to think about all that. All I need to know is that you love me, and that you want to be with me. Everything else, we can figure out."

He loves me. There were a thousand *but*s that went through her head. *But* what about his family? *But* how would they work it out? *But* what about what she wanted?

"You know I make my own decisions. I don't like how you took charge of the situation with my parents. I won't be controlled, Arjun."

"That's why I love you, Rani. You are your own woman.

I should have talked to you before I said something to your parents. I just couldn't stand to see you in so much pain."

Arjun pulled her into his arms and she savored the strength of his body, the beating of his heart. Its rhythm matched her own. She'd been herself with him. Never pretended to be someone she wasn't. And he still wanted her.

"Do you love me, Rani?" he whispered into her ear.

That's not the right question. The question is whether I can love you, whether I'm strong enough to love you.

"I've fought with myself. I haven't wanted to, but I've fallen in love with you."

He kissed her then. A soul-searing kiss that left no doubt in her heart about how she felt about him.

Neither of them noticed Anaya snapping their picture.

Fifteen

Arjun had to return to Las Vegas, but Rani remained behind until her father was released a few days later. He'd made a speedy recovery, but the specialist warned the family that he was still fragile and at high risk for another stroke.

Once he got home, Rani's parents insisted she stay, and she drank in the love of her family. Sohel had his own condo on the other side of town but he stayed in his old bedroom too. It was just like it had been growing up, with all of them together under one roof.

Anaya, Sohel and Rani were sitting on the brown-and-yellow shag rug in the family basement playing *Monopoly*. The room looked like it was stuck in the '70s, with a nut-brown couch that almost blended into the rug. The walls were covered in green-and-yellow wallpaper. It was an obnoxiously decorated room but it comforted Rani like a ratty stuffed bear. There were many childhood memories here: watching Bollywood movies with the family, laughing at vacation pictures and sleeping together on thin mattresses when the cousins came to visit from India. Her parents never had much in terms of money but they gave their children every spare minute of time they had.

"You've cut your hair so short." Rani's mother sat on the couch behind Rani and began braiding her daughter's loose hair. Rani savored the feeling of her mother's hands on her scalp. When she was a child, her mother braided her hair every morning before she left for school. At the time Rani complained and promptly undid the braids when she left the house because the kids made fun of her.

She'd only appreciated how much her mother had sacrificed when she'd had to watch Navin's two nieces for a week one summer. Rani had still been working and her mother-in-law had purposefully assigned Rani to take care of the two girls to prove to Rani that she couldn't work and take care of children. Her mother-in-law had succeeded. Rani had lasted all of four days and by Friday had slept through her alarm, missed all her morning meetings, and been late dropping the girls off to camp.

That was when she'd realized that her mother had been getting up hours before the children to make breakfast, get herself ready for work and then be available to braid Rani's hair. And she had done it for decades, first with Rani, then Sohel, and when they were finally old enough to take care of themselves, Anaya had come along and her mother started all over again.

"Rani, is Arjun coming back here?"

Rani had talked to Arjun every day. He was getting staff lined up for the hotel but he'd asked if she wanted him to come to LA to see her.

"He's busy with the hotel."

"I'm doing a *puja* tomorrow night to thank the Lord Krishna for making your dad better. It would be nice if Arjun could come. He should see our house."

Rani looked at her mother and knew instantly what she

meant. Her parents had researched Arjun and knew how wealthy he was. Rani thought about the flowered couch in the upstairs living room. The "good" couch that had been perfectly preserved underneath a plastic cover, the "new" kitchen that had been renovated fifteen years ago. There was nothing sleek, polished or grand about her parents' house. Which was exactly why she had to invite Arjun.

Arjun was well aware of her family's middle-class status but it was one thing to know it and another to see it first-hand. Plus an official event at the parents' house would take their relationship to the next level of seriousness and she wanted to see how he'd react to it.

She excused herself to go to her room and text Arjun.

Do you have plans tomorrow evening?

His response was immediate.

Yes but I could be persuaded out of them.

How about dinner and a puja at my parents' house.

Okay as long as there's dessert afterwards ;)

She smiled. It had been weeks since they'd been intimate. Surely she could find some private time for them.

Life is short. Dessert first.

She smiled as he sent back a winky face emoji with two hearts. She still couldn't believe that he loved her. When they were done texting, she booked him a room at the Beverly Wilshire. She wouldn't miss this chance to be with him.

When the next evening arrived, she decided to wear a pale pink chiffon sari with a lace trim. It was elegant and delicate. The sari had a rose-gold blouse that was skin-tight, sleeveless and cropped to a couple inches below the bra line.

She stood in front of the full-length mirror at the hotel and began getting dressed. She had purchased a pink bra with just enough support and lift to work underneath the sari blouse, as well as a matching thong. She'd blushed the whole time she was at the store, thinking of Arjun seeing her in them.

The sari also had a petticoat that started below her belly button and fell to her ankles. The main length of sari fabric was wrapped around and tucked into the petticoat to keep the sari in place. It had been a few years since Rani had worn one, and it took her a few tries to get the six yards of fabric wrapped just right.

She wore her hair loose, the way Arjun liked it. With just five minutes to spare before he was to arrive, she quickly slid some liner around her eyes and touched her lips with gloss. She went to put on her rose-gold heels and realized that she should have tied the sari after putting on the heels to get the length right but it was too late now.

She'd just grabbed the shoes when she heard a knock on the hotel room door.

She opened the door a little breathless. And there he stood, looking even more handsome than she remembered. He was dressed in a traditional Indian kurta pajama. The long tunic top was cream-colored with maroon embroidery. The legging-like pants were the same maroon as the embroidery on the tunic. He had a matching scarf wrapped around his neck. If possible, he looked even more handsome in Indian clothes than he did in his Savile Row suits.

He put his hand on his heart as he looked at her. "Wow. You are gorgeous, Rani."

Heat slid through her as his eyes roamed over her body. She waved him in. "Sorry it's not a suite but my credit card limit is not that high."

"I couldn't care less about the room right now," he said in a thick voice. He pointed to the heels she was holding in her hand. "Let me."

She felt a wave of disappointment that he wanted to leave already. She handed him the shoes and sat down. He bent down on his knee and took her foot. *My very own Prince Charming. Hope the shoe fits.*

"I talked to Hema."

Rani leaned forward.

"She was so relieved that I'm going to break the *rishta*," he continued. "The truth is that she's been seeing someone she has real feelings for. Now we just have to figure out a way to tell our parents."

Arjun took his time buckling the straps on the sandals, then ran his hand up Rani's leg. She shivered deliciously, craving the warmth of his body on hers. She took his hand and guided it further up her thigh.

"How much time do we have before we need to get to your parents? I don't want to be late."

She couldn't care less about being late. "We have time. I had you come early."

His face broke into a grin, his dimple sending heat racing to her core. He bent his head and kissed the inside of her thigh. Her carefully tied sari was already starting to bunch around her knees as his mouth moved upwards. She parted her legs and he gently rubbed the outside of her silky panties with his fingers, then slid them underneath the fabric and inside her. There was no hiding how she felt, just like she was sure that if she reached down and touched him, he would be hard as a rock.

He stood and hoisted her up with him. His hand was warm on her exposed lower back. He ran his fingers across her bare midriff. "Is this sari pinned?" She took out the clip that was holding the *pallu* in place. The decorated end of the sari began unraveling.

"Not anymore."

"I like a woman who knows how to tie a sari without a million pins."

The fact that he knew he'd have to undo a bunch of safety pins rankled her. Exactly how many women's saris had he taken off? Before, she hadn't let herself think about all those women because the affair was just temporary. But now? Would he be satisfied if she were the last woman he ever had?

"What's wrong?"

"Nothing."

"Rani…" He kissed her neck, then whispered across her earlobe, his breath warm and intoxicating. "I can tell when your mind has gone someplace it shouldn't." He pulled her close to him and kissed the space between her jaw and ear, and she curled her neck into his kiss, enjoying the quivers it sent down her spine.

"I was just thinking that you've had women who know how to please you in bed. Are you going to be happy with me forever? What if you stop being attracted to me?"

He took her hand and guided it down to his erection. "You feel that, Rani? You are so sexy. With most women, it takes me time to get to this point. I just have to look at you and I find it hard to control myself." He kissed the corners of her mouth. "After you, Rani, I don't want any other woman on this planet."

His words wrapped around her like a warm blanket. Never in her wildest dreams did she think she could be the one to drive a man hot with desire.

The *pallu* had already fallen to her waist, showing off the tight blouse that did nothing to hide her taut nipples. Her midriff was bare. He grabbed hold of the *pallu* and tugged. She twirled as he unwrapped the sari. He tossed the fabric on a chair.

He kissed her bare stomach and she shivered at his warm

breath, her entire body responding instantly. He unbuttoned her blouse, then filled his hands with her breasts and slowly rubbed his thumbs over her nipples.

"I can't wait to see you in a Rajasthani *choli*." He murmured.

A Rajasthani choli. Rani stilled. A traditional outfit from his home in India. The palace he called a home.

"What's wrong?"

"You know, we haven't talked about everything that's happened. About what it all means."

Arjun cupped her face and tilted it up so he could look at her. "I was kidding about the Rajasthani *choli*. You don't have to wear it if you don't want to. I'm not going to try and control you, Rani. That's not the kind of man I am."

"It's just, there is so much to work out between us. I wasn't brought up with your wealth. My parents' house is very different than yours…"

He bent down and kissed her lightly. "I don't care if you grew up in a cardboard box on the street corner. All that matters to me is that we love each other. We're going to take it step-by-step. Let's get through tonight, then we'll sort out how to break the news to my parents."

He was oversimplifying things. But when he bent his head and claimed her mouth with heat and desire and promise, her mind went blank. She was no longer able to think about what lay ahead.

This time their lovemaking was different. It wasn't furious, despite how their desire was driven to new levels of ecstasy. They both went slower, taking the time to enjoy each other and let themselves melt into one another. Rani let herself touch and explore Arjun like he belonged to her, and the love she felt in her heart was unbearable.

Could this be real? Or was her heart was about to shatter into a million unfixable pieces?

Sixteen

Rani had begged her mother to keep it simple. She had only been gone three hours but when she returned with Arjun, the house was chaos.

If Rani had been worried about the seventies-era decor being embarrassing, her mother had gone all out to decorate for the *puja*. Christmas lights hung around the entire living room. Midway through, her mother had run out of the white ones so multicolored bulbs were haphazardly strung on one side of the living room. A statue of Lord Krishna and his wife, Radha, was on the fireplace mantel, decorated with flowers. Tea light candles flickered at the base of the statues. The scent of incense permeated the room.

Her mother started the *puja* and everyone respectfully bowed their heads towards the statues but Rani caught Arjun looking around her living room. While there was no judgment in his eyes, Rani wondered how his parents would feel coming to a house like hers. They lived in a literal palace.

Thankfully her mother kept the *puja* to under thirty minutes rather than her usual hour plus. When she was done, she came around with a large steel plate that contained a burning candle, red vermillion paste, and *prasad*, a sweet offering to the gods that was now blessed thanks to the *puja* and thus ready for human consumption.

Rani's mother brought the plate to the participants one by one, who put their palms over the flame to receive the light from the prayers, then dipped their fingers in the red paste and touched their foreheads. They also each took a piece of the *prasad*. When she got to Rani and Arjun, her mother waved the plate in front of their faces, then used her own finger to dot their foreheads with the red paste. "I prayed for you two, as well," she said conspiratorially. "May God bless your union and you two have a very happy life together."

Their dining room table was filled with a variety of dishes that Rani knew her mother had spent all day cooking. They sat and filled their plates.

"So, Arjun, I read an article that your mother wants a very traditional *bahu* who will help her run the household. Will you all live together in your big *bangla* in Rajasthan?" The question was asked by Rani's father.

Arjun's gaze tangled with Rani's. He cleared his throat. "Rani and I have not made any decisions. This is all so new, I think we need some time to discuss things."

Her stomach dropped. His eyes conveyed what his mouth couldn't say. He hadn't considered the full ramifications of marrying Rani. And she hadn't, either. She was not moving to India. She'd been there a handful of times in her life and while she spoke the language and understood the culture, it didn't feel like home.

And what about his parents? While he may be able to extricate himself from his arrangement with Hema, would his parents accept her? Arjun was the most eligible bachelor in India, and by the community's standards, she was far from a prized catch.

A tense silence blanketed the room. "I think we should let Arjun eat before interrogating him," Rani's mother broke in. They switched to talking about Indian politics.

A little later, Rani caught up with her mother in the kitchen. "What are you doing? What's with the questions?"

Her mother placed her hands on her hips. "What's wrong with the questions? You think we haven't noticed that he is very evasive when we ask him about whether his family will accept you. He answers without answering. You are naive, Rani. You don't know how things work in traditional Indian families, especially *khandaani* ones like his. His parents' approval is very important and he should not be waiting too long to get it. We are just pushing him a little so he doesn't keep stringing you along."

She touched Rani's cheek. "We don't want him breaking your heart."

Rani sighed and turned away. How could she tell her mother that she hadn't thought things through? That she'd been so swept up in the moment that she had forgotten that everything her mother was saying was true? How was she supposed to tell her mother that there was a chance Arjun might not be the one walking away?

She couldn't make the same mistakes she'd made with Navin. She wasn't going to give up everything she'd worked for, and she wasn't moving to India. What remained to be seen was whether Arjun would stand up for her with his parents.

Her mother caught her arm. "Rani, we want you to be happy, above all else. Arjun seems like a decent boy, and marriage to him will leave your past behind. He cares about you. I see it by the way he looks at you, and the way he worried about your father. Did you know that he flew in the best stroke specialist in the country to see your dad?"

"What?" Rani had no idea.

"We wouldn't have found out but Anaya heard the doctors talking outside his room. We thought the hospital called Dr. McNeil but he was flown in from New York. He's a world-famous stroke specialist. Arjun got him a private jet and God knows how much he must have paid him. Doctors like that don't fly across the country for people like us."

Rani sucked in a breath. That sounded like something Arjun would do.

"No matter how rich he is, if he didn't love you, he would not have done that. And he would not have hidden it from us. He wanted your father to get better."

Her mother grabbed her hand. "I know you're afraid to go into another marriage, but you mustn't think like that. You need to consider the man you are marrying. He is pure gold. And this time, maybe you will be more understanding with your in-laws."

Tears stung her eyes. Rani extracted her hand from her mother's grip. It always came back to her needing to make the compromises.

She didn't argue with her mother then, but she did tell Arjun she wanted to leave as soon as they could. She couldn't let her parents fall more in love with Arjun than they already were. There were some difficult conversations that she and Arjun had been avoiding. It was time to have them.

Seventeen

Arjun stretched out in his seat as their plane took off towards Vegas. The night had been trying to say the least. When Rani suggested they leave, he had been happy to oblige. He hadn't fully thought through things when he had asked for Rani's hand in marriage and when he had agreed to the *puja* at her parents' house. In both instances, he'd let his love for Rani dictate what he'd done, rather than choosing the smart play. And tonight had been a good reminder of the consequences of his emotional decisions.

Rani's parents had every right to question why he hadn't told his parents about Rani. He should have called his mother the moment he returned the first time from LA but he'd decided to wait until he could fly to India and discuss it face-to-face.

There were several messages from his assistant to come back to Vegas, so he'd called for the jet immediately and Rani decided to return with him. His phone kept buzzing but he ignored it. Whatever crisis had brewed in the few hours that Arjun had been in LA could wait until the morning. Arjun was tired and wanted to enjoy a moment with Rani. Things would be hard enough for them in the next few weeks.

"Arjun, we should talk."

He nodded. "It'll be nearly midnight when we get to Vegas. Why don't you stay with me tonight? We can talk when we're both fresh in the morning."

"I don't have any of my stuff and I can't go around Vegas in this." They were still dressed in the Indian clothes they'd worn to Rani's house.

He tapped out some quick messages on his phone using the plane Wi-Fi. "I'll have someone buy some clothes for you to wear."

"At this hour?"

"It's Vegas. There are shops open 24/7."

"I meant you have people working at this late hour?"

He shrugged. "I have a personal assistant on call for things I might need." He saw the expression on her face. "What?"

"I can't even fathom this life that you have. An assistant at your beck and call to pick up clothes for your—" she paused "—for whatever I am."

He actually had several such assistants but he didn't bring that up now. He took her hand. "You are the love of my life. I know tonight was hard." He squeezed her hand. "I don't have all of the answers but I will soon. I've been getting things lined up. I'll fly to India next weekend and talk to my parents in person."

Rani's face brightened. "Really? Do you want me to come with you?"

"Not for this trip. My parents will be furious and I don't want you to bear their wrath. Once things have settled down and they've accepted the situation, then I'll take you to meet them. Or fly them here to meet your family."

Rani frowned.

"Trust me, Rani. I need to handle my parents carefully. The news is not going to be easy on them and I have to be very strategic about how I present things. It all has to be in a certain order."

"Why?" Rani whispered.

"It's all the reasons you already know."

"I want to hear you say it. What'll be the most important thing to them?"

"Probably the fact that my mother is breaking a *vachan* to Hema's family. And it's not just the promise she made, my mother loves Hema like her own daughter and she'll be heartbroken at the idea that Hema won't be her daughter-in-law."

"How will I ever compete with that?" Rani said in a small voice.

"You won't. My mother has known Hema since she was a little girl. It's not a competition between you, just like you wouldn't try to be equal with one of my sisters. Be your own person, Rani, and in time they will come to love you just like I have."

"And what happens if they don't accept me?"

"What happens if you don't accept them?"

"What?" The question had clearly surprised Rani, but it was one of the things that had him more worried than his own parents' reaction. There were a lot of things he'd have to work out with his family, his mother especially. But Rani would also have to compromise. He couldn't move to Vegas. Most of his family holdings were in India. He was also the eldest son, which meant that he was in charge of their familial home in Rajasthan. While he could work with his mother to loosen the house rules, Rani would still have to learn to live with his parents under more restrictions than she would like.

Will she accept the life I can give her?

"My family is very traditional, and I'll do my best to change that but it won't happen overnight. Are you willing to be patient with me? To go into this situation knowing you might have to make some compromises?"

"Like what?" Rani said, her eyes wide and panicked.

At that moment the pilot announced that they were landing soon and due to a dust storm in Vegas, the landing would be bumpy. Rani and Arjun buckled their safety belts, each lost in his or her own thoughts.

Arjun glanced at his phone to see that his executive assistant's panic level had risen. He'd call him once they were at his condo.

A car was waiting for them when they arrived at the airport. Rani was quiet on the ride into town, no doubt contemplating the loaded question Arjun had asked her. He didn't push. When they got to his building, he used his elevator key to get them up to his condo. When they exited the elevator, his executive assistant was standing in the foyer dressed in a business suit.

Arjun groaned. While he appreciated the man's tenacity, he was in no mood to deal with whatever red tape the gaming commission had thrown his way.

"Rahul, I need a minute," he said, holding up his hand as he punched the code to get into the condo.

"No, sir, I must speak to you before you go in."

Arjun waved Rani through the open door. "Go ahead, make yourself comfortable. I'll be right in." Then he turned to Rahul, who looked like he was about to go into cardiac arrest.

"Sir, your parents are inside," he whispered.

Eighteen

Rani had barely entered the condo when Arjun grabbed her hand. "Rani!"

"Don't bother, Arjun. We see you."

Rani turned towards the voice and recognized his mother immediately from the pictures she'd seen. Arjun's parents were not what Rani expected. Perhaps because of her experience with her mother and ex-mother-in-law, she expected a traditionally dressed woman in a sari or *salwar kameez* with the kind of jewelry that befit her status. But Jhanvi Singh was dressed in cream linen pants and a stylish light blue blouse. Her salt-and-pepper hair was stylishly cut in waves and fell around her shoulders. Her makeup was flawless even at this late hour and the only jewelry she wore were tasteful diamond solitaires. Dharampal Singh was an older version of Arjun, with nearly white hair. Tall and stately, he was dressed in a Lacoste collared shirt and khaki trousers. The couple looked like they belonged on a yacht in Monte Carlo.

Arjun moved towards his parents and bent down and touched their feet. They each placed a hand on his head. Only then did he rise and hug them. Rani knew the tradition but was surprised to see it. While touching feet was a mark of respect for elders, in modern Indian families it was only done during special occasions like marriage. Her parents, and even her ex-in-laws, didn't follow this custom on a daily basis. A deep dread spread inside her chest.

"And who is this?" his mother asked.

"This is Rani." Arjun motioned her over and Rani stepped towards them on leaden legs.

Rani joined her hands and bowed her head. "Namaste."

Arjun looked pointedly at Rani and then his parents' feet. She gave them a thin smile then bent down and did what was expected of her. They each touched her head and uttered a blessing.

"So she's the one you've been fooling around with?"

Rani froze then stepped away from them.

"Ma!"

Jhanvi's eyes blazed with anger. "We dropped everything and flew overnight from India to see if the story was true and we find you coming home in the middle of the night with her?" Then she turned to Rani. "And what good Indian girl is with a man in the middle of the night when he is not her husband?"

Rani shrank back, her mouth completely dry and her chest so constricted she wasn't sure if she was still breathing.

"What are you talking about?" Arjun came to stand beside Rani. He touched her and she tried to focus on the warmth of his hand in the exposed dip of her lower back.

His father clicked on a tablet and turned the screen to show Arjun. "There's a story of you circulating in the media. A picture of you and Rani kissing. The story claims you're engaged."

Rani squinted to look at the headline, which blazed in

red. *Hottie Arjun Getting Married to Average-Looking American Divorcée.* Right below it was a picture of them kissing. The hospital garden with its metal picnic tables was in the background. It was the day Arjun told her he loved her.

"How did this get out?" Arjun lamented.

Like that was what was important right now. Did he not see the anger in his parents' eyes?

"Someone named Anaya Gupta—I assume she's your sister—took the photo." Arjun's father looked at Rani with such anger that she felt like she'd been cut in half. She shriveled back, moving away from Arjun and towards the door as if willing it to open and let her escape. "She posted an Instagram picture saying how happy she is for her sister and used the hashtag *#IndiasHottestHottie.* That's when the story first broke. The story is all over the Indian news media. How could you be so stupid, letting people take pictures with you like that? Hema's family is furious. Her father wanted to come with us."

"What were our PR people doing? Why didn't they stop the story?" Arjun asked.

Why is that important? Rani shouted in her head. Why wasn't anyone addressing the real issue?

"That PR hack you hired isn't worth the dirt on my shoe." His father scoffed. "The paper called him for a comment and he was worse than useless."

"I'll fire him tomorrow."

"Already done," Dharampal responded.

I have to get out of here or I'll scream.

"We'll have to fix it. I'm thinking we call a press conference tomorrow morning and say the picture is being blown out of proportion. Maybe announce your engagement to Hema," his father said, all businesslike.

"How about just denying it's me in the picture. You can't see my full face."

What was Arjun saying? If they were going to be to-gether, what good would it do lying to the media? *Unless he didn't plan on going through with the engagement after all.*

"Arjun, this story has a lot of steam in India. The only way to settle things down is to announce your engagement. Besides, Hema's family isn't willing to wait anymore."

Say something, Arjun! Tell him that if you're announc-ing your engagement, it'll be to me! Rani's tongue was superglued to the roof of her mouth. Her body trembling, she was unconsciously taking small steps towards the door behind her.

"I'm not ready to announce my engagement to Hema."

Say the rest Arjun, say the rest, Rani silently pleaded.

"What's not to be ready about?" Arjun's mother stepped up to him. "Your wedding is set for two months from now. Do I need to remind you what's at stake here? Hema's fam-ily has been very patient with you but you know as well as we do that if they pull out of our business partnership, you'll have to sell the Vegas hotel."

Two months! The wedding date was around the corner and Arjun still hadn't talked to his parents about not want-ing to marry Hema? This wasn't just about him and Rani. It was about him having the courage to face his parents.

"Ma, why are we standing here talking about such im-portant matters? You must be tired from your journey. You should rest, and we can discuss this first thing in the morn-ing," Arjun said with maddening calm.

"I'm quite fresh," Jhanvi said. "It's early morning India time. I slept on the flight and so did your dad."

"Jhanvi, we are on India time but he's on Las Vegas time. Let him get a few hours' sleep. I'll send the jet back to get Hema. If we're going to make an announcement, she should be here with him."

Rani had never seen Arjun getting steamrolled and yet here he was, looking wearily at his parents like he wasn't going to tell them that the woman he loved was standing right there.

"Let's pick this up tomorrow morning," Arjun's father said with finality.

"What about her?" Jhanvi nodded towards Rani as if suddenly remembering she was there.

Yes, what about me? Were you going to remember that I've been standing here this whole time or am I always going to be invisible next to your parents?

Arjun stepped towards her and whispered quietly in her ear. "Rani, I will handle them, but not tonight. Why don't you go home? I'll have Sam take you."

Rani did not need to be told twice. She spun and Arjun had barely gotten the door open before she walked through it. She stabbed at the elevator button, silently cursing it for not lighting up. Arjun came up behind her and calmly punched a code into the keypad next to the call button.

"Rani, please understand. There is a way to deal with my parents."

"And that way is to pretend like I don't exist?"

"Believe me, this is not how I intended to introduce you to them. Right now they are only concerned about my media image. Remember, I'm the face of our hotel chain. Any scandal affects not just our family reputation but also our hotel brand and the partnership with Hema's parents' business. They're a publicly traded company and answer to shareholders. We need to deal with that situation first. If only your sister hadn't posted that picture on social media..."

I'm not going to cry. I'm not going to beg. And I'm not going to let this be Anaya's fault.

When the elevators dinged, Rani stepped into the carriage. "Your family image and hotel brand won't be helped by an average-looking divorcée."

He let the doors shut, and she let the tears stream down her cheeks.

Nineteen

The next morning Arjun woke up to his mother making chai in his kitchen. He kissed her on the cheek. "I'll call the housekeeper to bring us something for breakfast."

"I'm making you *aloo paranthas* with my own hands," his mother replied in Hindi.

Arjun smiled. The thin wheat pancakes stuffed with spiced potatoes were his favorite. It was a special treat in his house to have them made by his mother.

"I've taught Hema how to make these too."

Arjun sighed as he took the cup of tea she handed him.

"Ma, I'm not going to marry Hema."

He hadn't wanted to have the conversation with his parents in front of Rani. He knew how brutally blunt his parents could be and he didn't want Rani's relationship with them affected by what they'd say in anger. But he wasn't going to let them walk all over him. This was his life and it was time to get things under control.

His mother didn't miss a beat. "Don't be stupid. Of course you are."

"I've fallen in love. I don't think it's fair to Hema to marry her when my heart belongs to someone else." He didn't want to betray Hema's confidence by telling his mother that she didn't want to marry him, either. He'd talked with Hema earlier that morning and she'd promised to come clean with her parents and tell them she didn't want to marry him. He'd explained the potential business fallout if they thought he was the only one breaking the *rishta*.

"You've been in love before," his mother said coldly. "Besides, have you forgotten the implications of breaking the *rishta* with Hema's family?"

"Our business deal benefits them too. They're astute enough to know that pulling out now is a loss for both our families."

"That's not the point and you know it. This *rishta* was a way to permanently bind our families together in a way business deals can't. And have you forgotten what a lovely girl Hema is? She knows our family *parampara*. We will never find anyone better suited to be your wife."

"Hema is a good woman but I don't love her in the way a husband should love a wife."

She fisted the dough for the *paranthas*. "Who is this girl you're in love with? The one from yesterday?"

"Yes."

"The divorcée?"

"Her name is Rani, and she's an interior architect. She's intelligent, caring and my equal in every way."

His father appeared in the kitchen doorway. "Jhanvi, you beat that dough any further and you'll break the stone counter."

"Come and listen to what your son has to say. He's fallen in love with that girl from last night, that divorcée, and he doesn't want to marry Hema." Without waiting for his father to comment she continued. "What do you see in her, Arjun? Even if you don't want to marry Hema, every eligible girl in India is dying to marry you. This girl is not particularly beautiful, she's not that thin and I saw the way she looked at you when you asked her to touch our feet. What qualities does she have that make her right for our family?"

He took a breath to keep his voice calm, doubly glad that he hadn't let Rani hear this conversation. "You're talking about the woman I love. You don't know Rani. If you did you'd see that she is beautiful inside and out. She is intelligent, accomplished, she understands me…"

"And Hema is none of those things?"

"Hema is like my sister. We've grown up together. I just don't feel for her the way I do for Rani."

"Son…" Arjun's father had been listening silently to the exchange, but the deep baritone in his voice made Arjun cringe. He recognized it. It was the voice any father used when telling his son that he was in big trouble. Arjun suddenly felt like he was ten years old and had been caught beating on his brother.

"I know what you're going to say. We made a promise to Hema's family and we always keep our *vachan*. But—"

"You don't know what I'm going to say. And since when do you interrupt your father?"

Arjun took a breath. Now was not the time to get into an argument about pointless things.

"We have been fighting to make sure that the children of our house, our daughters especially, are not corrupted by the Western influences that have taken over India. Day by day we are losing our culture. You are the eldest son. It will be your job to keep the *parampara* of the house alive after your mother and I are dead. Your wife will be the eldest *bahu* of the house and more than you, she will keep the *izzat*, the respect of our family name. She will make sure that the next generation is raised with the same values that we raised you with. Is Rani going to be able to fulfill that role?"

This was the part that worried Arjun the most. It was the argument he had avoided having with his parents his whole life, and one where there would be no winners.

"Dad, don't you think that as times have changed, we too must evolve as a family? Not to change our values, but perhaps some of our traditions, our way of doing things."

"Jhanvi and my parents arranged our marriage. We've been happily married for thirty-six years."

"But your marriage was unconventional, was it not?" Arjun's heart hammered. He knew there was no turning back if he said the next words, but he had to. "Dad, you were from a wealthy family and in those days, you married in the same money class in order to consolidate wealth. But Ma, while from a family with lineage, your family had nothing. It took a change in tradition for dad's family to accept you. And for your family to accept that I already existed, which meant you would not give birth to the household heir."

"Arjun, how dare you?" his mother said sharply.

"Even traditions have to evolve with time to stay relevant. Ma, most women of your generation were married off by the time they were sixteen. But you didn't marry my sisters off. Why are you willing to break that tradition but not others?"

"And you see where your sisters are now? They want to work, and to have their own money."

"And what's wrong with that? You know we almost lost everything ten years ago when tourism crashed in India. We all need a career to fall back on. You educated me and Sameer, so it's right to do the same for my sisters. I work, why can't Divya? In fact, for the last month she's been incredibly helpful in the Jaipur office. So many things I couldn't take care of, she has handled even better than me. What gives me and Sameer the right to run your business, Dad? Why not Divya?"

"Because that's not the way society works. One day Divya will get married and have a household with her own husband and children to look after. They won't be part of our *gharana*. Why are you suddenly questioning our way of life?"

"This must be Rani's influence," his mother muttered bitterly.

"I have always felt this way but never questioned you."

"Because we raised you the right way. A few months with that girl and look at what's happening," Jhanvi said.

Arjun sighed. He'd expected the conversation to go badly but he was drowning.

"You know nothing about Rani."

"We had her investigated when the first picture surfaced," Dharampal said.

Anger boiled inside him and the only thing keeping him calm was the realization that flying off the handle would just make things worse for him and Rani.

"She divorced her ex-husband for no apparent reason. He came from a respectable family. What makes you think she can commit to you?" Jhanvi asked.

"You have no idea what kind of guy her ex-husband is. *Khandan* isn't the only thing that determines a person's character. Rani was right to leave him. I have no doubt that she's committed to me." Even as he said the words, he shifted on his feet. The very things he loved about Rani, her independence, her strength, would clash with his everyday family life. Would she be able to adjust?

"But is she committed to our family? To our traditions?"

Arjun wanted to answer *yes*, but he couldn't. He and Rani had been avoiding the conversation because she didn't want to disappoint him, and he didn't want to face the fact that he'd have to choose between Rani and his parents. A choice that was staring him in the face now.

"She will make some compromises, and so must we," he answered carefully.

"But why?" his mother asked.

"Why what?"

"Why must we compromise our values, our ideals?"

"I'm not as traditional as you want me to be. I agree with my sisters that they should have more freedom. Rani understands me. She can be my partner in life in a way Hema never can."

"We are not talking about this anymore. I'm making breakfast, and you will come to your senses, Arjun," his mother said decisively.

After a tensely silent breakfast, Arjun's mother excused herself. She had brought a few of her maids with her from India and the women efficiently went about cleaning the kitchen. He and his father stepped onto the balcony with a cup of chai.

"Son, I'm going to tell you about the time I married your mother."

Arjun sighed inwardly. He had heard the arranged marriage story a million times.

"Not Jhanvi, your birth mother."

Arjun looked at his father in surprise. He never talked about Arjun's birth mother. There weren't any pictures of her in the family archives, no mention of her among the older servants who knew his grandparents. The only evidence of her existence was Arjun himself.

"Your grandfather had arranged my marriage to Jhanvi when we were children. When I was barely eighteen, I fell in love with Savitri. She was beautiful and exciting, and she came from a good family who had money and status. I thought for sure my father would be happy to break the *rishta* with Jhanvi. By then her family had lost all their wealth and were no longer in the same social class as us. But my father said no. He said we made a promise to Jhanvi and her family and we didn't want their *hai*, the curse of their ill feelings."

Arjun shifted in his chair.

"But I was insistent. So much so that I ran away and had a priest marry us without our parents present. Savitri was always traumatized by the fact that her father wasn't there to give her away. The resentment from our families ate at both of us. Despite the fact that we were married, we were never happy. And then she died giving birth to you. I think our marriage was cursed from the beginning without the blessing of our parents."

Arjun saw the sincerity in his father's eyes. While he didn't believe in curses, he could see how parental disapproval could wreak havoc on a close-knit family. There was a child inside every adult who wanted nothing more than to please his or her parents. He'd seen that longing and pain in Rani's eyes every time she talked about her parents.

"I didn't know how to care for a baby. The *aiyas* took care of you, but a servant can't provide a mother's love. My father begged forgiveness from Jhanvi's father, and I from her. She not only married me, she loved you. In fact, we delayed having children because she wanted to give you her love exclusively. I didn't love Jhanvi when we married, but I love her more now than I ever loved Savitri. She made a home for me and my children. She brought our family together. My love for her has grown with age because each day I appreciate more and more how important the things my father talked about really are. I scoffed at him when he talked about *parampara* but it's only when I didn't have it, when there was chaos in my house that I understood what he was saying. Don't make the same mistake I did."

"How are you so sure that Rani won't do for our house

what Ma did? That she won't be able to bring our generations together? Maybe she is exactly what we need to bridge the divide between our *parampara* and the new world we live in. Rani grew up in a traditional household like us and she's struggled with this all her life. She understands how to handle it. She's the one who came up with the solution for Divya to work for us in the Jaipur office."

"A decision I don't agree with. I think we should have told Divya she can't work."

"And then what, Dad? Divya would meekly sit at home and be happy? She'd be miserable and fight us on every little thing, ruining the peace of the house. Instead, she's helping us run our family business and—"

"And every day she and your other sisters are feeling more emboldened to break the house rules."

"Dad, just like we modernized our hotels, we must change our household or—"

"Or all of the children will rebel like you. Arjun, have you forgotten that our wisdom stopped you from making a mistake with that other girl?"

Arjun fought the rage boiling deep in his belly. For the last ten years, he had worked tirelessly to secure and expand the family fortunes. To ensure the future for his siblings. He'd supported his parents even when he didn't agree with their decisions. He'd made a mistake with Lakshmi, but that was the inexperience of his youth. He was a thirty-eight-year-old man who managed a company worth nearly ten billion dollars.

Does Dad still see me as that foolish boy who fell for a gold digger?

"I'm not rebelling, Dad, I'm choosing how to live my personal life. You trust me to make critical decisions that affect our family business every day. Decisions that determine all our futures. Why can't you trust me to know what's best for me?"

"Because men cannot be trusted to differentiate between love and desire." Jhanvi's voice cut through the air. She was talking to Arjun but her gaze was fixed on her husband. She moved towards Arjun. "When you come back to India, you'll marry Hema. If you can't accept that, then I suggest you don't return."

Twenty

"You asked to see her?" Em asked incredulously.

Rani nodded, miserably picking at the pasta salad Em had made her for lunch. They were in the kitchen of their shared apartment. Em had decorated the room in a folksy style with small pictures of chickens and ducks that had been painted by her patients. The two-person dining room table was made of reclaimed barn wood. Rani loved the cozy warmth of this kitchen. Was she really ready to go back to large, shiny appliances that only chefs knew how to use? Then she thought about making lamb *saag* and masala chai with Arjun and tears stung her eyes.

"I'm tired of everyone thinking they know best how to handle my love life. I need to meet with his mother and decide for myself whether I can be with Arjun. So I called his condo and asked if I could come over to meet with her. She said she'd been about to call and ask me over for tea. I guess great minds think alike."

"Wow." Em had a rare morning off from the hospital,

and rather than sleeping or catching up on her never ending to-do list, she had spent the time keeping Rani company, listening with endless patience as she vented, then strategized, then cried about how to handle the situation.

"How much money do you think she'll offer you to remove your claws from her son?"

Rani cracked a smile. "How much should I accept?"

Em clicked on her phone, tucking her hot pink hair behind her ear. "Google says his family net worth is unknown but they're estimated to be in the top one hundred richest families in the world. I say you ask for a beach house in Hawaii."

"I jumped into things too quickly," Rani said miserably. "You should've seen him with his parents last night. They walked all over him. That's what it was like with Navin."

"And what you're like with your own parents," Em said gently.

"I've just gotten control over my life. I have the money to start my own consulting firm. I don't want to give all that up."

"You don't think true love is worth making some sacrifices?"

"That sounds great on a refrigerator magnet but you need more than love in reality. For the first time in my life, I don't have to answer to anyone but myself. I don't have to live my life because of obligations or traditions or because someone else wants to control me."

"Why does it have to be that way? You can still pursue your career dreams. As far as letting someone control your life, that's on you, Rani. You couldn't help how you grew up but you let Navin's family dominate you. I think you understand that now. This time, you're taking charge of this situation. What do you want Arjun to do?"

"I know this is wrong of me, but I want him to make the

big gesture and tell me he's going to give it all up. I need to know that he's willing to sacrifice for me. I'm not getting into another one-way marriage."

When she arrived at Arjun's condo, she was immediately struck by the change. The furnishings were the same, all his stuff was in the same place, but the air was literally different. The kitchen was fragrant with the smell of cardamom and cinnamon. A gray-haired woman in a navy sari Rani didn't recognize let her in and asked her to sit on the couch, then disappeared. As she looked over at the kitchen, two different women dressed in the same navy saris were moving about, preparing trays. Rani sat uncomfortably on the couch. Even the stunning view didn't soothe the churning in her stomach.

"Ah Rani, you're here." Arjun's mother was dressed in dark silk pants and a rich green tunic with gold embroidery. Her salt-and-pepper hair was pulled back into a bun, and elegantly simple emerald solitaires glittered at her ears. By comparison, after some panicked wardrobe flinging, Em had helped Rani pair one of her suit pants with a cream-colored silk button-down blouse. Her jewelry was a single pearl on a gold chain and small pearl earrings.

Rani's mouth was dry as she stood. She suddenly realized she didn't know how to address Arjun's mother. Mrs. Singh seemed too impersonal and Auntie seemed too casual. She managed a namaste.

Jhanvi nodded toward the couch. "Sit. What will you have? Chai or coffee?"

Rani didn't want anything but she smiled politely. "Whatever you're having."

Jhanvi clicked her fingers and yet another navy sari-clad woman appeared. "Gauri, chai." The woman vanished.

"Thank you for seeing me. I appreciate the opportunity

to clear the air." Rani delivered her practiced opening with a throat so tight that her voice came out in a croak.

Jhanvi gave her a tight-lipped smile. "When a son gets taken in by a woman, it's a mother's job to get to know her."

Rani's stomach knotted even tighter. Two women appeared carrying trays. One contained a tea service and another an assortment of sandwiches, cookies and Indian sweets.

Rani took a sip of the perfectly brewed masala chai that was handed to her, then set the cup on the table. "What would you like to know about me?"

Jhanvi took several slow sips of her tea before setting her cup down. She picked up a small plate filled with cucumber sandwiches and held it out to Rani, who shook her head. "Try them. My cook, Neelu, makes these with fresh cilantro chutney."

Rani selected one and set it on her plate.

Jhanvi took a delicate bite of her sandwich and Rani tried not to fidget.

"So, what are your plans after you marry my son?"

"Arjun hasn't asked me to marry him." Rani immediately regretted the glib words. She knew what Jhanvi's response would be before the woman even spoke.

"I think you know that we would not be meeting if my son wasn't serious about you, so let's talk frankly."

Rani nodded contritely. She felt like she was a teenager who'd been caught with a boy in her bed.

"What specific plans are you interested in?"

"Let's start with when you plan to move to India."

So much for easing into the conversation with a simple question. "Arjun and I haven't discussed where we will live, but I'm sure we can work something out."

Jhanvi leaned forward. "Our home, Arjun's home, is in India. Do you think he'll be happy living in America?"

No, he won't. "The hotel in Vegas will need oversight,

and as Arjun expands the business globally, we will have to be flexible with where we're based," Rani said evenly.

"That sounds ideal in theory but it's not practical. You are both quite old now and will want to have children soon. You can't take children from house to house. They will need a home and that home will be the one where Arjun, and his father, grew up. Our *khandani haveli*. The family palace."

Rani bit her tongue to keep from saying something she'd regret. She and Arjun had talked about the fact that they both wanted children. Although Rani was loath to admit it, she knew Jhanvi was correct in pointing out that children needed a home base. But settling the details of her future with Arjun was not the point of this conversation with his mother.

"These are all important decisions that Arjun and I will make," she said with a teary smile.

"But these decisions are not just for you and Arjun to make."

And there it is. What she had come to find out. Rani tilted her head and looked at Jhanvi.

"I understand you grew up in a respectable Indian household, so surely you know these are family decisions, and ones that cannot be taken lightly given how many lives this affects."

Rani bristled at the way Jhanvi said "respectable" as though she meant to put air quotes around the word.

"I understand completely. And while I *respect* the traditions and customs of your house, I think there are some things that a husband and wife must decide together. Surely you and Arjun's dad make many such decisions."

Jhanvi visibly bristled. "You aren't comparing this…this relationship you have with my son to the thirty-six years of marriage that my husband and I share? And we are the eldest generation in our house. When my in-laws were living, we bent to their every wish."

"And how did that make you feel as a daughter-in-law? Did you love your in-laws?" Rani knew she was really pushing the boundaries of appropriateness but she wanted to find some common ground with Jhanvi.

Jhanvi smiled. "I won't insult your intelligence by claiming that I loved my in-laws like a daughter would have. At first I resented and tolerated them, but as my children grew, I came to respect them and understand why they did things the way they did."

It was as honest an answer as Rani would ever get and hope bloomed in her chest. "But there are things you did differently. For example, educating your daughters."

Jhanvi reached across the couch to pat Rani's hand. "Rani, why don't we talk about what's really bothering both of us and stop circling around the real issues. I wanted to talk to you to see whether you're willing to make the sacrifices it will take to be a part of Arjun's life, and you asked to meet me to see just how tyrannical I'll be as a mother-in-law."

Rani smiled at Jhanvi, her directness reminding her so much of Arjun that she couldn't help but like the woman.

"Then how about I lay my cards on the table. I was married into a family where the parents controlled everything—the money, what we did, what we ate, who we were friends with. It was suffocating and I want to know if that's what your household is like."

Jhanvi took another cucumber sandwich; Rani hadn't touched hers. "And that is exactly why we are concerned about you, dear. We ran a background check on you and know that per your divorce decree, you parted because of irreconcilable differences. There was no mention of abuse or infidelity. Controlling in-laws are hardly a reason to leave your husband."

Rani took a breath. "It depends on one's perspective, and my situation was more complex than that. But it is also the reason that I hope we can come to an understanding about how we will interact. It's not a conversation I had before my prior marriage."

Jhanvi set down her plate. "Well, to answer your question, Dharampal and I are involved in all of the big life decisions. Arjun is in charge of the household finances and I don't care what he spends his money on or whether his wife tells the cook to make chicken tikka for dinner or *daal makhani*." She paused, as if trying to decide how to say the next part. "But we will have a role in determining who he will marry and his wife will follow the same house rules as my daughters. No late evenings without Arjun, and respectable friends. I don't want my *bahu* to work outside the house unless it's with Arjun like Divya is doing. We are a close family and are very involved in each other's lives."

Rani's mouth soured. "What if I disagree with your rules?" Rani hadn't meant to make it sound like a question and kicked herself for not being more forceful.

Jhanvi smiled. "I asked you before where you planned to live as a test question. There is no choice in that matter. Arjun will never live anywhere other than India. The fact that you think you have a choice tells me that you either don't know my son very well or you are living in a fantasy bubble that is about to burst. So I ask you to consider how much you're willing to give up for my son."

"I realize compromises need to be made, but why must I do all the sacrificing?"

"Ah, the optimism of youth." She took a bite of her sandwich. "Rani, dear, even in progressive societies like America, women talk about how they are responsible for too much of the domestic duties. More women leave their jobs when they have children than men."

"There are practical reasons why more women take time off to care for infants. They have to recover from childbirth and men can't breastfeed."

"Exactly, Rani. Arjun is responsible for not just his financial future but that of his siblings too. He's not going to become a stay-at-home dad, as you Americans say. So what type of life are you picturing together? Exactly what are you expecting he will give up for you? What are you willing to give up for him?"

"I love Arjun and I'm willing to give up the world for him." She paused, trying to find the right words. "But I expect equality in our marriage. And the big decisions about our life will be between me and him."

"Well, then you truly do not understand my son."

Rani stood, done with diplomacy. "I think we've both gotten what we wanted out of this conversation."

Jhanvi stood and smiled.

Rani thanked her for the meeting. Now she had to face Arjun.

Twenty-One

Arjun paced his office. Rani and his mother were meeting less than a mile away. *Should I go check on her?* He knew what his mother could be like. Yet he couldn't go. Rani had insisted that she wanted to meet with his mother alone and promised she would come see him afterwards. It was just as well; he wouldn't always be around to mediate disagreements between Rani and his parents and Rani had to make the decision about what she could handle.

She's strong. She stood up to me. She can do this.

He looked at his watch again. Only two minutes had passed since the last time he'd checked.

A knock on his door startled him. He had asked his assistant to bring Rani to his office as soon as she was done with his mother. He looked up to see her looking breathtakingly beautiful, and weary, like she'd been beaten down for hours.

He pulled her into his arms, not caring about the glass walls or prying eyes. Her body melted against his.

"That bad, huh?"

She pushed against his chest and lifted her face. "It wasn't bad. It was clarifying."

Acid churned in his stomach. "What do you mean?"

"Arjun, what are we thinking? How is this ever going to work? Every day will be a battle between me and your parents. I've done that before, and I can't. Not again. I don't want to give up my career to move to India and play housewife."

"You don't have to give up your career. You can open up your own design firm. My hotels alone have enough business to keep you busy for years."

She stepped back from him. "You don't get it. I don't want to be dependent on you. I want my freedom. I want to be able to work late if I need to, go out with friends at night if I want to. I don't want to fight over the simplest requests. I've lived that way all my life and I won't do it anymore."

"I'm not going to lie to you. My parents will always be a big part of my life. But we can work it out. As you Americans say, I come with baggage."

Her face crumpled. "You mother made it sound like I'd have no control over my life."

"I haven't asked you to give up a single thing, Rani."

"Okay, then tell me how it'll work between us?"

He blew out a breath, his chest so tight that he had trouble getting it all out. It was a conversation they should have had a while ago. A talk that he had avoided because he didn't like going into a meeting without having the answers.

"You can open your own design firm and we can live part time here and part time in India. If you don't want my business, that's fine. I'm not saying it'll be easy but we'll work on getting my parents to loosen the rules. If we live here part time, it won't be as bad."

"And what happens when we have children? We drag them with us on your private plane every time I get tired of living in India? Would you be happy having them grow up in a hotel?"

"We don't have to figure everything out right now. It'll be years before we have children."

"I'm thirty-six, Arjun. If we want children, there aren't a lot of years that we can wait."

Why was she being so stubborn? He was trying to meet her halfway and she was coming up with all the reasons why it wouldn't work rather than helping him find solutions like she usually did.

"I know your heart is in the right place and you want to make it work just as desperately as I do. But I think your mother has actually thought things through more than we have."

He clasped her hands. "I don't have it all worked out, but can you give me a chance to find a way?"

Her eyes were shining and the desperate look she gave him cut through his heart like a knife. He kissed her softly. "Give me some time to come up with a plan. Can you do that?"

She wrapped her arms around his neck and kissed him fiercely, her body pressed close to his, her mouth hungry on his, her fingers grasping his hair. When she released him, her face was wet. She turned and walked out, and he was left with a hole in the pit of his stomach.

Why did that feel like a goodbye kiss?

Twenty-Two

Arjun was drained. He stood at his kitchen stove watching the tea boil and looked at his watch. Rani had asked to come over and he was looking forward to holding her in his arms.

His parents had just left after a volatile two days. Hema had found the courage to tell her parents she didn't want to marry him but her parents had reacted the same way as his. They felt that Hema didn't know what was best for her and was making a rash decision. They'd called Jhanvi and Dharampal to reiterate that they'd given their daughter an ultimatum: to marry Arjun or be disowned. They had also expressed anger at Arjun for his indiscretions with Rani. Meanwhile, the media storm hadn't let up.

The only win for Arjun was that he'd prevented his parents from making an announcement about him and Hema. He'd told them in no uncertain terms that he would only marry Rani. Their response was that he wasn't welcome back into the family home if he didn't marry Hema. After her conversation with Rani, his mother was convinced that Rani would add fuel to the discord that already existed with his sisters, especially Divya.

As soon as the security guard downstairs alerted him that Rani had arrived, he took the tea off the stove and went to wait by the elevators. When the doors opened, his breath caught. Rani was wearing jeans and a V-neck shirt that showed off her curves beautifully. She smiled at him and he pulled her into his arms, savoring the feel of her against his body. He let her warm vanilla smell soothe the storm raging inside him.

She's the woman I love. How can I spend my life with someone else, knowing she exists?

He led her to the kitchen. "I didn't have time to make a full meal, but I made you some masala chai." She smiled and perched on the island stool while he poured the tea into two cups.

"It was rough with your parents."

He nodded. "They need some time." He tried—and failed—to sound convincing for her. "It'll be better once the media coverage dies down."

She shook her head. "You and I both know it's about more than bad publicity. I'm all wrong for your family."

His stomach clenched. He wanted to reassure her but his words would just sound hollow.

She reached out and grabbed his hands and he wove his fingers through hers.

"Arjun, I've been doing a lot of thinking. I've never loved anyone like I love you. And that's why I'm going to let you go." Her voice cracked.

His heart squeezed painfully in his chest. "You're going to have to explain that one to me."

She smiled sadly at him. "Have you looked at yourself in the mirror? You look horrible."

"Thanks so much. I haven't had time to get a facial," he joked.

"The stress is killing you and it's only been a few days." She looked down. "Think about how you're feeling right now. Can you imagine life like this every day? Constantly having to choose between me and your parents? This kind of burden will kill you, and I love you too much to do that to you. It was foolish for us to think that there was a magical way we could make it all work."

"So you want to give up? Throw it all away? Do you know how special it is to have what we have? To feel the way we do about each other?"

"Yes I do! But I also know what it's like to be trapped and feel like there's no escape. That's how it would be in your house. All my life, I've had no control over my own destiny. I did what my parents asked, and then I lived the way that my ex in-laws wanted. I can't do it anymore. I won't be the obedient *bahu* your mother is looking for, and it's going to create strife in your family. I'll be yet another burden on you and I don't want to become yet another person you have to manage in your life like you do with your sisters and brother."

Tears rolled down her cheeks. *She is unyielding*, his mother had said. He wanted to pull Rani close but she pulled her hands away from him and he let her. For the first time in his life, he felt beaten. He didn't want Rani to feel like a life with him would be the kind of prison she'd endured with her ex, yet he didn't have anything different to offer her. He'd been hoping that together they could come up with a middle ground where both their needs could be met.

"I wish more than anything that I'd never married Navin. That I didn't have the scars that are stopping me from believing that we can somehow make this work."

He wanted to beg her, plead with her to rethink what

she was saying. Convince her that things would be different. But the words stuck in his mouth. She needed him to give up everything for her. His family, his business, his life.

When she kissed him on the cheek and left, he didn't stop her.

Twenty-Three

How was it that the very person she went out of her way to avoid always ended up right in her path? Rani smiled as she passed Arjun in the hall. He gave her a clipped smile back then strode by. There were no more dimpled smiles for her.

She felt ravaged inside. The Mahal hotel was two days away from opening and for the last few weeks, she'd been onsite every day to make sure the finishing touches were done right. Arjun had moved his offices to the hotel and himself into the owners condo. Her heart squeezed painfully every time she thought of him sleeping in the four-poster bed where they'd made love for the first time.

She turned back to see him walking away. They had survived a month and a half of pretending they were just work colleagues. What was two more days?

After the opening, she was officially done at RKS. When Arjun had insisted she remain in charge, there had been some grumblings from Delia, which Rani calmed by announcing that she planned to leave at the end of the contract. That seemed to placate everyone. She had made it very clear to Ian Rabat that if he tried to tarnish her reputation like he had Bob's, Rani would do the same to him. She felt fairly confident that her break from RKS would be amicable.

In the last month, five different firms had given her amazing employment offers. Arjun's hotel had already been featured in several travel magazines and each piece had commented on the unique interior design of the hotel. It was fully booked for its first three months.

Rani had rejected all of the job offers. Instead, she had channeled the endless hours of sleepless nights into setting up her own interior architecture firm. She'd sunk every penny she had into buying basic computer equipment and software. She couldn't afford office space or staff until she got her first contract but things were looking promising on that front. She had already signed a small restaurant in Vegas and had meetings lined up with several other businesses. Nothing as big as Arjun's hotel, but she didn't have the team for something like that. She'd start off small and as she built her business, she could take on bigger projects.

Her career was finally taking off, but she couldn't find the joy in everything going well for her. It was as though there was a deep worm burrowing through her soul and emptying the happiness out of her. She felt like a shell with nothing left inside. Every cell in her body craved Arjun, longed and ached for him. *It'll get better with time*, Rani kept telling herself. Except each day she became hollower inside.

Her cell phone buzzed. It was a text from Anaya. Heads up! Amma saw this. Rani clicked on the link in the text. It was an article in a popular Indian magazine. After she scrolled past the ads, the headline stopped her heart. *Arjun and Hema, India's Hottest Couple, to Tie the Knot in a Month.* She had never seen a picture of Hema but there she was with Arjun's family. She stood tall by his side, classically beautiful in a Rajasthani *lehngah*, a red skirt adorned with mirrored jewels and a matching cropped top choli that left her stomach exposed. She had one hand on Arjun's arm and the other holding Jhanvi's hand. A perfect family.

Rani's phone rang. It was her mother. She hadn't told her parents about the breakup with Arjun but it was time to face the music.

"That rascal. How could he cheat you like this?" Her mother spared no niceties as she cursed out Arjun. Rani let her mother vent her frustrations.

"*Amma*, we broke up a month ago."

The line went silent and Rani's heart lurched. She had avoided telling her parents because she didn't want to lose them and Arjun all at the same time. She should've been nervous, afraid of what her mother would say, but she found herself not giving a damn. It was like she was going through the motions of life but not feeling anything.

"What happened, Rani?" her mother asked quietly.

"I met his parents and it was clear they would never accept me. Arjun was ready to go against them but I didn't want him to. I didn't want to make the same mistake I made with Navin. I would go into that house and be unhappy."

"Are you happy now without him?"

"No." Tears streamed down her face. It seemed to be the only thing she could do: cry until the tears dried up and then curl up on her bed and wait until she had fresh tears.

"Then what is the point of your stubbornness?"

Rani closed her eyes. "It's not stubbornness. It's self-preservation. I don't want to end up the way I did after Navin."

"So are you feeling better now than you did back then?"

The question gave Rani pause. She was in a better place. She had her career, she had future plans. And yet she'd never felt emptier in her life.

"I didn't mourn losing Navin. I mourned losing you and Dad. I need you to get through this. I don't want to lose you again, *Amma*."

"You won't, Rani. We were wrong in the way we treated you, I see that now. If something had happened to your father and you weren't here——" Her voice broke. "You are our daughter and we should have shared in your pain, not pushed you away."

Rani hung up with her mother and stared at Arjun's wedding announcement. She tried to picture herself where Hema stood. The article called Hema beautiful and elegant. Rani would always be the average-looking divorcée.

9>He likes the finer things in life. And he should have them.

Twenty-Four

It should have been one of the proudest moments of Arjun's life, but all he felt was restless. His hotel's grand opening was perfect. Nothing was out of place. Normally hotels did a soft opening to work out the kinks, but they hadn't had the time. It was a huge risk, but he'd spent every waking minute making sure they were ready. Not that he'd been able to sleep much anyway.

He glanced at the four-poster bed where he and Rani had made love for the first time. When he'd moved into the owners condos, he had taken one of the other bedrooms, unable to face the memories of his first night with Rani.

But then he'd walked into the master bedroom in the middle of the night and slept there. The linens had been changed but he could still smell and feel Rani in the bed.

His phone buzzed, reminding him it was time to go downstairs. The opening night party was tonight and his parents and siblings were waiting for him. He silenced the buzzer. He could be late.

He ran his hands over the luxurious bedding and closed his eyes. He could see her sitting on the bed, telling him how handsome he looked and fretting about her own clothes for the evening. They would discuss who they had to talk to at the party tonight and how to make sure that his brother, Sameer, didn't end up in the tabloids tomorrow. If he kept his eyes closed, he could almost see the life he could've had with her.

A knock on the door forced him to get back to the real world.

"Dude, you're five minutes late. Ma sent me up here to make sure you weren't dead." Sameer greeted him at the door with an easy smile. Like Arjun, he was dressed in a classic black tuxedo, except his white bow tie was a little crooked and his hair looked like he'd just gotten out of bed. Normally Arjun would have said something, but what did it matter?

"Hey, you okay, bro?"

Arjun nodded, then patted his brother on the shoulder. "Do you mind asking Ma and Dad to come up here? I need to discuss something with them."

Sameer rolled his eyes, then disappeared. It wasn't unusual for Arjun to meet with his parents before a major event.

Arjun ran his hands over the wood carving on the door. Diwali was his favorite holiday. The return of the Lord Rama, whose wife had followed him into a fourteen-year banishment. Would Rani follow him? He had heard through his staff that she was leaving RKS and that she was starting her own firm. He felt a surge of pride for her. She'd been right to end things between them. She could achieve so much more without his obligations weighing her down.

He left the door ajar for his parents, who arrived a few minutes later. His father wore a tuxedo and his mother glit-

tered in a black sari with Swarovski crystals on the *pallu*.
They looked at him expectantly.

He handed his laptop to his father, who gave him a puz-
zled look.

"That holds the proverbial keys to the hotel, and to our
entire empire. I organized all the files so you can easily
access anything you need."

"I don't understand," his father said, sounding bewil-
dered.

"I'm not marrying Hema. I don't know why you issued
a press release with that old picture of all of us together.
I've been very clear about my intentions. You gave me an
ultimatum that I either marry Hema or leave the family.
So I'm giving you back your empire."

"Arjun!" His mother sounded shocked.

"After tonight, you won't see me again."

His parents looked dumbstruck.

"*Beta*, what nonsense is this?" His father's voice was
louder now.

"You can't be serious," his mother exclaimed. "Is this
about Rani?"

"This is about me. And my life. I don't want to be bul-
lied into who I marry or how I live my life. I love you both,
and not being a part of this family will kill me. But if you're
willing to lose me over your stubbornness, then I'm your
son, and no less firm in my convictions."

Jhanvi sat on the chaise longue in the sitting area.
"You're willing to give up everything for that girl."

"Don't you see? I love Rani precisely because of who
she is, the way she thinks. I never wanted her to yield to
you or follow our family *parampara*. I wanted her to help
me change your way of thinking to be more like hers."

"Why are you speaking in past tense?"

"Because I took too long to come to the realization that
she was not the one who needed to change. I was."

* * *

Rani sat at the bar, nursing a cup of coffee. She would've left the opening night party hours ago but it turned out that several of the potential clients she'd been courting were here. In fact, most of the who's who of Vegas were here. She'd already set up two more pitch meetings.

She stared into the coffee cup, trying to find happiness in how far she'd come in the six short months since she'd first met Arjun. She'd gone from being a junior architect to starting her own company. But all she could think about was how she wished she could tell Arjun that the coffee was too bitter and he needed to find a new vendor, that his hotel was awesome, and that she was finding it really hard to give a damn about the career she cared so much about. More than anything, she wanted to tell him that she'd follow him anywhere he wanted to take her. So what if they moved to India and she had to endure his stifling household? She'd get to hold him every night. She had all the control she wanted and yet she couldn't get the one thing she needed.

"Rani, dear, do you mind if I sit here?"

Rani couldn't have been more surprised to see Arjun's mother take a seat next to her. She had seen Arjun's entire family from far away, taking the requisite publicity shots at the ribbon cutting earlier. But what could Jhanvi possibly want with her now that Arjun and Hema were getting married?

Jhanvi didn't wait for permission as she perched herself on the bar stool, and Rani couldn't help but admire the elegant way in which she managed the feat in a sari. Rani herself had dressed for the occasion in a floor-length royal-blue gown with a low back and a slit in the side.

Arjun's mother ordered a whiskey on the rocks. Her drink was delivered immediately.

"You look beautiful, dear. That color really suits you."

"Thank you."

"I noticed you earlier at the ribbon cutting so I told the security people to find you."

"You were looking for me?" She had not expected that. Surely the woman was too busy planning Arjun's big fat Indian wedding to worry about Rani.

She ignored Rani's question. "Do you know that I became a mother before I was a wife?" Rani sensed the question was rhetorical and kept her eyes on Jhanvi, giving the woman her undivided attention.

"The first time I held Arjun, he looked into my eyes with such innocent love, and I knew in that moment, even though I hadn't given birth to him, he was my son. I agreed to marry his father not because I loved Dharampal but because I'd fallen in love with Arjun. Among all my children, Arjun holds a special part of my heart. I always want to protect him." She gestured around her. "All this seems to attract the wrong sort towards him."

What was she saying? "I was never interested in Arjun's wealth…"

"You misunderstand me. I've been shielding him from having his heart broken for years. His father once broke my heart and I didn't want Arjun to go through that. But it seems that's exactly what I've done."

Her chest tightened. "What're you saying?"

"I'm saying it's clear that my son is in love with you and that he's willing to give up everything for you."

Rani's heart jumped into her throat and she sat straighter. "What do you mean he's willing to give up everything for me?"

"We gave him an ultimatum that if he didn't marry Hema, he would be disowned. So tonight, he left the family."

Rani gasped. *He did that for me?* Why hadn't he told her what he was planning to do?

"We wanted to scare him. Not in a million years did I think he would actually leave the family. So I've come to beg you to bring him back to us." Jhanvi's voice cracked.

Rani looked at her shining eyes and suddenly realized that the two of them shared something very powerful. A love for Arjun. And that made her feel a little closer to Jhanvi.

She reached out and grabbed Jhanvi's hand. "It was never my intention for him to leave the family. I just wanted him to stand up to you."

The big gesture she'd been waiting for was not for him to forsake everything he held dear. Then it hit her. Just like she'd been waiting for Arjun to make the big gesture, he had been waiting for her to tell him that she was strong enough to deal with what might come their way. He'd been waiting for her big gesture.

Rani looked into Jhanvi's eyes, and the jumble of thoughts and emotions that had haunted her for the last weeks tumbled into place. A sudden clarity swept through her. "We can find a way to share him, can't we?" She squeezed Jhanvi's hand.

A tear dropped onto Jhanvi's cheek and she wiped it away, smearing her makeup. She clutched Rani's hand and nodded.

She drank her whiskey in one gulp, then got down from the stool abruptly. Rani looked at her questioningly. "A mother should know when to not interfere," she said with a smile. Rani turned to see Arjun standing there. He was dressed in jeans and a T-shirt, looking like the man who lit her heart on fire from the first time she'd seen him.

He raised a brow at his mother, who motioned to the seat she'd just vacated then blew him a kiss and walked away.

"Ms. Gupta, do you mind if I sit?"

She smiled. "I don't know. It might cost you a billion dollars."

He grinned at her and she nearly fainted at the sight of his dimple. "It's worth the price."

He shooed the attentive bartender away. "I'm sorry it took me so long to realize what you were saying. I love you for who you are, and I was asking you to change that when what I should've been doing is showing you that I'll be there for you. Can I beg for your forgiveness? Am I too late to convince you to love a poor man with no home, no family and not a penny to his name?"

She smiled. "I see your new status as an improvement. Though I don't think it'll last too long." Rani turned to point at his mother, who had moved away but was hovering in the distance.

"You weren't the only one who handled it wrong," Rani continued. "I shouldn't have put everything on you and your parents. It's my life and I need to be the one strong enough to dictate the terms. And I am. All I need to know is that you'll be by my side."

He let out an audible sigh. "If there's anything I've learned in the last month, it's that I can't breathe without you, Rani."

She sighed. "This is how it'll work. My company is mine to run as I see fit. You will not interfere. We live here in Vegas part time, and I'm going to design a small house for us on your family property in Rajasthan. We'll live there the rest of the time. On your land but not under the same roof as your parents. We will raise our children there. Speaking of which, we will have no less than two but no more than three children. I get to name the girls and you get to name the boys, but I have veto power over names that sound dumb."

He grinned. "You forgot one thing?"

"What?"

He got up from the stool, then fell on one knee in front of her.

She gasped.

"Rani Gupta, I've loved you since the first moment we met. You make me whole. I want us to write the next chapters of our life together, to create our happy ending. Will you marry me?"

Her heart burst with love for him.

He pulled out a ring with a round solitaire. It was simple and elegant and just right for her.

"Yes, Arjun, I will." He stood and wrapped his arms around her. The telltale flashes of cameras clicked nearby but neither of them cared.

"I do believe you designed a tacky wedding chapel in this hotel, didn't you?"

She laughed. "Don't you dare call my designs tacky! It's actually a very tasteful chapel, complete with a traditional Hindu wedding *mandap*."

"Then what do you say we do this Vegas-style and spend the night as husband and wife?"

10>Once he gets what he wants, he doesn't let go.

* * * * *

CINDERELLA UNMASKED

SUSANNAH ERWIN

For Barbara Ankrum,
the best teacher and mentor
a romance novelist could ever have.

One

Nelle Lassen gripped the full skirt of her silver-and-turquoise ball gown as one strappy, high-heeled sandal landed on the first step of the stone staircase outside San Francisco's historic Ferry Building. Then she pulled her foot back.

If she turned around now, she could go home. Take off the borrowed finery and slip into her comfy leggings and favorite hoodie. Curl up on the sofa with her laptop open to her social media accounts and her TV streaming the latest British costume drama. It was just the way she liked to spend her free evenings.

Or at least the way she used to like spending them, before her life was turned upside down and then shot out of a cannon to splat against a brick wall. Her reputation had been blackened, her career wiped from existence, her self-confidence eroded like a sandcastle during high tide. It had taken her a few months to devise a way forward and she still had far to go, but thanks to her best friend and roommate, Yoselin Solero, she'd checked off two major hurdles: new job, new city. And to go with them, a new name: Nelle, short for her given name, Janelle.

A chime came from a hidden pocket underneath the layers of tulle and lace, and she dug out her phone. "I'm at the gala," she answered.

"Inside?" Yoselin asked.

Nelle put both feet on the step. "I'm on the property."

"Get up those stairs," Yoselin commanded.

Nelle laughed. "Are you spying on me?"

Two flights above her, the silhouette of a figure wearing a pirate hat and a billowy blouse over knee breeches appeared. "Yes," Yoselin said into the phone, then lifted her hand and waved. "Hurry up! It's cold outside. I'll wait for you inside the door."

As if in response to Yoselin's words, a breeze blew across Nelle's cheeks. She shivered. The calendar said late June, but winds off the bay meant San Francisco could be wintry even in high summer. She took a deep breath, bracing salt air filling her lungs. The first real test of Project New Nelle would come at the top of the stairs.

She squared her shoulders. One small step to take, but it would be a giant leap forward into her new life. Not even Yoselin knew what a big jump it would be. It had taken all the strength Nelle had to smile and say yes to attending when she learned tonight's gala would be honoring Grayson Monk, venture capitalist, philanthropist, and the subject of several breathless media profiles that started off praising his business acumen but ended up extolling his athletic physique, blond-surfer good looks and piercing dark eyes.

Grayson Monk, the son of the man who'd nearly destroyed her father.

Her phone rang again, and she laughed. "Almost there," she said and clicked Disconnect. She was being ridiculous. She was in San Francisco, not New York City. She now worked in fundraising for a children's charity, not personal financial planning for a boutique firm like she had back East. She was an invited guest, not the disgraced target of a jealous coworker who was also her ex. There was no need to fear anyone at the ball. Grayson Monk included.

No matter what their family history was.

She started up the stairs, her heels clicking with purpose. As she neared the top, she caught a glimpse of the decorated venue and a gasp of amazement escaped her. "I'm not in Kansas anymore," she whispered under her breath. "This would be amazing even for Oz."

The Ferry Building was a historic Beaux Arts structure, one of the few survivors of the 1906 earthquake and fire that had destroyed most of San Francisco. Its grand hall was a wide, rectangular concourse interrupted in the center by an atrium that allowed guests to look down on the market stalls below. The ceiling soared high above her head, the barrel-shaped steel supports dotted with bright, globe-shaped lights. There were also enormous half-moon windows covered by latticework that resembled rows of stars. The mosaic tile floor was dotted with cocktail tables draped in festive colors, matching the bright costumes of the mingling guests exchanging conversation and laughter. A stage set with a podium and various musical instruments occupied one end of the hall, with a space in front of it left clear for dancing. The theme of the masquerade was "Venice by the Bay," and flowers, twinkling fairy lights and shimmering cloth drapes completed the transformation from staid city landmark into a festive, carnival-inspired dreamscape.

Yoselin waved her over to the check-in table, her dark eyes sparkling behind a black half mask decorated with white skulls and crossbones. She looked like Captain Jack Sparrow, if Jack had been a woman with golden brown skin and tousled mahogany curls. "Finally. I was beginning to wonder if your shoes were glued to the stairs. The speeches are about to start, and I'll point out who is who."

The woman seated behind the table smiled at them, a pen poised above her clipboard. "Welcome to the Peninsula Society's Carnival by the Bay! May I have your names?"

"We're guests of Octavia Allen," Yoselin responded. Octavia was on the board of directors of Create4All, where both Yoselin and Nelle worked. It had been her brainstorm for the two to attend the gala in the hopes of garnering more money for the children's nonprofit. As the executive director, Yoselin had been invited to help Mrs. Allen charm their current donors into increasing their pledges while Nelle, as the new development director, was tasked with bringing in sizable donations from people who had previously resisted Mrs. Allen's arm-twisting.

The woman's smile deepened as she made a check mark. "Mrs. Allen is already here. You'll be seated at her table. Number seventeen, the first row in front of the stage to the right." She looked up at Nelle and her gaze sharpened. "Did you bring your mask?"

Nelle held it up. The children who took art classes at Create4All had decorated every last millimeter of the plain half-mask bought at a party store. Silver sequins, opalescent crystals and seed pearls created an ocean-inspired fantasy that made up in exuberance what it lacked in sophistication.

"How...original," the woman said. "Don't forget,

guests are asked to maintain the masquerade until the party ends at midnight."

"And then we turn back into our everyday pumpkin selves," Nelle said to Yoselin.

Yoselin laughed. "Let's find Octavia and the open bar. Not necessarily in that order." She strode into the party, her sword swinging in its scabbard at her side.

Nelle put on her mask, took a deep breath and followed in her friend's wake.

Grayson Monk waited in the wings of the makeshift stage and listened to the crowd noises coming from the other side of the heavy velvet curtains. The gala seemed to be going well. The food was top-notch, provided by world-renowned chefs. The wine and champagne as excellent as one would expect from Napa's and Sonoma's best vineyards. The crowd was glittering, the conversation scintillating, and smiles were plentiful. In short, it was what he'd come to expect from a Peninsula Society event. The usual.

But something was different. Off. What was it?

It took him a minute to realize the difference was him.

Previously he viewed his attendance at the annual gala as part of the cost of doing business in Silicon Valley. Anyone who was somebody—and those who wanted to be somebodies—made it a point to show their faces at the party. And not to be egotistical, but he knew they were there in part because they wanted his attention. Hungry entrepreneurs, hungry investors: they all hoped to dine off the high returns of Monk Partners, the private equity firm he'd founded right after graduating from Stanford.

Tonight, however, would change all that.

"Ladies and gentlemen, our philanthropist of the year,

Grayson Monk!" Applause sounded, and a young man wearing a headset motioned for Grayson to make his entrance.

He strode onto the stage and shook hands with the Peninsula Society's president and gala chairperson. Then he faced the crowd, and after thanking the society and complimenting them on a successful evening, took a deep breath and went directly to the reason why he'd agreed to accept the award.

The speech.

"As some of you know, I've managed Monk Partners for the last fifteen years. We're proud of our record of helping the audacious and the intrepid build industry-leading companies. Some of today's biggest names in technology received the capital they required to become the successes they are from us. Like our most recent unicorn, Medevco, which under Luke Dallas and Evan Fletcher's leadership has changed the medical technology industry as we know it. And we're more than honored to give back to the community we're privileged to call home."

He swallowed. So far, so boilerplate. These were words he'd said a hundred times over, at various events and conferences. The next part of his speech, however…

"But all good things must come to an end at some point. So, with the permission of the Peninsula Society to take advantage of my brief moment in the spotlight, I'm announcing I'm stepping down from Monk Partners."

Audible gasps echoed in the cavernous space. Grayson held up his hands and smiled. "Hey, don't worry, Monk Partners is still in the same smart, savvy hands as before. Philip Adebayo will be taking over for me, with the rest of the team remaining in place. They're as committed as ever to the firm, our portfolio companies and our limited partners." He paused. "They might change the name, however."

That got him some laughs. Not many, but a few. He relaxed. The worst was over. It was like pulling a plastic bandage off—it stung for a second, but the anticipation of the announcement had been worse than the reality.

Of course, now he had to deal with the fallout. "I know you all want to get back to the party, so I'm going to leave it there. If you have questions, my office is more than prepared to take them in the morning—"

"What are you going to do next?" The shouted question came from the back of the room. Grayson held his right hand to his forehead to shield his eyes from the lights as he tried to focus on the crowd. But even if he could see the questioner, the masks made it difficult to tell who was who.

"I see someone can't wait until morning." He smiled. "I believe most people know my father recently had a serious health scare. I know it's a cliché, but I'm going to focus on family for the near future."

He paused, expecting to receive muted murmurs of understanding. After all, spending time with family was often used by CEOs and others as an excuse when their professional lives took unforeseen swerves. But the crowd's reaction was subdued, the chatter so light he could make out individual words. Including a snippet of conversation coming from a table near the stage.

"—eah, right, focus on family. Focus on taking over the family seat in Congress is more like it. But El Santo doesn't need another Monk in Congress. The people deserve better than—"

Then the crowd noise surged, and the rest of the words were lost.

He blinked. The voice was feminine. Young-sounding. And…hostile. Very hostile.

That was not the reaction he expected.

"So, um." Damn it. He never fumbled for words. He cleared his throat to cover his confusion. "I'll miss every single one of you—well, maybe not you, Vikram and Helen." He pointed at where he knew his fiercest competitors were standing, and the crowd laughed. He relaxed. He was back on track. "Although I will miss how you both kept me on my toes. But as everyone in this room knows, start-ups are pretty common. Fathers are one of a kind. Thank you for the award, but most of all, thank you for your friendship and support."

Applause, accompanied by chatter, bounced off the stone floor and high ceilings, filling the room. Grayson gave a short wave and returned to the backstage area, glad to see who else was there. There was a reason he'd mentioned Medevco in his speech. Not only was it his most profitable investment, but the two men running the company had become his closest friends in the year since he suggested they work together. He was even happier to see that one of them, Luke Dallas, had a highball glass containing two fingers of whisky waiting for him.

"Congratulations," Luke said, handing him the drink.

Grayson downed the dark amber spirits, his adrenaline ebbing as the alcohol sent warmth flowing through his veins. "On the award? It half belongs to your wife. She was the one who bargained a half hour of your time if I matched her donation to the society at last year's gala."

"I'm happy to let you have the award." Luke's wife, Danica, appeared at her husband's side. "After all, I have Luke." The two smiled at each other, oblivious to everyone else in their vicinity.

Even though Luke and Danica had been married for over a year, it still stunned Grayson a little to see the taciturn Luke be so open with his emotions. True, Danica was a great partner for him. Smart, highly capable and attractive, she and Luke just…clicked. Like LEGO pieces you might not think go together at first, but join to create a solid structure.

Luke was lucky he'd found his complement in Danica. Grayson wasn't sure he would ever find his. And he wouldn't settle for anything less than permanent. Casual dating didn't work for him.

Not that he was looking. Especially not now.

"Luke meant congratulations on being the sole topic of conversation for the evening. You're all anyone wants to talk about." Evan Fletcher, Luke's partner in Medevco, joined the small group. He handed a glass of water to Danica, keeping a very full stem of red wine for himself. "I could barely make it backstage, so many people wanted to stop and talk about you and your announcement. As soon as you step outside these curtains, prepare to be pounced upon."

Grayson stared at the bottom of his glass. Why hadn't someone invented a perpetually refilling whisky tumbler? He would invest in it. "And so it begins," he said into the glass.

Evan took a sip of wine and made a face. "What begins? Your retirement at age thirty-five? Living the dream, my friend. Please tell me you're buying an island with room for a guest. Who would happen to be me."

Grayson shook his head. "I'm not retiring. Not the way you think."

"Then why the whole…" Evan waved the hand holding the wine, causing it to come dangerously close to the rim. A few drops splashed over and landed on the floor.

Grayson eyed him. "Are you going to drink that, or just use it as a threat?"

"What do you mean—oh." Evan looked at his glass, and then glanced around for a place to put it down. He settled on the low table next to the sofa. "Next year, I want to be on the gala committee so I can choose the vintage."

"I want Grayson to answer Evan's question. If you're not retiring, then why the announcement?" Luke frowned in Grayson's direction. "Retirement is the logical explanation why you would walk away at the top of your game."

He might as well tell them. It wasn't as if this would be a secret for much longer. "This isn't for public consumption. Not yet, anyway. But my father is about to announce his resignation from Congress. And when he does, it will trigger a special election to fill the seat for the rest of his term. There's over a year left in it." He inhaled, the burn of the whiskey nothing but a fond memory. "And I'll be running."

Danica gasped, while Luke grinned and shook Grayson's hand. "Congrats. You have our support, of course. Although you could have let us know."

"To be honest, I'm surprised you're surprised." Whoever he'd overheard in the audience certainly wouldn't be. "It's always been my intention to follow my father into politics."

"Hello, hello!" The cheery greeting came from behind them. Grayson turned to see Bitsy Christensen, the gala chairwoman, bustling into the backstage area with her ever-present phone in her hand. Behind her followed several people carrying musical instruments.

"I thought for sure you'd all be sampling the food stations by now." Bitsy indicated the musicians. "The band needs to set up, so I'm afraid we have to take over this space."

"Of course." Grayson motioned for Luke and Danica to go ahead of him, and then turned to usher Evan out. Evan bent to pick up his glass of wine. Bitsy looked down to scroll through her phone.

The next few seconds played out in slow motion.

Evan moved toward the exit, frowning into his wine glass. Bitsy walked farther into the backstage area, fully engrossed in her screen. Neither of them looked up to see where they were going. Until they collided. Right in front of Grayson.

The phone sailed into the air. So did the glass of wine.

Grayson dove and caught the phone before it could hit the stone floor. Unfortunately, the wine hit him. His white tuxedo shirt became splotchy pink. His black jacket and tie showed no damage, but he smelled as if he had bathed in a barrel of Napa's finest.

There was no way he could go out and face a room full of the Bay Area's brightest and smartest—all curious about the bombshell he'd dropped—appearing as if he'd just gone on the bender of all time backstage. He tried to blot the stains on his shirt with a paper cocktail napkin, but it was useless. The wine had soaked through the fabric to his skin.

"Oh, dear!" Bitsy appeared glued to the floor. "Oh, dear," she continued to repeat, as if on a loop.

"I'll ask the catering staff if they have dish towels," Evan volunteered. He disappeared behind the curtains.

Bitsy shook herself out of her shock. She took the phone Grayson held out to her and began to scroll through the screen. "We have extra costumes," she said. "In case someone forgot this was a masquerade. Always be prepared, right?" She fixed Grayson with an assessing stare, then fired off a text. "My assistant will be right here. I told her the Pierrot ensemble would be best, as it will hopefully accommodate your frame."

Pierrot? Great. Just how he wanted to appear to people he would soon be hitting up for campaign donations. A clown in baggy white pajamas.

He found a corner out of the way of the musicians and waited for the costume to arrive, his mind going over his goals for the rest of the night: talk to potential campaign donors, reassure nervous investors about his departure and—

"The people of El Santo deserve better."

The overheard words looped in his head, like the hook of a pop song turned earworm, despite his best efforts to concentrate on other thoughts.

Sure, there were people out there who were less than pleased with him. The entrepreneurs whose pitches he'd declined. The CEOs whose companies weren't right for an acquisition offer. His last girlfriend, who didn't appreciate having their week in Bali cut short by five days because he had to fly home to save a deal.

But in general, Grayson enjoyed a good working relationship with people. He'd been a leader since childhood, when he anchored his ten-and-under swimming relay team to a state championship. He'd started his own small venture capital fund in high school as a way to fund his swim meets, and when he decided to give up the pool, his skill at persuading entrepreneurs to work with him had led to the formation of Monk Partners. Now it had one of the best track records in Silicon Valley of picking winning investments.

But he'd always known he would follow his father into public service. It was the family tradition, after all. His great-grandfather had been Governor of California. His grandfather sat on the state supreme court. Taking over his father's seat in the House of Representatives would be the culmination of everything he had been raised to be.

The costume arrived neatly packaged in a clear plastic bag, breaking his reverie. Grayson took out a billowing white tunic, loose drawstring trousers and a tall cone hat. The outfit was even more ridiculous than he imagined. He was halfway to shoving the articles back into the bag, a wine-soaked shirt preferable to looking like a literal clown, when his hands stilled.

This was a rare opportunity. The next months were going to be a whirlwind of meetings and paperwork, shaking hands and kissing babies. His social life, which he already kept on the light and noncommittal side due to his long work hours, would become nonexistent. And if he won…well, he would have to say goodbye to the concept of taking time for himself.

A head-to-toe costume was the last thing anyone would expect to him to wear. It would allow him relative anonymity to spend time with his friends and enjoy a night out without worrying about, as Evan put it, being pounced on. There would be plenty of time to answer people's questions about the transition at Monk Partners next week.

Tonight was his for the taking. One last evening of freedom.

And maybe he could discover why someone had publicly voiced the concern he carried deep inside.

The guests seated with Nelle and Yoselin at Mrs. Allen's table burst into animated chatter as soon as Grayson Monk left the stage. Only Nelle stayed quiet, sipping her cranberry juice and vodka, hoping the ice in her drink would cool the heat still present in her cheeks.

She'd seen recent photos of Grayson, of course. Even caught a few of his television appearances. Who hadn't? He'd been a darling of the media since he made his first billion eight years ago at the tender age of twenty-five. But he was taller and broader in real life than any two-dimensional image could convey. Nor could the cameras capture the intensity in his gaze, the charm in his smile.

A deep flush filled every pore of her skin when he'd turned that smile in her direction. She knew he only looked her way because the man who had shouted out the question sat several tables behind her. But his sheer charisma had hit her like a tsunami, much to her chagrin. She held on to the knowledge that no matter how likable and charming he may seem when giving a speech, she knew the truth. It was a front so he could get what he wanted when he wanted, no matter the collateral damage.

Like father, like son.

And anyway, not that she would ever be this close to him again. She could start to relax and enjoy the evening. Now that she knew he was wearing a tuxedo, his dark blond hair uncovered by a mask or hat, it would be easy to spot him—and avoid his general vicinity.

Yoselin ended her conversation with the man on her left and turned to Nelle. "Is he really going to run?"

"Who?" Nelle widened her eyes, crossing her fingers Yoselin was talking about anyone else but the subject of Nelle's thoughts.

Yoselin indicated the stage, where musicians were now setting up additional instruments. "Grayson Monk. For Congress."

At the rate her drink was disappearing, Nelle was going to need a refill soon. Maybe two. "I guess? I wouldn't know."

"But you grew up in El Santo, right? I forgot until you mentioned he's from there, too," Yoselin persisted.

Nelle shook her head, aware her cheeks probably still matched the color of her drink. "I did, but he's several years older. Besides, we ran in different social circles. And speaking of running, did I tell you I want to run a marathon this year—"

Mrs. Allen leaned over the table. "Did you say you grew up with Grayson Monk?"

Nelle choked on a piece of ice. After coughing, she met Mrs. Allen's curious gaze. "We're from the same town. But—"

"Excellent!" Mrs. Allen clapped her hands together, her rings catching the glow of the stage lights and throwing small prisms of color onto the table. "I've been trying to secure Grayson as a key sponsor for eons. With his support, we are sure to receive the financing necessary for the East Bay facility." She nodded at Nelle. "I knew there had to be a reason why Yoselin demanded we hire you."

Nelle bit her lip and looked down at the table. What Mrs. Allen said was true: Yoselin had had to fight hard to hire her. Mrs. Allen in particular wanted another candidate, one with deep connections to the Bay Area's elite.

"There are many reasons why Nelle is perfect for the job." Yoselin held out her left hand and started to tick them off on her fingers. "One, she—" Her words trailed off as she spotted a tall black man wearing a judge's robe with a white collar and sporting a plain half mask making his way toward their table. "Jason!"

Jason grinned, and Yoselin got up out of her chair so she could kiss her boyfriend. "What are you doing here? I thought you couldn't be my date because you had study group after torts class," she said, somewhat out of breath.

"I can take one night off studying." He smiled and intertwined his hands with hers. "I borrowed an old robe from Judge Durham, and Mrs. Allen left me a ticket so I could surprise you."

Yoselin smiled at Mrs. Allen. "Thank you."

Mrs. Allen waved her hands in dismissal. "You've been working so hard it's the least I could do." She smiled at Nelle. "And now that I know that Nelle has a connection to Grayson Monk, I'm even happier. You two have fun. Nelle and I will take care of business."

The musicians took their spots and started to warm up. The room dimmed as streamers of purple, green and blue light shot outward from the proscenium outlining the stage. Jason held out his hand to Yoselin. "Shall we?"

Yoselin turned to Nelle. "You'll be okay if I leave you here?"

"Of course she will," Mrs. Allen stated. "She's with me."

"Farmer's market this Sunday, right, Nelle?" Jason asked. "Can't go to brunch afterward without you."

"It's on my calendar." Nelle smiled as she watched the couple walk toward the dance floor. Yoselin and Jason looked so…complete. A unit. And she appreciated the invitation. But while they never made her feel like the third wheel, she was well aware she was the odd woman out in their world built for two.

It might be nice to have someone of her own to put his arms around her, to sway with on the dance floor and laugh at a shared joke as Yoselin and Jason were doing right that minute.

It *might be*.

But first, she needed to make Project New Nelle a success. Put solid ground under her feet. Rebuild her reputation, career, confidence. Once she had her life back in order, maybe she could think about finding a partner to share it.

She caught Mrs. Allen's gaze and put on her best professional smile. "I'm here for work, so feel free to point me in the right direction."

Mrs. Allen glanced around the room, and then her face lit up. "Ah! There's Bitsy, by the other side of the stage. But I should speak to her alone. Why don't you mingle? We'll meet back here shortly." She rose from her seat and slipped on her phoenix mask, complete with towering red and gold feathers that shot toward the vaulted ceiling.

The other guests at the table also started to leave, some heading for the dance floor, others for the buffet tables and open bars dotting the perimeter of the hall. Nelle weighed her options and decided people were more likely to chat with a stranger if they had drinks in their hands instead of food on their forks. She fought her way through the crowd already forming at the nearest bar.

"Cranberry and soda, please," she said to the bartender, once she managed to get his attention. The vodka from her last drink was still making her head swim. Then she turned back to scan the concourse, hoping to keep an eye on Mrs. Allen so she could time her arrival back at the table to coincide with hers. But she didn't see her hostess in the sea of black tuxedos, brilliantly bright gowns and multihued costumes.

"Here you go," the bartender announced. Nelle turned around to reach for her drink. A sharp elbow landed in her side, causing her to stumble against the bar. Her fingers slid against the glass, sending it spinning down the polished, slick surface. It was headed toward a guest with his back to her. He was wearing a blinding white costume and was oblivious to the disaster heading his way. She opened her mouth to warn him—

—when he turned, assessed the situation with one

split-second glance, and caught the glass. Not a drop spilled.

He glanced to his left and his right. When he saw Nelle staring at him, her mouth still open in shock, he smiled. "Yours?" he asked, indicating the glass.

He was tall, well over six feet. Although he was dressed like a Venetian clown in a loose white top, his broad shoulders could not be hidden. Physically imposing men usually made Nelle wary, but there was something—perhaps the twinkle of humor in the dark eyes behind the mask, perhaps the way the one-sided smile gave him a slightly self-deprecating air—that allowed her to let down her guard. She smiled back. "Guilty," she responded. "That was some catch."

"One out of two isn't bad. I hope I don't have to go for three." He handed her the drink, careful not to let go until she had a firm grip on the glass. Their fingers brushed, just for a second, but long enough for a jolt of electricity to shock her into awareness. "This isn't the first drink thrown at me tonight."

Six months ago, she would have politely smiled and then walked away, secure in her staid but comfortable relationship. But Mrs. Allen had told her to mingle, didn't she? And while the old Janelle didn't flirt, she decided—spurred on by the lingering vodka mixed with his lingering touch—that Nelle did. She raised an eyebrow and leaned, ever so slightly, into his space. "Intriguing. Although in my case, it was an accident, I didn't throw it. What did you do to earn a drink thrown at you?"

"I tried to save a phone in distress."

"And the phone threw a drink at you in return? There really is an app for everything."

He laughed. It was a good laugh. A rumble of warm bass notes that resonated deep inside, the vibrations loosening the steel bands that kept her physical response to attractive men locked up tight. She couldn't help but grin in response, and his dark eyes took on a new light of appreciation as their gazes met and caught. He angled his body toward hers. "I was hoping for a bottomless whisky tumbler earlier tonight, but an app that throws drinks might be the idea the world is missing."

"Why stop at drinks? There are so many possibilities! Like, tomatoes."

"Tomatoes?"

"For, say, a bad movie. You could virtually throw a tomato at it."

"I think that app already exists. In a way. Rotten Tomatoes?"

She nodded. "Oh, right. So how about an app for... wedding cake?"

"Wedding cake?"

"You know, when the bride and groom cut the cake, and they feed it to each other but sometimes they purposefully miss and the cake is smeared all over? What if bridal couples could use an app instead? Think of the dry cleaning costs it would save."

His teeth flashed white in a very appealing smile. "You must go to very messy weddings. Did that happen at yours?"

She held up her bare left hand. "Not yet, and hopefully not ever. It's not my idea of fun. The cake thing, I mean, not the wedding. That is something I do hope... I mean..." Her cheeks grew hot. What made her talk about weddings with a man she'd just met? "Um, what else can be thrown...? I know. Milkshakes."

"Technically, milkshakes are a drink."

She tsked. "It's not just a drink. A good milkshake glides over your tongue, creamy and rich. It's so thick you can't suck it through a straw despite pulling as hard as you can. The spoon stands straight up—" She stopped, suddenly aware they were standing very, very close. So close, the sequins covering her bodice almost brushed the white canvas of his top.

"Go on," he said, his voice low and verging on rough. "Describe what you do to the straw again?"

"The straw." She swallowed, her attention caught by his chin and lips, the part of his face fully visible. His chin was square, firm, clean-shaven. His lips were neither full nor thin. If she were Goldilocks, she would pronounce them "just right." She wondered… "The straw is—"

"There you are. I've been waiting at our table for you."

Mrs. Allen's voice came from behind her. Startled, Nelle stumbled and almost fell against the man. He steadied her with a light grip on her bare upper arm. His touch delivered a quick lightning bolt of pure current. But she didn't have time to dwell on it as Mrs. Allen was joining her at the bar.

The older woman settled her cool gaze on Nelle, still leaning slightly against her conversational partner. "Shall we? If now is a good time for you, that is."

Nelle pulled herself upright, a tense knot forming between her shoulders. Her first work assignment and she was already failing. Her new life would fall apart before it began. "Yes. Of course. I'll follow you."

It wasn't until Mrs. Allen had led her to the other side of the venue that she realized she hadn't said goodbye to the man with the perfect lips, much less remembered to take her drink with her.

TWO

Grayson stared after the woman in the mermaid mask as she wove her way through the people clustered around the bar, tracing her movements until she was swallowed up by the crowd. He was intrigued by what he'd seen of her face, partially hidden though it was by the elaborate mask. Bee-stung lips, determined chin, sparkling light blue eyes that refracted light. And when he looked into those eyes, he could have sworn she was intrigued as well.

He'd had more than his share of casual encounters, enough to be bored with them. He didn't need to pick up women at bars, even an open bar at a charity gala. But he also could tell the difference between an encounter that inspired lust and nothing more, and one that intrigued his brain and soul as well as lower, less cognitively enabled parts of him.

"Who was that?" Evan managed to squeeze next to

him at the bar. "Let me guess—an ex who realized it was you under the mask."

"Funny. But no. I take it you didn't recognize her, either?"

Evan shrugged. "I have a hard enough time with faces when people aren't covering them up. Tonight? Not my optimum environment." He peered closer at Grayson. "You okay? I really am sorry."

Grayson held up his left hand, dismissing Evan's concern, as he searched the crowd in a vain attempt to trace the woman's steps. "Apology accepted an hour ago."

Where was she? How could she disappear so fast?

"Not about spilling the wine. I'm sorry an attractive woman noped out on you. Welcome to how the rest of us live."

Grayson focused on his friend. "How do you know she's pretty? You've seen her without her mask? When? Where?" A surge of electricity ran through him. If Evan was holding out on him...

Evan grinned and saluted Grayson with his newly acquired drink. "I've never seen her before. But you obviously find her attractive. I haven't seen you this interested in ages. Go after her."

Grayson shrugged Evan's hand off. "She's so interested she left without her drink."

"So take her drink to her. Look at this crowd. It's like a zombie flick, only they want alcohol instead of brains. You'd be a hero."

Grayson shifted on his feet. He should stay and talk to his colleagues and industry peers. He'd detonated the equivalent of an incendiary device with his announcement, and it was his responsibility to clean up any resulting damage. On the other hand, phones and email would still work on Monday.

He glanced at the crush of people hoping to take advantage of the open bar. Evan was right. Taking her drink to her would be the gentlemanly thing to do. He said goodbye to his smirking friend, picked up the abandoned glass and waded into the throng of the Bay Area's finest.

He started with the dance floor, literally heaving with gyrating bodies. The beat was fast and loud and thumped against the walls of his chest. Next he toured the concourse, not receiving a second glance from people who would normally have called him over to say hello or pitch him a new business idea. The costume definitely hid his identity. It was an odd but not unwelcome sensation to be this anonymous.

After several circuits, the glass was cold and slippery in his hand, the ice nearly all melted. He glanced at his watch and noticed it was nearing eleven o'clock. Maybe the person she briefly spoke to at the bar was her significant other. Maybe she'd already left the party with her partner. The thoughts made the whiskey in his stomach burn, and not in a good way.

Maybe the jolt of mutual appreciation when their gazes met had been all in his head.

He returned to the dance floor, intending to reveal himself to a group of investors in town from New York City who might be useful to cultivate, when a flash of silver and aqua dazzled his gaze.

He'd caught his mermaid.

She stood on the other side of the dance floor, her profile turned to him. Through the wall of dancers, he caught glimpses of details he missed during their first encounter: an hourglass waist defined by swirls of beads and pearls, full curves spilling over the strapless bodice, loosely braided chestnut hair wound with aqua and silver ribbons. A diadem of seashells and pearls crowned her head.

She turned and looked up. Their gazes met, held. He kept his steady, not ashamed to be caught admiring her. The connection he'd felt at the bar came roaring back, pinpricks of awareness coming alive all over his skin. No, he had not been imagining it. And she felt it, too. He could tell in the way she stood still, her gaze focused on his, her right hand pressing against the creamy skin of her throat.

The dancers disappeared. The entire Ferry Building faded away. They were the only two people in the entirety of the universe.

He smiled. And held up her glass, shaking it slightly. An answering smile curved her full lips, but she shook her head. The statuesque woman standing next to her in a phoenix costume followed her gaze and smiled, then said a few words to his mermaid, making shooing motions with her hands.

And his mermaid started to walk in his direction.

Did the crowd part for her? That was how he saw it. Or maybe it only seemed that way, the dancers melting to the sidelines as she advanced onto the dance floor. He met her halfway, the sharp shards of purple and red light turning to beams of soft blue as the band shifted from a pounding rock rhythm into a jazzy standard. The glow caused the pearls sewn on her dress to shimmer and made her appear even more like a mythological creature from the ocean depths. A sea goddess.

He swallowed, hoping to work moisture into his mouth. "You forgot this." He held out her drink.

"Oh. Thank you." She took it but made no attempt to take a sip. Their gazes continued to hold as the singer crooned about flying to the moon and playing with stars.

She finally broke the silence between them. "Are you, um, trying to go two for three after all?" She punctuated the sentence with a breathy laugh.

He shook his head, uncomprehending, still marveling he had found her. Still enjoying the frisson of energy that melded their gazes together.

"The drink? Two out of three? Throwing it at you? Not that I want to throw it at you," she said in a rush. "I mean, from before? You said at the bar that was the second time, so—" She stopped, looked down at the glass, and then her lips formed a perfect circle. "Wait. The ice is melted. Have you been carrying this around the whole time?"

He gave a nonchalant shrug. Or at least he tried for nonchalant. "Have you seen the line for the bar?"

"You know there's more than one, right?" She cocked her head, her chestnut braid falling over her left shoulder. A dangling silver ribbon came to nestle in her generous cleavage.

He had never been so jealous of a sliver of fabric before.

"Multiple bars? Really?" He looked around the room. He had been so focused on finding her he had ignored the various food and, yes, bars set up around the concourse. "Huh." He indicated the drink. "Well. That should save you from fighting through the crowd for a while, at least."

"Very thoughtful. Even though accepting a strange drink at a party is definitely on the list of things women should never do."

He hadn't thought about that. "Of course. You're right. I can have guests here vouch for me if you want."

She smiled, a dimple appearing in her left cheek. The room seemed to spin around them with her as its axis. "Maybe I shouldn't, but I trust you. Thank you again." She turned to go back to her friends.

"Dance with me." The request left his mouth before he had a chance to think it through.

She stopped at the edge of the floor. "With a drink in my hand? You do like living dangerously when it comes to beverages."

He stepped to her side, took the glass from her unresisting grip and handed it to a passing waiter. "Problem solved."

"Hey! You just gave that back to me." She folded her arms, but a smile played at the edges of her mouth. "And there's still a problem. I didn't say yes."

He held out his right hand. "Please. Dance with me?"

She regarded him, white teeth making an appearance to bite her lower lip. "Won't your date mind?"

He smiled. "No date. No significant other, here or anywhere. And you? Is someone waiting for you to come back?" *Please say no*, his brain chanted.

A sharp light flared in her gaze, and then she shook her head. Then she placed her hand in his. It was warm and soft, and her fingers wove into his like they were custom-made to fit.

The band's tempo decreased, the music changing from upbeat Sinatra to a lush ballad. She floated in his arms, her hands resting lightly on his shoulders, their movements in perfect sync. He held her waist, careful not to crush the beads and sequins, reveling in how her curves filled his palms. Their gazes met, and his stomach literally flipped. He didn't think such a thing physically possible.

He was not a romantic. Love at first sight was a creaky fairy tale no one over the age of twelve should believe. But when the song stopped, he didn't want his time with her to stop with it.

"Thank you. That was...thank you." Her hands

dropped to her sides, but she didn't step out of the circle of his arms.

"You're welcome." He was vaguely aware they were the focus of curious stares. They stood still as the music segued into country-western pop and the other guests assembled for line dancing. They needed to either join them or leave the floor. "Are you—" he swallowed, his mouth as dry as the Mojave Desert "—are you hungry?"

Her gaze fell to his mouth, a split-second flash, before meeting his again. "Depends on what you mean," she said, her voice husky with amusement.

"Would you like to have dinner?" he clarified.

She glanced around. The buffet tables that had earlier overflowed with delicacies from around the Bay Area looked decidedly barren. "I would, but it's slim pickings."

He smiled. "I think I know just the thing. Any objections to pork, garlic or rice?"

Her stomach growled in response. The sound was unmistakable over the rhythmic stomping of the guests and the twanging guitar music. Her eyes widened in horror before they both broke into laughter. He held out his left arm to her. "Let's see if we can do something about that."

Nelle allowed him to guide her out of the building, not sure what had come over her. The vodka should have worn off long ago. And while there were plenty of guests dressed as mages and witches, she doubted she was under a spell. Unless the Ferry Building itself had ensorcelled her, the majesty of the old building, the brilliant costumes, and the artful decorations and lighting combining to sweep her into a waking dream. Even Mrs. Allen had conspired to make the evening magical, telling Nelle to go have an unforgettable night when she saw someone was waiting for her on the dance floor.

And the reason why she hoped the dream would continue: her companion. Was it bizarre, perhaps even perilous, to let a man whose name she still didn't know guide her out of the party without letting Yoselin or Mrs. Allen know she was leaving? Normally, she would be the first to say yes. He was still wearing his mask, even. They both were. Spending time with an unknown man in disguise hadn't worked out well for the heroine of *The Phantom of the Opera*.

The old her would have refused to go with him.

But Nelle had never been held on a dance floor like that before. As if she were something precious, something to be treasured and respected. The touch of his large hand curved around her waist was solid and reassuring. She didn't want to miss the chance to grip his impossibly broad shoulders again, or watch his bicep flex when he offered her his arm.

"Are we going far?" she asked. "Because I'll need to change shoes." She opened her handbag and pulled out her pair of emergency slippers, folded into a tight square.

He laughed, a warm reverberation that made her stomach flutter. "No. In fact—" he indicated an empty bench on the large plaza across the Embarcadero from the Ferry Building "—your dining venue awaits."

She raised her eyebrows, even though he wouldn't see her expression because of the mask. He held out his hand and she took it, proud that she kept the trembling to a minimum. He had barely settled her on the bench's cool wood slats before a young man ran up to them and handed him a large brown paper bag.

"That looked like a rather illicit transaction," she said.

He grinned and opened the bag, drawing out a large, heavy cylinder wrapped in shiny foil and handing it to her. "Tosilog burritos. They're only illegal if you're on a diet." He took a second foil-wrapped burrito out of the bag, followed by two bottles of sparkling mineral water. But when he went to take his mask off, she reached out to still his hand.

"I was told the rules of the ball were quite strict. No unmasking until the clock strikes midnight."

His beautifully shaped lips quirked upward and he let his hand fall. "So you're a rule follower."

"I—" She was about to say yes. But then she remembered it was Janelle who followed the rules. Janelle who thought if she did everything right and followed the straight and narrow path, the world would reward her for her faithfulness to its strictures. Janelle, who had been shockingly wrong. "So few things in life are truly mysterious," she ended up saying. "Why not enjoy this while it lasts? It's just for—" she glanced at the Ferry Building clock in its tower, high above them "—fifty more minutes."

"Fifty long minutes," he replied.

"Are you saying you can't last that long?" She traced the seam of her foil-wrapped burrito with her fingers, seeking the best place to unwrap it.

His gaze followed the path of her fingers, then it rose and caught hers. "I'm coming to the conclusion delayed gratification might make the outcome even more satisfying."

She wet her lips, but whether in reaction to the heavenly smell of roasted pork and garlic or to his words, she wasn't sure. "Good things come to those who wait."

A dangerous, knowing smile curved his lips. "Good doesn't even begin to describe it."

She shivered, and it had nothing to do with the cool night air.

"You're cold." He started to look around as if to find a more sheltered spot.

"Maybe that's because I'm the only one sitting." She indicated the empty space on the bench next to her.

He smiled and sat down. Her full skirt threatened to spill over into his space and she gathered it up, noticing how the trousers of his costume drew tight over power-ful, well-muscled thighs when he was seated. Was the rest of him as muscular—she quickly turned her head to take a bite of her burrito. And then another. The heav-enly taste of marinated roasted pork and garlic rice took over her attention. But she remained aware of the solid heat of him pressed against her leg, the brush of his arm against her side.

They ate in companionable silence, breaking it occa-sionally to exchange observations about the people walk-ing by. Their senses of humor meshed well, although his was much drier than hers, and laughter punctuated their sentences. Then soft chords of music began to fill the small pauses in their conversation. After a quick mental check to make sure she wasn't hallucinating a roman-tic soundtrack for the evening, she spotted the source. A piano on wheels sat in the middle of the plaza, played by a young man who had a hat out on the ground beside him to collect tips.

She started to laugh. It was perfect for this dreamy, incredible evening. Almost too perfect.

As if he had read her mind, her mysterious stranger said, "I was just thinking the only thing this moment lacked was a Chopin concerto."

"It is a bit too on the nose," she agreed, after swal-lowing the last bite of her burrito. "But appreciated. And speaking of appreciation, that was delicious. Excellent delivery service, too," she added, wiping her fingers on the napkin he provided.

"It's my favorite food in the city," he said. "I try other places, but I keep returning to this food truck. It's no milkshake, however." He looked at her, and his gaze sharpened. "You have something on your cheek. Here." He pointed to the spot on his own face.

She tried to remove the offending stain with her napkin. "Better?"

He shook his head. "No. May I?"

At her nod, he cupped her cheek to hold her head still. His fingers rested lightly on her skin, but they lit up her nervous system like a match to a trail of gasoline. Her hands began to tremble as he gently passed his napkin once, then twice, over the offending spot. The piano music soared into a crescendo, echoing her heartbeat.

"There," he said.

Her gaze caught his. The streetlight high above cast a halo around his peaked hat. His mask caused shadows to fall on his cheekbones, but she was close enough to see how the gold highlights in his whiskey-brown eyes shone.

For her.

He wanted her. She knew, because the hunger in his gaze matched her own. Simmering since their encounter at the bar, it now roared, demanding to be satiated.

"I don't do this." The deep rumble of his voice sent a cascade of tiny earthquakes through her.

"Do what?" she asked. It came out as a breathy croak.

"Kiss women I'm not in a relationship with."

"Are you kissing someone?"

"If she says I can. May I?"

She answered by leaning closer to him on the bench and pressing her lips against his.

This was unwise, the tiny part of her brain not occupied by kissing and being thoroughly kissed in return tried to warn her. They both still wore their masks. She didn't know his name. She didn't know anything about him, except that he was a guest at the gala. He could be married. He could be a serial killer. He could be—

But then his strong hands reached out and pulled her to him and that tiny warning voice shut up. She let the electricity that had been building around them all evening take over, opening her mouth to the sweep of his tongue, exploring his mouth in return. There was nothing sloppy or awkward about his kiss, nothing overly practiced, either. He knew exactly the best angle, the right amount of pressure. This was a master class in kissing and not a single cell of hers wanted to be left out of the lesson.

She wound her arms around his neck, holding him against her, not wanting to let him go when he pulled back, just enough to whisper against her lips, "I'm going to stand up."

But before she could make a sound of disapproval, he had stood up, tugged her up with him, then sat back down on the bench and pulled her down on top of his lap.

The layers of tulle she wore compressed to nothing, and the thin fabric trousers he wore were an equally inadequate barrier between them. His thighs were indeed as firm and muscled as they looked. And warm. So warm. She wanted to burrow in the heat they created together, the ravenous flames he coaxed into life with his lips and tongue consuming all rational thought.

She wound her arms around his neck, pressing her breasts against his hard-muscled chest. She had forgotten how delectable a kiss could be. Or maybe she never really knew before now.

The clock in the Ferry Building tower gave a deep, sonorous clang. Once, twice, ten more times. It was midnight.

She lifted her mouth from his, just an inch, the effort taking enormous will. "The masquerade is officially over."

His gaze was dark and wild, but she could see it come into focus as he processed her words. "So it is."

"I guess that means…" She ran her fingers along the edge of his mask, across his cheekbones.

He drew in his breath, sharply. Then those firm, talented lips of his quirked upward. "I guess it does."

He untied the silver ribbons that held her handmade mask in place. She reached up and removed first his conical hat, already threatening to fall off, then slid the party store domino up and over his head.

Her gaze shifted to take in his entire face for the first time. And she froze.

She couldn't breathe. She couldn't move. She couldn't form thoughts, except for the one bouncing around her brain in a continuous loop.

She was kissing Grayson Monk.

Grayson's breath caught as he untied the mask, the silver ribbons slipping through his fingers as it fell to the ground.

She was beautiful.

But he already knew that, even before the mask came off. She was funny and charming, and time in her company sped by. The moments when conversation ceased and silence reigned weren't awkward, as they usually were when he just met someone, but comfortable, as if they'd known each other for a long time. Her beauty showed in her dry wit and breathy laughter, her sensuous lips that fit against his as if made for him and her mind-blowing kisses that made him forget his own name.

Now, without the mask, he could take in the rest of the perfection that was his sea goddess. Her aquiline nose, as regal as the rest of her. Her sharply angled eyebrows. Blue eyes the color of the Pacific immediately after the sunrise.

And she stared back at him in…horror. Shock. And loathing.

The antipathy in her gaze caused his arms to fall away from her soft curves. Without him supporting her, there was nothing keeping her anchored on his lap. She slid off in a cloud of tulle, nearly falling to the ground in her haste to put distance between them.

A chill cut through the passion keeping his brain pleasantly fogged. "Are you okay? Did I—if this was something you didn't want, I'm sorry—"

"You're Grayson Monk." Her voice was low, controlled, cool. Too cool, considering what they had been doing. She gathered her skirts in one hand and began to back away. "I… I have to go." Then she turned. Gathered her skirts. And started to run.

What the hell just happened? A few seconds ago, he was enjoying one of the most arousing moments of his life. Now this woman was literally running away, her face set in what could only be called horror.

He managed to catch the end of her stole, the flimsy fabric tangling in his fingers. It slipped from around her neck and she turned to grab at it. "Let go," she commanded.

"Don't leave like this. Talk to me." He handed the stole back to her.

She snatched it from him, balling it up in her hands. "There's nothing to say."

"I don't understand." She must have felt the same connection he did. Kisses like that were as rare as start-ups with ten-billion-dollar valuations. "Did I do something wrong? Tell me. I'll apologize. And it won't happen again."

She shook her head. Her gaze remained focused on the fabric tightly held in her grasp. "I made the mistake. But don't worry. This definitely won't happen again."

He opened his mouth. Closed it. Opened it again. "Do we know each other?"

She shook her head, even as he anticipated her answer. He knew they didn't. There was no way he would have forgotten her, for one. Then she glanced up at him. The streetlights above caught a wet shimmer in the corner of her eyes. "No."

Her gaze dropped. And before he could respond, she fled. There was no other word for it. She dashed across the plaza toward the front entrance of the Ferry Building, her diadem crooked and threatening to fall off. He started to follow her, but something white and sparkling near his shoe caught his attention.

Her mask. It must have slipped to the ground after he untied it. The pearls and crystals shimmered in the glow from the streetlight high above as he picked it up.

"Wait," he called after her. "You left this." This close, he could see the crooked lines of glue and the exuberant use of glitter that made her mask one-of-a-kind. It deserved more than to be discarded on a San Francisco city sidewalk.

She didn't hear him—or didn't want to hear him. She continued to run, a flash of silver and aqua weaving around the people on the plaza. He started after her, but a streetcar pulled to a stop on the tracks running parallel to the Embarcadero and cut off his route. By the time he got around the obstacle, she had disappeared.

The only sign she had been there was her mask, still clutched tightly in his hands.

Three

Grayson pulled his Tesla Model S into the parking space in front of the low-slung wood-and-stucco building set back from the main road and hidden by pine trees and tall shrubs. Tourists taking a detour off the freeway on their way between San Jose and San Francisco might drive by and mistake the building for an insurance agency, or perhaps a dentist's office. Little would they know that money amounting to the GDP of several small nations flowed in and out of it on a daily basis.

His name was still on the small brass sign next to the front door. He smiled at it, then at the receptionist who waved a greeting as he passed through the security gate. His smile faltered when he saw who was waiting for him in the lobby.

Finley.

His older sister was on the phone, holding a softly murmured conversation while scrolling through social media accounts on a second phone. When she saw him, she ended her call and put both phones down. "We need to talk," she said.

"I thought we were going to talk next week." Grayson strode past her and down the hall. He unlocked the door at the end and ushered Finley, who had followed him, into the suite of rooms he used as his office. His assistant wasn't in yet, so he busied himself turning on lights and powering up his laptop.

Finley positioned herself on the sleek leather sofa that occupied one wall, stretching her arms along the back and crossing feet clad in Italian-made pumps at the ankle. As usual, not one dark hair was out of place on her head. Her elegant gray suit, no doubt hand-sewn in Hong Kong by her favorite tailor, was a stark contrast to Grayson's Silicon Valley uniform of dark blue jeans, crisp cotton button-down shirt and running shoes.

The product of a first, disastrous three-month marriage, Finley had been just shy of a year old when Barrett Monk married their mother. Grayson came along ten months later. The half siblings shared brown eyes and little else except for a devotion to the Monk name and legacy. In Grayson's case, it was his heritage and birthright. But he was glad Finley cared as deeply as she did, even though her last name remained Smythe. Barrett had never formally adopted Finley, though he remained her legal guardian after their mother died. He blamed the demands of his political career for why the paperwork was never completed. Grayson didn't see that it mattered. She was his sister, nothing half about it.

Still, it didn't mean he was always happy to see her.

"I have a long day ahead of me," he told Finley. "We agreed I could take the necessary time to hand over Monk Partners to my team. What do you need?"

Finley brushed an imaginary piece of lint off her left trouser thigh. "I hear you had an interesting time at the Peninsula Society ball."

Grayson bit back his irritation. But he also didn't want to raise Finley's suspicions any more than they were already raised. She was adept at finding chinks in people's armors and exploiting them. Even his. "I announced I was leaving the company, as we discussed."

Finley smirked. "Is that what you call what happened in Embarcadero Plaza? An announcement?"

Of course, Finley had seen the story on the *Silicon Valley Weekly website*. Everyone in the Bay Area had seen it, judging by the text messages crowding his phone screen.

"Funny," Grayson growled. "If you're here to gossip, it'll have to wait. I have a job that requires my attention."

"So do I as your campaign manager, which means my job is gossip. Especially gossip about my candidate." The humor left Finley's expression and she leaned forward. "Who is she?"

It still hurt to recall how his sea goddess had left without a backward glance. "A guest at the ball. Obviously."

Finley gave him an assessing stare, then nodded. "As in obviously you don't know. And yet you were papped with her in a very public place." Finley handed Grayson her phone.

On the screen were two photos. The first was of Grayson and his companion before they unmasked. Her hands were cupping Grayson's face, and he was cradling her tight against him. They appeared oblivious to anyone else, wholly engrossed in each other. The intimacy of the photo took his breath away, like it had when he first saw the photo on his phone after his 5:00 a.m. workout.

But it was the other photo that caused him to regret his third espresso at breakfast as the acid rose in his stomach. In this image, he was clearly identifiable with his mask off, holding something white and silver in his hands and staring into the distance. The photo made him look resolute and strong. Amazing how the camera could lie. "Cinderella runs away from Silicon Valley's most eligible bachelor!" read the caption beneath it.

It took a concerted effort to keep his hand still as he handed the phone back to Finley. "Still don't know how the photographer knew it was me before I unmasked," he said, striving for nonchalance.

"Word to the wise for your next masquerade—Bitsy Christensen has most of the photographers in the Bay Area on speed dial. She probably had you followed to find out why you left her party early."

He shrugged. "Regardless, I've been kissing women for many years now. Some even publicly. It shouldn't be a surprise that while my last name is Monk, I don't behave like one."

"Leave the campaign slogans to me, please." Finley put the phone away. "But fine. Not knowing her name will make this more difficult, but not impossible."

Grayson opened his email. Three hundred and forty-two new messages stared back at him. At least half of them mentioned the gala in their subject line. "Spit it out, Finley. I speak four languages, but riddle isn't one of them. More difficult for what?"

"Setting her up as your campaign love interest."

Grayson blinked at his computer screen. "I'm sorry. I was reading my email and must have misheard you. Set who up as *what*?"

Finley sat on the edge of Grayson's desk and closed his laptop. "Focus, bro. Dad is going to announce his retirement soon. You have to be ready."

"Yeah, yeah, I know. What does that have to do with a—what did you call it? A love interest?"

"You're not married. You're not even dating someone seriously. Correct?"

"You know you are," Grayson growled. "So?"

Finley smirked. "So. It's a well-known fact the public loves a good romance. But they aren't so thrilled with a candidate who should be married by now—or at least in a serious relationship. It makes you seem like you can't commit. So why should they commit to you as their representative? Therefore, we need you to date someone. At least through the primary campaign. Hopefully until the general election."

Grayson stared at his sister. "I'm running for Congress. Not for *The Bachelor*."

"It's adorable you think there is a difference between the two—" Finley began.

Grayson stood up, intent on ushering Finley out of his office. This was ridiculous. And he didn't have time for ridiculous. Not ever, but especially not now.

"Wait, wait." Finley threw out her hands, palms up, in a placating gesture. "Please, sit back down."

Grayson remained standing. "You have five more minutes."

"Of course, there are differences between reality television series and running for office. But—" Finley held up her right index finger "—there are also similarities. Mostly in how the press shapes public perception. Sure, we'll put out policy papers, but take it from me. They don't generate clicks. However, a romance? And they're already calling her Cinderella? It's pure publicity gold. The story will dominate Facebook and Twitter." She took out her phone and held up the photos again. "And probably Instagram. You're disgustingly photogenic."

Grayson stared at his sister. "Please tell me you're still joking."

"Please tell me you aren't so naive." A hard light appeared in Finley's gaze. "I shouldn't have to remind you how important this election is to the Monk political legacy. You have the name. You look good on camera. And people like a self-made success story."

"Good. Then I don't need whatever it is you're proposing." Grayson sat down and reopened his laptop. Now he had 527 new emails.

Finley tried to close the screen again, but Grayson removed the computer from her reach. She folded her arms across her chest instead. "It won't be a slam dunk. An open congressional seat without an incumbent will receive a lot of interest from all corners. Barrett tasked me with getting you through the primary and onto the general ballot. This romance will help."

"Too bad I'll have to get by on hard work and addressing real issues instead." As he spoke, he received another twenty email alerts. His phone was set to silent, but the screen showed he had multiple missed calls. "Speaking of hard work, I need you to leave so I can get some done."

Finley shook her head. "The photos are blowing up on social media. We need to strike now, while the iron of public interest is hot."

Grayson stared her down. "Not going to happen. Even if I were to go along with your absurd plan, remember, I don't know her name." His chest twinged. Regret didn't get enough credit as a cause of cardiac pain. The pain sharpened when he remembered how the glow of passion in his mystery woman's gaze was replaced by horror as soon as she saw who he was. "Plus, you'd need to get her to consent to the scheme. That's even more unlikely."

Finley rolled her eyes, walked back to his sofa and

sat, half leaning on the cushions. "It's a romance for your campaign. You date her, you dump her, you're done. She doesn't need to know anything more."

Grayson's hands hovered in midair over his keyboard. "What are you… I'm not going to lie—"

"Who said it's a lie? You'd still be dating her, wouldn't you?"

"I'd know it's a lie. No. That's final."

Finley turned her gaze to the ceiling. "Give me strength." Then she turned her withering stare on Grayson. "Look, I know Mom filled your head with all sorts of garbage about good relationships being 'until death do you part' and yeah, she did die before her marriage to Barrett had time to fall apart, so no wonder you think she's a great example. But for once in your adult life, could you act like an unenlightened Neanderthal, the way almost every other guy of my acquaintance does? Can't you casually date someone without needing to have a vision of wedding rings to dance in your head first?"

A knock caused both siblings to turn toward the door as Grayson's assistant poked his head into the room. "Sorry to interrupt, but I've been trying to call and text you without answer. You have a guest sent by Octavia Allen who insists on seeing you."

"Tell them to—" But his assistant was already swinging the door open wide.

And then *she* stepped over the threshold.

His sea goddess.

If his heart twinged before, now it stopped. Completely. Then started beating again, faster than if he had just finished a marathon. He blinked, once, twice, seven times to ensure he wasn't hallucinating. But he knew it was her. The silver-and-aqua ball gown had been replaced by black trousers and a silvery gray pullover sweater, and her chestnut hair fell in soft waves below her shoulders instead of being constrained in a braid. Her eyes were the same, however. Crystal blue, framed by sooty eyelashes and sharply angled brows.

"A guest?" he repeated, not daring to move in case she was a mirage after all.

His sea goddess stepped forward. "I apologize for showing up without an appointment, but Mrs. Allen sent me to speak to you without delay. I'm…" She stopped, and he could see her swallow. "I'm from Create4All," she finished.

"Create4All." His brain struggled to make sense of her words; he was still stuck on the impossibility of seeing her materialize in his office. Then reason clicked into place and he rose from his desk, his right hand extended to shake hers. "Right. Octavia's nonprofit. Kids and art."

"Yes." She accepted his handshake for the briefest of seconds, keeping her gaze focused on an invisible point somewhere beyond his left shoulder.

In his peripheral vision he could see Finley suddenly straighten up and pay attention, as if she were a starving puppy and the mystery woman was a bag of treats. That wouldn't do. Not while she was banging on about manufacturing a romance. He cleared his throat and injected what he hoped was the right amount of boredom into his voice. "This couldn't wait?"

That got his mermaid to look directly at him for the first time. "No. Mrs. Allen is aware we…met…at the gala." Her gaze flicked in Finley's direction. "She asked me to follow up—I mean, we were wondering if Create4All can count on your support. Despite…" She bit her lower lip. "Despite…everything?"

"Despite everything?" Finley tapped her right index finger on her chin. "What everything?"

A tantalizing pink filled his guest's cheeks. "Despite the announcement, I mean," she said after a beat. "About Mr. Monk stepping down from Monk Partners."

Grayson didn't like the sharpening glint in Finley's gaze. "I can give you fifteen minutes," he said to the woman, and then turned to his sister, his tone much firmer. "See you next week."

"Of course. I'm sure we'll have much more to talk about by then. I'll just close the door behind me, shall I?" Finley said blithely. Too blithe for Grayson's liking. She ushered his assistant out of the room, then turned to waggle her eyebrows at him. "Later, bro."

And with a soft click of the door, he was alone with his sea goddess. Again.

And there wasn't a clock tower anywhere within earshot about to chime and remind her to flee.

Nelle cleared her throat. Her heart pounded so hard that it was a miracle her whole body didn't shake, and her palms alternated between numb from cold and slippery hot from sweat. She did her best to keep her voice on an even keel. "Thank you so much for your time."

It was a very formal greeting, considering the last time she saw him their tongues were wrapped around each other. But in a way, this was her first meeting with Grayson Monk. And it came with the added pressure of knowing her job was on the line.

She had hoped their previous interaction would go unnoticed. They were outside the party, after all, not making out in front of everyone. But she still should have seen it coming. Anyone with a smartphone could be a paparazzo. Anyone with a social media account could cause a photo to go viral. Especially when one of the photo's subjects was a very photogenic billionaire.

Mrs. Allen made it clear she knew Nelle was the Cinderella. And she had known at the party it was Grayson in the Pierrot costume, thanks to being clued in by the gala chairperson. She had been thrilled to see Grayson motion Nelle over for a dance, which was why she told Nelle to join him.

She was not thrilled to see a photo of Create4All's new development director with her lips glued to a potential key donor. Although, she sniffed, she could look past it since technically it wasn't a breach of Create4All's policy. After all, Grayson was not affiliated with the organization—yet. But what Mrs. Allen could not, would not stand for was a Create4All employee who was so unprofessional as to publicly reject one of the wealthiest men in the Valley. A man who could potentially be the linchpin of their fundraising goals for their five-year plan.

It took fast talking—very, very fast talking—but Nelle had managed to avoid being fired. And if Mrs. Allen ended the conversation believing the incident in Embarcadero Plaza was nothing but two old friends reconnecting and discovering sparks but wanting to keep their new relationship under wraps, only to have a minor spat caught on camera and blown up by the media, well, Nelle didn't disabuse her of the notion.

Unfortunately, Mrs. Allen also ended the conversation reiterating how much she was looking forward to receiving a very large donation from Grayson Monk in the near future. She didn't have to add, *or else*. Nelle received the message loud and clear.

She had to make that check happen. Not to keep her job, but so she could prove Mrs. Allen hadn't made a terrible mistake trusting Yoselin's judgment. For someone determined to avoid anything associated with the Monk family, things weren't working quite as Nelle had hoped.

It had taken every ounce of willpower to force herself to follow her phone's navigation system to the Monk Partners office and not stay on the northbound freeway until she reached the Canadian border.

And now that she was in Grayson Monk's office, their gazes locked on each other, it took every ounce of will-power not to lose herself in memories of how his firm lips had coaxed hers to open to him, how his arms flexed and tightened around her. How the world had shrunk until it was just him, her and the sensual spell they wove together.

How she had run, so determined to leave him that she'd forgotten her mask. She was crushed when she realized she had abandoned the children's hard work on a city street.

He was even more attractive than she remembered. His crisp white shirt was open at the throat, revealing a triangle of tanned skin, his broad shoulders even more prominent without the baggy clown costume concealing them. His dark jeans fit as though specially tailored for him, sitting low on his narrow hips and outlining his thighs.

He cleared his throat and she jumped, just a little, heat saturating her cheeks at being caught cataloging his physique. His whiskey-brown gaze contained not a little heat of its own, and with a strange flutter in her chest she realized he had been engaged in his own perusal. She thanked whatever impulse had caused her to reach into the back of her closet to find her most flattering trousers this morning, still covered by a dry cleaning bag from before her move back to the West Coast.

"You're from Create4All?" he prompted. "Funny. The other night I would have guessed Atlantis."

Her cheeks were so hot she was amazed she didn't spontaneously combust on the spot. "Yes. I'm the interim development director. Mrs. Allen is…she thought we… that is, after seeing the photos…" Maybe he didn't know about the viral social media posts? "I mean—"

"I saw them, too," he said, as if reading her mind. "So. You're here because of Octavia. Or is there another reason?" His smirk said he had already decided what her answer would be, and it wasn't Mrs. Allen.

Damn it. The smirk should have made him appear smarmy and arrogant. But along with the glint of unholy humor in his gaze, it only made him devilishly appealing.

She cleared her throat and gave herself a firm mental shake. It was one thing to flirt with an appealing stranger at a masquerade ball as a test run for New Nelle, but she wasn't shielded by a mask now. Her gaze lifted to meet his straight on. "You're right. I'm here to apologize for leaving so abruptly the other night."

His eyebrows rose and he nodded. "Apology accepted. May I ask why?"

She took a deep breath. She had tried so hard to leave El Santo behind, first by running to New York City, then by inventing New Nelle. Only to be confronted with everything she tried to forget in the person of the man standing before her. It didn't help that she viscerally knew how his kisses could make her knees dissolve. And that her job depended on getting his signature on a hefty donation. "You can ask. And I do owe you an explanation. But I please ask that it won't affect any support you might give to Create4All." She straightened her spine, and then held out her right hand for another handshake. A real one. "An introduction should make it obvious. Hi, I'm Nelle."

He took her hand in his. This time she knew to brace herself for the electric jolt of his touch. "Nice to meet you, Nelle. I'm Grayson. But you know that."

"Nelle Lassen." She watched him closely, but his expression didn't change. "Doug Lassen's daughter."

She dropped his hand and looked down at the polished hardwood floor, not wanting to see contempt fill his eyes as he finally figured out who she was.

But the anticipated reaction did not come. Instead she heard, "I'm sorry. That name doesn't ring a bell."

She blinked. The Monk-Lassen feud had been a cornerstone of her formative years. "Doug Lassen? He went to school with your father? They started a law practice together after graduation?"

There was still no recognition in Grayson's gaze.

"The law practice disbanded before either of us was born," she said. "When your father ran in his first election." Her palms were wet from nerves, but she resisted the urge to wipe them on her trousers. "When your father set mine up to take the fall for misuse of client funds. My father was disbarred as a result."

And my family was destroyed.

Grayson's smirk disappeared. "That's a strong accusation."

Finally, the ground was solid under her feet. This was the reaction she expected to receive from a Monk. "It's not an accusation, it's the truth. So, I was shocked when I discovered it was you under the mask. I apologize for running, however. That was wrong of me."

His narrowed gaze searched her face.

She kept her chin high. "Please don't hold my identity against Create4All. The organization is doing amazing work—"

"You ran away because our fathers had some sort of falling out before either of us was born. Is that what you're trying to say?" He sat down on a deeply tufted leather sofa and indicated to her she should take the matching chair across from him. His long legs sprawled, and she remembered what they felt like through the flimsy layers of her skirt, warm and firm and solid—

She shook her head to clear it and remained standing. "I'm not trying to say anything. That *is* what happened. I also said Create4All is doing ama—"

"You ran even though that was a damned good kiss, if I do say so myself."

The searing heat climbed back into her cheeks, hot enough to start a brush fire. "It was…adequate. Anyway, Create4All makes a positive impact on young children and their parents. We're expanding our commitment to the community and building a new center—"

"Adequate?" He raised his eyebrows.

"As far as kisses go. But back to Create4All. We believe in purposeful play, which builds self-confidence and—"

"Pretty sure adequate is not the right word." He stretched his arms along the back of the sofa and leaned back. "Or maybe you aren't familiar with damned good kisses."

A smile played at the corners of his mouth. It made her want to press her lips against his. To twine her arms around his neck as they crashed into each other, mouths open, their tongues competing to see who could coax the other to go deeper, harder, hotter. To show him just how spectacular she was at kisses that left her partner dazed and aching for more.

But.

He was a Monk. Trusting him would be like trusting a scorpion not to sting. She tore her gaze away from his and opened up her tote bag, taking out a colorful booklet. The cover featured photos of kids of all ages, genders and skin tones playing with clay, using computers to create illustrations and performing on stage.

"What I am familiar with is Create4All," she countered. Then, taking a deep breath, she launched into the speech she'd practiced a dozen times in the car before arriving at his office. "This is our prospectus. We've identified the perfect site for our new home. But to secure it, we need the guaranteed support of key sustaining donors like yourself. If you look at page twelve, you'll see where your money will be going. We believe in the strictest transparency—"

"I'll look at it." He took the glossy publication from her but didn't look at it. "I don't know what you think my father did to yours, or what stories you've been told, but—"

"Stories? Are you calling my dad a liar? He—" She slammed her lips shut. Standing up for what she believed in had already gotten her fired from one job. Antagonizing Grayson Monk further was a luxury she could ill afford. Not when her continued employment hinged on getting him to support Create4All. "I'm sorry, I didn't mean to—"

"No, I should apologize." He held his palms up in a placating gesture. "I wasn't saying—okay, it does sound that way. What I meant was everyone is the hero of his or her own story. That means someone else has to be the villain. I have no doubt your father is the hero of this story you're telling me. But this story doesn't have to be yours. After all, I'm not my father. And you're not your father."

He might not be Barrett Monk, but everyone knew it was a matter of time—a very short time—before Grayson would follow in his father's footsteps. "Technically, no, we're not. But blood is thicker than water. Isn't that how the saying goes?"

"Don't visit the sins of the father on the children," he retorted. "Whatever you think those sins may be."

And now he was back to insinuating she didn't know her own family history. "The apple doesn't fall far from the tree."

"In vino veritas," he replied.

"Chip off the old—wait. What?"

"In wine lies truth."

She narrowed her gaze. "Yes, I know what in vino veritas means. What I don't know is why you said it."

He put the prospectus down on the low coffee table in front of the sofa. "You're looking for sponsors, right?"

"Yes," she said slowly. She needed one sponsor in particular. Him.

He nodded. "And that's why you were at the masquerade. To meet people who can write large enough checks."

"It sounds so cynical when you put it that way," she said. "Create4All fulfills a vital need."

"Not saying it doesn't. But that's the bottom line. Correct?"

"If reduced to basics, yes."

He grinned. It warmed his expression, but there was a glint of wickedness that made her stomach flutter and tumble. "There's an event this weekend you should attend."

"Will you be there? If so, perhaps someone else should go. Mrs. Allen would be perfect." Despite her words, her heart started beating a little faster at the idea of seeing him again.

"I already turned down the invitation, but if you commit to being there, I'll bring you as my guest."

She regarded him for a beat, searching his gaze for any hint of an ulterior motive. "Why?"

He leaned forward. "Normally, I'd be happy to discuss a donation, but as you're aware I just resigned from the partnership. It's going to be a while before the new team starts making community development decisions. And my personal discretionary funds are…being held for another purpose at this time. I'm very sorry."

She took a deep breath, anticipating Mrs. Allen's reaction when she returned empty-handed. "I see. Perhaps we can set a future appointment—"

"However. If you're right and my father did commit nefarious deeds—" his mouth twisted to the side and she knew he didn't believe it for a second "—then I'd like to make up for it. This event will give you access to some of the heaviest hitters—and deepest pockets—on the West Coast."

He sounded sincere. But she knew well that sincerity could be faked. Knew it intimately. "But you said no to attending. I could go by myself."

"Not possible," he said, the glint in his gaze sharpening. "It's a drinks-and-dinner reception for an invitation-only summit of global CEOs. Very exclusive." He rose from the sofa and turned toward his desk, bending over to search through the papers on it. She couldn't help but notice how his dark jeans showed off one of the best examples of the male posterior it had ever been her privilege to see.

"You'll have plenty of opportunities for quality networking. And they're used to hearing pitches, so start practicing yours. It could use some polish." He wrote something down, then turned around and handed her a square of heavy card stock.

What the—her pitch was polished. She'd practiced it until her throat was sore. And to think she had been admiring his backside. She crossed her arms over her chest. "You cut me off before I could deliver it. Several times."

"Do you have experience pitching? To other people, not the mirror."

"Well, I…" No. She didn't. In her previous job, she did the writing. Other people delivered her words.

"You're not terrible. But I listen to pitches every day, and so do most of the people you'll be meeting. Every second counts. You'll be judged and weighed from your first word." He indicated the card. "That's the invite. And that's my cell phone number. I'll send a car for you. Text me the address where it should pick you up."

"St. Isadore Vineyards," she read off the invite. Her eyebrows rose. "This is in Napa."

"It takes about two hours to get there from here depending on traffic, so plan accordingly." He seemed to read her mind again, because he followed that with, "Business casual. Nothing fancy. Definitely no costumes." He paused. "And no masks."

Her head jerked up. It sounded more like a challenge than a joke about their previous encounter. "I don't wear masks as a rule," she said. "Do you?"

Their gazes met, hers searching, his amused but assessing. "I don't like having my vision impeded," he finally said. "I rely on it too much."

Was he talking about how he saw her? If so, what did he see? She rubbed her thumb over the embossed letters on the card she was holding. If the people putting on the reception spent this much money on a throwaway invite… "You're sure I'll meet potential sponsors for Create4All?"

"Guaranteed."

She looked up from the invite to catch his gaze. "You're very free with other people's money."

"On the contrary. I'm very careful with other people's money. That's why they trust me with it. I know a good opportunity when I hear one, which is why I'm positive you'll find receptive ears."

She felt a spark of excitement starting to kindle. Bringing in heavy hitters as sponsors would go a long way to appeasing Mrs. Allen's anger over the Embarcadero Plaza photos. And if she brought in enough donations to secure the new building…then she didn't need to continue to court Grayson as a sponsor. She could make Mrs. Allen happy, secure her job and go back to her Monk-free life. She shook off the sharp twinge of disappointment at the thought. "You're sure?"

He closed half the distance between them. He was so near she caught his scent, reminiscent of fresh salt air mixed with pine needles crunching underfoot. It took her back to their kiss on the bench, her arms wrapped around his neck, his large hands cupping her rear end through thin layers of tulle that seemed to disappear beneath his touch. "If I weren't, I'd be a very bad investor. And I'm very good at two things. One—" his low bass voice rumbled in her ears "—is investing."

Her lips were dry. She wet them with her tongue. His gaze followed its path. "And the other?"

He came half a step closer. She was once again mesmerized by how his brown eyes were flecked with amber and ringed by dark mahogany. "Let's say negotiating. Although apparently not today. You haven't said yes."

Her traitorous body leaned, ever so slightly, in his direction. Any farther, and she would brush against his broad chest. She stared at the white expanse of his shirt, wondering if its fine cotton weave was as soft to the touch as it looked, wondering how he would react if she—she blinked. "I'm sorry. Yes to what?"

"To Napa." He paused. "Unless you'd like to dance. Again."

"Dance," she repeated, parting her lips and tilting her head without thinking. His dark gaze turned black, the radiating amber flecks in his irises becoming hard spots of light. If she raised her arms and drew him closer, she could bring his mouth down on hers, lose herself once more in the heat of his kiss.

A knock at the door, followed by the sound of it opening, caused Nelle to blink and jump, putting a few feet between her and Grayson as his words finally hit her. Dance. It was a reference to their conversation at the gala, nothing more. Her cheeks heated at how she'd almost made a fool of herself.

Grayson's assistant poked his head into the room. His expression was even more harried than when Nelle had first arrived at the offices. "Grayson, you have thirty-seven urgent phone calls, and I swear the servers will overload if you don't start clearing your email inbox. Also, your ten o'clock is here."

"Not how servers work, but I get the message. Tell Adam to start the meeting with Hassan. I'll be there when I can." After his assistant exited, Grayson turned back to Nelle. His voice became slower, rougher. "So. Napa. Or would you prefer dancing?"

"I'm keeping you from your work," she said, rushing her words to cut him off. She had done everything but issue Grayson Monk a command to kiss her. Him. Grayson. Son of Barrett. A Monk. What was it about him that ten minutes in his presence made her forget every lesson her father ever taught her? "Yes to Napa. Thank you for the offer of a driver. I'll text you my address."

Then she turned and escaped through the half-open office door, almost but not quite running as fast as she had the other night.

Coward.

But if she didn't leave, she was in danger of losing more than a mask.

Four

The drive to Napa from Fremont, where Nelle was staying with Yoselin until she had enough saved for an apartment deposit, was two hours as advertised—and an entire world away.

Perched on the smooth leather rear seat of the luxury town car Grayson had sent, true to his word, to pick her up, Nelle took in the landscape flashing past her. If the gala at the Ferry Building had been Oz, all bright colors and flashing lights, then Napa was Middle Earth. Green and gold hills in undulating waves stretched out as far as the eye could see in all directions. Rows of vines, lushly verdant and heavy with fruit, imposed linear order on the landscape. The sky was the crystal blue of her favorite sapphire earrings with only the occasional puffy clouds, perfectly marshmallow-like, to break up the azure expanse.

In short, the day was so ideal it seemed created by a computer to precise specification.

She could only hope the evening would continue to be as picture-perfect. Mrs. Allen had not been thrilled when Nelle returned from her visit to Grayson's office without a firm commitment from him to sponsor their new building, but the invitation to St. Isadore smoothed over most of her irritation. Nelle learned from her that the event was even more exclusive than Grayson had indicated. So exclusive that Mrs. Allen had never received an invite despite angling for one for years.

Getting on the guest list after only two months in the Bay Area certainly raised Nelle's status in the board director's eyes, but also heightened her expectations. And going as Grayson Monk's plus-one—Nelle's stomach squeezed as she refused to allow the word "date" to linger in her brain—didn't exactly erase Mrs. Allen's impression that Nelle and Grayson were involved beyond a professional capacity.

Nelle dropped her head into her hands. So much was riding on trusting a Monk. A Monk who claimed to be oblivious of their families' history. Sure, his kisses were hot enough to smelt copper and cause her usual good sense to burn away, but he had to know how his father won his first election. And he apparently didn't care. That was a waving red flag, on top of a flashing siren, blaring an eighty-decibel alarm.

But she couldn't deny she needed him. For Create4All. Nothing more.

Or so she told herself.

The driver swung the car off the two-lane highway and onto a small, private road, allowing Nelle to catch her first sight of their destination. It took her breath away.

"I thought we were going to a winery," she said to the driver. The castle in front of her—there was no other word to describe it—did not look like a place of business.

It belonged instead in France's Loire Valley, the chateau of a long-ago noble. Whitewashed stone walls soared into the sky, topped by a slate gray roof. Dozens of neatly arranged windows reflected the sunshine. There were even turrets. Turrets! And was that…? It was. A moat. "No way," she breathed.

"This is the address, ma'am." The driver crossed the bridge over the moat, which at closer glance might be more properly called a very large pond, and turned into a sweeping, curved drive. Pebbles crunched under the car's tires as he pulled to a stop in front of imposing wood doors that must have been two stories tall and nearly as wide. Box hedges, trimmed into strict geometric lines, flanked the entrance.

The driver came around the car and opened her door, extending his hand to help her out. Clutching her tote bag to her chest, she stared up at the mansion, not knowing what to do next. When she worked in finance, her boss had attended events at estates like this, but she had happily stayed behind at the office to do more research and craft more spreadsheets. The one experience she'd had with palatial estates came from a high school field trip to Hearst Castle. And then she'd had tour tickets and volunteer docents to tell her where to go.

"Do I ring the doorbell?" she asked, only to realize that while she was staring, the driver had returned to the car and was now pulling away.

Her first instinct was to take out her phone and order a shared ride service to take her home. But that was what the old Janelle would have done. New Nelle, on the other hand, took a deep breath and, squaring her shoulders, walked up the flagstone steps toward the door and raised her hand to knock. Then she hesitated. How did knocking work at a castle? Was there someone assigned to sit by the door in case a neighbor dropped by to borrow the lawnmower?

"Nelle!" The wind carried the sound from a distance. She had never been so glad to hear her name shouted before. She turned and saw Grayson, coming toward her in a walk-jog from the left side of the building.

He looked…amazing. There was no other word to describe him. The late-afternoon sun lit him from behind, outlining his broad shoulders and narrow hips as he strode toward her. He stopped in front of her and his left arm came up as if to pull her in for a hug. She found herself leaning forward to accept his embrace, until at the last second he dropped it into a handshake. "Hey," he said. "Glad you made it. Drive was okay?"

His stance was relaxed, his words sincere, and when his gaze met hers it spoke of nothing but pleasure at seeing her again. She liked that light in his eyes. She especially liked knowing she put it there. She—no.

Nelle shook a mental finger at herself. The Monk family was well known for their charm. *Don't fall for it.* She was here to secure her job. He'd offered to help. Nothing more.

Nothing, except for the deep tug of attraction she'd first felt at the gala and again in his office, and was now practically a gravitational pull. "The drive was great," she said with her best professional smile. "We arrived faster than I thought we would. Hope I'm not too early."

"Right on time," he said.

"And dressed okay? I have to admit I rather miss wearing a mask." She tucked a strand of hair that didn't need to be tucked behind her ear. Yoselin had picked out her outfit, a dark plum dress paired with knee-high black boots. Nelle thought she would be too self-conscious in a dress that clung to her curves, but the appreciation in his gaze made her very glad she had listened to her friend.

A smile lifted the left side of his mouth. "I was rooting for the bunny costume you mentioned, but this works very well."

"Thanks." She resisted the urge to return the compliment. This was his world. Of course he was perfectly attired for it. Instead, she glanced at the imposing doors. "I was about to knock."

He shook his head and held out his right arm, elbow crooked. "The party is on the terrace. It's easier to take the side path."

She placed her hand on his arm, hoping he wouldn't notice the slight tremble in her fingers. Underneath her touch the finely woven wool of his sport coat was smooth, his flexed muscles firm.

Grayson led her down a stone path overhung with oak trees. It meandered along rows of grapevines, ending in a large flagstone terrace that wrapped the entire rear length of the castle. Nelle paused a moment to take in the view. It never ceased to amaze her how beautiful California could be, and Napa was one of its prettiest regions, rivaling landscapes painted by Impressionist masters. The air smelled of freshly cut grass mixed with wood smoke, coming from the massive cast-iron grill being prepared for the barbecue to come.

There were sixty, maybe seventy, people, arranged in small, animated groups. A few glanced up at Grayson and Nelle, their expressions welcoming. Still, beads of sweat dotted her hairline despite a welcome breeze. At the gala, she'd had Mrs. Allen and Yoselin nearby. Now... the only person she knew was Grayson.

She took a deep breath. This situation would have intimidated Janelle. But as Nelle, she threw her shoulders back, held her head high and—

The edge of her boot caught on an uneven flagstone, and she would have stumbled if it weren't for Grayson's steadying hand, immediately at her elbow. He glanced down at her. "Everything okay?"

She tried for a nonchalant laugh and then waved her hand, indicating the terrace before them. "What wouldn't be okay? So what's the plan? I mean, assuming you have a plan. Where do I start? Should I pick people to talk to, or will you bring them over to me, or should I wait until they come to me first, or—"

"Nelle."

She tore her gaze away from the crowd. "What?"

"Breathe in."

She did as he suggested, and it seemed to help. "Sorry. Just, I get nervous in front of big crowds."

"Give me your pitch." He dropped his arm in order to turn and face her. Her hand fell to her side, her fingers mourning the loss of the warmth radiating from beneath his sport coat and shirt.

"I'm sorry, you want me to pitch you? Now? But you've heard it. I don't—"

"Humor me. Create4All is…" He wagged his eyebrows in an invitation to complete the sentence, prompting a genuine laugh from her.

"Fine," she said and launched into her presentation. Yoselin had helped her to refine it, but she had to admit the video links Grayson texted her had been the most helpful. From them she learned she had fifteen, maybe thirty seconds to capture the other person's attention. Every syllable needed to count. As she delivered the pitch, she felt the knot of muscles holding her shoulders near her ears start to untangle. As no doubt had been his plan.

He nodded when she finished, and if she had stumbled over a word here or there under the intent warmth of his gaze, he didn't seem to notice. "That was good," he said. "You've got it down." His gaze fixed on a point over her right shoulder, and a grin appeared on his face. "Hey, Paco! Hassan!" He waved over two men, both dressed similarly to Grayson in khaki slacks, button-down shirts and sports jackets. "This is Nelle Lassen," he said to the newcomers. "She recently joined Create4All. Do you know it? It's like a start-up incubator but for kids. Helps them discover their creativity."

The taller of the two men extended his right hand to Nelle for a handshake, his dark gaze alight with interest. "Start-up incubator for kids. Intriguing."

"I can't take credit for that description, but I'm definitely stealing it from now on." She repeated the pitch she gave Grayson, her words increasing in confidence as the men listened and then started to ask questions.

Grayson remained by her side, so close that if she reached out her little finger, she would brush his thigh. As the conversation drew to a natural close, three more people joined their group and Nelle found herself pitching to them. Then others came over to be introduced. Throughout it all, she was acutely aware of Grayson. How he included her in the conversation even when the topic drifted away from Create4All and into the more esoteric ins and outs of buying and selling companies. How his body angled to ensure she was physically included in whatever group they were talking to. How he guided her wordlessly, seamlessly from one new arrival to the next with a light touch on her elbow.

As the sun sank in the sky, the last people to join their

group drifted away. She rifled through the stack of newly acquired business cards in her right hand. CEOs, heads of international funds, global tycoons—more than a few of the names were commonly seen on the Forbes 400 list. It would have taken her weeks, if not months, of careful courting of assistants, lower-level executives and other gatekeepers to receive direct access to these people. An adrenaline high spiked her veins. "Pitching is fun."

"It is. Especially when you have a good product, which you do. I read up on Create4All."

"Oh? I thought you weren't interested in becoming a sponsor?" She continued to flip through the cards, making notes on each one for follow-up.

"I said I can't right now. I never said I wasn't interested." His voice lingered on the last word. She looked up, catching his gaze.

That was a mistake.

The setting sun lit his dark blond hair so it almost looked like a halo. The same rays warmed his gaze, turning his brown eyes to molten bronze. The effect reminded her of paintings she had seen in her art history class. Of a Renaissance prince, perhaps.

Then he smiled at her, slow and warm, and her breath caught.

Damn it. She didn't want to like him. She really didn't want to be this attracted to him, but the knowledge was ever-present of how his touch kindled sparks, how his kiss ignited sparks into flames. Her hands itched to reach out, run her fingers over his jaw, his cheek, pull his mouth down to hers to ensure he really was flesh and blood and not a painting come to life.

It was impossible to return to their old relationship: the one where she despised him on principle from a distance and he had no idea she existed. But maybe she could still extricate herself before the night went further. Before *she* went further. She cleared her throat. "So. Thank you for inviting me. I appreciate it. This is my first time working in nonprofit development and I don't have a network built up yet."

"It speaks well for you that you got the job anyway. Octavia Allen is very particular." The appreciation in his gaze was like a soft velvet blanket. She wanted to pull it tight around her, lose herself in its depths.

She looked away instead, focusing on the pink and purple clouds hovering above the hills. "It speaks well for my best friend who got me the job. I had to…let's just say finding a job in my previous career would have been difficult. Nor could I remain where I lived. She hired me because she knew I was in a bad place."

"Physically?" The question was light, but there was a hard note underneath.

She shook her head. "No. Emotionally. Although when your ego is torn to shreds and eaten by hyenas, it can feel like a brick hit you. Several bricks." She glanced at him from under her eyelashes. "Not something you're familiar with."

"Of course I am. Everyone is."

"Right." She smirked at him. "C'mon. You're Grayson Monk, the fair-haired golden boy. Barrett's heir apparent. You know full well all you have to do is snap your fingers and people scramble to give you what you want. Be honest. Have you ever had your ego trampled? Truly?"

His gaze narrowed. "I thought your problem was with my father. It sounds like your problem might be with me."

"My problem with you is your father, as we discussed." She bit her lower lip. She didn't expect Grayson to understand that while she didn't have a problem with him, personally—on the contrary, she was begin-

ning to like him a little too much—she was very aware
of the vast differences in their upbringings. "But…am I
really that wrong?"

The sun disappeared below the horizon, and with it
went its remaining heat. A cool wind replaced it, coming down from the hills and sweeping across the terrace.
She resisted the urge to wrap her arms around herself,
both to keep warm and to protect herself from the still-
ness creeping into Grayson's expression. She especially
resisted the urge to lean into his warmth.

"No," he finally said. "You're not." Her head jerked
up. He continued, "I've had a lot of help. My family name
opened doors that were nailed shut to others. I've never
had to worry about money or a place to sleep." His mouth
twisted. "We just met, and you feel this way. I wonder if
others share your perception."

"Why do you care? It shouldn't matter what I or anyone else thinks. Not to you."

His gaze searched hers. Then he nodded, as if he found
what he was looking for. "It matters if I run for Congress."

She raised her eyebrows. "So the rumors are true? Barrett is stepping down and you're running for his seat?"

"Not officially. Not until he announces his retirement
next month. And definitely not as far as the press is concerned." His tone carried a warning.

"I won't say anything. But still, why would you worry?
You're a legend in El Santo. The entire county, for that
matter. Homecoming king, nationally ranked swimmer
in high school, now a titan of Silicon Valley. I'm surprised there isn't already a statue of you in Pioneer Park,"
she teased.

Too late, she realized she had said far too much. His
gaze was laser-focused on her. She shivered, remember-

ing their conversation in his office about masks and seeing beneath them. She would give anything to be safe behind a mask right now.

"Pioneer Park. You seem to be familiar with El Santo."

Busted. "I told you. Your father and mine were law partners. Where did you think that was?"

"My father started his law firm in Sacramento. El Santo became his home base during his first election."

She shook her head. "No, they practiced in El Santo. I grew up there."

"That's not—" He stopped, swinging his gaze to look over the grapevines. "The people of El Santo…" he said, barely audible. He turned back to her. "That was you. At the gala."

"You know it was me at the gala. You took off my mask, remember?"

"During my speech. I overheard, 'the people of El Santo deserve better.' You were the speaker."

She was no longer cold. Searing heat flushed her checks, neck and chest. "I… I didn't mean for you to hear that… I'm so sorry…what I meant was—"

"Do you still feel that way after meeting me?"

She blinked several times. "I…no, of course not."

"You hesitated."

"No, I didn't—look, I know the voters love your father. They're bound to love you, too."

He would not let her off the hook. "I hear a *but* at the end of that sentence."

She took a deep breath. *Might as well be completely honest.* After all, it was her intention to never see him again after tonight anyway. Wasn't it? "But. Deep down, have you asked yourself what the people *deserve*? Will you be able to deliver it? Because, so far, your father hasn't." She held up a hand to stop the protest she saw forming on his lips. "I know, you probably think he's doing a great job. After all, he keeps getting elected. But El Santo needs a representative who cares about its people. I grew up on the east side of town near the train yards, overlooked and underserved. And I'm one of the lucky ones. I was able to leave El Santo for college and found work elsewhere. But what of the residents who are stuck with falling property values and no jobs to replace the ones that went offshore decades ago? What do you really know about life there? You've spent most of your time here, with them." She waved her hand in a sweeping motion to indicate the well-dressed men and women on the terrace. "I mean, why do you even want to run? Are you doing it because you want to, because it's the right thing? Or are you running because everyone just supposes you'll follow in your father's footsteps when he retires?"

He regarded her for a moment, his gaze dark and steady.

She cleared her throat. "Is the car nearby? I'll say my goodbyes now."

His brow furrowed. "Are you leaving?"

She blinked. "Well…after what I said…don't you want me to leave?"

Grayson remained silent, struggling to organize his thoughts. Four in particular flashed through his brain, quick as minnows and as slippery to catch.

The first was he should be happy she wanted to leave. The longer she stayed, the more likely someone would post a photo of the two of them on social media or let slip an inadvertent comment about how cozy he and Nelle appeared to be. And the next thing he'd know Finley would be in his ear babbling about "campaign romances" and "building a narrative for maximum voter identification."

His second thought was how beautiful she looked in the twilight. The red and amber streaks low on the horizon created gold highlights in her chestnut hair and threw into silhouette the curves outlined by her dress.

The third: he would be a damn fool to let her get away, now that he knew she was from El Santo. Finley and his father insisted Grayson's election was a foregone conclusion. They wanted him to spend his campaign funds on ads and messaging, not focus groups and polls. But Nelle was suggesting it wasn't as much of a slam dunk as his family was telling him. He needed straight talk, not smoke blown up his ass, if he wanted to fulfill his legacy of serving the public.

His fourth thought was wondering if kissing her would be even better with her hair down instead of in a braid. With her hair down, his fingers could slip through the silken strands—

Thought three it was. *Stay on thought three.* "No. Of course I don't expect you to leave," he said. "I appreciate your honesty."

She shrugged slightly and looked away. "You'd be one of the first. I haven't had the best reaction when I point out truths."

He smiled at her. "I'm not that fragile."

She half chuckled, half snorted. "No. That's not a word I'd apply to you. Still, I should leave, let you be with your friends."

"The invitation was for wine tasting and a dinner." He indicated the crowd starting to form at one end of the terrace around long tables laden with wine bottles. Waitstaff handed out empty crystal stemware. "And the wine tasting is about to start."

"I thought the invitation was to pitch your colleagues. And I do thank you for the opportunity." She set her jaw and squared her shoulders. "If you don't mind pointing me toward the car?"

He recognized determination when he saw it. Perhaps other tactics might work better. He indicated a stone staircase to their right. "The car will be waiting for you. Take these steps and they'll put you on the path to the front of the house and the driveway."

"Thank you again." She held out her right hand to shake and he took it. Her fingers squeezed against his, creating a chain reaction that made him wish he was wearing the baggy trousers of the other night. "I really do appreciate everything you've done to help me. Good night."

"Good night. I'll be sure to let Reid Begaye know he missed you." He let her hand go and began to walk to where the rest of the guests congregated.

It took a few seconds longer than he thought it would. "Reid Begaye?" she said from behind him.

Bingo. He fixed his expression before turning around. "He should be here later."

"Reid Begaye, as in the world's second richest man? The Reid Begaye who used to run Metricware?"

"He's the keynote speaker for the conference tomorrow morning. I was told he's running late because his foundation had a conflicting event this evening."

She nodded. "Right. That would be the foundation that gives away tens of millions of dollars each year to education nonprofits. Like Create4All."

"That's him. But since you want to go home—" he shrugged with one shoulder "—I've heard your pitch. I'll give it to him if you want."

She crossed her arms over her chest and her right foot

started to tap on the flagstones. "Something tells me you know he's on Mrs. Allen's short list of dream sponsors for Create4All. She might want to land him even more than she wants to land you."

"Octavia isn't subtle about what she wants. Reid will be sorry to hear you had to leave."

Her delectable lips pursed into the most kissable shape. Then she unfolded her arms and began to walk toward him, taking an empty glass off a passing waiter's tray. "I only like red wine," she said as she passed by, heading to join the rest of the guests.

Grayson followed her. He couldn't erase the grin on his face if the fate of the world depended on it.

Nelle strode through the crowd at the wine tasting, but once she passed Grayson, her head held high, she slowed her steps. The crisp businesslike tones that had filled the air in the late afternoon as men and women talked deals and strategies had given way to laughter and soft conversation as evening fell. Strings of small globe lights crisscrossed the terrace, casting a golden gleam that softened the rough stone patio and low walls. Catering staff walked among the tall cocktail tables draped with black cloths, lighting candles in cut-glass jars. Even the woodsmoke she'd detected earlier seemed to change, becoming heavier and sweeter as the time for grilling the vast amounts of meat and vegetables visible on the prep table drew nearer.

It was as if she had been transported from a business conference in Northern California to a dream vacation in Tuscany. Never in her wildest dreams would she ever believe she'd attend an event like this. Or meet the people whose cards were still clutched tight in her hand, much less Reid Begaye.

Janelle had been a caterpillar, she decided. Afraid to leave her leaf, unable to move very far or fast, her scope limited to what was immediately before her. But Nelle could be a butterfly. Able to fly above, travel far, range beyond the limits she had previously set for herself. She could dare believe those dreams would turn into reality.

Thanks to Grayson.

A year ago, she would have rejected the idea that her career success depended on a Monk. But when caterpillars morphed into butterflies, their perspectives changed, as well. Caterpillars' vision was limited to grains of dirt and individual blades of grass. Butterflies could see whole mountains and fields.

But what flew up must, of a necessity, come back down. The higher she went, the worse the inevitable fall would be. Did this sudden change in perspective make actual butterflies as dizzy as she felt now? Or did the dizziness have a different origin?

A light touch came at her elbow, and with it her answer. Grayson was the cause. She knew he stood at her side without turning her head. Knew it from the way the brush of his fingers against her sleeve put her nerves on immediate alert. Knew it from the way the atmosphere changed, both lightening her mood and darkening her desire to be near him.

"I have it on good authority the best table is to the far left," he said, his voice a deep rumble in her ear.

"And what makes it the best?"

"The owner of the vineyard is standing at it." He turned and waved at a group clustered around the table in question, who waved back at him.

"But of course, you know the owner." She allowed him to steer her toward the table, where she was quickly introduced to Evan Fletcher, who'd recently purchased

St. Isadore Wines, and his business partner, Luke Dallas. Grayson handed her a stem of red wine before falling into a conversation with the other men about a possible new acquisition for Evan and Luke's company.

They included Nelle, but she was happy to let them catch up with each other without her. She drank deeply from her glass to avoid having to speak and reveal just how much she wasn't paying attention. But mostly she downed the wine so she would have an excuse to keep her hands busy, so she wasn't tempted to cling to Grayson's arm, to twine her fingers with his.

Maybe Grayson was right. Maybe the past was precisely that: the past. There was no reason why it should impact the present, much less the future. The previous generation's actions didn't have to dictate her view of the current one.

Did it?

Her thoughts chased each other, bouncing and skittering inside her skull. Before she knew it, her glass was empty. Oops. Weren't people supposed to sip and then spit out the wine when at a tasting? Or at least that was what the internet said.

She looked up to see Evan watching her with raised eyebrows. "I like a healthy appreciation," he said. "Here, let me top off your glass. I'm not sure you got the entire sensory experience with such a small sip."

Usually the suggestion she had made a social faux pas, no matter how slight, would be enough to send her shrinking into the shadows until she could back out via the nearest exit. But Evan's tone was light and teasing, Luke's smile was friendly and welcoming, and Grayson's gaze—Grayson's gaze made her lungs lose all sense of rhythm. Her breathing stopped, then sped up, then stopped again.

She held out her glass and searched her memory for phrases she read while researching what to expect at a wine tasting. "Full-bodied, nicely acidic with a touch of sweetness for balance, and pleasantly dry. In other words, fill 'er up." She tapped the brim. "To here."

"Ha!" Evan did as she requested, and then gave her an unopened bottle. "Here. Take this home. You earned it." He then turned to Grayson. "I like her," he said.

Nelle's gaze met Grayson's. If the intense light in his eyes caused her breathing to be erratic, now it caused her heart to beat three times faster than usual. He continued to hold her gaze as he answered Evan. "Me, too."

She sipped her wine slowly this time, very aware that her cheeks must be the exact same shade of crimson as her beverage. But the warmth in her cheeks was nothing compared to the heat building deep inside. A heat that only grew hotter when their arms brushed. If she had wondered if Grayson thought of this as a mere business excursion, she now had her answer.

This was a date.

And she was not unhappy about it.

Five

Grayson watched Nelle as Luke drew her into a conversation about child development and Create4All's recommended best practices. She laughed, throwing back her head, exposing the long pale expanse of her neck. He wanted to press his lips there. Taste her. Kiss a path from where a gold locket snuggled in the hollow of her throat to the curve of her jaw, follow it around to where that dimple teased him by appearing and disappearing as he watched. The kiss in Embarcadero Plaza would always be seared on his brain, but it wasn't enough. He craved more.

Evan clapped him on his shoulder and he reluctantly dragged his focus away from her. He and Evan had met at a similar function to this one, albeit when their bank balances were much closer to zero. Grayson had invested in two of Evan's previous start-ups, which performed well if not spectacularly, before coming up with the brainstorm to partner him with Luke Dallas. Together, their combined talents and complementary skills had created a medical technology company that rocketed straight from the gate into the stratosphere. And that had allowed Evan to buy St. Isadore.

Grayson lifted his glass. "This is good. I'm not usually a fan of blends."

"It's something the head vintner came up with. Only a few bottles are ready for drinking."

"He has a hit on his hands." Grayson finished his glass.

Evan watched the crowd gathered around his director of operations, who was leading them through a structured wine tasting. "You mean, she has a hit on her hands. Yeah, I know, she's told me."

Grayson raised his eyebrows at the coolness in Evan's tone. "Where is she? I'd love to meet her."

Evan's distant gaze snapped to Grayson's. "Working," he said, his consonants precise. "Or at home, since the workday is over. Or doing a thousand other things. How would I know?"

"I see." Grayson smiled as he poured himself another glass. Evan's speech only became clipped like that when something—or someone—had burrowed under his skin and continued to prickle.

"Speaking of seeing." Evan put his wineglass down, the better to lean his forearms on the table. "I wasn't expecting to see you. You said you weren't attending this year's summit."

Grayson shrugged. "Changed my mind."

"You don't do that. Not as a rule." Evan glanced at Nelle. "I don't have to be psychic to know why, though."

"If you were psychic, you'd know where your head vintner is."

"Ha, ha," Evan deadpanned. "Nelle is the woman from the gala, right? And the photos in *Silicon Valley Weekly.*"

Grayson started to answer, but Nelle caught his gaze and smiled. A wide, open, gorgeous smile. Her eyes shone, reflecting the glow of the candles and the strings of lights above. She raised her glass of wine to him and then turned back to her conversation.

"Yeah," Evan said, his tone dryer than a California drought, "she's the one."

"What's that supposed to mean?" Grayson's brows drew together. He didn't have many close friends. Oh, he had acquaintances and colleagues enough to fill several college football stadiums. But good friends? The kind who would be there at 3:00 a.m. to bail him out of jail, no questions asked? He could count those on the fingers of one hand. And he was about to lose one of those if Evan didn't explain himself.

Evan raised his hands in a conciliatory gesture. "It's bad enough I have to deal with Luke swooning over his wife on a daily basis at work. Now when we hang out, I'll have to listen to you wax poetic about true love. I won't be able to escape."

True love? Grayson glanced at Nelle, who was still intent on her discussion with Luke. His gaze traced the graceful contours of her face, the generous curve of her chest above her hourglass waist.

He liked her. He hoped he could persuade her to share her perceptions of El Santo and what the people of the district needed. And yes. He wanted her.

But like wasn't love. Lust definitely wasn't love.

Love wasn't on the schedule. He had a month to wind down his obligations to Monk Partners before he would be required to stand by his father's side as Barrett announced he wouldn't be seeking reelection. And then Grayson's campaign would begin in earnest.

He took his family's legacy seriously, and his responsibilities even more so. He had no time right now to discover if the electricity that arced between him and Nelle was a harbinger of deeper emotion or merely his libido demanding to get its way.

And he certainly wasn't going to enlist her in Finley's ridiculous plan. He would not use her as a prop, much less expose her to his sister's single-minded tactics. He really did like her.

Grayson tuned back in to hear Evan sigh. "Next thing I'll know, boys' night will be pizza for one and games of solitaire instead of Cuban cigars and hands of poker."

Grayson side-eyed him. "When have we held a boys' night? Or played poker?"

"It's metaphorical." Evan reached for the nearest open wine bottle.

Grayson took the bottle from Evan's grasp and moved it to the other side of the table, where it joined several empty ones. "I'm beginning to think a vineyard might not have been your wisest choice of investment."

"Remember how Luke looked at Danica the night of last year's Peninsula Society gala? I see the same thing in your eyes, my friend."

"I think you've seen the bottom of your glass too many times. Please tell me you're staying here tonight and not driving back to the city."

Evan laughed. "I'm as sober as a judge presiding over a patent theft trial." He indicated the guests migrating toward the tables of freshly prepared food. The night breeze carried the scent of well-seasoned steak and grilled vegetables, and plates were already being heaped high with food. "Dinner's on. But the real question is, have you decided on what—or who—you're having for dessert?" He wagged his eyebrows and clapped Grayson on the back. "I've got to mingle and sell a couple of bottles of wine to help pay for this thing. Talk to you later."

"Not if I can help it," Grayson muttered into his glass.

"What was that?" Nelle appeared at his side, Luke having left to join Evan in the crowd around the barbecue pit. She was so close he could reach out an arm, encircle her waist and pull her against him. He reached out his hand—

And motioned at the open bottle, still about half full. "I was saying I never leave good wine behind if I can help it. Want another glass?"

He was stalling, he knew. They should join the others eating dinner. But the sooner they ate, the sooner the end of the night would come. And the sooner he would have to say goodbye to her.

She glanced at the line for the food, then back at the bottle, and held out her glass. "I don't think I tried this one."

He poured a small amount in it, then glanced at the label. "This is a Cabernet Sauvignon blend. According to the tasting notes—" he picked up a sheet of paper dotted with ring-shaped stains and tried to read it in the dim light "—you should detect notes of plum, cherry and black currants."

She took a sip, considered for a minute, and gave him a half smile, half grimace. "Can I make a confession? I just taste wine."

He laughed. "Me, too. But we didn't go through the ritual wine tasting steps."

"Trust fancy people to make wine more complicated than it needs to be. You pour, you drink. What more needs to happen?" She reached across him to take the bottle and top off her glass. Her scent wafted over him, a light jasmine note that reminded him of spring and fresh beginnings. He remembered how it had filled his senses as her mouth crushed against his, his hands running over the hard peaks of her breasts—

Damn it. He was already responding to her. He cleared his throat. "Several things happen. For example, at a tasting you consider the wine's…" He dropped his gaze so he wouldn't be mesmerized by how the skin above the deep V of her neckline gleamed in contrast to the velvet of her dress. But when he looked down, he was greeted by the sight of knee-high boots, their supple black leather hugging beautifully shaped calves. "The wine's, um, legs."

She raised her eyebrows. "Wine has legs?"

"Some varietals do, depending on age. And then there's the—" He made the mistake of glancing up as Nelle drank deeply, her eyes closed in appreciation, her lips wet on the glass "—mouthfeel."

She threw him a glance from under her lashes. "My mouth feels like I just drank wine."

He would give anything to discover for himself how her mouth felt, right that very second. He put his hands in his trouser pockets and rocked back, hoping the tightness beginning to make itself known in the fabric wouldn't be apparent to her. "To properly assess mouthfeel, you hold the wine in your mouth."

Her right hand hovered in midair, the glass halfway to her lips. "Hold it in my mouth?"

He nodded. "To get the feel."

She put her wine glass down and slowly turned so they stood face-to-face. Barely a hand's width separated them. "And after I've held it in my mouth?"

He reached for the bottle of wine standing at her

elbow. It was either drink more or grab her hand, break into the winery, and find a secluded room in which to show her just what, exactly, should happen next. She reached for the bottle at the same time. Their fingers met, collided. Neither let go.

"You have a choice." His voice was raspy. He tried to work more moisture into his mouth.

"Do I swallow?" Her thumb moved where it met his, grazing over his skin, so slightly that he wondered if he were imagining it.

"That's a possibility. Although…" He paused. No, her thumb was definitely brushing against his. "Not recommended."

Her pink tongue darted out to wet her lips. He followed its path with his gaze. "Really. I would think differently. Otherwise, it's such a waste. Of wine."

"Not if there are hours—of wine tasting—to come." He leaned down, his mouth almost at her ear. "If you drink too much, there's a risk of finishing early."

Her lips curved upward in a slightly wicked smile. "I don't want that. The one thing I do know…about wine… is a lingering finish is preferred." Her fingers were now enmeshed with his where they held the bottle together.

At the gala she had appeared as a sea goddess, regal, almost unapproachable. Now, with her chestnut hair down and blowing in the breeze, her eyes dark and glittering in the glow of the string lights above, her lips stained red with wine—now she was unmistakably human, lusciously curvy flesh and blood. His hands ached to push aside the wide V of her neckline, exposing more bare skin for his mouth to worship. To free those glorious breasts that filled his hands in his dreams every night. He wanted to see if he could coax that dimple to appear by whispering what he wanted to do with her, here, now, despite the crowd gathered on the other end of the terrace.

The wind shifted, bringing with it the smell of mesquite smoke and tri-tip. He held her gaze with his. "Are you hungry?"

She audibly inhaled. "Depends. For what?"

He smiled at the echo of her words from the gala, his fingers remaining locked with hers. "There's a barbecue over there. Or…"

"Or?" She breathed the word.

"Grayson! There you are!"

With an oath, he dropped his hand from hers and turned to see who was hailing him. A man, wearing his signature Stetson along with his sport coat and khakis, waved at him from across the terrace. Of course. He always did have perfect timing.

Nelle turned her head to follow his gaze. "Who is that?"

"Who else? Reid Begaye has arrived."

Nelle didn't know whether to laugh with relief or cry with frustration as she watched Reid Begaye weave his way through the clusters of people, shaking hands and exchanging words, but staying on a clear beeline to where she and Grayson stood. If Reid had put off his entrance for even a minute longer, she had no doubt she and Grayson would already be in his car, driving through the night to the first place with an accommodating bed. In fact, with the way her legs still trembled and her breathing still stuttered, they might not have made it to the car, instead breaking into the winery's main building to find a secluded room.

Thank goodness for wealthy philanthropists who weren't named Monk, or she might have done something she would regret in the morning. And no, it wouldn't have just involved a forced entry.

She stepped away from Grayson, putting the bottle back down on the table. She also put a good foot of distance between them. A few deep, steadying breaths and she was ready to give Reid her most welcoming smile as he shook hands with Grayson.

"I hear you're looking for me," Reid said to Grayson, before extending his right hand to her. "Hi. Reid Begaye."

"Nelle Lassen," she responded. "It's a pleasure to meet you."

Reid was tall, about the same height as Grayson, but that was where the comparison stopped. Grayson was lean, his swimmer's shoulders lending the only appearance of bulk. Reid was well muscled, his sports jacket obviously custom-tailored to contain his broad chest and beefy forearms. Grayson's dark blond hair always looked as if he had just come from the beach, while Reid's was precisely cut without a hair out of place. Grayson's expression was generally open and friendly, as if he'd heard a good joke and couldn't wait to share it, while Reid's was opaque without a hint at his thoughts. It didn't help that his hat kept most of his face in shadow.

Still, she found herself liking him. His handshake was firm and no-nonsense, his gaze direct, and she began to relax despite everything she had at stake.

"So you're Nelle," Reid responded. "I thought so, seeing as you're here with him." He jerked a thumb at Grayson. "Luke Dallas said we should speak. You have a children's charity?"

"I work for one. Create4All. I'd love to tell you more about it."

Reid smiled. It changed his face, lighting it from within. Nelle hadn't thought of him as particularly hand-

some before, more interesting-looking than convention-
ally attractive, but now she changed her mind. It must
have shown, as Grayson closed the space between them,
angling his shoulder so he stood between her and Reid.

She bit back a smile, only to find Reid examining her
more closely. "Tell you what," he said, turning his back
so as to cut Grayson out of the conversation, "it's been a
long day for me. I flew in from Sydney and went straight
to an event and then came here. I can't tell my right hand
from my left hand. I'm only here to talk to folks like this
one—" he jerked his thumb at Grayson "—and for them
I don't need a working brain."

"Don't need a working brain? That explains why you
made the deal at last year's conference to sell Swynn In-
dustries when I advised against it," Grayson said with a
smile. "And the buyers ran it into the ground and declared
bankruptcy, like I told you they would."

Reid shrugged, his gaze still locked onto Nelle's.
"Fine, Grayson was right. Once. Let's allow him to enjoy
it while it lasts."

Nelle laughed. "I hope he's right about your support
of children's causes."

"That makes twice he's right." Reid turned and
clapped Grayson on the shoulder. "So. Were you asking
around for me just to rub my nose in a bad deal?"

Grayson shook his head. "No. Nelle is the one looking for a deal this year."

Reid nodded. "Ah. Got it." He turned back to Nelle.
"As I was saying, I can wheel and deal with guys like
this while I'm three-quarters asleep, but I like to be fully
awake when discussing my foundation. Let's have breakfast tomorrow before my keynote and you can tell me
about your organization. Seven thirty okay? Conference

hotel restaurant. I already have a reservation, but I'll cancel the existing meeting and put you in instead."

"She'll be there," Grayson said before she could respond. "Thanks for this, Reid. I know your schedule is tight. You're off to Asia after this, right?"

Reid's mouth twisted. "Yeah. Well, business—and good causes—stop for no man, even if life has another plan in mind." He clapped Grayson on the shoulder again. "Good to see you, even if it only reminded me of my lapse in judgment." Then he took Nelle's hand in his. "And very good to meet you. See you tomorrow."

He left almost as suddenly as he arrived, swallowed by another group of people who had obviously been waiting for him to join them. Nelle turned to Grayson. "Seven thirty a.m.?"

"It's your one chance to speak with him. He's currently embroiled in a fight for control of his family's assets—it's a long story. You must have impressed him to get on his schedule." His jaw tightened.

"You did the impressing. He's meeting me because of you," she pointed out.

"He doesn't do favors for just anyone. He liked you." A tiny muscle started to jump in his jaw.

"Is the car nearby? If I want to get any rest before the meeting, I should have left here hours ago." She'd need to wake up at 3:00 a.m. to get herself looking presentable and arrive on time in spite of any traffic snarls she might face. Better set her phone alarm while she was thinking of it. The last thing she wanted was to sleep through—

"Oh no."

"What's wrong?"

She showed him the news alert on her phone screen. "A brush fire broke out to the south of us a few hours ago" She clicked on the story and started to read. "It doesn't

sound too bad...no homes are in its path... Oh, wait,
here's an update." She read it and then looked up to catch
Grayson's gaze, feeling sick to her stomach. "Smoke is
drifting over the freeway and threatening drivers' vis-
ibility. The highway patrol is closing all lanes as a pre-
caution."

"May I see?"

She handed him her phone and squeezed her eyes shut,
trying to think of an alternative way to get home. There
were other freeways between Napa and the East Bay,
but it would mean taking a much more circuitous route.
She'd have barely enough time to grab a vat of coffee to
go and a change of clothes before needing to turn around
and head back.

"It sounds like it will be contained by morning." Grayson handed the phone back to her. "Freeway should be
open by then."

"That's good," she said. "Although it's going to take
forever to get home tonight." The wine in her stomach
sloshed in a very unappetizing manner. "I'm glad I came,
and it was very nice of you to invite me, but I really
should get going now and—"

"Nelle." It was one syllable, but it was warm and kind
and understanding. "Breathe."

"It's just...did you know the Begaye Foundation gave
ten million dollars to an organization similar to Crea-
te4All in Chicago? Granted, the Chicago nonprofit is
much larger, but if I can convince him to give even one
tenth of that to us, it will mean our capital budget will
be secure and we can go ahead with the new site. I can't
screw this up."

"You won't."

She tried to smile. It was wobbly. "Can you say goodbye to Luke and Evan for me? And could the driver stop

at a fast food drive-through on the way back?" She was going to miss dinner. "And, um, I know I'm forgetting something…"

Grayson considered her for a minute. Then he took out his phone, punched in a few numbers, and started to speak. "Hi, it's Grayson Monk. Can you add another room to my reservation for tonight?"

She whipped her head around to stare at him. He held her gaze as he continued speaking. "Thanks. Would you transfer me to the hotel's boutique?" He listened for a minute, then spoke again. "Hi. Did the front desk—great. I'm going to put a friend of mine on the phone. Send everything she asks for to my room and put it on my account."

He held out his phone to Nelle. "One solution is to stay at the conference hotel. There's a room available and I've got the hotel's shop on the line. They carry a wide range of clothes and toiletries. Order what you need for tonight and tomorrow." At her openmouthed surprise, he added, "On me. I insist."

She stared at him. So many conflicting thoughts and emotions jockeyed for attention that she couldn't sort through them all. She finally settled on, "I can't accept."

"You're in this situation because of me. It's the least I can do."

"I don't…" She shook her head, hoping to clear it. It only scrambled her brain more. On the one hand, it would make her life infinitely easier if she stayed at the same hotel where her breakfast meeting was taking place. On the other, it would put her even deeper in Grayson's debt. Yes, so far he'd followed through with everything he promised, not a hint of double-dealing in any of his actions. But he was still a Monk.

And someone she found very, very, *very* attractive. It

was one thing to heavily flirt over wine. It would be another to know they were sharing a roof, albeit in a hotel with numerous rooms. "I'm not sure—"

He held the phone to his ear. "Are you still there? Sorry to keep you on hold… Great. Send a selection of women's clothes in size…?" He raised his eyebrows at Nelle.

She folded her arms across her chest. "I'm not telling you my size."

"Let's say in an eight," he said into the phone. "Business casual. Plus anything else one might need for an overnight stay—yeah. Send some of those, too. Thank—"

She took the phone from him. "Size twelve," she said to the boutique employee on the other end, then handed it back to him. He finished the conversation and then had the audacity to grin at her.

"I still haven't said yes," she reminded him.

"But now you have a choice," he said. "If you want to leave, I'll have my driver take you home via the safest route possible. If you would like to stay—" his crooked grin deepened "—you can have a dinner prepared by a Michelin-starred chef and a good night's rest. Up to you." He shrugged.

Nelle pressed her lips into a thin line. It would serve him right if she called his bluff and asked for the car… Oh, who was she kidding? She was the person bluffing. There was only one good choice. Yes, he made the choice possible, but that didn't mean she had to shoot herself in the foot and not accept. "I'm paying you back for the room and clothes," she said. He opened his mouth, but she cut him off. "That's nonnegotiable."

Their gazes engaged in a slight skirmish before he relented, extending his arm to her with its elbow bent.

"As you wish. Meanwhile, the line for the buffet is now nonexistent. Shall we?"

She found her hand resting on his bicep before she could form a conscious thought. The now familiar electricity sparked anew. "Lead on."

She might as well enjoy his company for the rest of the evening before she said good-night to him—and goodbye. They would have separate rooms at the hotel. She could meet with Reid Begaye and then leave. She could even rent a car to drive home and not have to bother him again.

Ever.

Her heart constricted into a tight, painful knot at the thought.

Six

Nelle did not, as it turned out, have a separate room.

She stared at the hotel front desk clerk, her lower jaw somewhere between her knees and her ankles. "Could you repeat that?"

The clerk's gaze was wide with apology. "I am very sorry. The hotel is sold out. Between the conference and the guests who decided to stay an extra night thanks to the brush fire, I'm afraid there are no rooms left."

"But I called," Grayson interjected.

Nelle glanced at him. Their easy, flirtatious camaraderie had continued for the rest of their time at the winery. But when they got into the car for the ride to the hotel, they'd pulled away from each other to check their phones for messages and emails. Nelle quickly dealt with hers—Mrs. Allen wanting a recap of Nelle's evening, Yoselin wanting one, as well, but with an emphasis on activities featuring Grayson—but Grayson dove head-first into his phone with a crease forming between his brows and didn't resurface until the car pulled up in front of the hotel's main entrance. The crease was still there.

The hotel clerk typed on his computer. "Yes, Mr. Monk, I see that in your file. You asked for another room. So we upgraded you from a suite to a bungalow. There is separate living and dining space in addition to the usual sitting area found in our suites."

"I made it clear I wanted an additional hotel room. Not extra space." Grayson's words held the snap of a steel trap springing closed.

The clerk took a whole step back. "We're very sorry for the misunderstanding. The upgrade is, of course, complimentary, but we cannot accommodate a room change."

Grayson raised an eyebrow.

The clerk's Adam's apple bobbed. "I can try our sister hotel, if you like?"

"Your manager, please. I'll wait." Grayson had his head turned away from her, but Nelle still saw tight muscles in his jaw jump while the crease in his forehead grew deeper. She touched him on the arm to get his attention.

"It's okay," she said. "The bungalow sounds like it's more than big enough for the two of us. It's still a better plan than trying to get home while the freeway is closed."

He finally turned to look at her, anger and apology present in equal measures in his expression. "I want you to be comfortable. If I can't resolve this with the manager, I'll stay here in the lobby. You can have the room."

"It's not a room, it's a bungalow. Don't be a martyr. Especially not on my account." She turned back to the clerk, who was trying desperately to look like he wasn't eavesdropping. "We'll take it."

The clerk said a few words into his headset, then

smiled at Grayson. "If you would wait here, I'll have one of the staff escort you to where you're staying. We've already taken your bags from your car, Mr. Monk, and put them in the bungalow."

Under any other circumstance, Nelle would have been thrilled and amazed to find herself staying at the Auberge de la Lune. Even she knew it was one of the most exclusive hotels in the country, if not the world. And in a bungalow! Separate from the rest of the hotel, set back amongst tall trees and completely private from prying eyes, the cabin-like space was everything she could have known to imagine and then more. It was like stepping into one of her favorite Instagram accounts come to life, and she mentally cataloged the two rooms and their accompanying bathrooms to describe them to Yoselin later.

The smaller of the rooms held the bed, made up with crisp white linens, plush silver gray blankets, and plump, down-filled pillows. Nelle poked her head in and out, intending for Grayson to make use of it. The larger room was the living space, divided into distinct areas. A small kitchenette occupied one corner, next to a wet bar stocked with bottles from brands Nelle had only ever seen on the very top shelf at pricey bars. The refrigerator was stocked with various luxury snack foods, and its lower half was specially designed to store wine. She recognized labels from nearby wineries.

Blond hardwood furniture gleamed everywhere, tempting her to touch the expensive but inviting surfaces. There was a desk with a conference table extension along a second wall, while a square fireplace cut seamlessly out of the far wall was the focal point of the space. The gas logs were alight, throwing dancing shadows on the wide, overstuffed sofa, two easy chairs and a sheepskin rug placed in front of the fire. She peeked inside a sizable closet and found additional pillows and throw blankets.

But her gasp was reserved for the items on display on the various tables dotted around the room. On the console that stretched the length of the back of the sofa was an ice bucket containing a bottle of champagne and a bottle of white wine. A bottle of red wine, chocolate-dipped strawberries and a box of handmade milk chocolate truffles accompanied it. One table to the side of the sofa held a selection of mineral waters in various flavors and a basket of artfully arranged fruit. And on the other side table were several shopping bags bearing the name of the hotel's boutique.

She heard Grayson come up behind her. "What, no rose petals?" she joked, indicating the champagne. At least she thought she was joking. "The strawberries are a nice touch, though."

Grayson picked up a small folded card from where it was halfway hidden by the chocolates. "It's from the hotel's management. A small token of their apology for the mix-up." He let the card drop back onto the table and made a beeline for his luggage. He opened up the smaller of the two cases and took out a laptop, then settled at the desk.

She grabbed a water, keeping her gaze off the romantic display of fruit and wine. "I like the way they apologize. What's in the shopping bags?"

For the first time since they arrived at the hotel, a smile creased his face. "Your things for tomorrow."

She peeked inside the first bag. Fine wool trousers in various shades of gray, black and cream were nestled in sheets of tissue paper next to sweaters so soft they must be pure cashmere. The second bag contained makeup and basic skin care necessities, by a brand she knew from its mention by celebrities on beauty websites. And the third—searing heat rose in her cheeks and she was amazed she didn't set the place ablaze by proximity. It held silky scraps of lace tied with ribbons, so impossibly delicate they could only be called lingerie. They were the furthest things possible from her usual cotton underwear.

She looked up, hoping he would put the color in her face down to the nearby fire. "I'm sure something here will work. The boutique will take back the rest?"

"Of course."

She gathered the bags up. "Do you want me to wait until you finish your work before I make up the sofa?"

He looked up, his gaze distant. "Why would you do that?"

"Why would I wait for you to finish your work?"

"Make up the sofa." He nodded at the door to the bedroom. "That's where you're sleeping. I'm fine with the sofa as it is."

"I can't let you sleep out here. Have you seen that bed? It looks amazing—" She stopped, her thoughts going to earlier that night and her desperate desire to find a room, any room where they could slake the desire that seemed to always overtake them. She cleared her throat. "I mean, I'm infringing on you already. You take it."

He turned back to the desk, his back straight, his shoulders set. "I have work that can't wait. If I were alone, I'd be out here anyway. The bedroom is yours." His tone suggested he wouldn't discuss it further.

"If you're sure." She clutched the bags to her chest, not sure what to do next. Should she give him a hug goodnight? Or a kiss—a chaste one, to thank him for the evening? Or—

"Sleep well," he said, his gaze locked on his screen.

"If I don't see you in the morning, best of luck with your meeting. The car will be waiting for you when you're done."

He was dismissing her. She should be glad. This was what she wanted, a clean farewell with no hint of seeing each other again. So why did her hands shake and her eyes sting? She cleared her throat and put a cheery smile on her face.

"Sounds good. Good night," she replied, and closed the bedroom door behind her. Through it she heard him moving around the other room, typing on his keyboard. She sighed. So much for engaging in a session with her right hand, starring him in her fantasies. She'd have to find another way to lull herself to slumber despite knowing he was just a few feet away.

Several hours later, she was still wide awake.

She should be able to sleep. The bed was one of the most comfortable she had ever lain on. Firm but enveloping. Like a cloud, but with perfect support. The linens were crisp and cool and slid across her skin with a silken whisper. She had her choice of pillows, from ridiculously overstuffed goose down to memory foam that contoured to her head and neck. The room was dark, the blackout curtains shutting out not only light but apparently sound from outside the bungalow. There was nothing to disturb her slumber.

Nothing, except her knowledge of who was on the other side of the bedroom door.

She scowled and punched a pillow back to its perfect shape. She was dehydrated. That must be it. After an evening of wine and barbecue, she required additional water. She turned on a light. The room was as she remembered. No mini bar, as the bungalow had its own kitchen area. And she'd already noted the bathroom lacked water glasses.

Ugh.

She turned off the light, tossing and turning before she remembered what was also in the other room: the bottles of delicious flavored mineral water sent up by the hotel's staff as an apology.

She checked the time. It was 2:00 a.m. Surely Grayson was asleep by now. He couldn't possibly mind if she took another bottle.

She picked up her dress from where she had placed it on the bench at the foot of the bed. The selections from the hotel boutique were thoughtful and extensive but didn't include pajamas. Perhaps—she blushed—the boutique employee thought as Grayson's guest Nelle wouldn't need any.

She didn't bother with her bra, pulling the dress over her head before her courage failed her. Then, on a deep inhale, she opened the door to the living space.

The fire still burned in the hearth, the gas logs turned down to an amber glow. The flames illuminated Grayson, half sitting, half lying on the sofa.

Her heart twinged in the oddest way, in an almost pleasurable pain. He looked so…young. And vulnerable, never a word she would have associated with him. Any furrows previously in his forehead were smoothed away, his jaw relaxed, his expression still. The fire burnished his hair, creating molten gold highlights that framed his face. He dwarfed the sofa's frame, causing her guilt over taking the bedroom to spike once more.

She crept farther into the room. His laptop, still open on his lap, was in danger of slipping to the floor. Sleek and light, and very expensive. No doubt he could afford to buy and sell an entire chain of computer stores, but she'd still hate to see this machine come to a bad end. She tip-toed to the edge of the sofa, then knelt on the fluffy rug. Reaching out her hands, she gently lifted the machine—

—and stared into Grayson's eyes, open and dancing with reflected fire.

Grayson wasn't sure if he was still dreaming or awake. This certainly had all the qualities of a dream, his favorite one ever since the night of the gala. Nelle kneeling before him, her hair falling about her shoulders, her eyes wide and dark, her plump lips parted. He'd reach out his hand, cup the back of her head and pull her to him...

He was halfway to reenacting his dream when he realized it was Nelle's actual hair tangling around his fingers, Nelle's real gasp echoing in his ears. He blinked and let go, bringing his right hand up to run through his hair. One thing was for sure. He was no longer asleep.

"I'm so sorry... I was only trying to... I mean..." Nelle was babbling, as disconcerted as he was. "I didn't mean to disturb you. I wasn't..." She sat back on her heels. The fire threw her figure into relief, the dress clinging to curves outlined by the flames. "I saw the laptop and I was going to...um..." She mimed closing it and putting it on the side table.

His laptop was, indeed, about to hit the floor. He reached for it at the same time she did. Their hands met. Her gaze, a dark fathomless blue in the dim light, caught and tangled with his.

If saying good-night to her earlier had been difficult, knowing how she was just on the other side of the door, trying to find sleep now would be impossible. Not with his dream made real and within his grasp, not with her soft and warm and looking at him as if they were the only two people in the world. His groin tightened as he sat up on the sofa, slipped the computer from her grip and placed it on the table, holding her gaze with his. She was so close, all he had to do was lean forward and his mouth would be on hers, his tongue free to plunder her sweetness.

"Nelle."

"Yes?" she breathed.

"Either you go back to the other room or I'm going to kiss you. Your choice."

Her eyebrows rose while her delectable lips formed a perfect O. Then she rose on her knees as if preparing to get to her feet and leave.

That was the best option. He didn't have time for a relationship, and he didn't indulge in flings, finding there was always a hidden cost even when both parties had the most casual of intentions. And even if he did practice one-night stands as a matter of course, he wasn't sure he could do that with Nelle. He meant what he said to Evan. He liked her. He didn't want to hurt her, and she was already suspicious of him as it was, thanks to whatever she thought happened between their fathers.

On the other hand, if he didn't kiss her, he wasn't quite sure he would survive the night with his sanity intact. "Well?" he growled.

Her eyelashes fluttered and she got to her feet. She was walking away. Disappointment surged. But before it could swamp him, she returned and sat on the sofa next to him. In one hand she held the plate of chocolate-covered strawberries.

"I'm hungry," she said simply, putting it on the side table next to her. Then she picked up a strawberry and bit into it. With the berry's juice still glistening on her lips, she turned to face him and placed her lips next to his. "But not for food," she whispered against him.

He was starving. Starving for her, for the unique delight she and only she provided. His mouth met hers, the taste of strawberry and chocolate swirling around him as her tongue coaxed him deeper, harder. If kissing her in public had been thrilling, kissing her in private, with no one to see them except for a curious owl or coyote prowling past the windows, was pure erotic exhilaration.

They quickly became dissatisfied with the relatively chaste positions afforded by kissing while seated side by side. Her hands tangled in his hair as she straddled him where he sat on the sofa, her soft thighs on either side of him. He cupped her luscious ass, the slide of her velvet dress against his palms adding a new sensory thrill.

At the first taste of strawberry his cock sat straight up. With every stroke of her tongue he grew harder. Then he raised his hands to cup her breasts, her curves spilling over his palms, her nipples pushing against the velvet. He never knew his erection could be this heavy, this demanding. He took his mouth away from hers.

Her heavy-lidded eyes opened, her gaze dark and dreamy. "What is it?" she rasped, her chest rising and falling rapidly.

"We should stop now."

Some of the dreaminess left her expression. "Do you want to stop?"

No. No, he did not. He wanted to pull the velvet of her dress aside, draw her pebbled nipples into his mouth. He wanted to free his erection from its cloth prison and watch her berry-colored lips close around it. He wanted to lay her down on the sheepskin rug, open those soft thighs and draw her into his mouth, watch her scream her pleasure as the fire's glow burnished her skin. "It's late. You have a big meeting tomorrow."

"That's not a no." She rocked against him, her center pressing against his hungry cock, with only thin material separating them "Besides, are you sure I don't have something big now?" She grinned at him.

He cupped her face with his hands. "I want you. But I don't want you to think I planned this—"

She leaned forward and kissed him, taking the rest of his words away. "I know. I didn't plan this, either. But we're here. And I think I'm going to explode if we don't continue." She began to unbutton his shirt, her hands slipping below the cloth to caress his chest. Her thumbs found his nipples and she rubbed lazy circles around and over them.

If he thought his cock was already as hard as it could get, he was wrong. She wasn't the only one about to explode, and they were still mostly clothed. "If you insist," he managed to grind out.

She kissed a path from his jaw to his ear. "If you're really concerned about my rest, orgasms help me sleep." Then she slid off him, standing in the firelight. He watched, mesmerized, as she pulled her dress over her head. She wore nothing underneath.

Her breasts were even more beautiful than he imagined. Perfect round globes tipped with dark rose nipples that begged to be suckled and worshipped. Dark curls clustered in the V between her legs, below an hourglass waist and set off by beautifully curved wide hips. She smiled at him. "It's your turn."

She didn't have to ask twice. But he had more clothes than her. He busied himself shedding garments, looking up as he pulled off his shoes. She wasn't there. He frowned and stood up to look for her. "Nelle? Everything okay? Did you change your mind?"

"Of course not." She emerged from the bathroom off the living area. "I was looking though the amenity basket."

"Oh? Sudden craving for shower gel? Or a sewing kit?"

She bit her lower lip. "Well, I was thinking. I don't have condoms with me. I was hoping the hotel bathroom had some, but no. Or…you?"

He hadn't carried condoms in his wallet since he graduated college. "No."

"Oh." Then her gaze landed on him, almost fully nude. His male ego was gratified by how her eyes widened, her pupils dilating as she stared her fill. "You, um, still have one sock on," she choked out.

"Easily rectified." He moved to the sofa to sit down and remove it. "Unless the lack of condom made you change your mind."

She shook her head rapidly and moved to kneel in front of him, taking his foot into her hand. "Allow me."

She slowly rolled his sock down his ankle, her slender fingers caressing his skin as it was revealed. He bit back a groan. Who knew the lower leg was a major erogenous zone? His erection pulsed as she ever so gently tugged the article free.

She sat back on her heels and regarded him from under her eyelashes. "While I have you here… I've been thinking about this since the night of the gala. And considering we don't have condoms…"

She leaned forward. And then her mouth was on his erection, her wet, unbelievably hot mouth. She drew him in, her tongue swirling and licking, her fingers stroking, somehow knowing exactly how much pressure was needed and where to apply it to make him see stars behind his eyelids. He thought his fantasies were scorching, but the real thing was beyond anything his imagination was capable of conjuring. The pressure built before he knew it, demanding release and so he tugged her up, sweeping her the short distance to the sheepskin rug before them. He was not willing to end this night with her so soon. He had no idea if there would be another. This one shouldn't even be happening. But since it was, he wanted to make every minute last.

It was his turn to indulge his fantasy and so he gently laid her before the fire, kissing and nipping his way from her breasts to her inner thighs, stroking the soft skin and inhaling the sea salt scent he discovered there. Then he licked into her, finding her clit and ensuring it received the attention from his mouth that it deserved. She trembled, her breathing turning harsh and heavy, her hips starting to buck, and he let her guide him to what pleased her most until she shuddered and cried out. He traveled back up her torso, kissing the same path he had taken on the way down. Then he lay beside her, propped up on one elbow, tracing patterns on the gentle hill of her stomach as she came back to herself.

As he watched, something unfurled in Grayson. Something that had been present before, but easy to ignore. Now it straightened out, grew shoots, the roots digging in deeper.

He liked her. He really liked her.

This couldn't come at a worse time.

Her eyelashes fluttered. "Okay. That was…okay."

"Okay?" He grinned at her. "First you called my kiss adequate, now this was okay?"

She shook her head. "I mean, okay, let me get my breath back. Pretty sure it's in Nevada."

He kissed her forehead. "One orgasm, delivered. Do you think you can sleep now?"

She gave him a sleepy smile. "Maybe. But I hate to go to sleep with a guilty conscience."

He laughed. "What do you have to feel guilty about?"

"Unfinished business." She reached down between them, her fingers closing around his cock and finding his most sensitive places to stroke. He groaned and lay back. This time, he allowed her to complete what she had started earlier, coming so violently he was pretty sure he passed out for a minute or two. Then he guided her back to the bed, ensured she was tucked in tight, and fell asleep with his arm curving around her waist.

Until the phone rang, less than two hours later.

Seven

Nelle ignored the ringing phone, choosing to go back to her very compelling dream. She was in bed with Grayson Monk. Desire lit his golden-brown gaze. His mouth covered hers before moving to her neck, her breasts, and down her stomach—

The phone rang again. Nelle groaned and rolled over, punching her fist into the oddly hard pillow to find a more comfortable spot.

A loud male grunt caused her eyes to fly open.

Her head wasn't on a pillow, but a firm, warm and very male chest. She raised her head to find the object of her dream gazing down at her, sleepy amusement in his gaze.

"Good morning to you, too. And I think that's your phone."

"Sorry." Her brain went into overdrive, vibrating between two thoughts. She was in bed with Grayson. She had a meeting.

She. Was. In. Bed. With. Grayson.

And she was naked.

She pulled the sheets around her, scrambling to put some distance between them, only for Grayson to tug her head back down to his for a long, senses-drugging kiss. She blinked at him when he broke contact. What was she supposed to be doing again? His kiss drove all thoughts away.

He reached across her, found her ringing phone on the bedside table, and handed it to her. She took it from him with a discomfited smile. "Thanks." Then she looked at the screen and threw back the covers, heedless of her state of undress. "It's my alarm. For my meeting with Reid Begaye."

Grayson's gaze followed her as she gathered up the bags from the hotel boutique and ran-walked to the bathroom. She fought the urge to hide every imperfect bump and crease from his view, as she did when she had lived with Harry. Last night she'd done her best to embrace her new philosophy, telling herself to act confident, bold, unashamed.

Only she didn't have to act. He made her feel beautiful—no, that wasn't it, exactly. He made her feel like she was enough. Enough to be desired. Enough to be worshipped.

Enough for him.

Nelle liked being enough. It was a good change, feeling she didn't have to apologize for not being prettier or smarter or more sophisticated. And she had never been so aware of a man's appreciative gaze before. Harry's gaze hadn't lingered and it had certainly never caressed.

She could bathe in the light shining in Grayson's eyes all day.

She exited the bathroom, clad in gray fine wool trousers and a navy blue cashmere sweater so fine it floated over her skin as if spun from mist by angels. Grayson was in the living room, intent on his laptop. He was also shaved and showered thanks to the second bathroom, his dark blond hair showing the tracks of the comb he'd used to tame it for the time being. It was hard to believe the man who looked every inch a Silicon Valley executive in his crisp white shirt, sport coat and tailored trousers was the man whose skin she had explored with her fingers, lips, tongue.

"Hey," she said, a tentativeness she didn't feel when they were naked descending on her now that they were both clothed.

He looked up, his gaze distant at first but sharpening to appreciation as he took in her appearance. "My compliments to whoever picked out that sweater."

She did a slow pirouette. "This is okay for meeting Reid?"

"Okay is a highly inadequate description."

She tucked a lock of hair behind her ear. "I'm going to go to my breakfast now. I…" This was where she usually stammered and hesitated, wondering if he would ask to see her again, agonizing if he would call or text her. She hated one-night stands. She never got the hang of divorcing her expectations from the act of having sex. She wished she could learn how to enjoy a good time and walk away, chalking up the experience as a one-and-done moment in time.

But she had no other choice. She was not getting involved with a Monk. Sure, they had amazing chemistry, and now they knew it resulted in amazing sex. That should be enough. It would have to be enough.

She straightened her shoulders and held out her right hand. "I want to formally say goodbye, since the last time we…kissed… I rudely ran away. I can't thank you enough for inviting me to the wine tasting. And I'll send a check to your office for my new outfit." After getting an advance on her paycheck, that was.

Grayson looked at her outstretched palm, and then stood up without taking it. "That sounds final."

"Well, I mean…that is…" Damn it. She was babbling. Again. She took a deep breath, trying to force herself to meet his gaze and failing miserably. "We're both adults. Adults have sex. It doesn't mean anything."

He took her hand then, but instead of shaking it he used it to pull her in close. She resisted the urge to close her eyes and lean into him. Lean into him and wrap her arms around his neck and not let go for a very long time. "Then that's where we're different. It does mean something to me," he said.

Her gaze flew to meet his. "Wait. It does?"

He caressed her jawline with his thumb, then cupped the back of her head and brought her mouth to his for a long, deep kiss. He lifted his head just enough to speak against her lips. "It does."

Then he let go of her and returned to the low sofa, picking up his laptop again. "But if you don't feel the same way, I'll respect that. Either way, I'll be in the lobby after your meeting to make sure you get home."

She wasn't sure she could form coherent sentences after that kiss, much less make a cogent pitch for the nonprofit. But the promise in his words that this wasn't a one-night stand and he wanted to see her again—later today, even!—carried her on a cloud of hope she didn't even dare express to herself.

Reid was charming. There was no other word to describe him. At another time, in another place, he would have swept Nelle off her feet. He was smart and witty and listened intently to what she had to say. His questions were intelligent and pointed, and he made astute observations. Although it lasted well over two hours, at any other point in time breakfast would have flown by for Nelle.

But it didn't fly by, because every minute was a minute she anticipated seeing Grayson again. The anticipation made the hands on her watch seem to move so slowly that it felt as if a turtle could have completed a marathon between every tick.

Then Reid promised to pledge at least two million dollars from his foundation toward the completion of Create4All's new facility. That got her attention. Their conversation shifted to outlining the next steps.

Well, it got most of her attention.

"We'll have to see your books." Reid folded his napkin and put it down on the table next to his plate. "We need to ensure Create4All meets with the foundation's standards and guidelines for financial transparency and program spending. I'll warn you now, they're very stringent."

"Of course," Nelle agreed, folding her own napkin and placing it on the table. She'd barely touched her cheese omelet. "I'm sure the board of directors will be thrilled to give you all the information you require."

Reid nodded. "I'll have my grant director get in touch. Let me send a few emails while I'm thinking of it." He took out his phone, tapped on the screen for a few minutes, then rose from the table to help Nelle out of her chair. "I hate to leave so abruptly after such a great discussion, but."

"I understand." She smiled. "Break a leg at the keynote."

"More like break heads. The heads of the people I'm speaking to, that is. They're not going to like what I have to say to them." He smiled and held out his hand. "I'm not just saying this. I enjoyed our breakfast."

His large hand enveloped hers, his grip firm and warm. But no sparks traveled from where their hands met. The air remained free of electrical charge. "I did, too."

He nodded at the business card clutched in her hand. "You know where to find me Now tell Grayson he can call off the rescue party."

"Rescue party?"

Reid nodded at the nearby entrance to the restaurant. "He's been pacing in the lobby, glaring at me though those glass doors."

"He's what?" She swiveled in her chair to look behind her. Grayson was indeed in the lobby, but he was seated in a chair, speaking to what looked like a fellow conference attendee. But as soon as she spotted him, he looked up, catching her gaze with an easy smile.

Her stomach clenched, then fluttered in response.

"Okay, so he just sat down," Reid said. "Anyway, like I said, you know where to find me. See you around." He gave her a tip of his Stetson before he exited.

Nelle stayed seated, gathering her thoughts before she joined Grayson in the lobby. The image of his smile lingered before her. This was bad. She was more excited about the prospect of being in his company than she had ever been waking up on her birthday.

Be cool. Sure, last night had been amazing. But the lack of a condom had stopped them from exploring more of each other. Maybe he said those things to her so he could have the full experience before discarding her. Because he would. That's what Monks did to people like her.

Or at least, that's what his father did. Maybe—she glanced back at Grayson, who was engrossed in his conversation—maybe that didn't have to be their fate. After all, he said their night together meant something to him.

If she were being honest, it meant more to her than she could describe as well.

When she finally entered the lobby, Grayson broke off his discussion and stood up to greet her.

"Meeting go well?"

There was his grin. It warmed her insides, causing them to melt to the consistency of marshmallow fluff. All thoughts to channel her inner Elsa and cool their interaction in an avalanche of ice melted away. "It did. Better than any of my expectations. Thank you again."

"I had nothing to do with it. If Reid is making a donation, that's all your doing." He moved closer. Her nose caught notes of grapefruit and blood orange from toiletries provided by the hotel, plus a scent she recognized from the night before as uniquely his. Indescribable in words, but she would know it was him in the pitch dark.

Which made her think of other things she'd like to do to him in the dark. And in the daylight. At twilight. During the late afternoon. Or midmorning, like now.

Damn it. Last night should have lessened the urge. Dissipated the heat that seemed to materialize every time they were close enough to touch. Instead, the flames leaped even higher. "Still, you deserve my thanks. For bringing me. And for, well, last night. I mean, providing a place to stay. Among other things."

His mouth turned up in a lopsided smile. "I should be thanking you. After all, you saved my computer from a possibly fatal fall. Among other things."

She wanted to run her fingers along his stubbled jawline, explore with her own mouth where his smile dented his left cheek. She settled for, "My pleasure. Especially the…other things."

His gaze darkened, the golden shards in his irises standing out in bright relief. "I would very much like a physical demonstration of those other things, just to make sure we're on the same page. Unfortunately, I need to immediately return to San Francisco. The valet is pulling my car around now."

"Oh." She didn't know why her skin ran cold, as if an immense gray cloud dumped stinging rain on her head.

"I can give drive you home," he continued. "But I have to stop by my place in the city first. There's a video conference call I need to take from my home office. If you want to go straight home or to Create4All, I can have the driver take you instead."

The cloud lifted. She tilted her head to one side as she pretended to ponder the choice. "You know, I'd love to see more of San Francisco. The gala was my first time back in the city in years."

"If you don't mind waiting for my call to finish, I'm happy to play tour guide after." He offered his left elbow to her and escorted her to the lushly landscaped front entrance of the hotel, where his Tesla Model S awaited. The bellman placed a bag bearing the hotel boutique's label in the trunk as she sank down on the smooth leather of the passenger seat, marveling at the large touch screen that served as the car's dashboard. In some ways, the car was a metaphor for Grayson: sleek, unexpected, startling.

If she had a car capable of driving itself like a Tesla, she would get into trouble. She would let her guard down and put too much trust in it. She wouldn't be safe.

The same was true of Grayson. If she kept giving in to the temptation of his company, she was going to be in serious trouble. Although, if she were being honest, she'd flown past the signs warning of danger as soon as she opened the door to the bedroom last night.

They managed to drive to San Francisco without incident despite the distraction of being seated next to each other, close enough to run her hand along his thigh, near enough for him to lean over and capture her mouth at every red light. When they reached his place, a penthouse condominium on top of Nob Hill, she thrummed with desire. It was almost a relief when he left her in the open living area, promising to return as soon as he finished the call in his office. It allowed her to think straight again.

His home occupied the entire top floor of his building and was furnished in a masculine, minimalist style. Dark leather furniture and ebony wood shelves stood out against creamy white walls, decorated at intervals with abstract paintings featuring bold splashes of color.

She wandered to the floor-to-ceiling windows that lined one wall, offering panoramic vistas of the city below and the bay beyond. She had a bird's-eye view, and as if to illustrate the point, a seagull flew past as she watched tiny sailboats bob in the distant dark blue water.

Next to her stood an accent table with a display of several photos. She picked up one at random. A black-and-white Grayson smiled back at her. He stood next to his sister, who shared his square jaw and dark eyes.

Standing on the other side of Grayson in the photo— her heart skipped a beat—was his father. She'd recognize Barrett anywhere. From him, Grayson inherited his easy smile and dark blond surfer hair.

She ran a finger across Barrett's face, wondering how the demon of her bedtime stories could look so...normal. So relaxed, so happy to be with his children. Not a fang or evil eye in sight. But she knew the damage he'd done to her family. At least, she thought she did. The last week had turned her preconceptions upside down, inside out and sideways.

Perhaps Grayson was right. They were all the protagonists of their own individual stories. In telling a story that made himself the hero, did her father cast Barrett as the villain undeservedly?

"That was taken at Dad's last victory party," Grayson said from behind her.

"I wondered at the balloons. You, and your sister both look too old for it to be a birthday celebration."

"And just as I locked in the balloon shipment for my next birthday."

She laughed and put the photo down. "Is your meeting over? That was fast."

He made a noncommittal noise. "It's over for me. I have more pressing items to take care of."

"Take as much time as you need. I'm enjoying the view." She indicated the panoramic city scene before her.

"So am I."

She glanced up to realize his gaze was not focused on the hustle and bustle of the streets below them, but on her. A warm flush traveled from her cheeks to her chest.

"And the first urgent item on my agenda," he continued, "is the sightseeing I promised you." He came to join her at the window, his left arm brushing her right, causing the tiny hairs on her skin to rise up.

"I feel like I'm getting an aerial tour from here. Look, there's the Bay Bridge. And Treasure Island." She raised her right hand to point.

"That's Yerba Buena Island. Treasure Island is next to it." He took her hand in his, moving it a fraction of an inch. "Here," he said, low into her ear.

She shivered as his breath whispered against her cheek. "And the smaller island over there?"

"Alcatraz."

She knew that. But she liked having an excuse to keep

her hand in his. "What about the building shaped like a cylinder?" She turned her head to look at him.

Their mouths were millimeters apart.

"Coit Tower," he said.

"And that one?" She had no idea what she pointed at. She was focused on his lips, firm and beautifully shaped. Her mouth fit against his as if they were two pieces of the same puzzle. She suddenly very much wanted to kiss him again.

"I'm guessing… Transamerica Pyramid."

"You don't know?" Her gaze rose to meet his. Then her breath seized at the sheer want in his gaze. Want. For her.

"You're all I see right now." He lifted the back of his hand to her cheek, his thumb caressing the curve of her jaw.

Her heart skipped a beat then sped up, a timpani played at lightning speed.

"All I want right now is you," she managed to get out, and then she was kissing him, or he was kissing her. She didn't care, she only wanted the sweep of his tongue in hers, to suckle on his tongue in return.

The night before had been a waking dream. Midnight dark, the world silent and fast asleep, exploring each other on a luxurious rug in front of the fire: it was easy to tell herself sex with him was a once-in-a-lifetime indulgence of her imagination. The chance to fulfill her teenage wishful thinking, hero worshipping the hometown national swim star from afar.

But it had been pure fantasy, in a hotel bungalow that cost more per night than her share of monthly rent. Even as she shuddered underneath his insistent mouth, she refused to believe it had been real.

But now… He lifted her sweater and she helped him

remove it, breaking their kiss just long enough to pull it over her head. Then they were kissing again, his hands cupping her breasts, stroking her through her bra, her nipples hard and aching and begging for more. Then her bra was off and he gave her nipples what she desired, pulling them into his mouth, rolling them with his tongue.

She took the first chance she had to unbutton his shirt and tug it free from the trousers. He was now sporting a very impressive bulge. She caressed him through the fabric of his pants, loving the way he jerked against her, his arms pulling her tight against him, trapping her between him and the window. She gasped as her bare back met the glass, her superheated skin and the cold surface combining to shock her into even more awareness.

He glanced up from where he was unbuttoning her trousers. She stared back at him, unable to talk, only able feel the smooth coolness behind her, his warm fingers at her belly, her breasts bare and exposed to the air. He tugged her trousers down and then she was nude, save for the tiny wisp of silk covering her sex.

Despite the bright sunlight streaming in from the windows, his eyes dilated deepest black as they took in her newly acquired lingerie. "Is that from the hotel?"

She nodded, still unable to draw in enough oxygen to speak.

"Remind me to send whoever chose your clothes a thank-you card."

Then he was on his knees, his mouth kissing her though the soaked silk. His right hand came up to hold her still, pressed against the glass, as his right hand brushed the flimsy panty aside. Then his tongue and fingers took turns, licking, pressing, circling. It didn't take long. She had been on fire for him since the moment she punched him that morning. She gave herself over to the spiraling demand, crying his name as she came.

She would have fallen if it weren't for his arms. He held her up, stroking her back as she collapsed against him.

But she wouldn't let him see just how thoroughly he'd burned through all her defenses. How she was already halfway to being in love with him. She lifted her head and gave him a crooked smile. "That was decent."

"Decent, adequate, okay—I might develop a complex." He nipped at her earlobe.

"I like what's developing here." The bulge in his trousers was larger than before. She squeezed it gently, receiving a groan in return. "Please tell me you have condoms."

"Left pocket," he grunted. "Put them there after my phone call."

She slipped her hand into his pocket, brushing against his erection through the pocket lining as she did. He jerked against her.

"Let's get you undressed. And then dressed again." She carefully unzipped his fly, then pushed down his trousers and briefs. His erection sprung into her hand and she reveled in rolling on the condom, loving the velvet smoothness, the heavy firmness. "Bedroom?" she whispered against his lips when she was done.

He smiled, and the wickedness lurking there made her gasp with anxious anticipation. He kissed her, hard, deep, then turned her in his arms so she faced the window and he was at her back. "Since you seemed to like this last time," he rumbled in her ear. "Don't worry, the building was retrofitted for earthquakes. Not even an eight point zero will make this window fall out."

"I'm pretty sure that last one was a ten," she gasped,

and then she stopped forming coherent thoughts as he pressed her forward until her breasts grazed the glass, her already hard nipples puckering to points of painful pleasure. He nudged her knees apart and her palms flew up to rest flat against the window for support. Then he was at her entrance. Thick. Large. Demanding.

She cried out as he filled her. He rested his head against hers for a beat, letting her adjust to his size. Then he began to move, long strokes, hard strokes, building in heat and intensity. His arm came around to hold her, pulling her against him, helping her set the rhythm she required. His breathing was harsh in her ear, his scent surrounding her. Her knees started to tremble and he increased his tempo, pushing faster and faster. Her orgasm began to build again, a softly rolling one this time. Then he brought one of her icy hands down from the window to the front of her sex, pressed her cold fingers against her clit.

The orgasm hit her like a freight train without brakes. Then he shuddered against her, his movements gradually slowing until they collapsed together on a deep pile rug.

"I bet we shocked some pigeons," she said when speech returned to her.

"Someday we have to try that in a bed."

She glanced over at him. "My schedule is free for the rest of the day."

He shrugged. "I have an appointment to take someone sightseeing."

She lazily pointed at the windows. "You already showed me. San Francisco is that way. Your job is done."

"Well, there's one more place I might want to show you. And by coincidence, it happens to have a bed."

She got to her feet, still unsure whether her legs could support her weight. "Where do I buy my ticket for this tour?"

Eight

Grayson watched as Nelle slept, burrowing deeper into the covers as protection against the chilly morning air. He gathered her against him, luxuriating in the feel of her skin against his, smooth to his rough, and inhaling her spicy-sweet scent. Maybe he could call in sick. Maybe he could persuade her to call in sick and they could play hooky for the day, have a long, fortifying breakfast to make up for the meals they'd missed in favor of staying in bed. But even as he played around with the thought, he dismissed it. Nelle took her job at Create4All seriously. And he had too much work to do as it was. Starting with an early-morning meeting with—

"Hello? Grayson? You here?"

Damn it. Finley. He knew it had been a mistake to give her the access codes to his home.

"Grayson? You can't possibly still be sleeping."

Nelle stirred beside him, then bolted awake. "Did I hear someone?" she whispered to him.

"It's my sister. Stay here. I'll get rid of her." He kissed her on the forehead. Then he threw on a pair of old sweatpants and headed to the kitchen, where Finley was making herself a cappuccino. Badly.

"You're going to break that," he warned, and took over from her.

"I don't know why you have a car with no visible controls and a coffee machine that looks like something NASA uses to land vehicles on Mars," Finley complained.

Grayson prepared a cup of steaming caffeine for her, then made one for himself. "We aren't supposed to meet until this afternoon. Why are you here?"

"Now that's an interesting question," she said. "Almost as interesting as what you did this weekend."

"I was here for most of it." Not a lie.

"As has been noted." She handed him her phone. "By the way, do be careful when you leave. There are some rather persistent paparazzi who want a follow-up photo, so your building's exits are staked out. The doormen can only do so much."

"What are you talking about?" Then he looked at her phone screen—and saw red. "What the hell is this?"

Finley tapped her chin with her right index finger. "I have to confess, when we discussed campaign girlfriends, I didn't think you would jump at the idea so eagerly."

Grayson stared at the phone. Finley's web browser was open to the gossip page for *Silicon Valley Weekly*. And there, filling the screen, was a photo of him and Nelle at the wine tasting, their gazes locked on each other, the angle of the photo making it look as if they were just about to kiss. Next to it, much smaller, was the previously published photo of the two of them, in their masquerade finery, in Embarcadero Plaza. "CINDERELLA UNMASKED" screamed the headline in bold, stark lettering.

"It's a nice photo, isn't it?" Finley said, peering over his shoulder at the phone. "They got your good side." She took the phone from his nerveless grip and opened a note-taking app. "Must remember to remind other photographers to do the same."

"Did you do this?" He was surprised how calm he sounded. Still, Finley took a step back.

"Do what?"

"This. Place this story."

She rolled her eyes. "No, Grayson, I did not. If you don't want your photo on gossip websites, then don't continue to kiss people in public places. You're a person of interest. It's just going to intensify on Wednesday when Dad steps down."

"I may be a person of interest, but she isn't. This is your only warning. Leave her out of—wait. Did you say Wednesday?"

"That's when Dad is announcing his resignation."

What the... "That's the day after tomorrow. It was supposed to be next month."

"Change of plans." Finley busied herself adding sugar to her cappuccino. "And before you ask, the change is final."

No. He needed more time, damn it. Time to wrap up his business. Time to discover if the connection he felt with Nelle was real.

It wasn't on his agenda to date someone. And he didn't have flings. It was why he was so successful as an investor: he only committed once he was sure, and then he worked hard at making the partnership a success.

It had been a mistake to give in to the temptation of a sleep-warmed Nelle, kneeling before him with fire reflected in her gaze. To indulge the rush of need that engulfed him as she stood next to him, her fingers trembling in his. The wisest course forward would be to cut off the relationship now, before the hooks became more deeply embedded in his heart.

Right now, only one commitment mattered. And that was the one he made to his family. But he could try to claw back as much time for himself as he could. "We have a deal, Fin."

"Tell Dad's heart and the episodes of tachycardia he keeps having that you have a deal. He could have hit his head when he fainted over the weekend—" She clapped her right hand over her mouth. "I'm sorry, he didn't want me to tell you. He doesn't want you distracted."

"Dad fainted?" The room appeared to revolve. Grayson grabbed the back of a nearby chair for balance. "He sounded fine last time we spoke. His doctors said he was well on the way to recovering."

"He is. He will." Finley sighed. "But I believe the resignation hanging over his head is causing the tachycardia. That's why we're moving it up."

Grayson shook his head, still trying to process the new information. "You should have told me. *He* should have told me."

"And if we told you, you would've dropped everything to visit him, and then we'd have even less time to prep for the campaign launch. He thought it was for the best."

"You agreed with him?"

She bit her lower lip. "It doesn't matter what I think," she finally said. "This is about you and him and the Monk legacy. I'm just the facilitator. My job is to make the way smooth for him and now for you."

"You're not a facilitator, you're my sister. His daughter."

"If you want to get my titles correct, I'm your half-sister. His stepdaughter." Something cold and dark flashed in Finley's gaze. "And I'm also your campaign manager and his chief of staff until he resigns. Let's keep our eyes on the prize, which is your election."

"The election isn't more important than family—"

Finley scoffed. "This *is* family. If you lose you might not be disowned, but I definitely will be."

"C'mon, Fin. You know that's not true."

She opened her mouth, then shut it with a snap. Then she smiled, the kind of smile he recognized from long experience meant trouble for the person on the receiving end. "So, let's talk Cinderella. Is she the one until the election or do we still need to find you a campaign girlfriend?"

"A campaign *what*?"

Ice water replaced the blood in Grayson's veins. He turned, dreading what he knew he would see.

Nelle stood in doorway, dressed in his robe. At any other time, the sight of her wearing an article of his clothing—the sleeves falling down to cover her hands, the tie wound several times around her waist to keep the voluminous fabric somewhat contained—would have made him grin. Then he would sweep her up in his arms and carry her back to bed.

Now, he ran through various responses, discarding them as quickly as they popped into his head. No, she wasn't hearing things. No, she shouldn't leave and he'd explain later. No, Finley wasn't making a bad joke.

His sister broke the silence that hung in the air after Nelle's question. She held out her right hand for a handshake. "Hi, we saw each other in Grayson's office but I don't think we've been formally introduced. I'm Finley Smythe."

"Nelle Lassen." Nelle held herself as if she were clothed in couture rather than his bathrobe. "Or perhaps I should say Cinder-Nelle-a?"

Finley broke into a delighted smile. "That's good." She turned to Grayson. "Keep this one. I can work with funny."

The arch smile on his sister's face shook him out of his impersonation of a statue. "You're not going to do anything of the sort," he warned, picking up Finley's mostly untouched cappuccino and placing it in the sink. "Thanks for literally dropping in but call next time." He turned to Nelle, his heart thudding in his ears. "Let's get dressed, go out for breakfast, and I'll explain."

She ignored him and his stomach sank further. She perched on one of the barstools at the island that separated the kitchen from the informal eating area, rolling up the sleeves of the bathrobe and crossing her long legs as if sitting down for the final round of deal negotiations in the boardroom. "Work with that how?" she asked Finley.

"You know Grayson's going to run for Congress, right? I'm assuming he told you."

Nelle nodded. "Yes, for your father's seat."

Finley clasped her hands together and beamed. "So I'm going to be your fairy godmother. For the duration of the campaign."

"All right. Enough is enough." Grayson picked up Finley's tote bag and thrust it at her. "Goodbye."

"Grayson, it's okay." Nelle caught his gaze. To his stunned amazement, she wasn't upset or angry or even shocked. Instead, humor lurked in her blue gaze. "I've always wanted a fairy godmother," she said to Finley. "What does that entail, precisely?"

"First, I need to know if you are committed. To the campaign, that is. What you and my brother decide to do afterward is your affair. Pun fully intended."

"Gee, thanks for that," Grayson deadpanned. "Nelle, would you like an espresso or a cappuccino? Alcohol optional." Irish coffee was supposedly invented in San

Francisco. Probably because the bartender had a sister like Finley.

"Would caffeine help make sense of this conversation?" Nelle asked him.

He shook his head. "No. I'm hoping the addition of whiskey will."

"So, are you?" Finley persisted. "Committed to helping us with the campaign?"

"Don't say anything," Grayson suggested to Nelle. "If we ignore her, maybe she'll go away."

Nelle leaned her elbows on the island's marble counter. The bathrobe gaped open, teasing his gaze until she pulled it closed. "I can't commit to something if I don't know what it is."

"Date my brother. Until the general election is over."

"I might not make it that far," Grayson interjected. At least Nelle seemed to be taking the conversation in stride. He might as well try to do the same thing. And then they could hopefully laugh about it in the future. *If* they had a future. The fact that Nelle still sat in his kitchen was the only thing keeping Finley employed as his campaign manager.

"When you make it," Finley corrected him, then addressed Nelle. "I'm not asking you to do anything different from what you're apparently doing now, judging by your current ensemble." She waved a hand at the bathrobe Nelle wore. "Just don't break up with him until the winner is announced."

"What if I said your brother very kindly offered to let me crash here and this isn't what it seems?" Nelle accepted the mug Grayson handed her with a grateful smile.

"See?" He raised an eyebrow at Finley. "Logical explanation for Nelle's presence, so there is no need to involve her in your machinations. We can strategize about the campaign later. Right now, Nelle and I both need to shower, get dressed and go to work."

"You know fully well explanation isn't synonymous with truth." His sister narrowed her gaze at him. "And I'm not leaving until I get my answer. Look, your sentiment score has steadily climbed since the story broke late last night. People really like the idea of you and Cinderella." She held out her phone, the screen exhibiting a line graph trending upward.

"Sentiment score—do I want to know what that is?"

"Grayson, you need to start reading the materials I'm sending you—"

Nelle took a long sip from her mug, watching the siblings argue, thankful to be forgotten for the minute. It was one of the most delicious cappuccinos she'd ever had. Trust Grayson to even make hot beverages more amazing than she could have imagined.

She hadn't planned on intruding on his conversation with Finley. Nelle had been warm and cozy in his bed, propped up by enormous goose down pillows while texting Yoselin not to expect her in the office until the afternoon. But then an email had come in from Reid Begaye. She was so excited by its contents she only had one thought: to share it with Grayson. After all, he was the one who made the introduction. So she'd followed the sound of the voices, intending to wait until he had finished with his visitor.

Then she heard the word "girlfriend." Suddenly, interrupting him was of prime importance.

She wasn't really considering Finley's proposal to date Grayson for the duration of the campaign, was she? Yes, they had explosive chemistry. Even now, despite his sister's presence, it took everything she had not to run her hands over the well-defined pectoral muscles on display, let her fingers follow the dusting of dark blond hair from his six-pack abs to where it trailed into his low-slung sweatpants.

But no chemical reaction lasted forever, right? She ignored the tiny voice in the back of her head exclaiming this was more than mere lust.

Her old self would have rejected the suggestion that she date someone for an ulterior motive—and not just someone. A member of the Monk family. Janelle's indignant nose would be in the air as she stormed out in huff. And rightfully so.

What Barrett had done to her father was unconscionable. She could recite the story by heart. When the client funds were discovered missing, Barrett had produced a second set up of financial books that showed her father made the withdrawals. Her father had searched but couldn't find the real records. He'd narrowly escaped jail, but his legal career was over. And if he had turned to gambling to make extra money, so what? What other choices did he have?

Her parents had fought constantly over finances and her father's drinking at the gaming tables until her mother finally left when Nelle was in ninth grade. If it weren't for her late grandmother, who ensured she graduated high school and received a scholarship to college… Nelle didn't want to think about how her life would be different.

She came by her hatred of Barrett honestly.

But so much had happened over the last week. The gala, the trip to Napa, the aching tenderness of the night before. The look in Grayson's eyes when he said their time together meant something to him. The inalienable truths of her world were being torn down and worn away.

A sudden lull in the argument appeared and she seized the opening. "I have a question."

Finley and Grayson swung their heads to look at her, both sets of eyebrows raised.

"What does it matter if Grayson is dating someone or not? Do the voters of El Santo really care that much about his love life?"

Finley laughed. "You wouldn't ask if you knew El Santo."

"Nelle grew up there," Grayson informed her.

Finley's eyes widened so much she reminded Nelle of an animated film character. "Oh, this can't get any better. Really?"

"Go Saints," Nelle said, referring to the local high school team's football team.

"Then you should know the answer to your question," Finley responded.

Yeah. Nelle did. It was one of the reasons why she'd left as soon as she could and never returned. A town that placed a premium on appearances was not kind to a child whose mother ran off with a married man and whose father was more often found in the dive bars outside the city limits than he was at his paralegal desk. It was why she threw cold water at the thought of Grayson running for his father's seat when speaking to Yoselin at the gala. Barrett Monk had done nothing to help El Santo face the realities of the changing world, choosing instead to bolster the residents' illusions and stoke their resentments. El Santo deserved a representative who sought to provide what the people needed, not promise them what they thought they wanted and could never receive.

But Grayson, as he reminded her several times, was not his father.

She addressed Finley. "Speaking of El Santo, you should know I'm Doug Lassen's daughter."

Finley's expression remined blank. "Is there a reason that should mean something to me?"

"Nelle's father and Barrett have a long-ago history," Grayson replied.

"Barrett was my father's legal partner and my father was disbarred when their practice broke up," Nelle said evenly, refusing to look at Grayson. She knew he still didn't believe Barrett had set her father up. No need to go into the details with Finley.

Finley thought for a second. "I like it," she said. "If Cinderella starts to feel played out in the media, we can use Romeo and Juliet."

"Stop—" Grayson warned.

Finley held up a hand. "Fine, no Shakespearean tragedies." She turned to Nelle. "This is the first I've heard of your father. And if I don't know, then Barrett doesn't care. But if you think this will be a problem, we'll find someone else."

"No. There won't be anyone else." Grayson put his hand on Nelle's shoulder, angling himself as if to protect her from Finley. The warmth of his touch penetrated through the plush fabric. "I don't care about sentiment scores. You need to drop this."

Finley threw up her hands. "You need to trust me. I know what I'm doing." She appealed to Nelle. "Save him from himself. Say yes."

Nelle's heart pounded. A year ago, she would have said no way to Finley's scheme. But wasn't the point of becoming New Nelle to take risks, to change her luck? Besides, she owed Grayson. A lot. He introduced her to Reid Begaye, and in the process probably saved her job.

And maybe, if she helped Grayson, she could turn around the story of the Monks and the Lassens.

Maybe it didn't have to end so badly this time.

She swiveled in her stool to face him. "Do you want this? Me, I mean. Until the election. Not that it would mean anything. Because it wouldn't. I don't want you to think that I would think—"

"Nelle." Grayson's dark gaze caught hers. For a second, they were the only two people in the room. In the world, for that matter. "I like you. I like being with you."

Did the sun suddenly come out from behind a cloud? The entire room seemed brighter, sharper.

"Is that a yes?"

"I don't want to drag you into Finley's ridiculous scheme." But before the light could dim and winked out, he continued. "I do want to continue seeing you."

She wasn't sure if she stood up or if he pulled her off her barstool, but then she was in his arms and his mouth was on hers. Their now familiar electricity arced between them, crackling with heat.

"Fairy godmothering starts tomorrow. Be ready," Nelle heard Finley say, followed by the sound of a door closing. But then Grayson's hands were cupping her rear end, lifting her, carrying her back down the hallway to his bedroom.

It's only a favor, Nelle told herself while she was still capable of coherent thought. An opportunity to repay him while perhaps changing the trajectory of their families' entwined histories. Nothing more. But even as the words faded from her brain, replaced by a sharp jolt of pleasure as Grayson's mouth pulled on the diamond hard peak of her breast, she knew they were a lie.

Nine

Nelle ran one hand through her newly cut hair and tightened her grip on the straps of her overnight bag in the other. One deep inhale later, she knocked on the door of Grayson's temporary residence in El Santo, a sprawling ranch house on the west side of the small city.

He opened it. At the sight of his smiling face, she exhaled, dropped the bag and threw herself into his arms for a very thorough kiss. The knot between her shoulders that caused them to bunch up around her ears for the entire three-hour drive southeast from Fremont vanished, as if by magic. Crossing the city limits into El Santo was never easy for her, but as always, his presence caused her to melt into a gooey mess.

The six weeks since that fateful morning in Grayson's kitchen had been a whirlwind of nonstop activity. Barrett had announced he would not seek reelection. The governor had called a special election to be held in November.

Competitors flocked to file the paperwork to run. So far, no one caused Finley particular concern, although she was keeping a wary eye on a retired rancher who owned vast tracts of land in the district. Grayson began to spend the bulk of his time in El Santo, reacquainting himself with his birthplace.

Simultaneously, Nelle's job had gone into overdrive as the contacts she made at the gala and the winery began to bear fruit. Nearly every breakfast, lunch and dinner—and the hours between—were booked with meetings and follow-up appointments and new social events. She finally had enough money saved to afford renting her own studio apartment so she could give Yoselin and Jason their privacy, but she was too busy to house-hunt. Not that Yoselin noticed, as she, too, spent most of her time at the office.

Nelle and Grayson started meeting on Monday mornings via video call to synchronize their calendars for the week. Today was one of the rare occasions Nelle had enough free time to drive out to El Santo, while, as far as she knew, Grayson only had one appearance at a local craft beer festival on his schedule.

"Hi," Grayson said after kissing her until her legs forgot how to do their job. She clung to him, her arms entwined around his neck.

"Hi yourself." She pulled back to smile at him, but it turned into a frown. "You look tired. Much more tired than you did on the call last night."

"You look gorgeous, as always. Although FaceTime never does justice to the color of your eyes." He smoothed a lock of hair off her face before growling in her ear, "It doesn't capture other things as well. Can't wait to see—and taste—those in person."

She laughed even as the promise in his voice made her

shiver. "But you have to admit FaceTime makes phone sex far more interesting."

"Not a substitute for the real thing."

"No. Speaking of…" Her fingers traced the angle of his jaw, the curve of his lips. "When do we have to be at the festival and do we have time to start the in-person activities now?"

"Five o'clock, and sadly, no. Finley put a meeting with the county farm bureau on my schedule at the last minute. Which I have you to thank for."

"Me?" She laughed and allowed him to pick up her bag and then escort her to the house's vast main room, which held the kitchen, dining area and large living space. "How did I do that?"

"You asked me if I understood life in this district. So I asked her to set up meetings with the local associations and trade unions." He dropped her bag next to a sleek sofa that looked like it had just been delivered from a showroom and never been sat on. Then he drew her into his arms, tucking her tight against him. "I may have grown up here, but I have a lot to learn about the constituents."

She felt the rumble of his words almost more than she heard them. She closed her eyes and nestled closer to his warm strength. "You'll get there."

He kissed her forehead and let her go. "Which means I need to leave. I'm sorry."

"No worries. We have tonight."

"We do." His phone rang. He looked at the screen, declined to answer and sighed. "I told them not to call unless it was an emergency. Yet it never stops ringing. Will you be okay here by yourself for a few hours?"

"Of course. I wish I could help you somehow, though."

"Knowing you're here, waiting for me, will help me more than you know. And unless you want to go over my personal receipts before I turn them into the campaign treasurer, there's not much else you can do."

"As a matter of fact, I probably can." This…whatever they were involved in…had come so out of the blue, there was a lot they still didn't know about each other's pasts. "I'm a certified financial planner. I've been known to look at receipts before."

Surprise creased Grayson's brow. "You are?"

"Well, I was. It's a long story. I'm happy to tell you if you want—"

His phone rang again. He declined the call with an annoyed gesture. "I do want. Tell me tonight?"

"I'd rather do other things with our time together, but sure."

His mouth twisted in a crooked smile. "I'm a good multitasker. In the meantime—if you want and you're not obligated—printouts of the campaign finance reports are on my desk, in the home office. Second door to the left off the hallway."

"Got it."

He picked up his keys and shoved them in his pocket before turning back to her. Taking her face in his hands, he traced the contours of her face with his gaze, lingering on her lips before looking into her eyes. "It's hard enough to hang up after our phone calls. It's hell to leave when you're here next to me."

"I'll still be here when you get back. In the flesh." She turned her head to kiss the palm of his hand where it cupped her cheek. "And maybe nothing else."

He groaned before crushing her mouth with his. "I'm canceling the beer festival appearance."

She lost herself once more in his kiss, until something hard vibrated against her. "I'd say you're happy to see me, but I'm pretty sure that's your phone again."

"Right on both accounts." He kissed her again, hard and fast. "See you in a few hours."

"Bye." She watched him as he left, then turned to take in her surroundings.

As far as rented houses in El Santo went, it was a very nice one. Similar in style but far larger than her childhood home. Something sparkling out the window caught her eye and she smirked. She hadn't grown up with a fully landscaped swimming pool in the backyard, either. The lots on her family's side of town were barely big enough for an inflatable wading pool.

Still, there were certain touches—the fireplace made of local stone, the still-wrapped gift basket on the counter containing nuts and dried fruits from nearby orchards— that were wholly El Santo. She wrapped her arms around herself. According to the old saying, you can't go home again, and she was more than fine with that. She'd not only shaken the dust off her shoes and left town, she'd thrown the shoes away. And until she met Grayson, she hadn't had any reason to return.

She ran her fingers over the smooth leather of the modern couch and noticed how her feet sank into the deep pile rug. She might have grown up in a place like this if Barrett hadn't betrayed her father, if her mother hadn't subsequently left him for someone with a steadier paycheck. But the thought didn't bring its usual resentment. Yes, what happened then was awful. Her father wasn't able to recover. But the past didn't need to continue to hurt her. She and Grayson could figure out the future.

Smiling, she set off down the hall toward Grayson's home office.

Two hours later, she was knee-deep in receipts, making notes for Grayson of any questions she had, when she heard a man clearing his throat. She looked up with a smile. "You're back! I didn't hear—"

She froze, her blood congealing somewhere around her ankles.

It wasn't Grayson standing before the desk as she expected.

It was his father.

"Hi," he said with an easy grin, holding out his right hand for a handshake. "I'm Barrett Monk." She took his hand, her muscles acting on autopilot. Then he sat down in the overstuffed wing chair placed by the side of the desk. "You must be Nelle."

She nodded. She knew she should smile, speak. But she was frozen, her nerves encased in ice. She could only stare at him, her gaze fixated on the man whose name had haunted her growing up.

He was shorter than she anticipated. In her childish daydreams of revenge he had loomed over her, a monster of epic proportions. He was slight, too, for someone who'd taken his partner, one of the state's most promising litigation attorneys at the time, and broken him into pieces that couldn't be reassembled. But then his power lay not in brute strength but in his charisma, which hit her like a gust of wind from a winter storm. This was someone who got what he wanted because he made people gladly want to give it to him.

After what felt like an eternity but was probably more like ten seconds, she cleared her throat and forced her lips into a semblance of a smile. "Hello. Grayson's not here, but he should be back soon."

"Oh, I know." Barrett crossed one leg over the other and leaned back in his chair, as if he were an old friend stopping by to catch up. "I spoke to Finley before I headed over. She told me he was heading into a meeting with her and the farm folks. She also told me you were here."

He came here on purpose to see her? Nelle's stomach roiled. For a second she wondered if he was there to confront her about her father, but she dismissed it. Finley had said if she didn't know about the Lassen-Monk feud, then Barrett didn't care.

And Barrett's appearance wasn't a complete surprise. She'd been anticipating a meeting ever since Barrett's doctors gave him the all-clear last week to resume limited activities. She just wished Grayson was there.

Nelle made her smile bigger. "I hope this means you're feeling better."

"Eh, doctors." Barrett waved them off. "Bunch of old biddies, worried about the slightest blip and bloop. I'm going to live a good long time yet, don't you worry."

"I'm sure Grayson and Finley are happy to hear that." She straightened the keyboard on Grayson's desk so that it perfectly aligned with the edge of the desk, made sure all the pens had caps and were facing in the same direction. Anything to avoid being caught by Barrett's gaze. "I was about to get something to drink. Would you like something?"

"I'd like to talk to you. That's why I'm here, while my son and Finley are busy doing what they need to do."

"I—" Nelle began, but Barrett cut her off.

"Finley tells me you're doing a bang-up job for the campaign. You standing by Grayson's side has been a big help with the voters. I wanted to meet you and extend my thanks in person for your helpful contributions."

She blinked. Of the list of things she expected Barrett to say when they finally met face-to-face, this didn't make the top ten thousand. "But I'm not..."

She wasn't…what? Not acting the part for the campaign, but Grayson's actual girlfriend?

But was she? Really? He'd said he didn't want to go along with Finley's scheme. But on the other hand, they hadn't discussed their involvement beyond a vague "let's continue to see one another." They'd both been so busy. And when they did have limited precious time together, they were usually occupied with activities other than talking about their relationship.

She tucked a lock of hair behind her ear. "That's nice of Finley to say. Did Grayson agree?"

Barrett continued as if he didn't hear her. "The Cinderella thing is pure gold. Stroke of genius. My congratulations."

"I'm afraid that had nothing to do with me." Barrett's smile deepened. "You're modest. That speaks well for you. It's good to have you on the same page as us, Nelle."

The room was spinning, ever so slightly. "And what page is that?"

"The page where we all want Grayson to win, of course."

"I want Grayson to be happy," she countered.

Barrett chuckled. "Exactly. And for Grayson to be happy, he needs to fulfill the role he's prepared for his entire life. It's good to know you feel the same way, Nelle. I've got the feeling I can count on you. I can, right? Count on you?"

She finally looked him in the eye. His irises weren't the warm brown of Grayson's, but a dark, mesmerizing gray. His gaze pulled her in, as inescapable as gravity.

"Count on me for what?"

He spread his hands out and chuckled. "Why, just what we were talking about. Making Grayson happy by helping him win."

"I…he knows I'll help however I can. Whatever he thinks is best."

"Well, now, that's the thing. He doesn't really know what that is." Before she could interject, Barrett got out of his chair and walked to the front of the desk, placing his hands on the surface and leaning so they were face-to-face. "He may think he knows, but he's new to this game. I know, I know, he's a big deal up where you live, but around here, folks still think he's the kid who spends more time in the pool than on land."

"I don't think that's how voters see him—"

"I appreciate you defending my son. But I've been riding in this rodeo since before either of you was born. So can I count on you? This is Grayson's future happiness, after all."

Barrett's eyes twinkled with folksy charm, but hard-edged steel backed his words. She leaned back in her chair and crossed her arms over her chest. "Count on me for what?"

"Well now, you come to campaign events, you look pretty…" He ran his gaze over her. "Which you do, but Finley should gussy you up more. You smile at the cameras. And when the campaign is over, you go home. By yourself."

Her pulse thudded in her ears. "By myself? I'm not sure I know what you mean—"

"Nelle, let me tell you something about men. We are simple creatures. We can either think with what God gave us between our shoulders or between our legs, but not both at the same time. Now, it's fine you two are having some fun at the moment. But when the election is over it will be pedal to the metal and my son will need to think with his brain."

"What makes you think he's not doing that now?"

She held up her chin as she met the man's dark gray gaze head-on for the first time.

Barrett smiled, baring his teeth. It made her shiver. "You're a smart woman so I'm going to be straight with you. You're just fine for the campaign. I'm mighty thankful to have you on board."

"But?" Her heartbeat was almost deafening.

"But the Monks, well, we have a long, long legacy. Grayson's been raised to know his place. And when the election is over, Finley and I will find him a partner who can help him navigate Washington. He'll need one if he's going to succeed. And the more success he has, the happier he will be. We both agreed that's what we want for him." His gaze bored into hers.

"You're deciding what happiness looks like. I want him to decide that for himself."

Barrett leaned back in his chair. "I told you, he doesn't know enough yet to do that. But I think you do. Be honest, Nelle. Do you have what it takes to help my son be a successful congressman, heck, even president some day? To truly make him happy in the long run?"

She didn't answer. She'd be damned if she let Barrett see how many of her buttons he'd managed to push with exquisite precision. She focused instead on how Grayson's eyes lit up when he saw her, how he crushed her against him as if he never wanted to let her go. Their relationship, new as it was, did make him happy.

For now. The nagging voice in her head would not stop repeating the phrase on a loop.

In the silence, she heard the front door open. "Nelle? You still here? Ready for the festival?"

"In your office," she called, then stood up from the desk, knees trembling, and walked around it to face

Barrett. "Good. We can ask him together about what he wants—"

But before she could finish, Grayson appeared in the doorway. "There you are...oh. Dad. I didn't know you were dropping by. How are you feeling? Do you need me?" Concern flooded his expression.

Barrett beamed at Grayson as if he and Nelle had been discussing the weather, nothing more. "I'm fine, son. Just feeling lonesome rattling around in that big house by myself now that the nurses have been dismissed. Finley mentioned the lovely Nelle was in town and I knew you were busy, so I asked my driver to bring me here in order to introduce myself. Hope you don't mind."

Grayson looked at Nelle, and she saw the apology in his expression. "Your doctors want you to take it easy, Dad. I was going to ask them if I could bring Nelle by your place tomorrow. This wasn't how I planned to introduce you to each other." He reached out and took Nelle's right hand, squeezing it gently.

She knew he was asking if she was okay. She gave him a reassuring squeeze back. "We had an interesting conversation. We both agreed we want you to find happiness."

Grayson's brows nearly hit his hairline. "Sounds very metaphysical and 'follow your bliss,' which isn't like either of you. But I'll take it."

"Speaking of, how would you define happin—"

"Why don't you get changed for the festival, Nelle," Barrett drowned out her words. "I overhead Finley saying she left some new clothes for you in the guest room closet. My voters sure do like a pretty girl in a dress."

"Nelle looks great as she is," Grayson said. "I love Radiohead."

Nelle looked down at her vintage band tour T-shirt and well-worn jeans, paired with sneakers. "I thought this would fit the craft beer vibe. But Finley has been having such a good time playing fairy godmother, I hate to disappoint her." She squeezed Grayson's hand one last time before leaving the room. But he wouldn't let her go.

"You don't need a different outfit," he said. "Dad, do you want us to call your driver or should we drop you off on our way?"

"I'll take a ride, thank you, son. But before we go, there's one more thing I want to say to Nelle." Barrett folded his hands together in front of him. "Nelle, I am very sorry about what happened with your father."

Someone was breathing heavily in her ear. She gradually realized it was her, as her lungs strained to take in enough air. Grayson's palm was icy against hers. Or maybe the cold came from her own hand. She couldn't tell.

Grayson's gaze locked onto Nelle. "Dad? What do you mean?"

Barrett gave another of his expansive shrugs. "This happened before you were born, son. And you probably didn't hear the stories later because you were so busy with your practices and swim meets. But Nelle's dad got himself into some very hot water. Was even disbarred for stealing from clients. It was the talk of the town for a while." He turned to Nelle. "My big regret is I didn't do more to help him. We were friends in law school. We even thought about practicing law together. But your dad…he always did like the fine things in life a little too much. Taking off for the casinos as often as he did didn't help matters. Then your momma ran away. And if she couldn't change him… But I should have reached out, offered a hand. I always thought he resented me for not being a better friend, and y'know what? He was right. Please let Doug know I think of him often and wish him well. He's in Vegas now, if I'm not mistaken?"

Nelle stared at him, unblinking. Unmoving. That wasn't the story. Still, Barrett's description held some truths.

Her father did like to gamble and live beyond his means. Did he tell her his version so he wouldn't have to take responsibility for his own weaknesses? She could ask him, of course. But she knew what he would say. He never wavered in his telling of the tale, which was one of the reasons why she found it so convincing. His certainty fed hers. Now her worldview trembled, threatening to break into a thousand kaleidoscopic pieces as she struggled to take in Barrett's words.

Grayson's fingers stroked hers. At any other time, she would have welcomed his touch, leaning into it and returning it with caresses of her own. Now it felt like pity. She shook her hand free. "Yes, he moved to Las Vegas while I was in college. I'll give him your regards," she said, her words sounding as if they came from a distance.

"I'd appreciate that," Barrett said. "And I want you to know I do not hold your father's criminal actions against you. We are so proud to have an El Santo girl beside Grayson during the campaign."

"Dad—" Grayson warned, but Nelle cut him off.

"Look at the time," she said, pasting a bright smile on her face. "If I don't change now, we won't make it to the festival for your appearance." She had to get away. From both of them. She needed to think.

"We'll meet you out at the car," Barrett said. "We're going to have so much fun campaigning together, Janelle." His grin was back, as charming as before. But when his gaze caught hers, it was hard and opaque. "You don't mind if I use your full name, I hope? It just seems more you."

She fled the room.

Ten

Grayson rubbed his eyes and closed a window on his laptop. "That's enough for today," he told Finley.

Finley looked up from her own computer on the other side of the makeshift desk and frowned. "So soon?"

"It's almost ten. I'd like to get some sleep before I drive to Fremont in the morning." He yawned, then raised his arms over his head for a stretch. For once, they were alone in the campaign office. At best a stark and utilitarian space in the daylight, the rooms were even more nondescript at night without staffers and volunteers buzzing around the long folding tables and metal chairs. Campaign posters and flyers were tacked to the walls to add some color but the overall effect was still institutional beige, especially under the fluorescent lights. He took a doughnut from the pink box that had been sitting out since the day before, bit into it, made a face and threw the rest away. "Also, I need real food."

"You just want to call Nelle where I can't hear you."
Finley continued to type on her laptop. "Which I'm all
for, by the way. There are some things campaign man-
agers don't need to know about their candidates' lives."

Nelle. He missed her. He wanted to be with her. In
person, not on a video call.

But he was no longer certain she wanted to be with
him. Something had intruded on the relationship they
had been so carefully and steadily building. The problem had started when she came to El Santo to attend the
beer festival three weeks ago.

He knew meeting his father hadn't been easy for her.
Especially when Barrett explained the truth of his history with Nelle's father. But after her initial shock, she'd
seemed to take it in stride. They'd had a great time together at the festival until she developed a killer headache. He'd done his best to nurse her through it, even
though his contribution pretty much consisted of running a washcloth under cold water to put on her forehead
and bringing her two aspirin. When they said goodbye
the next morning, her kiss had ignited a blaze that still
burned.

But ever since he watched her drive away, a barrier
had sprung up between them. It wasn't high. It wasn't
even that thick. But it was growing. It was almost im-
perceptible at first, but lately he brushed against it every
time they spoke.

"Has Dad said anything to you about Nelle?" he asked.

Finley shook her head without looking at him. "Not
really. He's happy she's from here. It's one more point in
your favor for the voters."

The sugar in the doughnut made his empty stomach
roil. Or maybe it was hearing Finley speak of Nelle as
if she were an inanimate object, a mere bullet point on a

presentation. He'd stated repeatedly that his relationship with Nelle had nothing to do with the campaign, and yet Finley continued to discuss her as if she were just another volunteer eager to help the cause.

"She's not a 'point,' as you put it. Or a campaign asset. I like her, Fin."

"Good." Finley kept her gaze on her screen. "She's the current girlfriend, so liking her works out well."

"I'm in love with her."

That got Finley's attention. Her gaze flew to meet his. "That's…great. Really great. She's a great person."

"I know I was scheduled to return tomorrow night, but I'm going to stay a few days longer in Fremont. I need you to clear my schedule."

She stared at him. "Why? I thought you were going for Nelle's work thing, whatever it is. And Barrett wants you to meet with Jon Wurtz while you're up there. His PAC was a major donor to Barrett's campaigns."

"Nelle's 'work thing,' as you put it, is a surprise lunch for her. She closed a four-million-dollar partnership with the Begaye Foundation." He shook his head. "No meetings. Clear means clear."

Finley pinched the bridge of her nose. "Okay. Don't meet Wurtz. But the debate is in two weeks. I need you to commit to the prep schedule."

"I've been prepping my entire life."

Finley shook her head so rapidly it was almost a blur. "That's not the same as prepping for this specific debate. Look, I get it, you're thirsty. Take a day, get it out of your system. But you need to take down your debate opponents and you're not there yet."

"It's not up for discussion." Grayson shoved his chair back, the metal legs scraping on the scarred linoleum floor. "I'm going to get some food and rest, then leave first thing in the morning."

Finley opened and closed her mouth a few times as if struggling with how to phrase her next words. That was a first for her in Grayson's experience. "If you have something to say, spit it out," he said.

Finley's sigh rang through the empty space. "Here's the deal. You're far ahead in the polls. So, yes, perhaps debate prep isn't the most pressing thing ever."

"Good. Talk to you in the morning." He turned to leave.

"But." The note in Finley's voice made him stop short. "The election is only the first hurdle. The easiest hurdle, in fact. If you win, you'll be moving to Washington for a good part of the year. And it's a twenty-four hour/seven days a week job. There's not a lot of downtime for…let's say, trips to Fremont. Which isn't even in your district."

Grayson regarded his sister. "You still haven't spit it out."

"I'm just saying you need to consider the effect winning will have on your life. And hers. You've known each other, what? Two months?"

"Longer."

"Not by much. Use that big brain of yours and think it through."

"I have."

Finley raised a skeptical eyebrow. "Sure, if you say so. But has Nelle?"

Irritation mixed with the stale sugar in his stomach. It was not a good combination. "A girlfriend for the campaign was your idea. Not mine."

"Yes, and I told you not to get serious. Date her, dump her."

"That's not happening."

"Then you and Nelle need to have a serious conversation."

He knew that. Finley's confirmation only renewed his determination to spend more time with Nelle. And figure out how to bring down the barrier for good.

He nodded. "We'll be fine." They had to be. He wouldn't accept anything else. "Clear my schedule for the next four days, okay?"

Finley's gaze searched his face. He kept his expression impassive. "I'll clear two days," she said. "If you commit to prep when you return."

"Three days." He bent down and kissed her on the top of her head. "Thanks."

"Just don't stink up the debate."

"I promise I won't." He looked over at her screen. "What are you working on?"

"Finishing today's emails. The accountants haven't heard back from Al on his review of the campaign finance report. Let me remind him he needs to sign it and then I can walk out with you." She started to type.

Grayson frowned. "Why haven't I seen the report?"

She glanced at him. "Al's the campaign treasurer, so he's in charge of signing and then filing it with the Federal Election Commission."

"Yes, thank you, I did pay attention when you explained campaign finances to me. But shouldn't I review it? I'm the candidate."

Her brow creased. "Do you want to review it? Barrett never did. Al was Barrett's treasurer for years. He'll let us know if he sees anything the FEC might object to. You have enough on your plate, especially since you're taking too many days off for a booty call."

Grayson ignored her last words. "Dad didn't have his own venture capital fund. I miss looking at numbers.

Send it to me. I should be more familiar with the finances than I am, anyway."

"It's almost two hundred pages of names and dollar amounts. You sure you want to see it? We're coming up against the deadline to file for this quarter."

"You should've seen some of the business plans I used to receive. This sounds like light bedtime reading."

"Your eyeballs' funeral." She hit a key. "Sent. Let's get out of here."

Yoselin held her champagne flute out to clink it against Nelle's. "To you!"

Nelle laughed. "Shouldn't I be the one toasting you and Jason?" She nodded at the solitaire diamond winking on the fourth finger of Yoselin's left hand.

Yoselin held her hand out to admire her new ring. "It is pretty, isn't it? But this isn't about me." She took a sip and put her glass down. "Today is all about you, babe."

Nelle smiled. "It feels good to have a win, I have to admit." She looked around the private room of the elegant Indian restaurant. The table for twelve was set with a red cloth and china plates, and an elegant orchid arrangement in the center. A robin's-egg blue box tied with a satin bow occupied the far end of the table. "But you didn't need to do anything special."

"Oh, please, Octavia begged us to put this together. Oh, and she's insisting you call her Octavia now."

"Really?" Nelle's eyes widened. "That's not the champagne talking?"

"Bring in a major sponsor and you get special privileges." Yoselin winked at her. "She should be here soon."

"Who else is coming? People from the office?" But her question was answered when a man in a familiar Stetson entered the room. "Reid! What a terrific surprise."

"Hey, Nelle." He kissed her cheek and shook hands with Yoselin. "I wouldn't miss this. You're my favorite project we've promised to fund this year, and I'm not just saying that because I'm hoping to talk to your boyfriend when he shows up."

Nelle caught Yoselin's gaze. "Grayson is coming?"

She shrugged. "To see you accept a four-million check from an international foundation to help Bay Area children learn and thrive? Of course."

"Well, when you put it that way…" Nelle bit her lower lip. It was strange—a good strange! —to have so many things in her life headed in a positive direction at once. She kept waiting for the other shoe to drop. "But he's so busy. He's really taking the time off?"

At Yoselin's answering grin, something like a dam broke inside Nelle. A swell of happiness rose and crested, breaking down the wall of doubts that had crept higher and higher since her conversation with Barrett.

She hadn't seen Grayson in person since the beer festival, when she ended up sleeping in his guest room with a cold washcloth on her head to alleviate her migraine. They spoke every day, but his schedule was becoming tighter and tighter and the phone sex…well, that was still scorching hot and explosive. But then they would hang up and she would be back to wondering what, exactly, was her place in his life.

She knew he liked her. He'd told her that much. He might even like her a lot. But he liked a lot of people.

She, on the other hand, had zoomed past the point of no return long ago. She was in love with him. She'd fallen in love with his warm gaze and smart wit even when the rest of him was disguised as a clown. She fell deeper in love each time he held her, creating a world that was just the two of them. She was hopelessly in love with his kindness, his hundred different ways to be thoughtful.

Every time she allowed herself to hope that maybe, just maybe, this relationship didn't come with a hard expiration date, Barrett's words would echo in her head no matter how hard she tried to dismiss them.

It's okay to have fun now. But do you have what it takes to make him happy in the long run?

For the first time since that conversation, she dared to believe the answer might be yes.

"He did say he might be late, depending on traffic, and to start without him." Yoselin looked through the curtains that separated their room from the main restaurant. "And here's Octavia and the rest of the board of directors now." She waggled her eyebrows at Nelle. "Shall I tell our waiter to bring out the popadums?"

The wave of happiness kept Nelle buoyant throughout the various courses, from appetizers to *rasmalai* for dessert. But as the final plates were cleared and the last of the wine bottles were emptied, the seat next to hers remained empty. The wave receded, leaving her deflated and drained. It took all her energy to chat and laugh, to pretend nothing was wrong.

She smiled through the speeches and the toasts and the "a small token of our appreciation, really" presentation of the blue box. She smiled through the bestowing of the ceremonial check, with Reid demanding she come join him at the head of the table and accept a rectangle of cardboard that was almost too big to fit in the room. She smiled through the goodbyes, with Mrs. Allen—no, Octavia—telling her to take the rest of the day off. Finally, the room contained only her, Yoselin and a busboy clearing a few remaining dishes from the table. Her shoulders sagged.

Yoselin put her hand on Nelle's arm. "You okay?"

Nelle arranged her features into her most innocent expression. "Of course. Why wouldn't I be?"

"You know that wide-eyed thing doesn't work on me." Yoselin sighed. "I blame myself. I shouldn't have told you he was coming."

"I'm sure he got caught up in something to do with the election." She didn't sound convincing, even to her. "He'll call me when he can." She failed to mention that so far, her texts and messages had gone unanswered.

Yoselin folded her arms and regarded Nelle for a beat. "Be honest. You're not with him just because of Create4All, are you? As both your friend and your boss, if you're dating him for your job, don't."

"I'm not! I mean, yes, I met a lot of people through him who subsequently supported Create4All. But I'm not... that's not the reason we're..." How could she describe her relationship with Grayson when she didn't know their status? "Spending time together," she finished.

Yoselin gave her an assessing stare. "You sure?"

Nelle huffed. "If one of us is dating the other for their job, it's not me. He, on the other hand..." Argh. She pressed her lips together, to keep her thoughts bottled up so she couldn't voice them. They spilled out anyway. "For purposes of the election, he benefits from dating someone who grew up locally. And the whole Cinderella thing —" she waved a disgusted hand "—the media came up with after the gala plays really well with his voters."

"Are you fake-dating?" Yoselin's voice squeaked on the last word.

"No! At least, I'm not. And I didn't think he was. But then his father said..." She sighed. "My judgment feels broken."

Yoselin laid a gentle hand on her shoulder. "Your judgment works fine. Look at the ginormous check over there, and I'm not talking about the physical size of the cardboard. That was your work. I'm going to kick Grayson's ass for making you doubt yourself."

Nelle straightened up. She only had herself to blame for allowing Barrett's words to take up residence in her head. And maybe Barrett was right about her father being the unreliable narrator of his own story. She still hadn't received a straight answer from him.

But Grayson had never given her any reason to doubt his sincerity. To doubt the light in his eyes when he saw her. To doubt how he held her as if she held great value to him, the way his every gesture spoke of his thoughtfulness. The way they mutually ensured each other's pleasure.

She was falling into her old habits, she decided. Janelle would wring her hands and fret. That had been her reaction last year, when work turned into a disastrous nightmare. If she truly wanted to be New Nelle, to live her life as fully as possible, she had to stop being afraid and take action.

"If there are any asses to be kicked, it's mine. Can I have tomorrow off? I need to do what I should have done from the start."

She accomplished the drive to El Santo in less than three hours, thanks to minimal traffic and pushing her ten-year-old car as hard as she could. When she arrived at Grayson's rented house, she barely shut off the ignition before she was running up the path to the front door. She didn't concern herself with knocking, using the key he had given her the last time she visited and throwing open the heavy wood door. "Grayson!" she yelled into the echoing space. "We have to talk. Now."

Too late she realized he was probably at the campaign office. Or in a meeting with local officials. Or visiting a local school. Or at any other of the myriad places Finley had him running to and from, meeting voters and gathering donations. It had been a very dramatic plan, to burst into his house with a shouted demand, but the movie in her mind didn't contain any scenes past this one. Feeling slightly stupid, she turned to leave.

"Nelle?" Grayson emerged from the hallway that led to his office.

She bit back her gasp. He looked like hell. His eyes were bloodshot, his hair sticking up as if he had run his hands through it at frequent intervals, and his broad shoulders hunched as if trying to ward off a body blow.

She'd spent the entire drive building an impregnable stone fortress around her heart. One look at him and it crumbled. "What's wrong? Are you sick? Why didn't Finley call me?"

She'd never stopped to consider that something might have happened to him. Mostly because Grayson seemed so invulnerable, so impervious to the slings and arrows of life others encountered on a daily basis.

But she was wrong. So wrong. He was not invulnerable, but all too human. And she should have been the first to recognize that.

"Nelle. It is you." His gaze was alight with warmth and concern and, yes, caring. He held out his arms and she ran to him, throwing herself into his embrace. She wound her arms around his neck and buried her face in his shoulders, breathing in his scent. His clothes were rumpled, and a day's growth of beard darkened his jaw.

She ran her hand along the rough stubble, then lifted her head so she could kiss him. But he pulled back, keeping his arms around her but putting space between them. She frowned. "What's wrong?" she tried again.

Her earlier doubts tried to creep in. She shook them off. He might not love her, but there were feelings there. His grip wouldn't be so tight on her waist, as if she were the only life preserver in the middle of an ocean, if there weren't. "You're starting to scare me a little," she tried to joke.

He lifted his left hand to caress her cheek, as if to reassure himself it was really her. "It's so good to see you. But you shouldn't be—" He stopped. "But since you are, you can give me a second pair of eyes."

"Eyes for what?"

He let go of her then, his arms dropping to his sides. The gesture felt final. And that scared her a lot. "Come with me."

She followed him to his office and took the chair he offered behind his desk. Grayson took the wing chair to the side, his complexion gray despite the late afternoon sunlight streaming in from the windows. "I've highlighted the entries in question. You have a background in finance. Tell me what you see."

She glanced at the screen. The issue jumped out at her immediately.

"This doesn't make sense." She opened the calendar app on her phone. Maybe she had the date wrong…no. She was right. On the day in question, Grayson had been here, in El Santo. She knew because they had dinner plans in the Bay Area, but he had to cancel at the last minute when an opportunity to speak to a local women's club came up. So why was there a receipt for catering at one of San Francisco's most exclusive private clubs? A receipt for $4,462.34.

She glanced at some of the other highlighted entries.

There was the $2,3780.45 spent at a pricey Los Angeles store that catered to celebrities, characterized as office supplies. But Grayson was adamant about not flashing his wealth around, choosing instead to purchase from local vendors. First-class plane tickets to San Diego had cost $1,200.28, and another $1,534.87 had gone to room charges at a pricey San Diego resort, supposedly to attend a fundraiser. But she and Grayson spoke every day. Maybe other people would fake being at home or in the office while gallivanting around the state, but not him. She knew that with every cell of her being.

She caught his gaze, feeling as shocked as he looked. Someone was using Grayson's campaign as their personal piggy bank. They weren't exorbitant amounts, but they added up. Whoever did this had not only cheated Grayson out of his funds but was committing a crime. Providing false information to the Federal Election Commission, which oversaw campaign financial records, could result in an investigation—and a lengthy jail term for fraud.

Was Finley responsible? As campaign manager she would have access to the campaign's credit card. But Nelle discarded her as the culprit almost immediately. Finley's methods might be over the top and personally intrusive, but she cared about her brother. She wouldn't jeopardize his reputation, not to mention his freedom.

Someone else, then. Someone who didn't think they would be caught. She looked up and held Grayson's gaze with hers. "I see the problem."

"So, not my imagination." Grayson rubbed his forehead.

"Do you know who's responsible?"

He didn't answer her.

"Grayson?"

He stirred, shaking his head as if to jar something

loose. "You once called me a fair-haired prince. Or something like that."

She bit her lower lip. "Not my proudest moment, but yes."

"Growing up, I never questioned my place in the world. I accepted things were the way they were because that was how they were meant to be." A harsh chuckle escaped his lips.

"I think that's true for a lot of people," she said gently. "Especially those whose families provide them with a lot of advantages."

"I never thought to question why we lived in a big house. Or had private tutors. Or went on photo safari in Kenya over spring break."

"I wouldn't question a safari in Kenya. Sounds like fun." She tried to crack a smile.

"Maasai Mara. It's amazing. We should—anyway." He cleared his throat. "I believe you now. About your father's story."

"My father? You believe now that Barrett set him up?" She got up from the desk chair and came around to kneel at his feet, her arms folded on top of his knees. If only he would look at her. "Why now? What does this have to do with…" She stopped as an icy pit threatened to replace her stomach. "Wait. You don't think——"

He nodded. "Barrett misappropriated the campaign funds."

"How do you know?"

"Because he stole not just from my campaign, but his. FEC filings are online. I looked up his previous records. They have the same issue. Dates and receipts don't match." Grayson met her gaze as he cupped her cheek in his right hand. "I'm sorry I missed your lunch. Is Yoselin mad at me?"

"I'd wear armor the next time you see her, but she'll get over it. Reid was there, too. He might have been the most disappointed to miss you." She kissed his palm, then stood up. "Right. So what do we do now?" She knew from painful experience that the sooner financial irregularities were rooted out and dealt with, the better.

His gaze turned as bleak as a landscape after a brush fire. "We break up."

Eleven

It was the hardest thing Grayson had ever done.

Harder than pulling the plug on a promising entrepreneur whose idea proved not to be viable after three years of trying. Harder than walking away from Monk Partners, an organization he'd built from the ground up with sweat, tears and countless late nights. Even harder than calling his father and confronting him with what the reports made clear. He didn't know if his heart would ever fully mend the deep, jagged hole torn in it by the look in Nelle's eyes after he said they had to break up.

But they were out of choices.

Nelle's chest rose and fell rapidly. "I don't understand. Why would you say that?"

He couldn't look at her. He shouldn't have looked at her in the first place. One glance and he was intensely aware of her full lips that fit against his as if custom-crafted for that purpose. Of her crystal-blue gaze, begging him to tell her he was joking or mistaken. Her lush curves, warm and soft and delectable, a treasure-laden territory he would never tire of exploring.

The way she made him laugh. And challenged him to be a better person. In a way, if he hadn't met Nelle, he wouldn't have the strength to do what he had to do. He had to let her go.

His family had hurt hers. He knew that now. He would never stop kicking himself for doubting her story, for accepting his father's glib twisting of the truth. It was also made plain to him his family would continue to hurt her if she remained in their orbit. He had the opportunity to stop the cycle.

He pressed hard on the spot between his eyebrows where the headache had persisted since the early hours of the morning. "I called Barrett this morning, as soon as I knew he would be awake."

He heard her sharp inhale. "And?"

"He didn't deny it. He laughed. Congratulated me, even. Said he knew I was smart."

She slipped her hand into his. He didn't want to be reminded of her touch. They should make a clean break. But he twined his fingers with hers. One last time, to store the memory of her silken skin sliding against his, the warm strength of her fingers ironically lending him the courage to do what he must. "He and Al, the treasurer, have been conspiring for years to use the campaign funds as their personal checking account. They've been careful to keep the expenses just unremarkable enough that they don't draw greater attention. And that's how he took me diving on the Great Barrier Reef for my sixteenth birthday. He wrote it off as visiting a US naval station in the South Pacific."

"Here in El Santo, everyone thought your family was…"

"Rich? So did I." He sighed. The adrenaline that had kept him going for eighteen hours straight was starting to dwindle. "I discovered Dad lost the fortune he inherited before I was born. He invested it in a Ponzi scheme. And to get the money back, he stole from his law practice—"

"And framed my father." Her hand was cold in his.

"I'm so sorry I didn't believe you." And he was. More than he could ever put into words.

She took in a shuddering breath. "Okay. So now we both know the truth. But why did you say we have to break up?"

He let go of her hand and came around the desk to take the chair she had vacated. He sat down and opened a new set of files. "Barrett emailed this while I was on the phone with him."

She stood behind him and peered over his shoulder. "What the—oh. No. Oh no."

He turned and got up in time to grab her elbow as she wobbled. "Don't faint."

Her glare could turn sweet cream into sour. "I tripped over the rug. I'm not going to faint. I'm going to kick—"

"My father's ass? Get in line. But there's a problem—he's in the hospital."

Nelle gasped. "What?"

"Finley found him prostrate on the floor after we hung up. The doctors at the hospital said his life isn't in danger, but they're admitting him for the duration. He's undergoing tests now." Grayson had been heading for the shower to clean up before joining his sister in the waiting room when Nelle appeared. As if things weren't awful enough, he'd almost added causing his father's fatal attack to the list of the day's events.

"I wish him a fast recovery."

He ran a hand through his hair. "Yeah, well, I'd understand if you didn't."

"He's still your father." Nelle's gaze searched his. "You can dislike the person your father is but still love him."

"What if I had killed him?" The thought would forever haunt him.

Steel entered Nelle's gaze. "He brought this on himself. He took money that didn't belong to him. You have nothing to do with it."

He shook his head. "I can't turn and walk away from this family. But you can. You must. If not, Barrett will hold this—" he pointed at the computer screen "—against you. I can't let that happen."

Nelle looked back at the files open on the screen. There it was, in black-and-white plus a few color photos. Her life in New York City, well curated to show only the worst. A photo from a birthday dinner, after a few bottles of champagne with friends. She was half draped over a former boyfriend, her dress riding up and exposing her thighs, her eyes glazed from drinking. The ledger of the accounts her co-worker had doctored in order to sabotage her chances of receiving the promotion they were both pursuing. The letter terminating her employment. There was even the denial from the New York State unemployment office because she had been let go for work-related misconduct.

She pressed her lips together. Her past wasn't a secret. But it also wasn't something she volunteered. She pulled her sweater tighter around her, as if it could provide some of the privacy that had been stripped from her. "I never said I was perfect. But nobody's perfect. People make mistakes. That's why the human race was given the ability to forgive."

"There's nothing here to forgive. I know your co-worker orchestrated the whole thing. Yoselin told me."

"You knew?"

"I was waiting for you to tell me. I figured it would take time before you felt safe enough to trust me. I wanted to give you that time."

"I was going to tell you the night of the beer festival, but then…" She ran a hand through her hair. "I guess… I'll always be embarrassed the same thing happened to both my father and to me." She laughed, even though nothing felt like it would ever be humorous again. "Harry—that's my co-worker—probably got the idea from listening to me talk about my dad as a cautionary tale. How's that for irony?"

She turned back to the screen. "I'm surprised the media didn't dig this up first."

"Barrett bought their silence. For the length of the campaign."

Her mouth fell open, but she was too frozen with shock to form words.

Grayson continued, his tone bleak. "And if the campaign finance fraud becomes public, Barrett will put the blame on you."

That unfroze her. "What? How? I don't have access to the campaign funds."

"You helped with my personal accounts."

She did. It was the day she met Barrett. Right in this office.

"You've had access to my computer. So you had an opportunity to steal the credit card credentials."

Nelle's breath caught in her throat. All it would take would be a few well-placed whispers and the media would spin a story, using her history in New York City. Then bring in her dad's history. The financial fraudster daughter of a criminal embezzler.

"I told you the past was past and it didn't shape the present. I was wrong." Grayson closed the files and turned to face her. "But I'm stopping the cycle. For you."

For her? Flashes of red appeared in Nelle's vision. "Oh, no. You're not doing this. You're not playing the noble martyr. Especially not for me. I don't need saving and even if I did, I can save myself."

He drew himself up to his full height. "It's not under your control. This is my family, my problem, and it has to be my solution. You'll be hurt otherwise."

"But you *are* hurting me. This, what you're doing right now, hurts like hell. I love you, damn it! I've loved you since you handed me a warm, watered down drink." She held out her right hand. "Please. We can figure this out. Together. The past can only affect us if we let it."

So many conflicting emotions flew across his expression she couldn't keep track of them all. His gaze lifted to meet hers. The glowing gold shards in his eyes made them appear lit from within. Her heart beat in triple time as he lifted his hand to meet hers. "Nelle, I—"

His phone rang. He dropped his hand and the moment fled, as if it had never existed. He turned away from her and looked at the screen, then answered it with a curt "Yes?" He walked to a far corner of the room and spoke into the receiver in a hushed whisper.

She watched him, pretty sure her heart was in her eyes. And in her lungs. And in her stomach. Her entire body pulsed, waiting for him to finish his conversation and return to her.

But when he did, the look on his face caused her heart

to fall into her shoes. And stay there. "That was Dad. He's awake and wants to see me."

"I'll come with you."

He screwed his eyes shut. When he opened them, the light they had possessed was gone. "I'm ahead in the polls. Barring a disaster, the election is as good as won. I'll be moving to Washington, which means our relationship would be at an end regardless. It just came sooner than expected."

He would not meet her gaze. "I love you," she said again. "And I think you care for me."

"I have to go." He shoved his laptop into a leather bag. "Thanks for your help. I wish you all the very best. Always."

She ran ahead of him and blocked the doorway so he couldn't exit the room. "You told me in Napa after our first night together that it meant something to you. That I mean something to you. Look me in the eye and tell me those were all lies."

He stood very still. Then he lifted his head. His whiskey brown gaze burned hot with pain and regret, searing her heart. "I'm sorry."

The world faded to a pinprick as oceans roared in her ears. She leaned on the doorjamb for support, allowing room for Grayson to pass before she could process what was happening. He didn't mean it. He wasn't really going through with the breakup. She ran after him as soon as her muscles unfroze enough to move. "Grayson—"

The sound of the front door shutting and his car starting in the driveway was the only response she received.

This couldn't be the end. He was exhausted and in shock. His emotions were at the breaking point. In a few hours, when he had more information about Barrett's health, he would see things differently. There was too much between them for him to walk away. Too much that was real. She could wait.

And wait.

And wait some more.

When morning rolled around and Grayson still hadn't returned to his house nor answered any of her calls or texts, she got in her car and drove back to Fremont.

"And in the race for California's fifty-fourth district, Silicon Valley venture capitalist Grayson Monk is far out in front of the pack to fill his father's congressional seat in the upcoming special election. The debate this evening is seen as just a formality. Former congressman Barrett Monk is still in the hospital recovering from—"

Nelle turned off the television, a giant fist squeezing her heart into spiky shards. Even in her new apartment, with zero things in it to remind her of Grayson, he still managed to be present. She told herself it would take more time. Two weeks wasn't nearly long enough to heal her gaping wounds. Although, who was she kidding. She would never fully be over him at the rate she was going.

Her phone rang. The screen read, "No Caller ID." She answered anyway. Living by herself was a bigger adjustment than she'd anticipated. Even a computer-generated voice telling her she'd won an all-expenses-paid trip if she would just provide a credit card number would be a welcome break in the silence. "Hello?"

It wasn't a computerized voice. Nelle almost dropped the phone in surprise, but not before she heard Finley ask, "Where are you?"

"What do you mean, where am I?"

"You're not here, which means you have to be somewhere. When will you get here?"

Nelle sank down on the secondhand couch Octavia had insisted on giving her. "Get where?"

She could practically hear Finley's eyes roll. "El Santo. The debate is tonight." Her tone implied a "duh" at the end.

Nelle burst out laughing. She liked Finley a lot, but her tolerance of the other woman's audacity had its limits. "How about never? Is that a good time to arrive?"

"That isn't funny," Finley snapped. "This is the debate. It's a big deal as we head toward election day. And did you or did you not promise me you would show up for the *entire* campaign?"

Nelle stared at her phone in disbelief. Finley couldn't be serious. Could she? Nelle slammed the phone back against her ear. "Your brother and I are not involved anymore. He said goodbye."

"Yes, well, I don't care. Sleep with him, don't sleep with him, that's between you two. But I'm in charge of the campaign, not him. And you promised *me*. He had no power to release you from that promise."

Nelle didn't know whether to laugh or cry. "I can't. You have to understand why. Somewhere under your shark suit is a human."

"Clever." Finley's tone implied it was anything but. Then she sighed, and the snap in her tone softened. "Look, I know this family is a lot. I know Barrett is a master manipulator who can make you swear on a stack of Bibles that the sky is chartreuse and the grass is fuchsia."

"And a thief and a fraudster. When are you turning him in to the Federal Elections Commission?"

"Who says we haven't? Not everything is on the internet. The real question is why haven't *you* turned him in?"

Nelle shut her eyes. It was true. She hadn't called the

FEC. Despite the finality of Grayson's goodbye, she would never do anything that might harm him or his chances of success. "I'm going to hang up now."

Finley huffed. "Fine, don't come. But if you don't, I'll let the FEC know you had material evidence about campaign finance fraud and didn't tell them. So, talk to you later—"

"Wait!" Nelle ran through what she knew of FEC regulations in her head. "I don't think that's a thing. Is it?"

"There's one way to find out. If you don't come to the debate, that is."

"This is blackmail, Finley."

"No, it's enforcement of a verbal contract between two parties. So. You coming?"

Nelle looked down at her outfit. She was wearing her oldest pair of jeans, topped by vintage Pearl Jam T-shirt. "It would take me at least an hour to get ready, and then three hours of driving. By the time I get there, the debate will be long over. You can't blackmail the laws of physics into obeying you."

"Don't you know me by now? Go downstairs. Take your purse and lock your door."

She should say no. She should have ended the call as soon as she knew it was Finley, for that matter. But she left her apartment and went downstairs to her building's front entrance. Her curiosity would never forgive her otherwise.

She burst out laughing when she opened the door and saw what awaited her. "Nice one," she said into the phone.

A man in a military-style pilot jumpsuit wearing aviator sunglasses was standing by a large Mercedes sedan. "CC's Helicopter Tours" read the magnetic sign affixed to the side of the vehicle. "Ma'am," the man said, giving her a salute. "Ready to go to the airport?"

"Laws of physics solved," Finley said. "The helicopter will get you here in time. See you soon." The phone disconnected.

"Ma'am?" The man opened the rear passenger door.

Nelle shook her head. "I don't think so. But please tell Finley she gets an A for effort—" She stopped. What was on the rear seat? Was that…?

It was. An aqua and silver dress. Not her ballgown from the gala; this one was more appropriate for day wear. But it had a full skirt and silvery-pearl buttons on the bodice.

A note was attached. "Courtesy of your friendly neighborhood fairy godmother," it read on one side. And on the reverse: "I never beg but I'm begging now. Please come to the debate. I know he messed up but he needs you. And then I promise you never have to see any of us again if you don't want to."

The man cleared his throat. "Excuse me, but the copter is waiting."

Nelle took a deep breath. Her soul was still raw and bleeding from Grayson's goodbye. She didn't owe him or Finley a thing. By every right, she should march back into her apartment and put her phone on silent. She had tried being New Nelle. She had tried going after what she wanted. She had failed. And it still hurt.

Her gaze fell on the note. *He needs you.*

She entered the sedan, sat down and buckled the seatbelt.

Twelve

Grayson glanced in the mirror of the dressing room assigned to him for the debate. It was being held in the local community college's auditorium and apparently the last occupants of this room had worn some sort of costume made of feathers, because yellow and purple and orange ones were everywhere. He straightened his tie, then decided he didn't like the knot and undid it. He'd just finished tying a new knot when Finley walked in.

"How are you doing?" Her usually precise haircut was a touch shaggy, and her tailored suit hung off her frame instead of being fitted to her contours. However, for the first time in days, a hint of her usual spark was back in her gaze.

"I could ask the same of you."

"Doesn't matter how I feel. You're the main event." Finley brushed at the shoulders of Grayson's jacket. He allowed her ministrations, knowing it was as much a nervous tic of hers as it was ensuring his suit was lint-free.

"I'm fine." And he was. For the first time in a long time—since he found Finley trying to make coffee that morning in his penthouse in San Francisco—he was utterly calm, cool and collected. "Don't worry."

"I'm not," she said. But she wouldn't look him in the eye. If he didn't know better, he'd think she was hiding something from him. "I'm looking forward to this debate being over, however. You're going to kick ass."

"I know." He also knew by the time the night was through, Finley might be looking to kick his ass. He took a deep breath. "Fin, why aren't you the one running?"

"What?" This finally got her to look up. "What are you talking about?"

"Why aren't you the one running for this seat? You know the district. You know Washington. You know the job, inside and out. You'd be an amazing congresswoman."

Finley chuckled. "Jokes to loosen up before you go on stage. That's a good tactic."

"I'm not joking. Why aren't you Barrett's heir apparent?" He grabbed her hands and kept them still in his.

She laughed again, but this time there was no mirth in the sound. "You know why. Barrett may be the only father I know, but I'm not his blood. There's only one heir, apparent or otherwise, in this family."

"It should be you. You should be the one going on this stage."

Finley snatched her hands away. "Let's go over your position on farm subsidies again. You promise to…" She lifted her eyebrows. "C'mon, fill in the rest."

He shook his head. "I'm sorry for being so blind."

She huffed. "That's a terrible answer, especially when your toughest competition is a rancher who knows subsidies inside and out. Try again."

"I'm sorry I didn't pay attention to how Barrett treats you. He constantly takes but never gives."

For a second, Finley's air of amused superiority slipped. Then a knock came at the door, and a production assistant ducked his head in to let them know Grayson had ten minutes to get to the stage. She lifted her chin and smirked at him, the armor back and wrapped even thicker around her. "All I know is you're about to go on that stage and show the people of this district their next congressman. Break two legs and an elbow."

He hugged her. Finley stiffened, her arms hanging at her side, before tentatively returning the hug. They weren't a demonstrative family. He couldn't recall the last time Barrett showed fatherly affection. Maybe not since their mother died. But that was going to change. Finley deserved her full place at the family table. And she would get it. He'd make sure of that. "Thanks, sis. For everything. Your faith in me has meant a lot."

Finley's cheeks were bright red, but she waved off his words. "You sound as if you're about to leave on a trip to Mars. It's just an hour's debate. Get out there."

He nodded. "Right." He took a quick glance in the mirror, straightened his tie and opened the door. Oddly, he wasn't nervous. The speech at the gala had caused him more apprehension, even though the stakes tonight were much higher. Clarity of purpose was a terrific antidote to nerves. One last check of his inside suit jacket pocket, ensuring its contents were still there, and he was ready to go on stage. "See you on the other side."

Nelle arrived at the auditorium just as the outer doors were being closed and no more audience members were allowed in. She had to wave her backstage pass at a grumpy attendant or she would have been left out on the sidewalk with the other latecomers. She pushed open the door to the main auditorium to the sound of recorded horns and brass playing patriotic-sounding riffs. Too late to go backstage, she looked around for an empty seat. The only one she spotted was in the middle of a row, which meant she had to climb over purses and backpacks while trying and failing to avoid stepping on toes to reach it.

The stage was brightly lit, illuminating the black curtain backdrop and the podiums draped with red, white and blue bunting. The debate moderators sat at a long table set up before the stage, two cameras from the local television station flanking them as they faced where the candidates would stand. Nelle's palms were wet, but she didn't want to wipe them on the delicate fabric of the aqua and silver dress.

The helicopter got her to El Santo with an hour to spare to change into her new finery. Finley had thoughtfully also provided make-up, hairstyling tools and silver sandals with stiletto heels. However, Nelle's hands had shaken so much, she used up most of time putting on and then taking off lipstick and mascara.

The lights in the audience dimmed. The music changed to a fanfare. A disembodied voice began the night's announcements.

And there he was.

Her heart constricted as Grayson waved and smiled at the audience. Really, no one should be that handsome. Or maybe he was so attractive because it came from his inner self, not just the accident of genes that led to the symmetry of his facial features.

She leaned forward, her pulse beating so loud in her ears she could barely comprehend what was being said, despite the excellent acoustics and expertly mixed sound system. Other candidates joined him on stage, but she barely noticed them. Her entire focus was captured by him.

Too late, she joined in the applause after the field was introduced. Then the audience settled, a hush descending upon the auditorium as the debate moderators began to explain the procedure for the evening and the rules they would be following.

Nelle closed her eyes. She just had to survive the debate. She wasn't sure why Finley said he needed her as Grayson looked just fine. More than fine. Thriving. Certainly not as if he'd spent the last two weeks pining for her.

Next time, she would not answer the phone. No matter what name was on the screen.

"Next, let's hear from Grayson Monk. Mr. Monk?"

The moderator's voice cut through what little Zen Nelle had achieved. Her gaze flew to Grayson, tall and lean and exuding calm confidence. He took the microphone from its stand. "Mind if I step out from behind the podium?" When the moderator gave his assent, Grayson moved downstage. "I know the question is about my position on the national defense budget. But I'd like to beg the audience's—and my opponents'—indulgence for a minute."

The audience around her started to murmur as Grayson stepped to the edge of the stage. Both cameramen focused their lenses on him. "It has been a privilege coming back to El Santo. You have all taught me so much. When I began this campaign, I thought being your representative was what I was meant to do. It was what I was raised for, growing up as Barrett Monk's son—to carry on the legacy of public service that began with my great-grandfather, who was governor of this state."

On the stage his opponents were starting to shuffle their feet, their expressions ranging from confused to annoyed. "This is highly irregular—" a former city council member started to say.

Grayson turned to him. "You're right. I'll be brief." He faced the audience again. "But what I learned as I got deeper into the campaign is you don't need someone with a family name or a legacy as your representative. You need a representative who is deeply involved with this district and its people, who has been here, fighting the good fight alongside you. You all taught me I have so much more left to learn about El Santo, its resources and its people. Your hopes and your dreams, your past and your future." He stopped and cleared his throat. Nelle edged forward until she almost fell off her seat, her bottom lip numb from biting it so hard.

"Someday I might stand before you and ask you to vote for me. But now is not the time." He paused to raise his right hand, cutting the glare from the bright lights shining in his face. He looked down at someone in the front row, his gaze laser-focused. "To paraphrase someone I care about very much, you deserve a representative who will put you, the voters of this district, first. Not their family name, not their power over others, not their appearance. The masks need to come off."

Nelle inhaled, a sharp, audible gasp. The people seated next to her turned to glare in her direction.

Then Grayson swung his gaze up to sweep the entirety of the auditorium. "I'm withdrawing from the race and taking my name off the ballot. You have great candidates up here, and I urge you to vote for the person you feel will do the best job of taking your voice to Washington. As for me, I'm going to find the woman who wore this mask and spend the rest of my life making up to her for taking two weeks to figure out what really matters. Thank you."

And he pulled out an aqua-blue mask decorated with seashells and crystals and faux pearls.

The auditorium spun around Nelle as the crowd erupted into a cacophony of noise. The lights, the decibels of sound, the heat of a room filled to capacity with people packed into tight rows: her senses couldn't keep up. Only two things cut through the overload: one, he had her mask. The one she thought lost forever on a San Francisco street. She struggled to breathe. It was as if her ribcage was too small to contain her heart.

He did care. From the moment they met. That kiss the night of the gala was as special to him as it was to her.

And two: Grayson was giving up his dream. For her. A dream that would also benefit others, as he would be a damn fine congressman. Did Finley know he was going to do this? Is that why she wanted Nelle here, to stop him? "You can't step down!" She was on her feet and climbing over the people in her row, heedless of stepped-on toes, before she had time to think through her actions. She flew down the aisle toward the stage. One of her stiletto heels caught on the carpet and she stopped herself from falling just at the last minute. She kicked off the sandals to regain her speed. "You have to stay in the race."

Too late, she realized she had drawn the attention off Grayson and onto herself. One of the cameras swung to focus on her, while the other remained on him. She glanced to her left and then to her right and saw hundreds of pairs of eyes staring back at her. She stood still, her chest heaving. "Don't do it," she said in a quieter voice.

"Nelle?" Grayson still shielded his eyes, trying to find her in the auditorium.

"Yes," she said, her gaze seeing him and him only.

Then hands were at her elbows and she was being helped onto the stage, guided forward until she stood facing him. She instinctively reached out to touch him, but when the audience started to "ooh" and "aah" she pulled back and gave him a half wave instead. "Um, hi."

"Hi yourself," he said. He looked around. She followed his gaze. His former opponents exhibited various stages of shock, some leaning on their podiums with wide gazes and open mouths, others frantically texting on their phones. The moderators shuffled though their scripts while the camera operators spoke intently into their headpieces, keeping the lenses focused on Nelle and Grayson. He took off his lapel mike, tossing it aside so they wouldn't be overheard. "I thought you didn't like big crowds," he said with a lopsided grin.

"I don't. But this is too important to let a fear of crowds get in the way." She shook her head. "I mean it. Don't drop out. Not for me. This is all you've wanted. This is your dream—"

He tucked a loose strand of hair behind her ear. "It's not. It's what other people dreamed for me."

"But you worked toward this your entire life. Your education, running the fund—"

"Only because I thought I had to be the person I was supposed to be."

"Right. And you can't give that up. Especially not for me."

He smiled and cupped her face with his hands. "Nelle, darling Nelle. Will you believe the truth? I'm not doing this for you."

She narrowed her gaze. "You broke up with me for my own good."

"And that is unforgivable. But then I remembered

something a very wise woman said to me. About doing the right thing versus the supposed thing."

Nelle rolled her eyes. "Oh. Her. She's a bit of a know-it-all."

"Hey, don't talk that way about the love of my life." His expression turned sober. "Running for office, protecting my dad because he threatened you to hurt you if I didn't—those were things I was supposed to do. It's time to do the right thing."

"But are you sure pulling out of the race is the right thing?"

"It should have been Finley in the first place. Not me. Politics are her passion, not mine."

"Oh?" Nelle's shock was wearing off, replaced by a warm, fizzing sensation she could only identify as joy. "And what are you passionate about?"

He glanced up at the crowded auditorium, then bent down so his mouth was by her ear. "Ask me in an hour when I have you naked in my bed and I'll show you."

She shivered at the promise in his tone. "By all means, follow your passion."

He grinned. "Believe me, I fully intend to explore it." Then his smile faded. "But we should stop by the hospital to see how Barrett took my announcement first."

She took a deep breath. "Of course."

"He knows he's going to be indicted. The FEC is investigating as we speak." Grayson straightened up. "He's still my father, though."

"I know."

"It might be a rough few years as the case winds through the courts."

She nodded. "You'll get through them. You and Finley both. Speaking of Finley, where is she?" Her gaze searched for Grayson's sister in the sea of TV cameramen, assistants, candidates, and the occasional audience member who had wandered out of their seat. It was clear the debate's producers hadn't made a decision yet whether to go forward with the remaining candidates or cancel.

"Not sure. My guess is she had the same concern as me and went to visit Dad. She knew he'd be watching the debate on television."

"I hope he's okay with your decision."

"He doesn't get a say. Especially since after his latest heart episode he gave me power of attorney over his estate." Grayson cupped her cheek with his left hand. "That's one of the reasons why it's taken this long to withdraw from the race. I needed to secure the power of attorney first. We're going to liquidate his assets. The proceeds will go to schools and social services in this district."

"Grayson," she breathed.

"The money rightfully belongs to them anyway. I made more than enough with Monk Partners to take care of him for the rest of his life. I'd like to set up a pension for your father, too. If that's okay with you."

She nodded, her heart too full to form words.

"And speaking of rest of one's life…" He dropped to one knee.

The background auditorium noise, humming steadily since Grayson made his announcement, tripled in decibels. Cameras appeared as if by magic, pointing at the two of them. And then Nelle could only see and hear the man in front of her, holding out a familiar mask.

"Once upon a midnight, masked strangers shared a kiss and I fell in love. Now that I know you, Nelle Lassen, that love only grows stronger and deeper every hour. I can't imagine spending another minute without you by my side. Will you marry me?"

She heard music. Maybe it came from the auditorium speakers, maybe it was angels singing hallelujah, or maybe it was just her heart, a song of joy so overwhelming it filled her ears. She shook as he reached for her hand and placed the mask in it. "Yes! I love you, Grayson." She smiled at him, even as tears fell down her cheeks. "And I can't wait to write our future story. Together."

He kissed her then, in front of the other candidates and the cameras and crowd. A chorus of *awww*s rose from the audience, ringing in her ears. Then his kiss deepened, and he pulled her tight against him, his hands tangling in her hair, and the world narrowed to just the two of them. The mask dangled off the fourth finger of her left hand.

* * * * *

COMING SOON!

We really hope you enjoyed reading this book.
If you're looking for more romance, be sure to
head to the shops when new books are
available on

Thursday 6th
August

To see which titles are coming soon, please visit

millsandboon.co.uk/nextmonth

LET'S TALK
Romance

For exclusive extracts, competitions
and special offers, find us online:

f facebook.com/millsandboon

🐦 @MillsandBoon

📷 @MillsandBoonUK

Get in touch on 01413 063232

For all the latest titles coming soon, visit
millsandboon.co.uk/nextmonth

JOIN US ON SOCIAL MEDIA!

Stay up to date with our latest releases, author news and gossip, special offers and discounts, and all the behind-the-scenes action from Mills & Boon...

 millsandboon

 millsandboonuk

 millsandboon

It might just be true love...

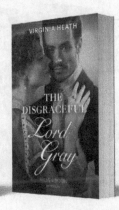